"It's true that I no longer require the services of Rixidenteron, lord of Pastinas Manor.

Or perhaps I should say the soon-to-be *former* lord of Pastinas Manor." Merivale sighed, as if mourning the passing of his nobility. Then she flashed that brilliant smile of hers. "But I *do* require the services of a certain thief and scoundrel who sometimes goes by the unlikely name of Red."

"Oh?" Red was surprised by how thrillingly the idea struck him.

"I will sneak you out of Stonepeak, past imperial soldiers and biomancers, and get you safe passage to New Laven," said Merivale.

"And in return?" Red knew her well enough to know there was always a price.

"You will find these two women, Bleak Hope and Brigga Lin, that worry our enemies so much. You will warn them of the Vinchen that are hunting them, and recruit them to our cause. Preferably before Ammon Set puts his new plan into action."

By Jon Skovron

THE EMPIRE OF STORMS

Hope and Red

Bane and Shadow

Blood and Tempest

Struts & Frets

Misfit

Man Made Boy

This Broken Wondrous World

BLOOD
AND
TEMPEST

THE EMPIRE OF STORMS: BOOK THREE

JON
SKOVRON

www.orbitbooks.net

Copyright © 2017 by Jon Skovron
Excerpt from *The Tethered Mage* copyright © 2017 by Melissa Caruso
Excerpt from *Age of Assassins* copyright © 2017 by RJ Barker

Cover design by Lauren Panepinto
Cover illustration by Bastien Lecouffe Deharme
Cover copyright © 2017 by Hachette Book Group, Inc.
Map copyright © 2017 Tim Paul

Orbit
Hachette Book Group
1290 Avenue of the Americas
New York, NY 10104
orbitbooks.net

First Edition: November 2017

Orbit is an imprint of Hachette Book Group.
The Orbit name and logo are trademarks of Little, Brown Book Group Limited.

The publisher is not responsible for websites (or their content) that are not owned by the publisher.

The Hachette Speakers Bureau provides a wide range of authors for speaking events. To find out more, go to www.hachettespeakersbureau.com or call (866) 376-6591.

ISBNs: 978-0-316-26820-2 (mass market), 978-0-316-26819-6 (ebook)

Printed in the United States of America

OPM

10 9 8 7 6 5 4 3 2 1

For my stepmother, Doctor Sandra Skovron, who never draws attention to her good deeds, so it took me far too long to notice them.
Thank you.

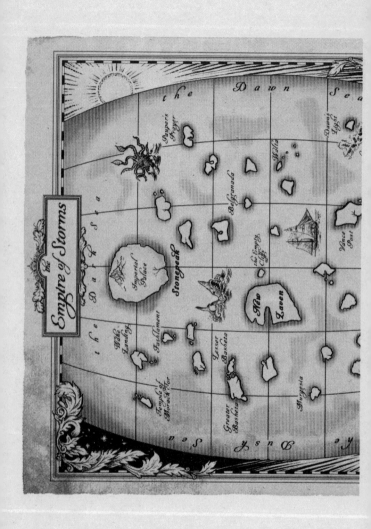

a. Broadside Inn

b. Imperial Trade Commission

c. Sleeth Harbor Hotel

d. Abandoned Temple

e. The Past Is Forgotten Tavern

f. Visionary Square

g. Police Station

the Breach

Rugby Isle

the Southern Isles

Vance Post

PART ONE

My fellow brothers strive to avoid doubt. They think doubt makes them weak. They do not understand that doubt is the beginning of true understanding, and therefore true strength.

—from the private journal of
Hurlo the Cunning

1

"They say he spawned from the blackness of night itself, and that he oozes in and out of the dark like he was part of it."

Old Turnel the mason put down his tankard of ale, wiped the foam from his bushy mustache, and fixed the other three wags at the table with a knowing look. They all nodded into their own tankards. They'd heard similar things.

The Wheelhouse Tavern was crowded that night, as it had been nearly every night the last few weeks. Folks in Stonepeak didn't feel safe lately, so it was natural for them to gather. And yet they couldn't stop talking about the thing that filled them with such dread.

"Someone told me that he makes no sounds and has no mouth," said Mash the ink maker.

"No, I heard he had *three* mouths," disagreed Trina the cobbler. "One mouth spits acid, one spits poison, and one screams so loud, it makes your ears bleed."

"I seen some of his handiwork myself, and them poor gafs weren't burned or poisoned or anything like that," said Old Turnel. "Every last one of them had the life choked out of 'em, but without no finger marks on their necks."

The people had given this new killer the nickname

Stonepeak Strangler. His victims had been turning up every night, from Artisan Way all the way down to the docks. Not just men and women, but children, too. That Shadow Demon from a few months back had been bad enough. But he'd always targeted dissidents and troublemakers. This Stonepeak Strangler seemed to have no motive or pattern, and he was all the scarier for that. Parents had started keeping their children indoors at night, and even the mildest mollies carried a knife with them when they were about town. Over the course of the last month or so, the capital city of the Empire of Storms had become gripped in a fear that seemed very close to boiling over into citywide panic.

"I heard he can't abide the sun, though," said Mash. "That's something, ain't it?"

"If it's true," said Trina.

"My tom heard a funny thing down at the docks," said Hooper, the dressmaker. He was a quiet wag, but greatly respected by the others as the most successful among them. He'd even made dresses for Lady Hempist and Archlady Bashim, two of the most fashionable nobles in the empire. "You know that old warehouse along the west bank of Trader's Fork?"

"The one slowly falling in on itself these past ten years?" asked Trina.

"That's the one," said Hooper. "Anyway, my tom was down there bartering with Jacklow the fisherman. You know him?"

"He's my cousin!" Mash said, always eager to impress Hooper any way he could.

Hooper gave the youngest member of their group a steady look, then said, "Be that as it may, my tom and I have known Jacklow to be a truthy wag who always speaks crystal. And he said someone's been lurking down in that warehouse for the last month or so. Someone who ain't entirely...natural."

"That's about the same time these killings started," observed Old Turnel.

Hooper nodded gravely as he drank from his tankard.

"How does he know someone unnatural's been lurking?" asked Trina. "He seen 'em?"

Hooper shook his head. "He only *hears* him, just around sunset, crying and moaning like some kind of beastly thing. Happens nearly every night, he said."

Mash shuddered. "Like to give me nightmares, we keep talking in this direction."

"Don't be a ponce," said Hooper.

Mash turned to Trina with an appealing look. "Don't you think so, Trin? This one's even worse than that Shadow Demon."

Before Trina could reply, a new voice cut in:

"You think so?"

The speaker sat at the next table over, leaning back in his chair, his arms crossed. He wore the fine jacket and cravat of a lord, which made him a little out of place in the Wheelhouse. But even stranger, he wore glasses that were tinted so dark, they hid his eyes. "And who would win in a fight, do you think?"

The artisans all looked at each other.

"Between the Strangler and the Shadow Demon?" asked Hooper.

"Personally, my money would be on the Demon," said the newcomer.

"Why would they fight?" asked Mash.

"Like as not, they'd be in league," agreed Trina.

The newcomer shrugged. "I suppose that's possible."

"But see now," said Old Turnel, finger and thumb rubbing his mustache thoughtfully. "They could be *competing*, you know. For territory."

"Could be," said the newcomer. "Or *maybe* they'd fight because the Shadow Demon wants to make amends for his past crimes."

They all looked at each other again.

"Ain't seen you around here, stranger," said Old Turnel finally. "You got a name?"

The man grinned. "You can call me Red."

———

Red went down to the docks the next evening. The sky had that peculiar gold color of twilight that made things seem not quite real as he walked past small, one-masted sloops being loaded or unloaded. He wore the soft gray clothes the biomancers had given him when they'd forced him to be the Shadow Demon. His lacy clothes would have stood out in the dockyards, and if he ran into trouble, they would have hindered his movements.

He'd always considered the docks of Paradise Circle big, with over twenty piers, and upward of fifty ships coming and going at any given time. But the docks of Stonepeak stretched all the way down the Burness River from the heart of the city, through the remains of the Thunder Gate, to the coast. There were even piers built up on some of the larger tributaries that fed into the Burness. And where the Burness met the sea, docks stretched for miles along the southern coast. All told, there were nearly eighty piers and over a hundred warehouses. Red couldn't even guess the number of ships that came and went.

Thankfully, Trader's Fork was one of the smaller tributaries, mainly used as a trading post between artisans for items unrelated to the needs of the nobility. That meant it wasn't well policed, or nearly as crowded. It was, Red decided, a perfect place for a monster to hide. Red hoped that Jacklow the fisherman had been right about hearing something "unnatural" coming from the abandoned warehouse. Lady

Hempist had assigned the mission to him weeks ago, and this was his first promising lead.

He made his way along the riverbank, skirting the people still working on the docks. There were more than he'd expected this close to sunset, and that worried him a little. Merivale had made it crystal that this mission was to be carried out unobtrusively, like a proper spy mission should be. He wasn't supposed to draw any unnecessary attention or increase the panic of a city already on edge. He also had to hide his identity by wearing a gray scarf over the lower half of his face. Apparently, it wouldn't do if anyone recognized the lord of Pastinas Manor out hunting monsters. At first it had seemed silly to keep his mouth and nose covered, yet leave his eyes visible. They were by far his most distinguishing trait. But Merivale had pointed out that, as Lord Pastinas, he was hardly ever seen without his tinted glasses, so most people didn't even know his eyes were red.

Red finally reached the warehouse around sunset. That cobbler hadn't been exaggerating when she said the place was collapsing. Most of the roof was gone, and the walls were beginning to cave in on one another. There were two entrances. One at the riverbank, where goods had likely once been loaded into the warehouse from boats. The other entrance was on the opposite side, where those same items might have been loaded onto wagons for transport into the city. Given the fact that all of the victims had been inland, Red decided to approach from the landward entrance, cutting off the escape route that led directly to innocent people.

Red had been trying to construct an image of what this creature might look like in his mind, but the various descriptions he'd heard had all been so conflicting, he still had no idea what he would find inside. The only thing he was fairly certain of was that it had been made by a biomancer, with their usual lack of compassion or basic decency.

As he drew closer to the warehouse, he heard an unsettling keening sound from inside. It was somewhere between the cry of a child and the whine of a wounded animal.

He saw a large window above the entrance. The glass had already been broken, and he decided it would be a little better than just walking in through the door. He climbed up the wall, his heightened sense of touch allowing his fingers and soft-shoed toes to find any crack or ledge that would help his ascent.

He perched on the window ledge and surveyed the inside of the warehouse. His red, catlike eyes worked especially well in the dim light. It was a large, open space cluttered with rusted boating equipment, coils of rotting rope, and chunks of roofing that had already fallen. There were windows near the ceiling that let in the last faint rays of sun, drenching everything in crimson.

The painful cries came from beneath an upturned rowboat by the wall. There was enough space under that boat to allow for a fairly large creature, but whatever it was would have to flip the boat over to get out. That would leave it vulnerable for a moment, giving Red the perfect moment to strike. So he settled in to wait.

It wasn't the most comfortable thing, perched up there on that ledge. He had to shake his legs several times to keep the circulation going. And when the last rays of sunlight did finally disappear, the boat didn't flip at all. Instead, Red watched with sick fascination as something pale and veiny oozed out through the small gap between the boat and the floor. It spread across the wooden floorboards like a lumpy pool of flesh, only occasionally pushing the edge of the boat up as one of the larger chunks passed through.

Once it was completely free of the boat, Red realized that it wasn't a blob or pool exactly. There was a shape to it. A *human* shape. But it was malleable, as if all the bones had been turned soft and pliable. This person lay on their belly, drooping and heavy, arms and legs bowing out to the sides like rubbery insect legs. Then Red saw the mashed-in face.

"Brackson?"

Red remembered Progul Bon casually mentioning that Deadface Drem's old lieutenant had been punished after prematurely revealing Red's vulnerability to high-pitched sounds. Red had assumed it was something terrible, but even so, he hadn't expected them to keep him alive afterward.

The thing that used to be Brackson turned sluggishly when Red called out his name. Instead of walking, or even crawling, the creature had to squirm and undulate across the floor like some kind of human-octopus hybrid. With such a soft rib cage, the weight of his own flesh must be pressing down on his innards. Red guessed it had to hurt like all hells. And the way Brackson's head sagged to one side like a deflated pastry suggested his brain wasn't getting much protection either.

"Brackson, can you speak?" Red had always hated Brackson. But *nobody* deserved this. He pulled down his scarf to show his face. "Do you recognize me?"

Brackson made a grunt that didn't sound particularly friendly. His mouth flapped around. Maybe he was trying to speak, but his jaw was too soft to form the words.

"Listen. I know we ain't ever been wags, but what's been done to you is plain wrong. Let me help you." He had no idea how, but he knew the prince and the empress. There had to be *something* he could do.

Brackson shuffle-slithered toward the door like he was ignoring Red. Or maybe there'd been so much brain damage, he didn't understand. Either way, he seemed intent on getting out of the warehouse, probably back into town where he could mindlessly strangle anyone he came across with his rubbery arms.

Red sighed and pulled his scarf back up. "I should've known you wouldn't make things easy for me even now." He jumped down from the windowsill, blocking Brackson's exit. "Sorry, old pot. Your murder spree ends tonight."

Brackson's rubbery face stretched into something that might have been a frown, and he gave a low, gurgling growl.

Red drew a throwing blade in each hand. Brackson paused when he saw the gleaming steel and scrunched back into himself.

"There, now," said Red. "You may not understand much, but you still know danger when you see it. Maybe we can settle this peacefully after all."

Brackson scrunched even farther into himself. Then he shot forward like a spring, slamming into Red's chest and knocking him over.

Brackson trampled over him, and would have escaped, but Red plunged one of his blades into the creature's soft shoulder and used it as leverage to get on the creature's back as it passed him. He then stabbed his second blade into the other shoulder and held on tight. He was grateful he still wore his leather fingerless gloves, or the blades might have cut right through his palms.

Brackson made a warbling sound of protest and took off faster than Red thought possible. It was a strange sort of lurching gait in which Brackson compressed himself, then shot forward, his rubbery arms and legs scrabbling at anything in reach for additional purchase. By this point, Red's plan was to put a blade or two in Brackson's soft skull, but at their current frantic, uneven speed, he'd get thrown if he let go of even one of the blades planted in the creature's shoulders. For the moment, it was all he could do just to hang on.

Red and his unwilling ride smashed right through the rickety door and down the wagon path toward town. Town was the last place Red wanted this to go, so he leaned hard on the blades in Brackson's shoulders, steering them in a wide arc through tall grass back toward the docks along the west bank of Trader's Fork. Brackson had some trouble moving in the grass, and Red thought he was about to get his opening. But before he could take advantage of it, they reached the docks. Brackson's rubbery fingers and toes hooked on to the widely spaced planks of wood, and the pair lurched forward with even greater speed.

"Clear the way!" yelled Red as they neared a group of dockhands unloading something from a small sloop that, at this hour, was probably smuggled goods.

The dockhands dodged to the side, and Brackson smashed through the crates, sending the fine pink powder of coral spice into the air.

"No loss there," muttered Red. He still held a grudge against the drug that had claimed his mother and nearly killed him as an infant. He was sentimental that way.

The dockhands stared incredulously as the bizarre pair raced past them. The dock stretched along the banks of Trader's Fork for a quarter mile or so. Red saw that there were four or five other groups of workers ahead of them, all blocking the way. He had to end this before every drug runner in Stonepeak saw it. It was time for some risky, and possibly ostentatious, acrobatics.

Red jerked his blades out of Brackson's shoulders and jumped straight up. In midair, he threw the blades, which both sank into the base of Brackson's soft skull. Red landed on the dock, rolling to cushion the impact. Still sprawled on the dock, he looked up in time to see the lifeless monstrosity carried forward by momentum into another stack of crates on the dock. The angry shouts of the workers quickly turned to yelps of alarm when they saw what it was that had knocked over their cargo.

Red staggered to his feet, hurried over, and shoved Brackson's body off the edge of the dock into the water, where it quickly sank out of sight.

A proper spy probably would have slipped away right then, silent and mysterious. Well, a proper spy probably wouldn't have allowed themselves to get into this mess in the first place. But seeing as how he was already in the muck of it, Red couldn't resist a little flourish.

"Well, my wags," he said to the smugglers, his red eyes gleaming in the moonlight above his gray mask. "I think that about takes care of your Stonepeak Strangler problem!"

He gave them a quick bow, and ran off, his laughter trailing into the night.

"You certainly have a curious idea of what it means to keep a low profile," said Lady Merivale Hempist.

She and Red were in her apartments, which were impeccably neat and minimal to the point of austere. She sat at her glass table, delicately dismantling and eating a roast quail. Despite her cool demeanor and steely gaze, there was a lush allure to Lady Hempist that Red could never quite ignore. It didn't help that she always favored gowns that showed off her extremely inviting cleavage.

"My lady, I'm sure I don't know what you're referring to," he said airily as he slouched nearby in a upholstered chair, one leg hooked on the arm.

He idly swirled the last bit of red wine in his glass and then drank it. Merivale really had the best wine. It was one of the things that made these debriefings bearable. He had enjoyed Lady Hempist's company so much back when she was pretending to woo him. Now that she was his boss, she seemed less inclined to appreciate his humor. He knew this was the *real* Merivale. A brilliant tactician and spy with an almost frightening lack of empathy. He was one of the few people in the world who got to see her true self, and more often than not, he was in awe of her. But she certainly was less fun now.

"I'm speaking about your little *performance* on the docks last night, of course," she said.

"Performance?" he asked innocently.

"It's the talk of every tavern in the southern half of the city."

"It *was* probably a rather heroic sight to behold," he admitted. "But it couldn't be helped."

Merivale patted her lips with her napkin. "Heroic. Yes. That reminds me, there is also a rather surprising rumor making the rounds that the person who killed the Stonepeak Strangler is none other than the Shadow Demon."

"How strange." Red ran his finger around the lip of his wineglass so it gave a light hum.

"*Apparently*," continued Merivale, "people are saying he wishes to make amends to the good people of Stonepeak. I can't imagine where they might have gotten such an idea."

Red flashed his most benign smile. "The imaginations of the common folk certainly are vivid, aren't they."

She gazed at him for a moment, then stood up from the table, walked over to a nearby window, and looked out into the bright, cloudless blue. "You have a great many talents, my Lord Pastinas. But I am coming to believe that spying is not one of them."

"Maybe I would be better suited to leading the search for Bleak Hope." He said it lightly, as if it had not been the topic of several heated conversations in the past.

"I told you, it's being handled," said Merivale. "Right now, we have more pressing concerns."

"Oh?"

"Your lack of discretion notwithstanding, I'm deeply concerned by this latest act of the biomancers. Sending you out to kill predetermined targets as the Shadow Demon had been one thing. But releasing a mindless creature to wreak havoc on the general populace?"

"It does seem reckless," said Red. "Not something Progul Bon would have done."

"Exactly," said Merivale. "As much as we all loathed Bon, I worry that he was a restraining influence on the other biomancers."

"They were *restrained* before?"

"Bon's death has clearly altered their strategy. This creature is not the only indication. They have also apparently decided to allow the emperor to begin treaty negotiations with Ambassador Omnipora."

"That *is* surprising," agreed Red.

"I want to know why this sudden change of policy," said Merivale. "I also want to know what their plans are concerning this new alliance with the Vinchen."

"I've been trying to get them to open up to me during training sessions, but they're a slippery bunch," said Red.

She turned from the window to look at him. "I think it's time to utilize your unique connection to them in a more…direct manner."

"Merivale, you know as well as I do that if I start pushing too aggressively, it could completely destroy that connection. If they figure out that I'm no longer at their beck and call, it's all over."

"I am willing to take that risk," said Merivale.

"You're that worried?"

"Do you know the last time the biomancers and Vinchen worked together?" she asked quietly.

"The time of the Dark Mage," Red said.

"Yes," said Merivale. "And centuries later, we are still recovering from that cataclysmic event. If something on a similar scale erupted now...it's entirely possible the empire wouldn't survive."

Red stared at his empty wineglass for a moment, then looked at her. "What do you need me to do?"

———

That night, Red sat in his apartments and painted. He'd been doing it regularly since he got back from Lesser Basheta. Whenever he felt the darkness within him begin to rise up inside like a tide, painting helped drain away the excess. Not that he really thought he'd lose control of himself again. But it was an unpleasant feeling, and Red was generally the sort of wag who liked to feel sunny, even when bad things were happening. He'd never seen a whole lot of point in brooding.

"Drown it all, but that's a frightening creature!" Prince Leston peered over Red's shoulder at the painting.

The prince had a tendency to come and go as he pleased. Red was fine with that, because it meant he could do the same. And the prince had better food and drink, so it generally worked in Red's favor. Besides, the casual ease of it reminded him of simpler times when he and Filler shared an apartment.

"Don't you like it, Your Highness?" Red asked as he continued to work on the painting of Brackson emerging from under the boat. He'd thrown aside his jacket and cravat and now worked with his shirt-sleeves rolled up.

"It's very well done," Leston said quickly. "But generally speaking, people paint *pleasant* things, like flowers, or scenery."

"Of course," said Red. "Those people want to sell their paintings, so they paint things people want to look at. But I don't plan to sell any of my paintings, so I don't have to worry about what other people want to see. I just paint for myself."

Leston pulled a stool over and stared at the picture of Brackson.

"But why would you want to paint such an unpleasant image?" he asked.

"If I can get it on the canvas properly," said Red, "then it doesn't feel quite so stuck in my head."

Leston was quiet for a moment. "It must be a great and terrible thing to be an artist."

"Oh, come on, my wag. I'm sure being prince has its moments." Then Red's expression grew serious and he put his paintbrush down. "Listen, I may have to . . . go away for a little while."

"What do you mean *go away*? Leave the palace?"

"Leave Stonepeak altogether. I've got to do something that could get me in a lot of trouble. Like as not, I won't be too welcome around here for a while."

Or ever again, but he didn't say that.

Leston frowned. "Lady Hempist is putting you on another assignment already? Something even worse?"

"The one she hired me for in the first place, I reckon."

"Something to do with the biomancers?" He shook his head. "It's too dangerous. I forbid it."

"Sorry, Leston," said Red. "This is something that

must be done. And the order comes from Her Imperial Majesty, so it outranks you."

"What about Hope?" Leston gave him a pleading look. "Didn't you strike a bargain with the biomancers that they wouldn't harm her as long as you remained here?"

"Yeah, and they wiggled out of that one by having the Vinchen go after her instead. So even though they technically kept their word, the bargain is as good as broken to me."

"But can't someone else do this?"

"I'm the only one who can get close enough."

"But..." The prince's face creased with frustration. "After everything you've already gone through..."

In all Red's life, with all the crazy things he'd dreamed about, he would never have imagined he'd one day become friends with the heir to the imperial throne. And what surprised him even more was how much he truly liked the wag. Sure, the prince was sheltered beyond reason, entitled beyond bearing, and spoiled beyond belief. Yet, somehow, he was still a good person.

Red squeezed the prince's shoulder. "Thanks, old pot. I'm glad *somebody* agrees with me. But it doesn't change a thing."

"So...when are you leaving?" Leston looked heartbroken. Red was painfully aware that he was the prince's only true friend.

"Tomorrow, most likely."

"Are you going to say good-bye to Nea?"

Red gave the prince a wry smile. Even after several months, things between him and Nea were still distant. He didn't blame her, of course. Biomancer control or not, it was understandable that she might not want to be around the person who nearly killed her. But Nea was not some poncey coward, and Red wondered if she might have also learned that Red was working as a spy for Merivale. If that was the case, her avoidance was more political than personal. In a way, he hoped that was it, because he rather liked the ambassador of Aukbontar.

Regardless, she *was* the ambassador of a foreign country, and absolutely didn't need to get wind of something this sensitive.

"You know what," he said at last. "Could you do it for me, Your Highness? I'd appreciate that. But not until after tomorrow."

———

The next morning, Red stood alone in his small sitting room and stared at the furniture. It was really nice furniture. There were two chairs and a love seat. The frames were made from the fine dark wood exported from Merivale's island of Lesser Basheta. The wood had been smoothed and stained until it gleamed almost like glass. Both the seat and back were upholstered with a soft, silken fabric of a dark midnight blue from the island of Fashlament, where, according to Merivale, it came out in threads from the asses of worms. Or maybe she had been joking. It was hard to tell with her sometimes. That was one of the reasons he liked her.

Beside the chairs was a rectangular glass tabletop set in a fine wrought iron frame with little seashell shapes etched into the corners. A silk runner stretched from one end of the table to the other. It was decorated with images of seabirds and fish, and Red had always wondered whether it was supposed to be flying fish, or underwater birds.

Not that Red was complaining. About any of it. He'd never had such fine furniture in his sitting room before. Hells, he'd never even had a sitting room before. And he expected it was unlikely he ever would again.

He sighed and brushed some nonexistent dust from the back of one of the chairs.

"Well, it was nice while it lasted."

"What was that, my lord?" asked Hume as he walked past with a stack of clean bed linens in his hands.

"I wouldn't bother changing the linens, Humey, old pot," Red said cheerfully. "I won't be sleeping in that bed tonight. Or any night after, most likely."

Hume turned to him, his iron-gray ponytail perfectly in place, his posture erect. Only a few folds in his forehead suggested he was genuinely worried. Red had been trying his damnedest over the last year to shake him, and there was a certain rightness that this is what did it.

"My lord?" Hume asked carefully.

"You were good to me, Hume," said Red. "A pissing angel, really. Better than I deserved. To be perfectly honest, as much of a show as I made about not needing you, I'm going to miss you."

"If I may say so, my lord, your words have a certain...finality to them."

Red gave him a wan smile. "Merivale needs to know what the biomancers are up to. I've always fancied myself a silk talker, but I've been trying for months to wheedle something out of them without success. Those cock-dribbles are better at keeping secrets than the owner of the Slice of Heaven in Paradise Circle. And let me tell you, that's saying something."

"I am familiar with the person you are referring to," Hume said dryly.

Red's eyes lit up. "See now? What a shame I'm only finding out now that you and Mo were once wags. Ah well. Anyway, Merivale needs results, and it's my job to get them."

"You are about to do something rash, aren't you, my lord," Hume said gravely.

Red grinned. "Humey, my wag, it's what I do best."

He was fond of dramatic exits, so with that, he turned and headed for the door.

"One question, my lord," said Hume.

Red paused and turned back to him.

"What would you like me to do with these?" Hume pointed to the stack of paintings leaning against the wall.

"Whatever you want, Hume. I paint to keep myself myself. I don't need them after that."

"Perhaps I should give them to Mr. Thoriston Baggelworthy of Hollow Falls? He seems particularly appreciative of the Pastinas inclination toward the arts."

"Only if you sell them to him for an outrageous sum of money and buy yourself something nice with it," said Red.

A thin smile curled up at the corners of Hume's mouth. "As you wish, my lord."

2

*S*he hadn't been to the island of Bleak Hope since she was eight years old. And yet, somehow, it felt as though she had never left.

She had been named after this place so that she'd never forget it, or the terrible events that occurred there. Perhaps the idea had worked too well, because she had not only remembered, but carried the burden of the island's fate all these years.

That was why she returned now. To lay down that burden. Maybe then she could find new direction and purpose.

As the island came into view, she didn't sail straight for the dock. Instead, she guided her small boat along the barren coastline until she saw the rocks she used to climb on as a little girl. It was high tide, so she steered carefully between the jagged black boulders until she reached the waterline. She hauled her boat up onto the shore, then sat on the small prow. She pushed back the hood of her black robe, and waited.

She watched attentively as the tide gradually revealed the base of the rocks. She had been doing this a lot lately: watching the slow processes of nature. Sunsets and sunrises, the movements of clouds across the sky. Once she had even watched ice melt. There was something about the steady but unstoppable flow of these things she sought to understand. In his journal, Hurlo remarked that he used examples in nature as a means to elevate his mind. After all, what could be more elevated than a sunrise?

When she first began the practice of observing these slow processes of nature, it had felt tedious. So much time spent watching something that she couldn't even perceive was changing from one moment to the next. But she forced herself to continue observing the movements of the sun, the moon, the tides, and anything else she thought might help her to understand...something. She couldn't say what, exactly.

She had continued to watch these natural processes every day, week after week, month after month. Gradually, she lost her impatience and began to truly *see* their movements. She adapted her perceptions to fit the event she was observing. Words like *slow* and *fast* lost much of their meaning for her when she was in that state. Time became elastic, and perception became unique to the individual moment.

So now she watched the tide reveal what lay at the base of the rocks as if it were the flourish of a magician performing a trick.

She smiled as she caught herself, even after all these years, scanning the rocky sand eagerly for sea glass. Her pulse sped up when she caught sight of a piece, but she didn't immediately run to it. Instead she stood up and slowly walked over, enjoying the delayed gratification even as her hand longed to touch it.

She knelt down and picked it up. This one was not red or blue or green, but colorless. She held the small opaque triangle in her hand and rubbed it with her thumb, enjoying the satin feel of it.

Colorless. Uninflected. Perhaps it was a sign. Or a reminder.

She slipped the sea glass into the deep pocket of

her robe. Then she pulled the hood back over her head and turned toward the ruins of her village. As she walked, the tall grass didn't seem as tall as it did when she'd been a girl.

When she reached the village, she found that it had remained undisturbed by human hand. The sign of biomancery was still planted on the dock, and that was enough to keep people away. Her home had been left to slowly, quietly dissolve from the wind, rain, and snow. Among the burnt-out husks of buildings, several walls had collapsed. A few others now housed nests for seagulls. And yet, even so changed, the sight of it brought back memories so vividly, it was as if she were looking at two images superimposed on each other. Then, and now. Living, and dead.

She walked slowly down the village's one dirt road. With only twenty buildings in total, it wasn't long before she reached the mass grave at the far end that she had dug for her people. Strangely, it was the only thing that seemed bigger than she remembered. She marveled that she had been able to do such a task alone, small as she'd been. Of course, it had taken her a long time, and throughout it all, she hadn't been able to truly comprehend the enormity of what she was doing. She'd only known it needed to be done.

She looked at the mass grave now and comprehended it completely. How could someone kill this many people? She knew the answer to that question, because she had done it herself. Few set out simply to massacre, but through their arrogance and entitlement, through their rigid adherence to ideals or ideology, they did so because they truly believed that the sacrifice was worth it. Teltho Kan had been developing a weapon that he believed would save the whole empire. Fifty lives must have seemed a paltry cost. Perhaps he had even talked of the "greater good," just as she had when she led all those people to their deaths against the biomancer Progul Bon, the Jackal Lord Vikma Bruea, and their army of the dead.

But sacrificing lives to save lives was no longer a solution she could accept. There had to be another way. In the end, Hurlo had believed that as well. He hadn't been able to find that new way, and perhaps neither would she. But if she had to die while searching for the solution, she couldn't think of any cause more worthy.

She turned away from the graveyard and walked back through the village. She looked into the broken huts as she went, curious to see what remained. Mostly it was plates and cups, pots and tools. Some rotting clothes and a few moldering dolls. She went into her own hut and found her trunk of treasures. The wood was blackened from fire set by the imperial soldiers, but the contents, mostly shells and bones, remained undamaged. She considered taking a few, but when she picked up one of the shells, it felt impossibly heavy. She reminded herself that she was here to lay down burdens, not pick up new ones.

The home of Shamka, the village elder, was the biggest and sturdiest. It had survived better than the other buildings. Even the roof, sheets of overlapping slate, was intact. She had never been allowed into his home when she was a child, so she found herself unable to resist taking a peek now.

His accommodations of an iron-frame bed and feathered mattress were far from luxurious, but had probably been the envy of everyone else in the village. No books, of course. No one in her village had been able to read. But there was a finely crafted table and cabinet made from a wood that she was certain didn't grow on the island.

She surveyed this "opulence" with wry amusement until two items on the top shelf of the cabinet caught her attention. The first was a small hand sickle. The blade was etched with what appeared to be lettering of some kind, although the language was unfamiliar to her. Next to the sickle was a painted wooden mask with a pointed snout decorated with real animal whiskers and sharp canine teeth. Was it a wolf or a dog?

She picked up the mask and examined it carefully.

Or no, perhaps it was a jackal.

She'd planned on returning to the monastery at Galemoor once she had finished with Bleak Hope. But the objects she discovered in Shamka's hut seemed to lend credence to Vikma Bruea's claim that the people of the Southern Isles shared a direct connection with the Jackal Lords and necromancy. And therefore with the hundreds of girls who had been murdered on Dawn's Light.

It was an idea that had haunted her in the months since their confrontation, but she'd been unable to find any evidence. She'd checked the library on Galemoor, which was the second largest in the empire. But the only thing she had found was a crumbling scroll that contained a rather poetic account of the forming of the empire. It spoke of "angels" with golden hair from another world who helped Cremalton unite the islands. But it didn't say how they had helped, or what happened to them after. They seemed little more than a footnote in the history of the empire. She couldn't even be sure those golden-haired people were connected to the Jackal Lords or the people of the Southern Isles.

She knew there might be information about the origin of the Jackal Lords at the library on Stonepeak, but that was the last place in the empire she wanted to go right now. Progul Bon had claimed that

Red was "so changed" that she wouldn't be able to recognize him. Since biomancers didn't lie she knew that his words were true. After losing Filler, Sadie, and, in a manner of speaking, Nettles, she didn't think she could endure seeing Red so perverted by biomancery.

It was cowardly, of course. To avoid facing the evidence that she had failed Red. But if her other recent failures had taught her nothing else, it was to know her limits, emotional as well as physical. And while the Jackal Lord's claim of kinship had troubled her, it hadn't seemed so pressing that it warranted a voyage across the entire empire to the one island she dreaded to visit.

But the evidence she found in Shamka's hut brought new urgency to the idea. The sickle looked like the one held by Vikma Bruea when he slit the throats of those innocent girls on Dawn's Light, and the more she examined the wooden mask, the more it seemed apparent to her that it was a jackal.

Perhaps libraries weren't the place to look. After all, the people of the Southern Isles were mostly illiterate. Maybe instead she needed to talk to her kinsmen. So rather than return to Galemoor, she continued east to the neighboring island of Gull's Cry.

It was summer, so the ice was broken up enough for her to reach the island within a few days. She tied up her boat at the small dock and walked the short way to the village. She felt like she was in a dream as she looked around, because it was almost exactly like her own village, except alive. People wore the plain, rough cloth she remembered so clearly from her childhood. Many of them worked next to their mud and stone huts, smoking fish or boiling strips of whale blubber for oil.

People looked at her with their guarded blue or green eyes. Their faces were etched with the hard life of the Southern Isles, made all the more prominent by the gray sand that found its way into every line and crevice of their pale faces. While she looked like one of them in some ways, her black robe and mechanical hand clearly set her apart. Moreover, in a village this small, it would be unusual to see anyone you hadn't grown up with.

She stopped in front of a hut where an older woman sat in the open doorway mending a fishing net.

"Excuse me. My name is Hope. May I ask where I can find your elder?"

The woman looked up at her with rheumy eyes, her fingers never stopping their work. "That'll be Maltch, young miss. What do you need with him?"

"I'm from the next island over," said Hope. "And I wanted to ask him a question about the history of our people."

"Next island over, eh?" Her old fingers continued their work, surprisingly nimble considering how knotted they looked. Her expression gave nothing away. "In which direction?"

"West of here."

"That so?" She looked back down at her work, her expression still unchanging. After a moment she said, "I reckon you ain't got your own elder to ask anymore, then."

"No," agreed Hope. "I don't."

"Didn't think there were any survivors."

"Just me," said Hope.

The woman continued to work in silence for a few moments. "Maltch is down the way. Third to last on the right. Can't miss it. Biggest home in Gull's Cry."

"Thank you." Hope turned and began walking in the direction the woman had indicated.

"Used to see the folk of Bleak Hope once a year," called the woman.

Hope paused and turned back to her.

The woman's face was slightly more creased than before as she examined her work. "We'd hold a festival at the end of the summer before the waters got impassable, the two villages coming together for one great big celebration." She looked up at Hope, and maybe her expression softened just a little. "Your people are missed."

The woman went back to her work, but Hope stood and watched her for a little while longer. In her head, the massacre of her village had always been something that had happened in isolation. Something no one else had noticed or cared about. The idea that the people of her humble village had been missed, even just by the people of the neighboring humble village, had never crossed her mind before. Now the notion of it left her stunned and oddly grateful. It was several minutes before she finally turned and continued on to Maltch's home.

This elder's house was much like Shamka's, with far more stone than mud, and a roof that clearly wouldn't leak even in the harshest weather. She knocked on the thick door with her clamp, realizing belatedly that the sound of metal striking wood might sound alarming to the inhabitant.

It took a few moments, but the door slowly opened, and an old man eyed her warily.

"I come from the village of Bleak Hope, and I have a question about the history of our people."

He looked at her awhile, as if he was taking in what she said and what she looked like, trying to find some way for it all to make sense. He stared longest at the metal clamp she had for a hand.

Finally, he said, "Bleak Hope, huh?"

"Yes."

"What you been doing all this time?"

"Surviving."

The loose, wrinkled skin on the corners of his

mouth and eyes creased into something that might have been a smile. "What's your question?"

She pulled the makeshift sling bag from her shoulder and opened it to show him the sickle and mask.

"What are these?"

He stared at those two items even longer than he had stared at her.

"I'm sorry," he said finally. "The only person I can tell is the one taking my place. Nobody else. Not even if they're from Bleak Hope."

Now it was her turn to stare at him. He hadn't even tried to feign ignorance. He knew something. She was certain she could force it out of him. The impulse was there. A blade to his throat would get him to talk quickly enough. Or merely slam him against the door frame a few times.

But that was not how she wanted to do things anymore.

"I thought we were a simple people, without secrets or pretensions," she said.

His eyes stayed on hers, unflinching and cold. "That what you thought?"

She tried a different tack. "I have some gold..." She reached for the pouch at her waist.

"And what do you expect someone would do with imperial coins way down here?"

His voice dripped with scorn, and rightfully so. Hope should have known better. This wasn't downtown New Laven, after all. People around here bartered and traded. Money wasn't any use in the Southern Isles.

"Sorry...," she said awkwardly. "I'm just—"

"I don't know what you've had to do to survive the fate of your island. I expect it wasn't pleasant," he said. "But that don't give you special rights. We all suffer. That's just how it is. Now you best go on back to wherever you came from."

He turned and began closing the door.

Again the impulse toward violence surged through her. One quick blow to the stomach would make him much more pliable. But she swallowed her anger and impatience. Instead she asked, "Is the answer so shameful?"

He stopped in the doorway, his back to her. He didn't respond except to take a slow breath. The wet, gurgling sound made Hope wonder how much time he had left, and if he'd found his successor yet. Someone to burden with whatever this terrible knowledge was.

"I'll tell you this," he said finally. "You might find what you're looking for on Height of Lay."

"Height of Lay?" That was the name of the island Vikma Bruea had told her the Jackal Lords had been exiled.

"Head east from here," said Maltch. "When you get to an island with nothing to the south but ice, and nothing to the east but water, you're there."

"What will I find?"

"Maybe nothing. Maybe more than you wanted. Either way, you best get going. Summer's almost over, and once the dark season sets in, nobody gets on or off that godforsaken place." He glanced back over his shoulder and eyed the sickle and mask in her sling bag. "And cover those up. Show them to no one else on this island. Understand?"

Hope nodded wordlessly. She understood one thing, at least. It *was* that shameful.

———

Height of Lay was the most inhospitable island Hope had ever seen. It looked like a small mountain range rising up from the water. She couldn't see any level terrain. The only foliage appeared to be the coarse brambles that clung stubbornly to the rocks. How could anyone live there?

She found a tiny spit of gray beach for her boat. Then she looked for the shortest peak, and began her ascent. She climbed without stopping that whole day, but her clamp slowed her down, so she was only halfway up by sunset. She rested that night on a small bit of cold rock that jutted out from the cliff.

When she woke the next morning, her black robes were covered with frost. Her limbs were stiff when she started to climb again, but they loosened as the exertion warmed her. She reached the snow line near midday, and shortly after that reached the summit. Taller peaks continued to stretch up on either side, but now she could see that there was a valley in the center of the island that cut nearly down to sea level. The valley was sheltered from the wind, but open to the sun. As she began her descent, the air warmed noticeably.

The valley floor was thick with dark green vegetation. She scanned for any sign of habitation as she waded through the knee-high grass. There was a simple beauty to the valley, with yellow, purple, and white wildflowers sprouting from small trees, and hard red berries glistening on bushes. Hope suspected that in the winter, it was just as harsh and unforgiving as the rest of the Southern Isles, but here in the summer months, it seemed like a hidden paradise. If this was where the Jackal Lords had been exiled, they could have been sent to worse places.

After walking for about an hour, she saw a large cave opening in the cliff face along the eastern boundary of the valley. The same unfamiliar letters that were on the sickle had been carved into the rock around the cave entrance. That might have captured her attention, except there was something even more interesting underneath.

Or rather, some*one*.

A boy of about five or six sat in the grass in front of the cave entrance. His bare, pale legs stuck out beneath a rough gray smock as he sat cross-legged. His feet were covered by thick black boots that seemed almost comically large for him. His shaggy hair was an eerie bone white, paler even than the typical blond hair of someone from the Southern Isles. His head was bowed, so she couldn't see his face. He held something small and dark in his lap, and he hummed to himself in a cheerful but somehow disconcerting voice.

Hope approached slowly so as not to alarm the boy. As she got closer, she noticed that the object in the boy's lap was a dead bird. She also caught a glint of metal in the grass next to him, perhaps a knife or other hunting tool.

She had assumed the bird was dead because it had been so still in his hands. But suddenly it began to move. The boy laughed delightedly as he released it up into the sky. He leaned back on his hands and smiled up at the bird as it circled overhead. Strangely, the bird only continued to fly around in a circle, its head tilted at an unnatural angle.

"Who are *you*?" the boy asked in a chirping voice. There was a feral, almost deranged quality in the way he grinned fixedly at her. Now that she was closer, she saw that his bare arms and legs were covered in thin pink scars, as if he had been cut countless times. Perhaps by Vikma Bruea? Was this the Jackal Lord's son, or a victim of his cruelty?

She drew back her hood and regarded him for a moment. "You can call me Hope, if you like."

He pointed a finger at her. "You are a *girl*!"

She nodded.

He kept his finger pointed at her. "Then you are *not* my lord. He is a *boy*." He seemed very pleased with his deduction.

"What's your name?" she asked as she stepped closer.

"I am called Uter." Then his expression became pleading. "Will you be my friend?"

"Perhaps," she said.

"Hooray!"

With unexpected speed, he grabbed the blade that lay in the grass next to him. It looked like the same small sickle she'd seen before. Still smiling, he lunged forward and took a swipe at her throat. She leaned back, avoiding the curved edge.

For a moment, he looked surprised that she'd avoided his attack. Then his face curled into a pout.

"I thought you were going to be my friend!" He came at her with a rapid series of swings, the blade hissing in the cold air.

"I never promised I would." She calmly dodged each slash but did not retaliate. "And anyway, how can we be friends if I'm dead?"

"Silly, that's *how* we become friends."

She continued to avoid his attacks as she thought about that for a moment. "What if I know a *better* way to be friends?"

He abruptly stopped. His eyes narrowed suspiciously. "What better way?"

"Why don't you explain the way you know, and I'll explain the way I know, and then we'll decide together which is better."

His manic grin returned. "Like a contest?"

"Sure," agreed Hope.

"Okay, great!" He plopped back down on the ground, his big boots splayed out in front of him as he negligently dropped his sickle back in the grass. "*My* way is to kill them, then bring them back to life. When I do that, they always do what I say."

Hope looked up at the bird wheeling overhead. "Is that what you did with the bird?"

"You bet!" He lay back into the grass, stretching out his arms and legs, and stared up at the bird.

"It certainly seems effective," admitted Hope.

"So I win?" He reached for his sickle.

"You have to listen to *my* way first."

"Right!" He dropped his sickle back into the grass, rolled onto his stomach, and stared up at her, propping his chin up with his hands. "Your turn!"

"Here is my way of making friends," said Hope. "I do nice things for you, and you do nice things for me."

Uter continued to gaze up at her for several moments, until he realized that was all she had to say. Then his eyes widened. "That's *it*?"

"That's it."

"And . . . when does it end?"

"As long as we keep doing nice things for each other, it never has to end."

"You mean *your* friendship is forever?"

"It can be."

He let his head drop to the ground. "Fine," he said into the dirt. "You win."

"Your way doesn't last that long, I take it?"

He shook his head, his forehead still pressed into the dirt. Without looking up, he pointed unerringly at the bird, his finger following its slow circle. "Just watch. It's almost over."

Hope watched the bird make a few more rounds. Then it suddenly dropped out of the sky, lifeless once again.

"Is it difficult to make it alive again?"

"Nah."

"I thought it took days, and the body needed to be treated with various chemicals."

He lifted his head up, smiling once again. There was a large smear of dirt on his ghostly white forehead. "That's the *normal* way. But I have a special way."

"A special way?"

"Yes. Because I've been wighted!"

"Wighted?"

"I'll show you." He snatched up his sickle, held it between his clenched teeth, and scrambled across the grass on all fours to the dead bird. He sat down cross-legged again and placed the bird in his lap. He sliced open his palm with the sickle, then tossed the blade to the side. He held his now-bleeding palm over the bird, letting the blood drip on its open beak and eyes. Then he stared down at the bird, smiling with anticipation.

After a moment, the bird shook itself and once again flew into the air.

"I can do it as many times as I like," he told Hope. "But the body keeps rotting, so after a while they can't move, and that's no fun."

"Did Vikma Bruea teach you how to do that?"

He leaned forward eagerly. "You know my lord? When is he coming back?"

"He isn't coming back," Hope said quietly. "I killed him."

"You killed him?" He didn't look upset by the news. If anything, he looked impressed. "Nobody has ever killed the lord before! I tried five times!" He held up one hand, the fingers splayed out. "Five! And it never worked!"

"Was . . . Vikma Bruea your father?" asked Hope.

"Father?" Uter didn't seem to understand what the word meant.

"Was he your parent?"

"Oh, I don't have parents. Because I've been wighted."

"What does that mean? To be wighted?" she asked.

He looked confused. "It means *me*."

"I see." Although, really, all she saw was that the boy didn't know what it meant either, and didn't appear to comprehend the larger ramifications of his ability.

The boy had lost interest in their conversation and was now pulling out long strands of grass and braiding them together, humming eerily to himself again. Hope watched him for a little while, wondering what she should do. It was abundantly clear that the boy was damaged in some way and, despite his youth, might already be beyond repair.

She looked down at her clamp. Being irreparably damaged was something they had in common. And she had killed his only guardian. Perhaps, in a way, that made him her responsibility. It didn't seem right to leave him here alone. He might be able to survive by foraging and hunting, but he seemed desperate for friendship. He needed to be among other humans.

Maltch was the one who had sent her here. Perhaps he knew what wighting was. Perhaps he could be a mentor to the boy as well. Gull's Cry was not luxurious by any means, but there was a community there that Uter would most likely benefit from.

"Uter?"

"Yes?" He didn't look at her, and instead kept his eyes on the braid of grass he was weaving.

"Would you like it if I took you away from here? To live with other people?"

"More people?" He leapt to his feet and squinted hard at her. "You mean it?"

"I do."

His face widened into a big smile. "So many friends!"

Then he capered across the grass, jumping, summersaulting, cartwheeling, and beheading wildflowers with his sickle as he went.

"I think we'll leave the sickle behind, though," she said.

3

*R*ed had no idea how many times he'd stood in this shooting range far beneath the palace in the biomancers' underground lair. How many times he'd loaded this revolver. How many times he'd hit the bull's-eye at the far end. How many times the biomancer Chiffet Mek was still able to find some small criticism. He'd never even thought about counting before. It was funny how the knowledge that this was the last time held a certain bittersweet tang on his tongue, even for this.

"You're still compensating slightly with your left hand when you pull the trigger," Mek said in his rusty voice as he stood in his habitual spot ten feet behind Red's right shoulder.

Over time, the biomancer had become less and less concerned with hiding his face in the deep shadow of his white hooded robe. Now Red could clearly see the strange bits of metal that poked out here and there, and the strands of wire that laced through patches of the biomancer's skin. It looked like it hurt like all hells, but Chiffet Mek never gave any indication of it. Maybe it didn't actually hurt. Or maybe Mek was so accustomed to living in constant pain, he was no longer aware of it. Red had come to understand the biomancers to some degree during his captivity. They were cruel to everyone around them, but first and foremost, they were cruelest to themselves. The entire order was built around that premise. In some ways, it reminded Red of the Vinchen, with their punishing self-discipline. But where the Vinchen used that masochism to hone themselves into weapons, the biomancers used it to turn themselves into monsters. Red used to think one was better than the other, but after seeing Racklock and his followers, he realized that it really just depended on how the "Vinchen weapons" were used. Now that they were being wielded by the monsters, he wondered if anything could stand in their way. After all, together they had united an empire, then centuries later vanquished a near-omnipotent tyrant.

"Are you even listening to me?" demanded Chiffet Mek.

"I don't know why you even care, now that you've got the Vinchen at your beck and call," Red said offhandedly as he continued to load his gun.

Mek paused for a moment. Poor gaf. Of the three biomancers who had taken charge of him, Mek was the least skilled at talking clever. Progul Bon had been the best, by far, but according to Merivale, Bon had been slain by Hope at Dawn's Light. Ammon Set had a tendency to talk a lot, but did it in circles, with at least half his words used to obscure meaning instead of providing it. Mek spoke little, and Red suspected it was because he didn't trust himself to keep all the secrets. It didn't help that biomancers couldn't lie.

"Which Vinchen are you referring to?" asked Chiffet Mek finally.

"Come off it, old pot. You and I were both there when Racklock and his wags came strolling into the council chamber." Red still kept his tone light, but he had just crossed the line, and now there was no turning back.

"How could you remember...," began Mek. Then

his bloodshot eyes widened. "You've broken Bon's control!"

"And such a shame he's no longer alive, or he'd have noticed months ago." Red turned and fired four shots: one into each of Chiffet Mek's shoulders and one into each of his knees.

Mek fell back into the stone wall behind him, and slid to the ground. He couldn't stand or lift his arms, but he didn't cry out from the pain. Instead, he glared up at Red.

"After everything we've taught you, you ungrateful street trash."

"Oh, sorry, I was supposed to be *thankful* that you tried to turn me into your own personal murder puppet?"

"In time, you would have been truly *great*," said Mek with a ferocity that suggested he honestly believed what he said. "With our guidance, you could have become something the world had never seen before. A warrior of the *future*. Something the empire sorely needs as we plummet headlong toward chaos and war for the first time in centuries. But apparently you have chosen to remain just another smart-mouthed criminal who cares nothing for the empire that has always protected him from the darkness that exists beyond its borders."

"You mean Aukbontar? At least they don't torture and mutilate their own people."

"If you think Aukbontar wants peace, you're a fool. They want to dominate us. *Use* us. If we give them a foothold, it will be the end of the empire as we know it."

"Maybe that's not such a bad thing," Red said quietly.

Mek's eyes widened. "Treason!"

"An empire that no longer looks after its people is about due for a change anyway."

Red looked down at his gun. He'd learned from
Merivale that the only reason the empire had revolv-
ing pistols was because Chiffet Mek had obtained
an Aukbontaren model and reverse engineered a
biomancery-based version of it. That single advance-
ment had allowed the imperial police to dominate
the lower classes of New Laven in a way previously
impossible. Those same revolvers had enabled Deadface Drem to capture Paradise Circle and turn it into
a laboratory for the biomancers. God only knew how
many other terrible things had come from it. And
therefore from Chiffet Mek.

He pointed the gun at Mek's head. "Now, let's
talk about why you're suddenly letting the emperor
negotiate with the ambassador. What's the new
strategy?"

"Threatening to kill me is not a very smart way to
get me to talk," said Chiffet Mek.

"I don't have as much experience in tormenting
people, so I'll defer to your judgment." Red shot Chiffet Mek's foot. "Now, are you ready to tell me?"

Mek's face didn't change, but a harsh grunt
escaped his throat. "You'll still kill me anyway, so
what does it matter."

"That's where you're wrong, old pot. I prefer not
to murder defenseless people. Even when they're
complete cock-dribbles. Call it my sensitive artistic
nature." Then he shot Mek's other foot. "Not *that*
sensitive, though, I guess."

Another grunt escaped Chiffet Mek's throat, but
he continued to glare up at Red.

"Looks like we'll be at this awhile," said Red. "I
better reload." He turned back to the small table that
held the powder cartridge and bullets. As he worked,
he said, "I can't stop thinking of all the people I've
seen biomancers kill. There was Thorn Billy. I think
that was my first time seeing it all the way through.

And then all those poor wags when we stormed the Three Cups. There was also that sailor Hope knew. And then those imps you turned into beasts to attack Hope and Brigga Lin. I know you're not personally responsible for every one of those horrible deaths. It's probably not fair to take it all out on you. But as a professional gambler, the first thing you learn is that life is anything but fair."

He turned back to Chiffet Mek with his loaded gun. The biomancer was sweating, his chest rising and falling with harsh pants. No doubt the blood loss and accumulated pain was taking its toll.

"Ready to tell me why you've changed your mind about letting the emperor negotiate with the ambassador? No? Where next, then, I wonder." Red pointed the gun between Mek's legs and watched the biomancer's eyes go wide. "Just kidding, old pot. What kind of a tom do you think I am, shooting a man's cock off? Some things just aren't done. Maybe one of the hands."

The moment he pointed his gun at Chiffet Mek's closed fist, the biomancer's face crumpled. "Wait! I'll tell you!"

Red wondered why he was more protective of hand than cock, but he wasn't going to miss the opportunity. "Okay, why, then?"

"It was Bon! He was the one who managed the emperor."

"So he did to His Majesty what he did to me?"

"Not exactly, but the same general idea."

"I would almost be flattered, if it hadn't been so pissing awful," said Red. "Okay, so you're telling me you've actually lost direct control of the emperor?"

"Yes," admitted Mek.

"So your old plan is out. But obviously you're not just going to give up and let Nea negotiate with the emperor. Not with all those terrible warnings from the Dark Mage burned into your addled brains. I need to know the *new* plan."

Chiffet Mek glared at him and said nothing.

Red slowly moved his gun back and forth. "Which hand would you rather I take first?" he asked. "I guess it depends on whether you favor your left or your right. If I remember correctly, you typically use your right." He pulled back the hammer on his gun and aimed it at Mek's right fist. "So let's go with this one."

"Fine! We *do* have a plan!"

"And it is?" Red pressed the barrel to the back of Mek's fist.

"Ammon Set will make the ultimate sacrifice, and he will be forever revered for it," Mek said quietly.

Then Chiffet Mek suddenly rotated his hand, opened his fist, and grabbed the barrel of the gun. Red released it just as the weapon began to wilt and liquefy. Mek was able to raise his hands high enough to touch his knees, and they healed instantly. Mek smiled grimly at Red as he stumbled to his feet.

"A disobedient dog must be put down," he said through gritted teeth as he forced his hand up to touch first one shoulder, then the other. "What a waste you are, Lord Pastinas. You could have been among us, exalted beyond ordinary men. But it's too late for that." He reached his hand for Red.

Red dodged the hand that no doubt carried with it some slow and gruesome death, and stepped back, wishing he'd had a second gun or some knives on him.

"Better to be among ordinary men," he said, "than a dog to the supposed exalted ones."

He flipped the small table at Chiffet Mek. He'd left the powder cartridge open on the table, so black gunpowder sprayed up at Mek's face, causing him to stumble backward. Then Red ran.

Red didn't bother to knock when he reached Lady Merivale Hempist's apartments. He barely broke stride as he threw open the doors and pushed past startled servants. It wasn't until he reached the dining room that he stopped to catch his breath. That's when he realized Merivale was entertaining. And probably working, as well. She was *always* working.

She sat at the head of her table, a glass of wine halfway to her bright red lips as she calmly regarded the sweaty, disheveled Red. To her right was the corpulent Lord Weatherwight of Wake Landing. Next to him sat the elderly high steward, looking as disapproving as ever. To Merivale's left was the thin, anxious-looking Archlord Tramasta of Fashlament. Next to him was Archlady Bashim, who it appeared had given up hope of catching Prince Leston and had now set her sights on the archlord. From what Red knew of Tramasta, however, he wasn't the marrying kind, and preferred his mollies young, without title, and easy to bully.

There was a moment of awkward silence as they all stared at Red. He smoothed his jacket and straightened his cravat as he tried to think of something clever to say. For once, he was at a loss.

But then Merivale put her wine down and stood up.

"My apologies. Lord Pastinas and I must speak for a moment concerning a pressing business enterprise we have undertaken together."

"Business, my lady?" asked Tramasta. "*You?*"

She gave him a mysterious smile. "I have discovered that managing assets can be just as entertaining as managing men. Now, if you'll excuse me, I'm sure this will only take a moment. Please continue with dinner."

"You don't have to tell *me* twice, eh, Steward?"

Weatherwight said as he held up his empty wineglass for a servant to fill.

"Indeed, my lord," said the steward, helping himself to another quail from the platter in the middle of the table.

Merivale motioned to Red, and he followed her into the small library next to the dining room. She shut the doors, then turned to him.

"Since even you are not normally this indiscreet, I assume this is a matter of desperate urgency," she said quietly.

"I pushed Chiffet Mek as far as I could," said Red. "Got some information, but I'm not sure it was worth blowing my cover."

"Don't worry about that. What do you have for me?"

"They haven't been *letting* the emperor negotiate with Nea. Progul Bon was the key to controlling him. Now that Bon's dead, the old man has gone rogue. They've got something else in the works, but I wasn't able to get the details. Mek said Ammon Set would be making the 'ultimate sacrifice.' Maybe dying in some grand biomancer experiment?"

"Perhaps…" Merivale seemed to have other ideas, but as usual kept them to herself.

"Sorry," said Red. "I know it's not a lot. I wish I could help more, but now that my cover's blown, I don't know what else I can do."

"It's true that I no longer require the services of Rixidenteron, lord of Pastinas Manor. Or perhaps I should say the soon-to-be *former* lord of Pastinas Manor." Merivale sighed, as if mourning the passing of his nobility. Then she flashed that brilliant smile of hers. "But I *do* require the services of a certain thief and scoundrel who sometimes goes by the unlikely name of Red."

"Oh?" Red was surprised by how thrillingly the idea struck him.

"I will sneak you out of Stonepeak, past imperial

soldiers and biomancers, and get you safe passage to New Laven," said Merivale.

"And in return?" Red knew her well enough to know there was always a price.

"You will find these two women, Bleak Hope and Brigga Lin, that worry our enemies so much. You will warn them of the Vinchen that are hunting them, and recruit them to our cause. Preferably before Ammon Set puts his new plan into action."

Red stared at her, openmouthed. "Merivale..."

"Come now, you *are* the logical choice. You didn't think I'd missed that, did you? I just needed to make sure I'd used up as much of your previous position with the biomancers as possible before I sent you on this new mission."

"So no one else has been looking for them," Red said evenly.

"Resources are limited," she said primly. "No point in duplicating efforts."

Red sighed. "You've bested me again, my lady."

Her expression softened slightly and she patted his cheek. "If it makes you feel better, I once again had to expend genuine effort in it. Very rare for me." Then the smile returned. "But perhaps this will make up for my callous manipulations."

She walked over to her desk and opened the larger bottom drawer. She pulled out a tightly wrapped leather bundle. She carefully unrolled it and pulled out a pair of shiny new revolvers and a leather belt with two holsters dyed a deep crimson.

"My lady," he said as he accepted the guns and holsters. "This is the finest gift I've ever received."

"I expect results, Red," Merivale said. "A Vinchen and biomancer of our own to help in the coming conflict."

Red bowed deeply. "It will be both an honor and a pleasure, my Lady Hempist."

———

Merivale helped Red clean up a little, then they returned to the dinner. Red was cognizant that this might be his last meal among the nobility and ate nearly as much as Lord Weatherwight and the high steward combined. He and Merivale chatted with the lords and ladies as if they weren't constantly expecting shouting soldiers and a pounding at the door. Thankfully, neither happened, and soon Merivale was able to shoo the other guests out of her apartments.

Archlady Bashim was the last to leave, and just before the door closed, she gave Merivale and Red a speculative look, then a knowing smile.

Once they were alone, Red said, "I do believe Archlady Bashim thinks we're having a tryst."

"I hope it won't sully your honor too much if I encourage that rumor," said Merivale. "I doubt the biomancers will openly accuse you of anything, and love gone awry would be an excellent alibi for your sudden departure. You might even get to hold on to that lordship after all."

"Actually, I'd prefer it be restored to my cousin, Alash Havolon. Or better yet, give it to my aunt Minara."

She rolled her eyes. "Very well, *Mr. Red*. But I must say, you can be tediously altruistic at times."

Red strapped the belt and holstered guns to his waist, then examined himself in a mirror. It was a curious look with the guns and the jacket and cravat, but not necessarily bad. He wished he had his gloves, but going back to his apartments would probably be a death sentence.

"Are you quite finished preening?" Merivale asked. "Just because the biomancers won't accuse you publicly doesn't mean they won't send out search parties for you."

"How am I going to get past them?" asked Red. "They're probably all over the city by now."

"I promised you *safe* passage," said Merivale. "I didn't say comfortable. Follow me."

Merivale led him out of her apartments and down the long hallway. The lift would likely be watched, so they took the stairs from the thirty-second floor all the way down to the second floor.

Floors two through five were given over entirely to the kitchens, laundry, and other menial tasks required to run the palace. Generally, the only people who entered those floors were the people who worked there. Red was surprised at how confidently Merivale led him past massive tubs of soapy water filled with dirty clothes. It was as if she knew the layout of that floor intimately. Was there anything that woman didn't know?

Past the vats of laundry was a doorway that led outside to a wide balcony on the side of the mountain. Since it was only the second floor, they were still quite close to the courtyard that encircled the front half of the mountain, and a wide ramp connected the two. All around him on the balcony were row after row of clothing racks where laundry dried in the crisp evening air.

"My lady, what brings you down here?" asked a cheerful older woman as she hung a blue silk gown on a rack.

"Ah, Hester," said Merivale, sweeping over to her with Red in tow. "I'm afraid I've been terribly indiscreet."

Hester sighed. "Again, my lady?"

"Well, he is rather handsome," said Merivale, indicating Red with a negligent wave of her hand.

Hester eyed Red. "And a bit of a rascal by the looks of him."

"Seducing ugly, rich, old men is wearying work,

Hester. A woman needs a break now and then." Merivale's eyes narrowed conspiratorially. "But I'm afraid Lord Weatherwight would be most distraught to find my little plaything still lounging about when he arrives at my chambers."

"The jealous type, is he?" asked Hester.

"Please, Miss Hester," said Red, looking as frightened and humble as he could manage. "Won't you save a poor, bludgeon tom from the gallows?"

Hester laughed. "This one's full of balls and pricks," she told Merivale. "But how can I say no? Don't you worry, I'll have him at the docks in time for the morning cargo ships to depart."

"My thanks, as always, Hester," said Merivale. "And how does your daughter like working in the grand ballroom?"

"It's a damn sight better than the laundries, my lady, begging your pardon. I'm forever grateful to you for securing that job for her."

"Always happy to help a smart young woman find a better place," said Merivale. She turned to Red. "I'm afraid I must be off, my darling. Hester will see you safely to the docks. Once there, look for the ship called the *Harrowing Sky*, where you will find Captain Yevish. Give him this paper." She handed him a short note in her own handwriting. "That should see you safely on your way. I hope when you have made your fortune, we may meet again."

"I shall win the prize and return directly, my lady," Red said as he bowed deeply.

"See that you do."

He watched her return the way they'd come, weaving swiftly between the vats of laundry.

"Alright, you leaky tom," said Hester chidingly as she pulled him deeper into the forest of damp, hanging clothes. "She's better than you deserve, I'm sure."

Red smiled. "You think so?"

Hester led him to a ramp. There was a wagon at the bottom filled with large bins of clean soldier uniforms. "Lady Hempist is better than *any* man deserves."

"Maybe that's her tragedy," suggested Red.

"It's not for the likes of you or me to say."

Hester pointed to one of the laundry bins on the wagon. "In you go. I've got a schedule to keep. Cover yourself up until I tell you it's safe to come out."

———

It was a long, bumpy ride to the docks at the bottom of the wagon. The piles of uniforms weren't nearly as comfortable as Red had expected. He hadn't realized there were so many decorative bits of metal threaded into them, and the faint sulfuric stench of gunpowder still clung to the fabric.

They stopped at a few imperial garrisons along the way to drop off bundles of clean clothes. Red worried there wouldn't be enough to cover him by the time they reached the docks, but Hester had brought along a large sailcloth tarp to cover him for the last leg of the trip. When they reached the dock garrison, the sun was just coming out, and he could make out faint shadows against the rising sun as Hester chided the soldiers with the same ornery concern she'd shown Merivale. Finally, they continued on to the docks.

"Alright, you leaky tom, out with you," she said from her seat at the front of the wagon.

Red slipped out of the wagon, wincing at the new sun as he hurriedly put on his tinted glasses.

"I wish there was some way I could repay you," Red told the woman.

Hester shook her head. "Nothing to repay." Then she gave him a hard look. "Just make sure you do whatever Lady Hempist has set you out to do."

Apparently Hester hadn't believed a word of their cover story. Rather than insult her further, he merely bowed as low as he had to Merivale. "You can be sure of it, Miss Hester."

"Get on with you, then." She flicked the end of her reins at him, then at the horses. The wagon began its slow trip back to the palace.

Red scanned the docks and soon found a large, clumsy three-masted cargo ship with *Harrowing Sky* painted across the stern. The crew were hustling to get the last of the cargo on board before the tide started to go out. Captain Yevish was easy enough to spot among them. Partly because he was the one barking orders, and partly because he was the tallest man Red had ever seen. He was even taller than Filler, although he wasn't nearly as muscular.

Thinking of Filler gave Red a sharp jolt of eagerness. He'd already decided that the first place to start his search for Hope and Brigga Lin would be New Laven. Someone there would have heard about where they were. And while he was there, he'd probably see some of the crew. Maybe even his oldest wag in the world, unless the salthead was still off keeping Hope out of trouble. No, that's what he *should* be doing, Red told himself. Not waiting around for him to suddenly and unexpectedly show up. Red needed to steel himself for the possibility that none of the people he held closest would be there. But hopefully he could at least pick up a lead on where they were. Maybe from Old Yammy, or whoever was running the Circle now.

"Captain Yevish!" he called to the tall man.

The captain gave him a suspicious look. "What can I do for you?"

"I was asked to give this to you." Red held up the sheet of parchment with Merivale's message.

Yevish made his way slowly down the gangplank to the dock, barking a few more orders to his men as he went. He took the parchment from Red and squinted at it for a moment. Then he rolled his eyes.

"Ever at the beck and call of Her Imperial Majesty, I suppose. It was *one* time I got caught with goods I shouldn't have. And that conniving Hempist somehow turned it into a life of service to the throne."

Red grinned and offered his hand. "You and me both, my wag. I think we'll get along just fine."

Yevish gripped his hand. "You drink? I could do with some drink and conversation on the voyage."

"Those are two of my specialities, Captain," said Red.

"Welcome aboard, then, Mister..." He looked at the parchment again. "Red?"

"Red'll do fine, Captain. A wag like me doesn't go in for formalities. Especially after having to spend as much time at the palace as I have."

"Got any good stories?" asked Yevish as he led him back up the gangplank.

"Captain, stories are what I'm *best* at."

The tall man smiled for the first time. "Well, now. I do like a good story."

A short time later, Red stood at the stern and watched Stonepeak recede into the distance. He'd spent more than a year on that island, and it saddened him to see it go. He was glad he'd at least said good-bye to Leston. And he felt a pang of regret that he hadn't said anything to Nea. If Leston didn't tell her, no doubt Merivale would make up something colorful.

It occurred to him that he'd actually spent more time with those three people than he ever had with Hope. If he was being honest with himself, he was a little nervous about seeing her again. He had changed so much, and probably so had she. Would he still be sotted with her? And what would she think of him?

He sighed and turned his back on Stonepeak. He would find out one way or the other, and soon. Then at least he'd know how it was.

4

*H*ope and Uter sailed west from Height of Lay back to Gull's Cry. As Hope guided their small craft through the slate-gray waters, she watched the white-haired boy pretend that a small bit of rope was a snake. He hummed quietly to himself, punctuating the song occasionally with a playful hiss from his rope snake.

They tied up at the rickety dock at Gull's Cry and walked through the small village toward the elder's hut. Uter walked beside her, holding on to her metal clamp. He had been fascinated by the clamp ever since he noticed it during their climb out of the valley. Later, he'd spent hours on the boat trying to understand its mechanics.

Now he held on to it tightly as he stared at the clusters of squat huts that lined both sides of the dirt path.

"So many people," he whispered excitedly as he watched the hard-faced villagers that pretended not to notice the new arrivals. "Aren't they *amazing*?"

Hope smiled, wondering if he'd ever seen this many people before. "I suppose *all* people are amazing, when you think about it."

"Do you think they'll be friends with us?"

"Perhaps," said Hope. "But first we must go and talk to their elder."

"Why?"

"Because it's the polite thing to do, and because I think he may be able to help us understand where you come from."

"I already know where I come from," Uter said boastfully.

"Is that so?" Hope doubted his answer would be accurate, but she was curious what his perspective might be.

"Yes." Uter nodded. "I come from the land after death!"

"That may be true," Hope said carefully. "But you came from somewhere else before that."

"Did I?" He seemed thrilled by this idea, as if it was something he'd never considered before.

When Maltch answered his door, he gave Hope an uneasy look. Then he noticed the boy, and his expression became panicked. He tried to close the door, but Hope held it open. He strained with it for a moment, then all the fight suddenly left him, and he let go.

"May we come in?" asked Hope.

He glared at her, then sighed and turned his back on her. "Might as well. It's too late anyway." He shuffled over to the table in the center of the room and sat down.

As Hope walked into the hut, Uter scampered in ahead of her. She watched him move around the room, examining the contents of cupboards and pantries. Since he no longer had his sickle, she decided he wouldn't do any lasting harm by poking around, and let him be.

She sat down at the table across from Maltch. "There were no written records on Height of Lay. Nothing to be learned about the Jackal Lords or their relationship to the people of the Southern Isles. Only this boy."

"He *is* the relationship between the Jackal Lords and the people of the Isles."

"So you *knew* he'd be there?"

"I never been to Height of Lay myself, so I didn't *know* anything."

He watched the boy for a moment. Uter peered through the bottom of a glass bowl at them, his face oddly distorted by the convex shape.

Maltch's eyes remained on Uter as he said, "I never actually seen someone who's been wighted before."

"He used that word, too," said Hope. "What does 'wighted' mean?"

Maltch looked back at her briefly. Then his eyes strayed to a nearby shelf, which had a sickle and mask exactly like the ones Hope had found in Shamka's hut.

"I understand your reluctance to speak," Hope said quietly. "And I would rather not resort to violence. But understand, I am not leaving without answers."

He nodded wearily and rubbed his eyes. "All the islands of the south must pledge their allegiance to the Jackal Lords. They protect us, keep us safe. And in return, once every seven years, a child is chosen from among the islands. A little boy no older than two years. He is taken to Height of Lay and left there on the beach. It's been like that for as long as anyone can remember. No one's ever been sure what happens to these boys. Some say they're sacrificed. Some say they're trained as necromancers. And some say they're wighted. I guess now I know which it is."

"But what *is* it?" pressed Hope.

"The way my dad told me, when someone is wighted, they're treated with all kinds of strange potions, medicines, and ointments. Things only necromancers know how to make. These things are poisonous, and they push the person to the very brink of death, where they suffer for days in more pain and torment than you or I could imagine. Most of them eventually die. Their bodies just can't take the suffering and give out. But every once in a while, one of them comes back."

He watched as the boy pulled open a drawer filled with cookware and utensils, examining each one with fascination.

"It's said that those who come back are given the power to raise the dead with only a drop of their own blood. But they are marked with bone-white hair, and their minds are broken beyond repair."

"Is there any way to help him?" asked Hope.

Anger flashed across the old man's face. "You still don't get it. He belongs to the Jackal Lords. A child that survives the wighting is a rare thing. They'll be coming for him. And when they do, they'll kill *all* of us. And if we're very lucky, they'll let us stay dead."

"You don't need to worry about that," said Hope. "They won't be coming for him, because the Jackal Lords are all dead."

He leaned back in his chair and looked at her as if she'd gone mad. "The Jackal Lords don't die. They are *masters* of death. It bends to their will!"

"Even so," Hope said. "I met Vikma Bruea, who claimed to be the last of the Jackal Lords, and I slew him. Since there was no one else on Height of Lay besides Uter, I can only surmise that he was telling the truth, and the Jackal Lords are no more."

Maltch looked stunned. "You...really *killed* a Jackal Lord?" He shook his head. "That's not..." His face pinched with fear and he suddenly stood up, knocking his chair over. He backed across the room, his eyes locked on Hope. "Get out, you... blasphemer! You've doomed us all!"

Hope stood up slowly. She kept her hand open in front of her to show she meant no harm, but she suspected it wouldn't make much difference. "Calm down. Tell me how I have doomed us."

"The..." He looked so enraged now that he could

hardly get the words out. He jabbed his finger off to one side. "The *Northerners*, you idiot! They'll sweep down on us without mercy! It was only their fear of the Jackal Lords that kept them at bay!"

"That's ridiculous," said Hope. "Listen, I know the Northerners, and—"

"Of course you know them!" His face was flushed and sweating now. "You...you must be a servant of theirs." He grimaced with a strange satisfaction. "Yes, that's it. This is where you've been all this time, hiding up north. You're a traitor sent to assassinate the Jackal Lords and bring us to heel!"

"Don't be absurd," said Hope. "If you just calm down—"

"Get out, I said!" He was screaming now. "And take that little *monster* with you!" He pointed at Uter.

Uter stared at him quizzically, more curious than offended. Then he turned to Hope. "Is he going to be our friend?"

"It doesn't seem like it," Hope said.

"My turn, then!"

Taking her by surprise with his speed, the little boy grabbed a meat cleaver from the kitchen drawer and threw it at Maltch. It lodged in Maltch's forehead and the man fell over, his limbs twitching. Uter laughed gleefully as he hurried over to the corpse.

"Uter, stop!" said Hope.

"Just watch!" He yanked the cleaver out of the elder's forehead and used it to cut open his own palm. Then he squeezed his hand so the blood dripped into the corpse's gaping mouth and eyes.

"Maltch?" came a female voice from outside. "What's all the yelling in there?"

The front door opened behind Hope, revealing a young woman. She stared first at Hope, then at the grinning, white-haired boy who crouched down next to the dead body of her elder.

"What…" The woman seemed paralyzed with horror.

"Please…," said Hope. But what could she say?

Then the dead Maltch began to move. Uter let out a cackle of delight. The woman gave a piercing scream.

"Let's go." Hope lunged across the room, grabbed Uter, and pulled him past the shrieking woman in the doorway.

"Help! They killed Maltch! Help!" shouted the woman.

"She sure is loud," Uter observed as he allowed Hope to pull him into the dirt road that ran through the center of the village.

"She's upset," Hope said tersely.

The woman came running out of the hut. *"Murder! Necromancy!"*

"Why?" asked Uter.

People rushed from their homes, looking both afraid and very angry.

"You there! Stop!" shouted one of the men, a tall, burly fellow in a fur vest.

"We'll talk about it later," said Hope. "Right now we need to get out of here."

They were surrounded by several men, armed with hammers and pikes. They clearly weren't warriors and had no idea what to do with their "weapons." But they were completely justified in their anger, so Hope was loath to hurt them.

"What the hell did you do to Maltch?" demanded the one who had spoken before.

"They killed him!" shouted the woman as she backed away fearfully from the hut. "Then they *raised* him!"

"It was an accident," Hope said lamely. "The boy doesn't know what—"

She was interrupted by more shouts of fear and

anger as the raised Maltch stumbled to the doorway, the cleaver wound in his head spilling blood and bits of brain.

The look that the villagers gave her then said that she couldn't talk her way out of this. Not that she was particularly good at talking her way out of things under the best of circumstances. That had always been Red's specialty.

One of the men let out a wordless yell and swung his sledgehammer at them with both hands. Hope dropped to the ground, knocking Uter's feet out from under him so that the swing missed him as well.

"Run for the boat," she told him. "Now!"

As Uter scrambled to his feet, a different villager thrust his pike down at Hope. She knocked it aside with her clamp so that the blunt end slammed into the side of the hammer villager's head. She then knocked it the other way so that it hit a villager on the other side, sending him stumbling back. She'd hoped not to hurt anyone, but at this point she'd settle for just not killing any of them.

The hammer had fallen on the ground next to her, so she grabbed it and swung it in a wide arc, sweeping several other villagers off their feet. She saw Uter was already on his way toward the boat, his pale little legs pumping, a delighted grin on his face, like this was all great fun. Fortunately, the villagers seemed more focused on Hope now.

She vaulted to her feet, dodged to one side to avoid the swing of a hatchet, then blocked the thrust of a rusty knife with her clamp. She almost had a clear run for the docks, but there was one particularly large fellow directly in front of her. He wasn't armed and came at her with a right roundhouse punch. She blocked the punch with her left forearm while slamming the palm of her right hand into his chin. She chopped the side of her hand into his neck to soften him up further, then grabbed the back of his head and pulled him forward so that she could jam her knee into his stomach. She didn't even wait for him to drop before she took off running after Uter.

Uter was already in the boat as Hope neared the docks with half the village right behind her.

"Untie the line!" barked Hope.

Hope leapt for the boat just as Uter released the line from the cleat. When she landed, her momentum pushed the boat away from the dock and out to sea. She hurriedly ran up the sail, grateful for the simplicity of this tiny boat.

As the wind took them away from Gull's Cry, Hope looked back at the villagers gathered at the dock. They threw things at her and shouted curses, their fear completely overcome by frustration and rage.

All Hope felt in return was a quiet sadness. More death. No matter how she tried to avoid it. And now she had nowhere else to take Uter except back with her to Galemoor.

They sailed for a while in silence, with the dark gray of the water transitioning almost imperceptibly to the lighter gray of the sky. Uter had apparently taken a small earthenware cup from the elder's hut and hidden it in the large pocket on the front of his smock. He pulled it out now and examined it curiously, tracing the paint swirls in the baked clay with his finger. He seemed completely indifferent to what he'd done back at the village. Or perhaps, merely uncomprehending.

"Uter?"

"Yes, Hope?" He looked eagerly up from his cup.

"You shouldn't kill people."

He looked surprised. "Why not?"

"Because, even if you bring their body back to life, their soul is still gone forever."

He frowned under his white bangs. "What's a soul?"

She thought about how best to answer that question as she trimmed the sail. "It's what makes you... you," she said. "It changes and grows, just like your body. But you can't see it because it's on the inside."

"Do *I* have a soul?" he asked, fascinated.

"Every person has one," said Hope. "But when you kill them, they lose that part."

He frowned. "I wouldn't want to stop being me."

Hope nodded. "That's right. And most people feel the same way. You wouldn't want someone to get rid of your soul, so you shouldn't get rid of other people's souls."

"Not even if they won't be my friend?" asked Uter.

"Not even then," said Hope. "Do you understand?"

He beamed at her. "I understand." Then his eyes darted over her shoulder as he caught sight of something behind her. "What is *that*?" He stood up in the boat and pointed excitedly, making the small craft rock back and forth. "It's a moving island!"

"Sit down, Uter, or we'll capsize." Hope followed the direction he'd pointed and saw the black hump of a whale in the distance. They watched as it slid smoothly below the surface, followed by the wide, flat tail, which slapped the water with a loud splash before sinking out of sight.

"Hey, islands don't have tails!" He turned to Hope. "Do they?"

"It wasn't an island, Uter. It was a whale."

"A what?"

"It's like a giant fish."

Uter shifted around excitedly, making the boat rock again. "Can *it* be my friend?"

Hope sighed and shook her head. "Just leave it alone, Uter."

———

"That's an island, right?" asked Uter as they drew near Galemoor. "Not a whale?"

"It's an island," agreed Hope as she steered them into the small bay. "The biggest in the Southern Isles. Although it's nowhere near as large as some of the islands in the north."

"And this is where you live?" asked Uter.

"It's where *you'll* be living, too," said Hope. "At least for now, this will be your home."

He gazed up at the brooding, black, rocky shore of the island and smiled contentedly. "Home."

Hope tied their boat to the small dock, then led Uter up the long, winding path toward the monastery. As they walked, Hope thought of all the times she had taken that same path as a little girl with Hurlo. Not that she had any intention of teaching Uter the ways of the Vinchen. The boy was already dangerous enough. But still, walking side by side with the boy along the stony path felt unexpectedly right to her in a way she couldn't quite define.

"What is this *place*?" Uter yelled excitedly as they approached the monastery.

The black stone walls were still charred and cracked from when Racklock and the other Vinchen brothers had set fire to it before leaving. The wooden support beams had all been burned or torn away, leaving many of the stone structures to lean in on themselves. Hope had replaced the roof on a few of the buildings since her return, but most were still only hollow shells. That didn't seem to bother Uter, however. Once they passed through the front entrance, he scampered around the compound in a state very close to ecstasy.

"It's beautiful!" he crowed, doing cartwheels across the open courtyard. "We live in a beautiful palace!"

"I'm glad you think so," said Wentu as he emerged from the temple that stood in the center of the compound. The old monk's black hood was back, and he smiled serenely. "You may be the first boy to ever have that reaction."

"New friend!" shouted Uter gleefully. He'd somehow secreted a large hook into his smock and now brandished it like a sickle.

"Uter, no!" Hope was too far away to stop him, and the boy was much too excited to listen to her. He closed the distance between himself and Wentu in moments. The pointed hook gleamed in the wan sunlight as he brought it down.

But Wentu's peaceful smile never faltered as he stepped nimbly to one side, grabbed Uter's wrist, and disarmed him, all in one fluid motion. A Vinchen was a Vinchen, no matter the age.

Uter stared at his empty hand for a moment, then at the still-smiling Wentu.

"Do it *again*!" he pleaded.

"Perhaps another time, my child." Wentu turned to Hope. "It appears your trip to the island of Bleak Hope yielded unexpected results."

"It's a long story," said Hope. "And the boy and I haven't eaten since yesterday."

"It just so happens I made your favorite stew," said Wentu. "And you know I always make too much. Both of you come in and you can eat while you regale me with your adventures."

"*I* made friends," boasted Uter as Wentu guided him gently into the temple.

"Indeed?"

"But I think Hope is my *favorite* friend. Did you know she has a hand made of *metal*?"

"She is a remarkable woman in many ways," said Wentu as he turned and gave her an oddly knowing smirk.

———

Hope had replaced the roof on the dormitory so that they wouldn't have to sleep in the temple. But there didn't seem to be much point in moving the iron stove back to the enormous kitchen when it was just the two of them, so they still took their meals there.

That night, Uter dozed contentedly on the meditation mat in front of the black stone altar, his belly full of warm fish stew. Hope and Wentu sat in the corner by the glowing iron stove, sipping from wooden bowls and talking quietly.

"This elder...Maltch," said Hope. "He genuinely seemed to believe that without the supposed protection of the Jackal Lords, the north would swoop down and conquer the Southern Isles."

"Ah," said Wentu.

She gave him a searching look. "It's a preposterous notion, of course. First, the Isles are already part of the empire, so there is no need to *conquer*. Second, on the whole, most Northerners would prefer to completely ignore the Southern Isles. Few are willing to travel here, and then only for trade."

"True," agreed Wentu.

"So why do you not seem surprised by Maltch's fear of invasion from the north? What am I missing?"

Wentu closed his tired, gray eyes and sighed. "I heard a story once. I don't know if there is any basis of fact in it. But I suppose a story can be true without being factual. It was a tale my mother told me when I was a boy on Greater Basheta."

"You were a boy once?" Hope asked teasingly.

Wentu smiled. "It was a *very* long time ago. We were walking through the market by the docks when I saw someone from the Southern Isles for the first time. I asked my mother why he was like that, so pale, and with yellow hair. And to explain it, she told me this story."

He paused for a moment, as if gathering the memories, and then said, "People tell of how the great Vinchen, Selk the Brave, and the fearsome biomancer, Burness Vee, helped Cremalton unite all the islands of the Storm into a great empire. But few people talk of the *other* group that assisted him. A clan of angels from another world."

"They were mentioned briefly in that history you recommended," said Hope. "But I didn't really see a connection. Were the people mistaken for angels because they had yellow hair? Was it the Jackal Lords?"

Wentu shook his head. "These people were not from the Southern Isles. They did have golden hair and pale skin, but they were from a land far away, on the other side of the Dawn Sea. These people had a knowledge of spirits and the dead that went beyond anything known by either the Vinchen or the biomancers. When they arrived, they offered Cremalton their support and were a tremendous asset in bringing some of the more unruly islands under control."

Wentu paused again, staring up at the stained glass windows above them. "My mother said, 'Wentu, my boy, people will tell you that after the empire was united, the angels returned to their distant land. But the truth is, they couldn't. They were trapped here by the prevailing currents that pushed ever westward. Not even angels can command the sea.'"

Wentu smiled to himself, and Hope tried to picture him as a boy, standing with his mother in that market.

"According to the tale my mother told me," continued Wentu, "when the angels realized they were trapped, they turned on Cremalton and tried to take the empire for themselves. It took the combined power of the Vinchen and biomancers to prevent their coup. When they were defeated, the angels fled down into the remote, uninhabited islands of the south. It was there they began calling themselves the Jackal Lords."

"So the people of the Southern Isles today are descendants of those foreigners from across the Dawn Sea?" asked Hope.

"It's one story that explains these islands and their inhabitants. There are others. I recall one scholar who claimed that thousands of years ago, everyone in the islands of the Storm was as pale as the Southerners, but that in the north, they intermingled with dark-skinned settlers from Aukbontar until everyone there was neither dark nor light skinned, but somewhere in between." Wentu shrugged. "Who can say which is true? They both sound equally implausible to my ear. Perhaps the truth lies somewhere else entirely."

"Do you think Maltch believed in the story of these exiled angels?" asked Hope.

"Probably. The Jackal Lords encouraged that belief," said Wentu. "As I recall, they talked a great deal about reclaiming past greatness during the uprising that Hurlo and I put down. There was even a song about it that we often heard them sing when they were preparing for battle." His eyes grew distant for a moment. "It was a strange tune, at once sad and forceful. Let's see, how did it go..." He cleared his throat, then in his worn, cracked voice, he began to sing:

Tumble down, ho!
Rumble down low!
The ground gives all our wanting.
Tumble down, ho!
Rumble down low!
Now it's time for hunting.
For the angels talk
So the dead can walk,
The living will quail,

And their courage will fail,
When the dead come for the living.
Yes, the dead come for the living!
Tumble down, ho!
Rumble down low!
Glory has always been our fate.

Then Uter's voice joined in, light and sleepy, but clear as a bell:

Tumble down, ho!
Rumble down low!
Glory to the Haevanton Triumvirate!

Uter smiled, his eyes still closed, and curled up on the meditation mat as if it were as comfortable as a feather bed.

"The Haevanton Triumvirate?" Hope asked quietly. "Vikma Bruea spoke of that as well. What is it?"

"Perhaps the land your distant ancestors came from? What does it matter? We haven't had contact with them for over a thousand years. Perhaps the place no longer even exists."

Then he gave her a hard look, which was unusual for him. It reminded Hope uneasily of Hurlo when he was scolding her. "Of course, this is nothing but a distraction for you. The Jackal Lords, the Haevanton Triumvirate, even this boy, though it was sweet of you to take him in. It's all a way to avoid your true, and far more immediate, concerns."

Hope wished desperately that she could change the subject, but even now, the courtesy that Hurlo had beat into her held. She couldn't disrespect her elder brother, so she said nothing, and instead stared into the orange glow that showed through the vents in the stove.

Wentu's face softened. "I'm not your teacher, and

I cannot tell you what to do. But Racklock is out there somewhere, perverting the Vinchen order and everything it stands for." He placed his wrinkled old hand on her shoulder. "I know you have suffered and lost a great deal. But you cannot hide here forever."

"I'm not hiding," she said, perhaps too quickly. It sounded defensive, even to her own ears. "I'm just preparing. And I'm not ready yet."

She glanced at Uter, who snored softly, his expression a picture of innocence.

"Besides, I have this one to look after now. You've seen what he's like. I can't just unleash him on the world."

Wentu nodded, but said nothing. He didn't need to, because they both knew she really was hiding after all. And not just from Racklock. Red was still out there, turned into something terrible because she had failed to rescue him. If worse came to worst, she would face Racklock and probably death. But she didn't know if she could summon up the courage to face whatever had become of Red.

———

After their return to Galemoor, things settled into a routine for Hope, Uter, and Wentu.

Hope spent much of her day rereading sections of Hurlo's journal, meditating, and training. The last was not out of any conviction that she would be fighting anyone in the near future. Rather it was a comfort for her. A way to release the slow buildup of worry that she was always trying to convince herself she didn't feel. Wentu occupied himself happily as he always did with domestic chores such as cleaning and cooking. Uter was thrilled merely to have a whole new island to explore. He would often be gone all day and stumble into the temple for supper shortly after sunset, covered in dirt and fresh scrapes.

Hope wasn't sure she was getting through to the boy about his cavalier attitude toward death. When she spoke to him about it again, he seemed to understand. But the next day, he came home with a pack of resurrected snakes slithering dutifully behind him, and was genuinely surprised when Hope scolded him for it.

Wentu was far more patient, and Hope would have thought the boy would prefer the gentle old man's presence. But Uter still preferred Hope, and he seemed desperate to share activities with her. At first, she wasn't sure what those might be. But when she discovered that Vikma Bruea hadn't taught him to read, she decided to set aside time each day to teach him.

He picked up the letters easily enough, but once they started combining those letters into words, things became more challenging. They sat on the floor every morning in the dormitory and worked with a small slate and chalk.

"The cot says moo."

"Cow," Hope corrected him.

He looked down at the short sentence written on the slate and shrugged. "Cow, then. The letters are mostly the same."

"They're very different words with very different meanings." Hope could hear the irritation in her voice.

"I know, I know," he said, his eyes already trailing off to stare at the ceiling.

She had a hard time understanding why he didn't seem all that interested. She remembered feeling *starved* for the knowledge when Hurlo had taught her.

"Uter, learning to read is *important*," she said.

"Why?"

"Because then you can learn about everything else."

"Like what?"

"History, science, poetry. It's all open to you once you learn this basic skill."

He gave her a dubious look. "Could I learn about whales?"

"Yes, reading will help you learn about whales."

"I *guess* it's worth it, then," he said.

"Thank you. Now, let's try a different one. And this time, pay attention to *all* the letters."

———

That afternoon, Hope confessed her frustration to Wentu.

"It is an excellent exercise in patience for you," he told her as the two hung laundry up in the breezy courtyard.

Hope watched Uter run past the open gate after a pack of seagulls.

"It is," she agreed. "I'd always considered myself even tempered, but this experience has shown me otherwise. When he cannot grasp something that seems so obvious to me, my frustration is immediate, and I'm afraid it shows more often than not."

Wentu smiled as he hung up a heavy black robe on the line. "We all have our weak points. There was a young brother named Stephan who could not cook to save his life, and it drove me mad at times." He hung up one of Uter's new makeshift smocks made from the scraps of an old Vinchen robe. "I *do* think you and the boy are good for each other, though."

"I suppose so."

Uter ran past the gate again in the opposite direction. But then the boy jerked to a halt and stared at something farther down the path. After a few moments, he turned to Hope and jumped up and down, waving his hands above his head.

"A boat!" he shouted, then began running toward her. "Someone's here to visit!"

Hope and Wentu exchanged surprised glances.

"Perhaps the Vinchen have returned?" she asked.

"Doubtful," said Wentu. "They made it pretty clear that they were finished with this place."

"Merchants, then?"

"We haven't had those in years. Not since Racklock shut down the distillery."

"What, then?" asked Hope as Uter came up to her and began pulling excitedly on her clamp.

"Come on, Hope!" he pleaded. "Come see!"

Wentu nodded. "Perhaps we should do as the boy asks."

"Alright," said Hope. "But, Uter, stop trying to pull my clamp out."

He immediately let go, his face concerned. "Could I do that?"

She ruffled his mop of white hair. "Of course not. But you don't need to drag me."

As they walked toward the gate, Hope was keenly aware of the emptiness at her waist where the Song of Sorrows used to hang. If these visitors were hostile and well armed, she didn't know how she would defend against them.

But when they reached the entrance and Hope looked down the path, all her anxiety left. The small boat at the dock was already turning back out to sea. It had left behind only a single person.

Old Yammy was walking unhurriedly up the path toward them.

"Well, look who it is," said Wentu, an odd twinkle in his eye.

"You know Yammy?" Hope asked. She would

never have imagined that someone from Red's past also had connections to Wentu. But she supposed if anyone was capable of straddling such different worlds, it would be Old Yammy.

"How long has it been, Yameria?" Wentu called to her as she came near.

"Apparently long enough for you to become quite distinguished and wise-looking, Brother Wentu," she said.

"Still such a flatterer, I see," he said.

Hope turned from one to the other. "How...do you know each other?"

Wentu laughed. "It's hard to *avoid* her." He turned back to Yammy. "Still everyone's favorite meddler."

"This is the last time," she said mildly. "I promise."

Wentu gave her a strange look, like she'd just said something troubling.

"Will you be my friend?"

Hope thought she'd locked up all the sharp objects on the island, but Uter pulled a small paring knife from his pocket. Before he could lunge at her, Old Yammy smiled down at him.

"Sweet boy, we're already friends."

"Are we?" He looked surprised and lowered his knife.

"Of course," she said. "Anyone who is friends with Hope and Brother Wentu is automatically friends with me."

"So...I can get more friends just by having friends already?"

"Only if you do it *my* way," Hope said as she snatched the knife from his hand.

Uter gave her a grudging look. "Maybe your way really is better. When it works." He turned back to Old Yammy. "*My* way always works, though."

"I'm happy to see you, Yammy," said Hope. "Or should I call you Yameria?"

"Whichever pleases you," said Yammy. "It doesn't matter to me."

"What are you doing here, though?" asked Hope.

"I'm here for *you*, of course," said Yammy. "Don't you remember? I told you months ago that we would have our time together. And I always keep my promises."

"I see," said Hope. "Where is Vaderton?"

"I have given Brice his own set of tasks. But you and I must begin ours immediately if we are to be of any help in the struggle to come."

"Begin what?" asked Hope.

Yammy put her hand on Hope's cheek and smiled fondly. "It's wonderful that you have resolved to turn away from the path of vengeance and death glorified by the Vinchen code. But as you've discovered through your work as Dire Bane, simply adopting someone else's path won't yield the result you're looking for either. You must find your *own* way."

Hope looked out at the distant ocean as she massaged her forearm. It didn't really bother her the way it used to, but she still found the action soothing. "I've been trying. And at times it feels almost maddeningly within reach. I've meditated, I've studied Grandteacher Hurlo's writings. But I just feel like there's...something missing."

"Yes, dear," agreed Old Yammy. "You've been missing me."

5

*W*hat in God's name *is* it?" Stephan asked.

Hectory shook his head and said nothing.

The two young Vinchen warriors stared at what appeared to be a forest of fifteen-foot-tall mushrooms arrayed in a random assortment of bright colors.

"Has to be some kind of biomancery," declared Hectory. Then he suddenly looked unsure. "Right?"

"I don't know what else could make such a thing," said Stephan. "Let's get a closer look."

Stephan wasn't too clear on what had actually happened on Dawn's Light. Some sort of clash between the biomancers and the blasphemer. This was the last place anyone had seen her, so Grandteacher Racklock had told them to comb the entire island and look for clues as to where she had gone next.

"Do you think the *real* biomancers did this?" asked Hectory. "Or was it that female biomancer allied with the blasphemer?"

Stephan didn't respond because something caught his eye at the base of the nearest mushroom. He moved closer and knelt down to get a better look. His new, untested black leather armor creaked quietly.

It was teeth. Too small to be adult. No, it was a set of...children's teeth embedded in the base of the thick mushroom stalk.

"What in all hells...," he whispered to himself.

"What is it, Steph?" asked Hectory.

"Shut up for a minute," Stephan said tersely. Still on his knees, he moved to the next stalk. Was that a small skull partly sticking out? And the next one, was that a tiny, shriveled hand? As he moved deeper into the rainbow mushroom forest, a sick dread grew in his stomach.

"I don't know if that's such a good idea," said Hectory. "We don't know what kind of biomancery this is. It could still be dangerous. I mean, why put a bunch of giant mushrooms in a field? Maybe they're poisonous. Or...*alive*."

But by now Stephan was deep into the heart of the forest, and he had seen enough to have a pretty good idea what kind of biomancery it was.

"They're all children," he said.

"What?" Hectory had reluctantly moved a short way into the forest, but the thick stalks seemed to absorb the sound, making the words between them muted.

"Every one of them." Stephan gestured to the mushrooms that loomed over them. He tried to sound brave, but his voice was tinged with horror. "These used to be children."

"Oh, God." Hectory flinched back from the nearest stalk, suddenly unwilling to touch it. "So it must be that female biomancer with the blasphemer who did it."

"Don't be an idiot," said Stephan. "Don't you think *regular* biomancers would be capable of something as awful as this?"

"I...don't know."

But Stephan knew. His father had worked with a biomancer many times. He had seen the horrible things his father's "friend" could do firsthand. Even as a young boy, he'd known it was wrong, and he'd spoken out against it as often as he could. Eventually

his father had tired of his attitude, and shipped him
off to be a Vinchen. It was ironic, really, that many
years later, his grandteacher would also decide to
align with the biomancers. But what could Stephan
do now? When he took his final vows as a Vinchen, he
had sworn to obey the grandteacher in all things.

"What's that over there?" Hectory pointed to a
small clearing in the middle of the forest.

Stephan caught a glint of metal and approached
the clearing. As the object came into view, he moved
faster, forcing his way through the thick stalks.
He dropped to his hands and knees beside a sword
handle that protruded from the ground. The handle
was intertwined with white and black fabric. He
brushed the loose dirt away to reveal a golden hilt
and pommel.

"It can't be..."

He grasped the handle and pulled it free from the
earth. Dirt fell away from the shining blade, which
hummed mournfully even though there was no wind
within the mushroom forest.

"The Song of Sorrows!" He held it triumphantly
over his head.

"We must take it to Grandteacher Racklock immediately," said Hectory.

"Yes, of course," Stephan said quickly. He felt
ashamed that he'd allowed himself to feel—even for a
moment—that he had claimed the treasured blade as
his own. Obviously it would go to the grandteacher.

To prove to Hectory (and perhaps himself as well)
that he was honored to deliver the Song of Sorrows
into the hands of his grandteacher, he leapt to his feet
and shoved his way back through the stalks of rainbow mushrooms that had once been children until he
reached the open field. Then he ran across the rocky
soil toward the dock.

He held the blade aloft as he ran so that any brothers he passed would recognize it. When they saw it, they immediately stopped their own search and followed him. The shame of having the Song of Sorrows wielded by the blasphemer all these years had weighed heavily on everyone in the order. Seeing it returned to its rightful hand was a momentous occasion that none wanted to miss.

A small military pavilion had been erected for Grandteacher Racklock in a clearing near the dock. It kept the sun and wind off him as he waited in quiet meditation for his warriors to bring what information could be gleaned from this island. His hair was mostly gray now, but his broad shoulders were still thickly muscled, and none had yet been able to best him in a sparring match.

A grandteacher usually received his honorific either from his predecessor, or by consensus from his fellow Vinchen. But Racklock had given himself the name "Racklock the Just" when he'd taken power. None dared contradict him, especially after he reinstituted some of the older, harsher disciplinary measures of the Vinchen code that Hurlo the heretic had abandoned.

Now, as Stephan approached the grandteacher's tent, he thought of the other honorific that he and some of his fellow brothers whispered when they were alone and safely out of hearing: Racklock the Cruel. It was difficult to know how the man would react in any given situation, and several brothers had accidentally irritated or offended him. Punishment for such slips, even unintentional ones, was swift and painful.

Stephan could feel the tension twist up his spine the closer he got to the entrance. When he saw the grandteacher in silent meditation, Stephan even considered letting one of the other brothers deliver the blade.

But no, that would be cowardly.

So he quietly entered the tent and knelt in front of Grandteacher Racklock. He bowed his head and presented the sword with one hand on the hilt and one hand on the tip of the blade, as was customary. Behind him, he could hear the other brothers gathering just outside the tent. He guessed they all felt a mixture of jealousy and trepidation for him.

"Forgive me for intruding on your meditation, Grandteacher," said Stephan.

Racklock slowly opened his eyes. When he saw what Stephan held out to him, his eyes grew even wider.

"There is no need for forgiveness," he said. "Not for the one who brings affirmation of the righteousness of our cause."

Racklock's thick hands shook with what Stephan could only assume was eagerness as he took the sword. Stephan guiltily acknowledged to himself a tiny pang of loss when it left his hands.

"Grandteacher, why would the blasphemer release the Song of Sorrows now, after all these years?" he asked. "Do you think she is beginning to see the error of her ways?"

It was bold to ask even such innocent questions of the grandteacher, but it truly troubled Stephan. Why now? How could anyone give up such a magnificent weapon?

Thankfully, this time Racklock didn't seem bothered to be asked a question. His eyes were riveted to the sword in his hand. He responded almost absently, "It makes no difference *why* she did it. Only that it has made her death all the more certain. This sword was her last, best chance of survival. Now her fate is sealed."

6

*R*ed decided to disembark from the *Harrowing Sky* when it made port at Hollow Falls. It was tempting to stay on until Paradise Circle, but he thought it best to check Pastinas Manor first. If Alash had returned, he might have a good idea where Hope was. And if Red's cousin still hadn't come back, his aunt Minara might know where he was. Even if she didn't, Red felt he owed his aunt a visit. The biomancers had murdered his grandfather, which she probably hadn't minded too much. The gaf had been a complete cock-dribble, after all. But he was sure she hadn't been happy to learn that Alash's inheritance had been stripped and given to her wayward illegitimate nephew. If nothing else, he could tell her that he'd managed to fix that part.

Besides, the *Harrowing Sky* was a largo cargo ship, much slower than the *Lady's Gambit*. It had taken nearly a week to get from Stonepeak to New Laven. Captain Yevish was a decent enough wag, but his constant complaining over the last few days had set Red's teeth on edge.

Merivale had paid Red very well these last few months, so rather than walk all the way from the harbor to the manor, Red decided to hire a carriage. That way, even if he didn't get any leads from his aunt, it would be a fairly quick ride down to Silver-

back, where he might get some information from
Old Yammy. There was no reason for her to know
anything about Hope's whereabouts, of course, but
Yammy had a habit of knowing a lot of stuff that
probably wasn't her business.

As Red watched the pastoral countryside of Hollow
Falls slide by from the comfort of his carriage, he
thought back to when he and Hope had come skulking
up from Silverback, following Hope's sword. He remembered how intimidated he'd been by the vast, open mead-
ows and stately mansions. Hollow Falls now seemed
charmingly provincial. Being a lord was at the very top
of the social ladder here. But at the palace, among the
nobility, it hadn't been anything remarkable at all.

When the carriage pulled in front of Pastinas
Manor, it felt like he was looking at a different place
from the one he'd approached a year ago as well. It
was well kept, certainly, and tastefully decorated.
But it was nothing compared to the palace, or
Empress Pysetcha's "home in seclusion," or, truth be
told, even Hempist Manor on Lesser Basheta.

Red climbed out of the carriage and walked up the
neatly paved path to the front door. Before he could
knock, the door was opened by an elderly serving
woman that Red vaguely remembered from the last
time he'd been there.

"Welcome home, my lord," she said in a carefully
neutral voice as she gestured for him to come inside.

"Uh, thanks, but..." Red trailed off when he saw
his aunt Minara waiting for him in the foyer. She
wore a nice gown of lavender, her hair done up in a
careful, if slightly out-of-fashion arrangement. She
was perfectly composed, but judging by the tension
around her eyes, it was costing her a lot of effort.

"What a delight to see you again, my lord," she
said. "We get so few visitors these days, I was surprised to see a carriage coming to call."

Red glanced around at all the servants who stood in attendance. Probably the entire household, by the look of it, all come to "welcome" their lord to the manor. Red had never felt easy about his lordship, but he'd grudgingly grown accustomed. Now it felt strange all over again. Even more so because by now he'd probably officially been stripped of his title anyway.

Red gave his aunt a meaningful look, then said, "I hate to cut things short, Aunt Minara, but I'm in a bit of a hurry. Is there somewhere we can talk privately?"

She gave him an unsure look.

"It's partly about my cousin," he added.

Her eyes narrowed for a moment, then her expression settled back into careful decorum.

"As you wish, my lord. Please, follow me."

Red was surprised when instead of leading him toward the parlor, she led him down the servants' hallway to Alash's workshop. Was his cousin hiding out there? That would be a stroke of luck.

But the workshop was filled only with the mechanical odds and ends that Alash had left behind. A light film of dust covered everything.

Aunt Minara firmly shut the door behind them. "Sorry about the decor." She gestured to the piles of metal, sheaths of worn leather, and swatches of sailcloth. "I had Alash insulate the walls of this room so I wouldn't have to listen to all the racket he made in here building his ridiculous contraptions. It's as close to truly private as we can get, I'm afraid. I presume whatever you have to say is something not even the servants should be privy to."

"This is perfect, Aunt Minara," said Red.

"Wonderful." She folded her arms and gave him a stern look. "Now, nephew, care to tell me what in all hells has been going on?"

"Look, before I get into anything else, I want you

to know that none of the lord stuff was my idea. I've actually been a prisoner of the biomancers for the last year or so."

"Prisoner?"

"Well, maybe that's not the right word, since I was living in more luxury at the palace than I'd ever seen in my life."

"You lived in the *palace*?"

"Yeah, but I couldn't leave it. Sort of a gilded cage, I guess you'd say."

"Why couldn't you leave?"

"It's a long story, so I'll just say that the biomancers had to keep me close so they could use me for something. And giving me Alash's inheritance and killing Grandfather was the way they could justify my presence there."

Red watched the shock slowly spread across his aunt's face. Maybe he'd been going too fast there.

"W-what do you mean *killed*?" she finally asked, her voice trembling. "My father . . . died in his *sleep*."

"Of course he did. Right after someone poisoned him or something like that. Look, trust me on this, the biomancers that he helped all those years wouldn't hesitate to kill him if it suited them."

Red had never seen his aunt so rattled. Ripples of tension ran across her face as she struggled to put the words together.

"What . . . Why would the emperor allow them to get away with such things?"

That reminded Red that most people in the empire still thought the emperor was in charge. People needed to know the truth, of course, but he didn't have time for that right now.

"Listen, I think I've managed to fix it up so that you've been officially named lady of Pastinas Manor. You should get the official word after they get around to declaring me a traitor."

"Traitor?"

"It's not true, strangely enough," said Red. "Because I'm actually on a secret mission sanctioned by Her Majesty."

"You...work for the *empress?*"

Aunt Minara's eyes were practically rolling back in her head by that point. Red remembered how patronizing she'd been on his last visit, and he was tempted to push her right over the edge. But he knew enough about lacies now to understand she hadn't meant to be an insufferable bore. And besides, he still needed her.

So instead he said, "That's right. Now, do you know where Alash is?"

She blinked rapidly as if coming out of a trance. "Alash? Why? What does he have to do with all this? What have you gotten him into?"

"Believe it or not, it wasn't me. At least, I don't think so..." He shook his head. "Regardless, if you know anything, I need you to tell me. For once I'm not exaggerating here. This is for the good of the whole empire."

"I don't know *exactly* where he is, but a few months ago, I received a letter from him."

"What did it say?"

"Just that he was okay, but wouldn't be coming home anytime soon. He didn't leave a return address, but the letter arrived on a ship from Vance Post."

"Did he happen to say who he was with?" asked Red.

She shook her head. "He was very vague about everything. He sounded sad, so I assumed he just didn't feel like going into details...but perhaps he was doing it on purpose?"

Red nodded. "Since he's a wanted criminal."

"What?"

He put his hand on his aunt's shoulders to steady her. She looked like she was about to faint.

"Don't worry," he said. "As long as he doesn't do

anything reckless before I find him, he'll be fine, and
I promise we'll get his name cleared."

"And then...then he can come home?" Her expression was almost pleading. Like she already knew the
answer, but wanted him to tell her differently.

"I can't make him come home," said Red. "And
after everything that's happened, he might not want to
come home. At least, not to stay."

She nodded, her eyes gleaming with suppressed
tears. "I didn't realize...about the biomancers. I
thought it was just stories to scare the peasants.
I thought surely Father would never get mixed up in
something if it was truly awful."

"I know, Aunt Minara. It wasn't your fault."

She took his hands in hers. He could feel a tremor
in them. "Will you stay a few days?"

"Sorry, I really am in a hurry. This mission can't
wait."

She forced a smile. "Naturally. But...perhaps...
maybe just lunch at least?"

He'd always thought of his aunt as aloof. Above
it all. But he saw something different now. A lonely
widow struggling to accept that her only child had
found a life outside of the tiny manor she clung to so
desperately.

"Of course I'll stay for lunch," he said. "Nothing
but ship's rations all week, I'd have to be slippy to turn
down a proper lacy meal. And you'll be happy to know
my table manners are much improved."

That small gesture only cost Red a few hours, and it
lit up his aunt even more brightly than he'd expected.
As he watched her order the servants around, preparing their lunch as if it were a grand imperial ball, Red
got the feeling that he was the first person to eat with
her in a long time. Maybe the other lords and ladies
shunned her when her son was stripped of his title. If
so, she really was completely alone out here.

As they ate, Red regaled her with some of his many exploits at the palace, finishing it off with his dinner at the empress's own table. He left out many details, of course, and made certain not to blow Merivale's carefully constructed cover as a shallow, husband-hungry socialite.

"Why on earth didn't you agree to marry Lady Hempist?" asked Minara. "She sounds like quite a good match for you."

Red sighed dramatically as he nibbled on a sandwich. "That's what His Highness said as well. But I'm afraid once she learns I've been de-lorded, her interest will cool considerably."

"Still a rogue, then, I see. I can only wonder what sort of woman would actually get you to settle down." She took a sip of wine and stared off at nothing in particular. "To think Gulia's little boy, getting matchmaking advice from the prince himself. I wonder what she would have thought of all this."

"I'm not sure about most of it," said Red. "But I think she'd be pleased that I've taken up painting again. Just as a hobby," he said quickly. "I know how much you dread having another artist in the family."

Aunt Minara laughed for the first time since his arrival. "I think I would have preferred my nephew take up painting over dangerous secret missions for the throne."

"Don't worry, Aunt Minara. I can handle myself."

"I'm certain you can. But my poor Alash. I hope he hasn't gotten himself in too deep."

"You might be surprised. If he's still keeping company with the people I think he is, then he could have come a long away. I'd be willing to bet that he's quite the adventurer himself by now."

She smiled sadly. "It's hard to let go of the boy I knew, but perhaps you're right."

After lunch, Red said good-bye to his aunt and climbed back into his hired coach.

"Where to now, sir?" asked the driver, a solid old wrink with a short gray beard.

"Silverback, my wag. Need to check in on an old friend."

"Very good, sir."

Red gazed out the window as they rode south. He remembered it being a long walk from the pastoral Hollow Falls to the neat, even streets of Keystown, but in the carriage, it took only an hour. He felt a little uneasy entering the neighborhood that was more or less one giant military barracks—a place he'd been taught most of his life was to be feared above all others and avoided at all costs. But as they rode down the clean, well-kept streets, he realized it really wasn't much different from the palace. Even if he was a wanted man again, the idea that such a criminal would be casually riding by in a carriage wouldn't even occur to them. And true enough, not a single imp stopped him or even looked into the window. Of course, if they were stopped, Red still had the commission letter from Merivale with Her Majesty's seal. But that sort of thing might draw the attention of the biomancers, and he needed to avoid that for as long as possible.

The carriage skirted around Joiner's Bay until it entered Silverback. The streets became narrower and more haphazard, with fewer imps and more performers. He directed the driver west, and as they rode past Bayview Gallery, he wondered if Thoriston still had his mom's paintings up. Probably not, since the exhibition had opened over a year ago. Red was surprised to find he was a little saddened by the idea. Now that he'd embraced being a painter himself, he felt the urge to go back and look at that early work he did with his mother with a more critical eye.

But he really didn't have time for artistic exploration right now anyway. If Old Yammy didn't have any information for him, he would find a ship heading for Vance Post. Even if Alash wasn't with Hope anymore, he probably had a better idea than most where she might be.

They reached Madame Destiny's House of All well after dark. As the carriage pulled in front of the building, Red was surprised to see that the sign was gone. Its absence gave him an uneasy feeling.

"Stay here and keep the horses quiet," he told the driver, then climbed out of the carriage.

He approached the building cautiously, his red eyes scanning the outside of the building for any clues. It didn't look all that different, other than the missing sign. The curtains were drawn, but that was typical. He could see light faintly around the edges of the curtains on the first floor, so he knew someone was there.

He pressed his ear against one of the windows and was struck immediately by a familiar voice:

"You scoundrel! You *criminal!*"

It was Broomefedies, the theater master from across the street. Red hadn't seen the man in years, but there was no forgetting that distinctive, booming voice.

"Shout all you like." It was a male voice that Red didn't recognize, but it had the clipped precision of an imp in the officer class. "You'll find no rescue."

"Please, sir, have mercy!" said a female voice that sounded too young and tremulous to be Old Yammy. One of Broom's mistresses, maybe?

"You'll find none of that here either," said the male voice. "Your death will be slow and painful."

Whatever was going on, Red clearly needed to put

a stop to it. He took a few steps back, then ran forward and jumped, catching the shallow awning above the door. He hauled himself up to the second-floor window. The lock was old and rusty, and after a few hard tugs, it broke. Red slid the window open and climbed into the unlit room. It still looked like Old Yammy's room, but there were also some men's clothes in the wardrobe. Red had never known her to take a tom, but maybe she'd just never told him about it. And where was she? Maybe downstairs with the others, only remaining quiet? Or perhaps unable to speak. Or even...

He moved quickly but silently from the bedroom into the tiny hallway that led to the narrow spiral staircase down to the ground floor.

"I beg you, sir!" Broom's voice sounded like it was directly below.

"Beg all you like. It amuses me," said the male voice in a not-very-amused tone. "But it will do you no good."

"You won't get away with this, you monster!" said the woman.

"Oh, but I already have. Now, prepare to die!"

Red jumped down, skipping the staircase and landing in a crouch.

"Not quite yet, you haven't," he said as he drew his revolvers and pointed them at the stranger with the black beard.

"Good God!" shouted a woman in a low-cut gown.

"Piss'ell!" said Broom. The tall man wore a vest without any shirt underneath, and his large, hairy belly shook slightly.

The stranger merely stared at Red uncomprehendingly. He wasn't holding any kind of weapon. Just a sheet of parchment. Red glanced at Broom and the woman, and noticed they also held sheets of parchment.

"Wait," he said. "Is this a pissing *read through*?"

"You must be Red," said the stranger. While he'd been startled by Red's entrance, he didn't seem particularly alarmed to have a gun pointing at him.

"Damn it, Red, where in all hells did you come from?" asked Broom.

"From the palace," said Red as he holstered his guns. "I was looking for Old Yammy."

"She's not here," said the stranger.

"This is Captain Vaderton," said Broom.

"And I am the Luscious Lymestria, *jewel* of the Silverback theater!" Lymestria offered Red the back of her hand, her smoldering eyes fixed on his.

Red grinned as he kissed her hand. Actresses. He sort of missed that world. "Luscious indeed," he said, eyeing the cleavage that she was shoving at him. "A pleasure to meet you."

"An uncommon resemblance to that lacy boy from a while back," she said to Broom.

"Cousins, I think," said Broom.

"That explains it," she said. "Although this one is clearly more skilled at talking to women."

"Wait, you know Alash?" Red couldn't quite reconcile those two worlds.

"He came here with that Southie calling herself Dire Bane," said Broom.

"Dire Bane?" Was Broom talking about Hope? But why would she be calling herself that?

"They were looking for Old Yammy as well, as I recall," continued Broom. "She'd been sent to the Empty Cliffs, and Captain Bane rescued her."

"She also rescued me," said Vaderton.

Red felt like he was missing a lot of the pieces, but right now he had to cut through to the most important thing.

"Old Yammy isn't here?" he asked Vaderton. "Do you know where she is now?"

"She wouldn't tell me. I'm sure you know how she can be sometimes." There was a tone of fond resignation in his voice. "She only told me to wait here for you."

"Me? You're saying she knew when I was coming?"

"Not exactly, of course. I've actually been waiting for months."

"The poor captain's been a bit restless," said Broom. "A man of action doesn't like sitting still, right, my wag?" He leaned over and gave the captain a hearty slap on the arm.

Vaderton smiled graciously. "Precisely."

"So that's why we enlisted his help in doing a read through of my new play."

Red gave him a critical look. "*Prepare to die*? Who actually says that?"

Broom looked hurt. "It was realistic enough to convince you, apparently."

Red laughed. "I suppose you got me there. Maybe I was a little eager for some action myself." He turned back to Vaderton. "So why were you supposed to wait for me?"

"She said you'd need a ship, in a hurry."

"I think my cousin is in Vance Post. I take it you have a ship to get me there?"

Vaderton nodded. "I do. But Yammy was also very clear that before we leave New Laven, there's someone you have to talk to."

"Oh?" asked Red. "Who's that?"

"The Black Rose of Paradise Circle."

7

The morning after Old Yammy arrived, Hope awoke at dawn and began to meditate, as she had nearly every day since her return to Galemoor. But that morning, unpredictable sounds out in the courtyard kept intruding. Voices and laughter.

Hope tried her best to simply acknowledge the sounds and not get wrapped up in them. It was pretty clear that Old Yammy, Uter, and Wentu were engaged in some sort of activity. She didn't quite know what it was, though, and when she caught herself trying to figure it out for the fourth or fifth time, she sighed and gave up on meditation.

She slowly stood and walked over to the doorway that looked out onto the courtyard.

It was a sunny day, probably one of the last before the summer ended. The three of them were spread out across the courtyard and appeared to be playing catch with a ball about the size of an orange. Wentu gave it an easy toss, and it sailed over to Old Yammy, who caught it neatly with two hands.

"Oooh! Me!" pleaded Uter. "Throw it to *me*!" He jumped up and down, frantically waving his arms.

But Old Yammy turned to Hope, nodded once, and threw the ball to her.

Hope caught the ball with her one hand and

examined it. It appeared to be stitched-together scraps of black leather from the old tannery.

"Please, Hope!" begged Uter. "Throw it to *me*!"

Hope threw him the ball. He made what seemed to her a completely unnecessary dive to catch it, then rolled up onto his knees and held it up triumphantly. "I got it!"

"You two continue," Old Yammy told Uter and Wentu. "I must begin Hope's training."

As the old man and the boy continued to throw the ball back and forth, Old Yammy walked over to Hope with her usual, unhurried calm. Her thick scarf flapped in the hard winds that often raked Galemoor in the late summer. Signs of the weather turning to autumn and the cold and darkness that would follow.

"Are you good at math?" asked Yammy as she drew near.

Hope used to think she was exceptional at math, but after seeing Red in action during a game of stones, she knew better.

"Adequate," she said.

"Then it's rather amazing how quickly you did all those calculations in your head just now."

"Calculations?" asked Hope.

"Certainly," said Yammy. "When you caught the ball, you had to consider trajectory, velocity, and of course take wind speed into account. Quite a lot to work out in only a couple of seconds."

"But I didn't do any of that," said Hope.

"No?" asked Yammy. "So it was luck that you caught the ball?"

"Well, no . . ."

"Whether you realized it or not, somewhere inside you, those calculations were made. Our heads are not the only parts of our body that have intelligence."

"Are you talking about instinct?" asked Hope.

"An unflattering name," said Yammy. "And one

that still does not provide the whole picture. That's my main objection to the way Vinchen train. They presume that the mind is superior to the body. That the body is a base and shallow thing that must be mastered by an indomitable will."

"Do you know a lot about Vinchen training and technique?" Hope tried to keep the doubt out of her voice, but suspected she was not completely successful because Yammy gave her a knowing smile.

"Your teacher and I would argue about that particular topic endlessly. He was young then, and arrogant, as I suppose most young Vinchen are."

Not for the first time, Hope wondered just how old Yammy really was. "It's hard for me to imagine Grandteacher Hurlo as arrogant."

Yammy nodded. "This was before he accomplished any of the feats he was so famous for. Interesting, don't you think? That the more he achieved, the less arrogant he became? Worth pondering. But walk with me, Hope. Tell me what you have learned since the last time we met."

As Hope followed Yammy across the courtyard and out of the monastery, she told her about the trap of vainglory she had fallen into as Dire Bane, and the shame that followed when she realized what she had become. They walked along the path beside the monastery, and she told Yammy about Hurlo's journal and his unfinished quest to find a new path for the Vinchen. They continued down the rugged, stony trail to the dense forest that lay to the south of the monastery, and she told her about her meditations and contemplation of the quiet moments of nature. Old Yammy was silent through all of it, and when Hope ran out of things to say, the silence remained.

The soil in that part of the island was much too rocky for crops, so the brothers had left the forest alone, entering only now and then to catch small game when the fish and octopuses were scarce. Hope used to spend hours in the forest when she was a girl, and she was fairly certain this was where Uter spent a large part of his time when he was out exploring. There was something about the rocky black crags and gnarled, twisted gray trees that made it seem enticingly creepy.

At last they reached a small, flat clearing in the forest.

Yammy said, "What I find most intriguing about your studies is your contemplation of time."

"Time? I'm not sure what you mean."

"Your exercises in watching the sunrises, the movements of tides, and so forth. You said it yourself. That during those periods, time feels more elastic to you. Malleable."

"I'm not sure about *malleable*, exactly."

"'Elastic' means something that expands spontaneously to fill the available space, doesn't it? And in a sense, that's precisely what time does. It expands or contracts to fit the available moment."

"That...*does* fit with my observations," admitted Hope. When she focused on watching a sunset, it seemed to her as if the sun moved with impossible speed. "But that's merely my perspective. It's not as if time is actually speeding up."

"Perhaps you haven't grasped yet that time is not objective. While it's muddling things a bit, we could say that everything has its own time. You, me, that bird, and even that rock. We each operate in our own subjective time. Usually, they all flow together. But they don't *have* to."

Hope narrowed her eyes. "What are you suggesting? That I can manipulate my own time?"

"You're doing it already. You slow yourself down as you watch the sunset. Who's to say you couldn't speed yourself up to match, say, a bullet?"

"Impossible."

Old Yammy looked suddenly sad. "Really? After all you've seen, you still think that word has any meaning? Are you so certain of your understanding of the relationship between time and space?"

No matter what else Hope had been in her life, she had always been a good student. So it pained her to see her new teacher look so disappointed. "It's just...there are physical limitations to, well, *everything*, aren't there?"

"There are limits," agreed Yammy. "I doubt anyone could maintain such speeds for more than a few seconds. But a bullet's entire existence unfolds in less time than that."

"Still, it seems so..." She looked helplessly at Yammy. "I'm sorry. I don't mean to be difficult."

Yammy laughed. A deep, throaty sound. "Not nearly as difficult as other students I've had. That Brigga Lin of yours, for example. Stubborn as anything. Anyway, Brice told me he saw you slap a bullet right out of the air once. How did you do *that*?"

"I'm not sure," admitted Hope. "The first time I did it, it was instinct. I imagine I was able to do it because of the Song of Sorrows."

"Certainly that sword is strong enough to turn aside a bullet. But a sword can't move on its own. So what, other than you, could account for the speed?"

"I don't know."

"You don't know how you caught that ball either," said Yammy.

"If I accept for the moment that it's possible for me to alter my time," said Hope, "how would I go about actually developing such an ability?"

Old Yammy gave her a wicked grin that reminded her of Red. "Like anything else. With practice." Then she drew a revolver from inside her cloak and fired.

Hope's entire body locked up as the gun went off.

A moment later, a tree trunk about four feet away exploded.

"Piss'ell," Hope wheezed quietly.

"Oh, relax," said Yammy. "I'm not aiming for *you*. I don't expect you to get this on the first try. Or even the tenth try, really."

"Tenth?" asked Hope. "How much gunpowder do you have hidden in that cloak of yours?"

"Only what's in the gun. But I didn't just bring you back here for the scenery. There's a hidden weapons cache nearby that includes gunpowder. Thank God Racklock didn't know about it, or he could have blown the entire temple straight to Heaven. Come on."

Hope followed Old Yammy through the woods for a little while before she asked, "How did *you* know about it?"

"Shilgo told me about it," she said offhandedly.

"You knew Shilgo the Wise?" He had been Hurlo's teacher.

"Oh, I *knew* him all right." She gave a coarse chuckle. "I was a bad girl in those days, and Shilgo was not yet so wise."

"You're saying that he violated his vow of chastity?" Hope was unable to hide her shock.

Yammy leered at her. "On *many* occasions. But surely you already know that the best, truest sort of wisdom comes from making mistakes. And as fun as it was, he and I were definitely a mistake."

Hope had to admit that her own mistakes as Dire Bane, arrogant and grotesque as they had been, certainly taught her a great deal.

"We'll bring the gunpowder and bullets back to the monastery," said Yammy as they continued south through the forest. "Perhaps we'll put that boy of yours to work cleaning and loading the gun. That's always been my least favorite part."

"He's not *my* boy," Hope said.

"Oh?" asked Yammy. "Then whose boy is he?"

Hope couldn't bring herself to say *no one's*. It sounded too cruel. And it wasn't really true either. Hope had originally planned to leave him with someone on Gull's Cry, but that became impossible when he killed their elder. Not knowing what else to do, she'd just brought him back to Galemoor. She had been alone often enough as a child. She wouldn't abandon Uter to a similar fate.

"I suppose he *is* mine, then. For as long as he chooses to stay with me."

———

The weapons cache was in a concealed cave at the edge of the forest, near the southern shore. The rock rose up from the ground like a black blister. There was no door on the cave mouth, but the twisted trees grew up in front of it so densely, Hope thought it was likely they had been cultivated to do so.

She and Yammy pushed through the spindly trees, then walked a short way into the cave. Only a faint bit of light made it to the back, but it was enough for Hope to see the outline of several wooden crates, their seams sealed with pitch to keep them airtight. In addition to a box of bullets and small keg of gunpowder, there was a crate of old-fashioned flintlock rifles and pistols, and several crates of sturdy but unadorned swords and knives.

"I've never seen Vinchen use short swords," remarked Hope as she held one up to examine it in the dim light.

Yammy nodded. "They're used in pairs, one in each hand. It's a lesser known technique, typically used by Vinchen who favor agility over strength. Wentu knows it, if I remember right."

"Really? Perhaps we should bring a pair back so he can demonstrate."

Yammy narrowed her eyes. "I thought you were done with swords."

"That doesn't mean I don't still appreciate the form," said Hope. "Besides, I wasn't thinking so much for me, but for someone else."

"Uter?" Yammy looked alarmed.

Hope shook her head. "No, I was thinking of Jilly."

"Oh?" asked Yammy. "So you haven't forgotten your promise to the girl after all?"

"I haven't forgotten *any* of my promises," Hope said sharply. "Why would you think I have?"

Yammy looked like she was about to reply, but stopped herself. She carefully tipped over the gunpowder barrel so it lay on its side. "We'll get the swords another time. This and the box of bullets will be about all we can manage in one trip."

Yammy began rolling the barrel toward the mouth of the cave. The box of bullets was small, but extremely heavy. Hope found it awkward to pick up with only one hand, and the only way she could carry it was by keeping both arms out in front of her and holding the box in the crook of her elbows.

"It looks like your prosthetic could use some adjustments," said Yammy as they maneuvered the barrel and box through the trees. "Now that it doesn't need to be dedicated solely to wielding a sword, perhaps it could be modified for more generalized use."

"There's only one person still alive that I trust to fiddle with it, and I have no idea where he is," said Hope.

Old Yammy nodded but said nothing.

———

Uter was thrilled with his new job as official gun
loader. At first, Hope was nervous about giving the
occasionally homicidal boy not only access to firearms, but also the knowledge of how to load them.
Yammy insisted that it would be fine, and after
watching him closely for the first few days, Hope saw
how seriously he took his responsibility. Apparently,
as long as there weren't any sharp edges involved, he
wasn't that interested in the weapon.

So every day, Uter would load the gun and give it
to Yammy. Then Yammy and Hope would return to
the clearing in the woods. Yammy would fire a shot
and Hope would try to watch it. They would repeat
that until the gun was empty. Then they would return
to the monastery, Uter would load it again, and the
two women would go back out again. They did this
several times a day for weeks. The barrel and the box
slowly grew emptier, but nothing else changed. Hope
grew accustomed to the sulfurous smell and the
harsh sound, but she felt no closer to achieving what
Yammy claimed was possible.

Hope noticed that the impact point of each shot
was getting gradually closer. Originally, it had been
about four feet to her left. But after a few weeks, she
realized it was now three feet away, as if it had been
inching over, a little each day. When Hope pointed
that out to Old Yammy, the woman smiled sweetly
and said, "You can't just practice forever. Eventually
there needs to be some sort of test."

If that was Yammy's idea of motivating Hope, it
worked. She didn't really know Yammy all that well.
She wasn't sure a regular person *could* know her all that
well. And Hope couldn't say for certain that the ageless
woman wouldn't follow through with the threat.

Hope began to push harder on any aspect she
thought might help. If her contemplation of gradual
movements of nature was what started this, perhaps

returning to that would help her in some way. So she began once again to watch the sun rise and set each day. If a true connection between body and mind was necessary, then both her body and mind needed to be perfectly in sync. In his journal, Hurlo had observed that he saw no difference between practicing his sword forms and meditation. She reasoned that attempting to meditate at the same time as training her body would help foster the connection she was looking for. She still refused to pick up a sword, so instead she went back to the hand-to-hand combat forms he had taught her when she was a little girl. She moved slowly, treating it less like combat and more like dance, and she was surprised at the tranquility it brought her. Once she was accustomed to it, she found that hours would pass without her even noticing.

But still, even with all that work, she could not see the bullet as it sped toward its target.

One day, as they stood in the same clearing before yet another session, Hope found herself in particularly low spirits. Oddly, whenever she began to doubt Old Yammy, she found herself instead looking for a way to compliment her.

"I'm impressed with the consistency of your aim," she said.

Old Yammy shrugged as she examined her revolver. "One of the benefits of a long life is the time to accumulate a wide variety of skills. Shall we begin?"

Hope nodded and moved so that her back was to the tree line and Yammy was about twenty paces away. They had been doing this for over a month now, and the target was only a foot and a half to Hope's left. She calculated about two weeks before Yammy was aiming directly at her. Would *that* finally give her the incentive or inspiration she needed to break through this barrier? Or would she just end up with a gunshot wound?

These thoughts rambled around in her mind as Old Yammy lifted the revolver and pulled back the hammer.

"Hope, you've got to see this!" Uter popped out of the tree line about a foot to her left.

Then the gun went off.

The world seemed to freeze. Uter was looking at Hope with his bright, excited eyes. Yammy's eyes, however, had just begun to widen with horror. The gunshot sounded like the endless roar of death itself coming for its victim. Fire and smoke were emerging from the gun along with a small, round piece of metal that was headed directly toward Uter.

Hope reached her arm toward the boy, but it was like pushing through a wall of wet sand. Her body moved with infuriating sluggishness, and the air pressure made it feel like she was being slowly crushed beneath the weight of invisible stone. Inch by inch, her hand drew closer to Uter. He still hadn't moved. Neither had Old Yammy. But out of the corner of her eye, Hope could see the bullet drawing near, the metal glowing a searing red as it cut through the air.

Finally, her fingers gradually curled around a fold in Uter's gray smock. Even this action strained Hope's body to the limit. It felt like she was grabbing hold of something much harder than fabric. Her fingers throbbed with pain as she forced the fabric to move, and it did so grudgingly. By this time the bullet was only a few feet away.

Hope leveraged the stronger muscles in her shoulders, back, and thighs to reel him slowly back toward her and out of the line of fire. The bullet continued to close the distance, screeching like a hawk as it neared Uter's still-excited face. It wasn't until she saw the bullet scrape the side of Uter's ear that she knew the danger was past.

Then everything snapped back to normal. The bullet struck a nearby tree, Uter stumbled, and Yammy yelled out, "Oh God!"

Hope swayed for a moment. Every muscle in her body felt bruised and swollen, but she refused to let herself fall.

"Ouch!" said Uter as he clapped his hand over his ear. "What was that?" He turned toward the sound where the bullet had impacted, then back to Hope. "Anyway, Hope, you have to..."

He trailed off when he saw Hope's furious expression.

"You *knew* we were shooting guns out here." Her voice crackled like fire. She had never felt a fury quite like this before. "You *knew* how dangerous it was."

"Yeah, but you hadn't started yet," he said sheepishly. "So I thought—"

"We were just *starting*!" Hope's voice rose to a scream. She knew this was not the proper way for a warrior, a mentor, or a guardian to act, but she couldn't help herself. She grabbed him by the scruff of his neck and hauled him over to the tree with the fresh, scorched bullet hole. "Take a good look, because that was almost *you*!"

Uter stared at the bullet hole for a moment. When he looked back at her, his eyes brimmed with tears.

"I...don't know what I'm supposed to do now."

"Say you're sorry, dear." Even Old Yammy sounded a bit flustered. "And promise her you'll be more careful next time."

"I'm sorry, Hope," he said dutifully. "I'll be more careful next time."

Hope pulled him into a rough embrace.

After a moment, he said, "You're squeezing me."

"You'll live," she said, her voice thick, and didn't let him go.

"On the bright side," said Yammy, "it looks like you found it."

"I did." Hope finally released Uter. But then she swayed and nearly fell. Both Yammy and Uter instinctively reached out and steadied her. Now that the crises and resulting anger were dissipating, her limbs felt heavy, like she'd used up several hours' worth of energy in a few moments. Perhaps she had. She would need to do more stamina training if she planned to use this reliably.

"*Now* can you come see this thing I found?" asked Uter.

Hope smiled wearily. "What is this thing that was so exciting, you forgot about the danger of gunfire?"

Uter's expression returned to blissful wonder. "A two-headed snake!"

Exhausted but curious, Hope followed him through the forest with Old Yammy bringing up the rear. After a little while, they came to a small outcropping of black rock. On the lee side were two snakes copulating.

"Ah," said Hope.

Old Yammy suppressed a chuckle.

"Uter, that's two snakes...cuddling," said Hope.

Old Yammy didn't even bother to suppress her chuckle that time.

"Oh..." Uter looked disappointed.

Hope patted him consolingly on the shoulder. "Come on. Let's go home and have dinner."

"I am pretty hungry," he admitted, and allowed himself to be led away.

———

Now that Hope knew what it felt like to change her speed, she needed to be able to use it reliably. It was like exercising a muscle. First in tiny flickers, with an effort hugely disproportionate to the result. But over time, she grew more comfortable with it until finally she was able to call upon it at will. It was still physically exhausting, and she was never able to do it for more than a second or two. But as Yammy had pointed out, a second was the entire life of a bullet.

The weather grew cooler and the nights grew longer as summer turned into fall. Yammy suggested they have a cookout on the beach before it got too cold. "It can be a celebration of Hope's achievement."

"A cookout?" Wentu looked slightly scandalized. "We've never had a cookout on Galemoor in the many decades I've been on this island."

"Well, then, it's long overdue," she said. "Unless there's something in that Vinchen code of yours against it?"

"Not specifically, no . . . ," admitted Wentu.

So the four of them gathered on the black, rocky northern shore, which was slightly warmer than the southern shore. They built a large bonfire, which Uter capered around wildly until he nearly burned himself. They roasted fish on sticks, and Wentu cracked open a cask of fine Vinchen ale he'd been saving for a special occasion.

As the adults sat on the rocks and watched Uter toss things into the fire, Hope took a long drink of ale from her wooden cup.

"In all my travels, no ale ever equaled this," she said quietly. "I'm sad it's not being made anymore."

"You're not the only one," said Old Yammy. "People were openly weeping in Silverback when word got around."

"Perhaps someday . . . ," said Wentu. Then he sighed and shook his head.

They sat in silence for a while, with only the hiss of the fire and Uter's chirps of delight as he threw strands of seaweed into the flames.

"I've been thinking about what you said regarding

your prosthesis," Old Yammy said at last. "That there's only one person you trust to alter it."

"Alash," said Hope. "Red's cousin."

"What if I told you where he is? Would you find him and ask him to redesign it for you?"

Hope sat up. "You know where he is? How?"

Old Yammy smirked. "You might be surprised to learn that he wrote a letter to the Luscious Lymestria."

"Really?" asked Hope.

"Apparently, Brigga Lin has become quite... involved with that pirate, Gavish Gray. That left poor, shy Alash lonely and despairing. I suppose his memories of his night with a famous actress are something that comforts him now."

"That's heartbreaking," said Hope.

"She didn't write him back, of course," said Yammy.

"Even worse," said Hope.

"But she did mention to me, rather offhandedly, that it came from Walta."

"*Walta?*" asked Hope. "The huge mole rat warren? What on earth is he doing in a place like that?"

"Lymestria was a little vague on that. I think she only skimmed the letter. Something about him believing mole rats to have some disease-curing properties."

"He'll get himself eaten," said Hope.

"Well, then," said Old Yammy. "If you want him to fix your prosthesis, you'd better get to him before that."

"It'll take me weeks to reach Walta," said Hope. "Will you look after Uter while I'm gone?"

"No," said Yammy.

"What?" Hope hadn't really expected her to decline, especially since she seemed so fond of the boy.

"And neither will Wentu. We're too old to raise children."

"Old? You?" asked Hope.

Yammy smiled, but it didn't seem as energetic as usual. In fact, the woman almost seemed to shrink a little before Hope's eyes. "Just because I don't look old, doesn't mean I don't *feel* old."

Hope didn't know what to say to that. Had Yammy been forcing herself to go on when all she wanted to do was rest? Hope almost asked that question, but realized to her shame that the idea was so upsetting, she didn't actually want to know the answer. All she could do, then, was accept what Yammy said.

"I suppose I must take him with me, then. But I'm worried he will be difficult to control. What if he kills people again? He doesn't do it out of meanness or spite, but..."

Uter had run out of seaweed nearby, so he was forced to run farther down the beach to gather more. He charged back and forth along the beach many times. He would sleep well that night.

"The boy minds you a lot better than he used to," said Wentu.

"Ever since I almost shot him," said Yammy quietly.

"If anyone is to blame," said Hope, "it was me for allowing him to sneak up on us."

"Don't be foolish," said Wentu. "It was an accident. Sometimes there is no one to blame."

Hope bowed her head in respect. It was rare for Wentu to take a teacherly tone, and she always heeded him when he did. "Uter and I will go to Walta and retrieve Alash. We should be back in a few months."

"When will you go?" asked Yammy.

"We'll leave at dawn," said Hope. "Every day we wait is another day Alash might end up in the belly of a mole rat."

"That makes sense," said Yammy.

Hope stood up. "Come on, Uter."

"Time for bed *already*?" he asked, giving her a petulant frown.

"No, we must prepare for our trip tomorrow."

He perked up at that. "We're going on a trip? To where?"

"Come with me, and I'll tell you while we pack," said Hope.

He seemed to forget all about the fire as he followed Hope back to the sleeping quarters.

———

After Hope and Uter went to the dormitory, Wentu and Yammy sat for a while and watched the fire slowly die out.

"I've been meaning to ask you, Yameria," Wentu said finally.

"Yes?"

"When you first arrived, you promised this would be the last time you meddled. I'm sorry to hear that."

"Not even I can do this forever. That accident with Uter..." She shook her head. "Stupid mistake. I should have seen it coming. That's when I knew for certain that my time is nearly up, and if I was going to help this one last time, I needed to wrap it up."

"That was brilliant, by the way," said Wentu. "I've been trying to get Hope to leave the Southern Isles for months."

"She's been hiding here long enough." Then Yammy gave Wentu a tired smile. "And frankly, I've been living long enough. You don't mind if I let it all go here, do you?"

Wentu looked sadly at the woman he had known, off and on, for his entire life. "It would be an honor, Yameria."

8

*A*s Red rode with Vaderton into Paradise Circle, it reminded him of the last time he'd come home after a long adventure. He'd been just a boy back then, and it was in the back of a wagon full of fruits and vegetables with Sadie instead of a fine carriage. But despite those differences, when he saw the familiar streets roll past the window, and smelled the earthy scent of them, his chest filled with a warm, comforting glow. No matter where else he went, Paradise Circle would always feel like coming home.

"I believe the Black Rose has set her base of operations at Apple Grove Manor," Vaderton was saying.

"Hmmm?" asked Red, pulling his gaze from the window for a moment.

"Do you know where that is?" asked Vaderton.

"That old wreck? Sure…" Red's eyes were drawn back to the window. "But I tell you what. Let's continue on a ways through the old neighborhood for a bit. There's not a huge rush to meet her, is there?"

"I suppose not."

Red didn't really know this naval captain, but if Yammy trusted him, then he had to be all right. Still, there was something about his demeanor that made Red suspect he knew more than he was letting on. And that whatever he knew, it wasn't good news. Red wasn't eager to find out what that was.

"Driver, why don't you leave us at the Drowned Rat. We'll find our own way from there." Red was eager to walk the streets once again, but he was also looking forward to a grand arrival at his favorite tavern.

"The Drowned Rat, sir?" asked the driver. "Are you sure? That place has quite a reputation."

Red laughed. "I'm one of the people that *made* its reputation, my wag."

———

There were a lot of eyes on the fine Hollow Falls carriage as it pulled up in front of the Drowned Rat. It was possibly the finest carriage that had ever graced the block. But those eyes shifted from narrow scheming to wide surprise when Red leapt boldly from the door in his jacket and cravat. He was pleased to hear more than one person mutter "Piss'ell" under their breath.

"Coming, Vaderton?" he asked over his shoulder.

"Of course." Vaderton stepped unhurriedly down to the street. Although he wore a plain shirt and unadorned dark blue jacket, anyone could recognize his proud naval bearing. Red was greatly amused by the odd picture they presented as they stepped inside the tavern.

But while he'd expected to turn a few heads, he hadn't anticipated the whole place would go dead quiet and stare.

As they stood there awkwardly, Vaderton whispered, "I can't tell. Is this friendly recognition, or the other kind?"

Red held his smile as he muttered back, "Wish I knew, old pot." He cast his eyes desperately toward the bar and was relieved to see Prin.

"Prinny!" He swept over to her. "My sweet provider of ale."

The rest of the tavern went slowly back to their business. Or at least, they made some show of doing so. But Prin looked a little queasy as she tried and failed to meet his gaze.

"Hey, Red."

"What's the matter, Prin? Someone been telling you I was dead or something?"

She flinched at the word *dead*, but then forced a thin smile. "Course not, Red. And I wouldn't have believed them if they had."

"Glad to hear it." Red leaned his elbows on the bar. "Piss'ell, but it's good to see a friendly old face."

"It's...good to see you, too, Red," she said haltingly.

Why was she and everyone else in this place so askew? he wondered. "How about a round of..."

Red trailed off when he saw another familiar face at the big table in the back of the tavern.

"Well, well, Nettie!" He hurried over to her, grinning and feeling almost giddy. "Aren't you putting on the lords. Sitting at Drem's old spot like you own the place."

Nettles sat at the table, her expression oddly distant. Almost detached. He was surprised to see her with two gafs from his old pickpocket gang. Moxy Poxy had gotten even rangier and more ragged since he'd seen her last. Mister Hatbox, with his black top hat and pristine black jacket and white shirt, looked as creepy as ever. Red had never really liked them, but it didn't seem like they were wags with Nettles either. The way they deferred to her made them seem more like loyal boots.

"Why don't you have a seat, Red?" Nettles asked, her voice just as distant as her expression.

Red decided to play along until he had a better sense of things. If she was playing it pat, so would he. He pulled out a chair and slouched into it. It appeared Vaderton was content to remain at the bar.

Nettles signaled to Prin, who hurried over immediately with a tankard of dark for him.

"Thanks, Prinny," he said when she handed him the drink.

She flashed him another thin smile, then hurried back to the bar.

"How'd you escape Stonepeak?" asked Nettles.

"Made some friends on the inside." He grinned.

"That so?" she asked.

"You know me," Red said airily. "I make friends everywhere I go." He leaned in conspiratorially. "So what is all this, Nettie? Are you running the Circle now?"

"These days, wags call me the Black Rose."

"Really? *You're* the one Vaderton wanted me to talk to?"

"Who's Vaderton?" asked Nettles.

"That gaf over at the bar with the black beard and the pole up his ass. Friend of Yammy's, apparently."

Nettles glanced over at him. "Looks vaguely familiar. Can't remember from where, though. He say why he wanted you to talk to me?"

Red shook his head. "Just that there was something important you had to tell me."

She looked at him for a moment, then said, "I reckon there is." She gestured to Prin again. When the bartender hurried over, Nettles said, "Red and I need to talk privately. Can we use your office?"

"Of course, Black Rose. I'll get the key." She headed back toward the bar.

"And a bottle of whiskey," said Nettles.

Prin stopped and glanced first at Red, then at Nettles. After a moment, she nodded tersely, and brought over a key and a very quality bottle of whiskey.

Nettles stood. "You two, stay," she told Hatbox and Moxy. "Nobody goes near the office until I say. Keen?"

They nodded silently.

"You," she said to Red. "Come with me." Then she turned, the keys in one hand and the bottle in the other, and headed toward the office door at the side of the tavern.

As Red followed her, he decided she'd taken rather well to ordering people around. An effortless surety combined with a total lack of pretension.

The office was small, with room for little more than a desk, a large filing cabinet, and a safe. To this day, Red was impressed that Prin had run the tavern all by herself ever since her parents passed away. Everything from serving to accounting. Not many people could do such a wide assortment of jobs.

"The old office, huh?" he said as he sat down on the desk. "Only time I was ever back here was when Prin and I tossed a few times. I wanted to do it on the bar after closing, but she said it wasn't hygienic or something."

"Drink." Nettles shoved the bottle at him. He'd expected her to drop the pat ganglord act once they were alone, but she didn't. He was beginning to suspect it was more than just her neighborhood status that had changed.

"Yeah, alright." He uncorked the whiskey and took a sip. He held the bottle out to her, but she shook her head. She was still standing, too, even though he'd left her the chair.

"Would you sit down at least?" he asked. "You're making me nervous."

"Have another drink," she advised, and continued to stand.

He took another sip, the burn of the liquid almost enough to smother the dark unease that was growing in his stomach.

"You know I was never good at speaking nice," said Nettles. "And there's no nice way to say some-

thing like this anyway. So I'll just come out with it."
She took a slow breath. "Filler and Sadie are dead."

When Red had been a little boy, he found his mom
dead on the couch. Her nose and mouth had been
caked with dried blood, her eyes glassy, and her fingers curled in like claws. When he'd seen that, it had
been like someone had put a bellows to his lips and
opened them so that all the air was sucked out. It had
felt like he'd been suffocating where he stood.

It felt like that now.

He couldn't speak, or even breathe. He stared at
Nettles, desperate for some warmth or comfort in
those brown eyes. But there was nothing. Maybe
that's why she'd been acting so distant. Maybe it
wasn't just toward him. She'd taken a step back
from everything. It had been too much for her. She'd
strangled the part of her that hurt. She might have
even killed it.

But Red wouldn't do that. Or couldn't. It hardly
mattered which. He'd come too far, worked through
too much pain already. He wasn't going to run from
it now. So he let the shock, the confusion, and the
horror wash over him. And it just kept coming in
waves, over and over again.

Filler and Sadie. Dead.

He longed to hold on to Nettles like a sailor clings
to a mast in a storm. But there was nothing in her
demeanor that invited him to reach out. And when
she did begin to speak again, it wasn't to provide any
words of comfort. It was only to give him the facts.

She spoke to him about the details that led to the
deaths of the two people he loved most in the world
in a voice that he barely recognized as hers. In that
sense, it felt like he'd lost not two people he loved,
but three.

The details did help in a way, though. They took
the abstract and made it more concrete. A world

without Filler and Sadie? At first, the idea simply
didn't make sense. But as Nettles continued to talk
quietly about the clash with her brother, and Hope's
desperate raid on Dawn's Light, he started to see
that such a world already existed, even if he hadn't
known it yet.

"Filler was properly avenged," Nettles said, "I saw
to that myself. I wasn't there when Sadie rammed
her ship into that imperial frigate at the Breaks, but
Gavish Gray sent word of it and said she saved a lot
of people that day, including Hope, Alash, and Jilly."

"Jilly?" It was the first thing Red had said since
two people-shaped holes had been cut in his world.

"We picked her up on an imperial frigate." She
narrowed her eyes. "Come to think of it, that's where
I've seen that Vaderton of yours."

Red nodded and took another drink. It seemed
like the sort of thing he should ask more about, but
he just couldn't bring himself to do it.

There was silence in the office for a little while,
broken only by the occasional slosh of whiskey in the
bottle as Red took another drink.

"Well, that's all there is to say, I reckon." Nettles
looked at him again, and there was still nothing in it.
"I'll have this Vaderton of yours put up for the night at
Apple Grove Manor so you can, uh, have some time
alone."

Red's only response was to take another drink. So
Nettles left, closing the door quietly behind her.

Red thought he could face the pain of it all head-
on. He'd come so far, grown so strong. But this was
worse than anything he'd ever experienced because it
didn't stop. Each moment brought a fresh new wave
of shock and horror. A new realization of something
else lost. No one to needle him into action like Sadie.
No one to lean on like Filler. There was that mischievous old gleam in Sadie's eye he'd always loved, ever

since he was a boy. And the musky sandalwood smell of Filler that was as familiar and more comforting than maybe any other scent in Paradise Circle. All of that was gone forever. It no longer existed in his life. In the world. Like it had never been there at all.

This thought unfolded endlessly, over and again, with different variations, each one causing its own special sharp spike of pain. A wag can only take so much of that, and so he kept drinking. Red was no stranger to whiskey, but that night he drank with the single-minded purpose of someone who wished to smother every burning thought that came out of his head. By the time Prin came in, he could barely focus his eyes.

Prin sighed when she saw him. "Should be *her* taking care of you," she muttered, more to herself than to him. "But I reckon the Black Rose can't be a shoulder to cry on, so I'll have to fill in."

She got behind him and hauled him to his feet with the precision of someone who was accustomed to dealing with drunk people. She ducked under his arm and half carried him across the tavern and up the steps to her small bedroom.

"You don' godda do this," he slurred as she helped him out of his jacket and boots, carefully placing his holstered guns on the small bedside table.

"Hush, you," she said and gave him a gentle push.

He fell back onto the bed and lay there while the world began to spin very unpleasantly. He felt so heavy, it seemed possible he could sink through the mattress and fall to the floor beneath, through all the floors, and into the cold, dark earth.

"It's a small bed, but it's all I got," she said as she pulled her dress over her head. "You'll just have to share."

She rolled him over on his side, then curled up behind him so her cheek was pressed against his upper back, and her legs were tucked up behind his. She reached her arm around and squeezed his hand.

"I miss 'em, too, Red."

"God, Prin." His voice cracked as he finally began to cry. "I don't know what to do."

She let him sob for a while, still holding him. It was an ugly sound, throaty and raw.

When he eventually quieted down, she said, "If you ask me, there ain't no good left in the world. Certainly none I ever see anymore."

Those words echoed in his ears as he drifted off to sleep.

———

The next morning, Red slumped against the bar, nursing a brutal hangover. He could feel the Shadow Demon pressing against the back of his skull. It was always there, of course. It was a part of him. But it was louder than usual, strengthened by the dark and miserable thoughts that wandered through his brain. There was a cold smugness to it that said, *See, I told you the world was nothing but piss and death.*

As he stared down at the bowl of watery stew that Prin had given him to ease his hangover, Red let the Shadow Demon have its way with his mind. He let it run circles, repeating and reshaping slivers of memory it considered proof of the awfulness of life. It was like a dog chewing on a favorite bone. He could feel its hard, chilly grip creep out into his limbs. It was tempting to let it come. He could already feel his hands longing for some kind of vague retribution. That was what a true wag of the Circle did, right? Pain for pain, death for death. But to whom? And for whom? Who, exactly, would gain right now from even more death?

As the sunlight came in through the grimy tavern

windows, it struck the broth in just the right way so that he could see his own reflection on its oily surface. He leaned away from the bowl, uncomfortable with the haggard expression he found there.

He found himself instead staring at the back wall of the tavern. It was a large, flat, blank space, stained and scraped here and there. It looked exactly the same as it had when he'd come here the first time, so many years ago, just a boy, following Sadie around like a lost, red-eyed puppy. It had been the night she lost her ear. There were so many memories in this place of Sadie. And Filler, too. All those memories would slip away and vanish forever. It wouldn't be long before even their faces would be hard to remember.

Unless...

"Hey, Prin," he said.

"Yeah?" she called from the other end of the bar, where she was setting a fresh cask of ale to be broached.

"Can I have that back wall?"

She looked at him over the barrel. *"Have?"*

"I want to paint it," he said.

"Really?" She looked at the wall as if she'd never really noticed it before. "Yeah, I reckon it could do with a fresh coat of paint."

A tiny hint of a smirk curled up at the corners of Red's mouth. She'd figure out what he meant soon enough.

———

Red had to go all the way to Silverback to get the kind of paint that would last in that dirty, smoky hole of a tavern. But the walk in the chilly, fall air did him some good, and by the time he'd returned, he'd mostly shaken off his hangover. He felt alert, focused, and ready to work.

It was early evening by then, and the tavern was full. But Nettles's table in the back was empty. He shoved it aside, which gave him a bit more room to work.

"You sure that's a good idea?" asked Prin as she walked by with three tankards in each hand.

"She won't be coming by tonight," he assured her.

He reckoned she was giving him some space, like she'd said. Maybe deep down she felt a little guilty, and worried that he blamed her for Filler's death. But Red remembered when Filler got shot during the storming of the Three Cups. Red had tried to blame himself for that one, and it was one of the few times he'd ever seen Filler angry. "*My* choice to fight for the Circle," he'd said. "Don't you dare take that away from me." Red had no doubt that Filler had chosen to stand by Nettles for the same reason. Clearly he'd believed in what she was doing, and what kind of a wag would Red be if he didn't honor that? So he couldn't put the blame on Nettles.

Still, it was nice to have the space to work. That's all he really wanted right then. First, he scrubbed the wall down. It took a while to get the buildup of smoke and grime off the surface, but he knew it would be much easier to paint if he did, and it would last longer, which was the whole point. It was nearly closing by the time he finished, and his shoulders ached. As he sat down at Nettles's table to rest, he noticed many of the patrons glancing curiously in his direction, but none of them risking an outright stare.

Red couldn't quite take the temperature of the Circle since he'd gotten back. It felt strangely subdued. The storming of the Three Cups and the subsequent riot and attack by the imps, followed only a year later by what sounded like a particularly vicious gang war between Nettles and her brother. It had taken a huge toll on the people. He wasn't the only one grappling with loss. That made what he was about to do feel all the more urgent.

Once Prin had pushed the last of the customers out the door, Red got to work. He decided to start with a bit of distance. He would ease into the things he *really* wanted to paint with something a little less personal. It wanted a nice big centerpiece anyway. Someone larger than life...

He began painting Bracers Madge from memory. Truth be told, it probably wasn't the most accurate likeness. But there were few alive now that remembered exactly what she looked like anyway. He made her impossibly big, nearly to the ceiling, so that she loomed over everything with her stern face and massive bulk, just like he remembered from when he was a boy.

On one side of her, he painted Sadie as she had been when he'd first met her. Vicious and rowdy and oddly joyful. He put her in the captain's hat, coat, and boots she'd been so proud of. The ones he'd stolen for her with Filler's help.

On the other side of Bracers Madge, he painted Filler in the place he was always happiest. In front of the smithy forge, where he could be equal parts brute strength and careful craftsman. He painted him shirtless and pounding steel on the anvil with a hammer. He might have exaggerated Filler's sweaty, muscled physique somewhat, but it gave him an odd pleasure to think that toms and mollies for years to come would be ogling his best wag's biceps.

He'd originally thought that would be it. Just the three images. But when he looked at it, he knew that it wasn't finished, and there was plenty of wall space left. So he took an area and painted Deadface Drem, with his haunted eyes and blank face, along with Brackson, half transformed into that blob creature, and Ranking, half transformed into that bug creature. Above the three of them he painted a ghostly figure in a white hooded robe that everyone would recognize, because the fear and hatred of biomancers would never leave the Circle.

But even *that* wasn't enough. So he started over on the other side, painting everyone he remembered who was dead now: past ganglord Jix the Lift; Jilly's mother, Jacey; Sadie's rival Backus, who died of old age, that rarest of deaths in the Circle; and Neepman, who owned that bakery and butcher shop he and Nettles had robbed. There was still space, so he painted a whole scene of people marching on the Three Cups. He was surprised at how many faces he remembered. Faces that would *always* be remembered now.

He finally ran out of wall space as the pink light of dawn came in through the windows. He collapsed into a chair at Nettles's table, his hands sore and paint-stained, and fell asleep.

———

"Red, I think it's time you got up." Prin's voice was gentle, as was her hand on his shoulder.

Red opened his eyes slowly and winced at the afternoon sun as he fumbled for the smoked glasses in his pocket.

"Did I sleep the whole day?" He slowly sat up. His neck was stiff, and it felt like there might be an imprint of the table wood grain on his cheek.

"You were up all night, so I thought it best to let you sleep, but uh…" She glanced nervously behind him. "I think she wants her table back."

Red nodded, then rubbed at his sore neck as he got to his feet and turned around. Nettles stood nearby, flanked again by Moxy Poxy and Mister Hatbox. Vaderton was nearby at the bar, drinking a tankard.

Others had begun to filter in at the other tables for their first drink after a long day of work.

"Well, now," said Nettles. Her expression was unreadable as she stared at the mural.

"See now, Mister H," said Moxy Poxy in a voice that had only gotten more grating and unpleasant in the years since Red had last heard it. She walked closer to the mural, her hands on her hips. "This here is true *Art*, the like of which you and me don't get to see too often."

"It moves the very soul," agreed Mister Hatbox in his quiet, dead voice.

"I tell you, Rixie." Moxy patted Red's shoulder good-naturedly. "I've never been happier that Filler wouldn't let me kill you all them years ago. This here is nothing short of inspirational to a fellow artist."

Red knew that her "art" was mainly composed of the fingers of her victims, and gave a wan smile. "Thanks, Moxy."

Then he turned back to Nettles. Like many artists, he often acted like he didn't care what people thought of his work. And like many artists, it was a load of balls and pricks. "What do you think?"

Nettles didn't speak right away. Instead she continued to stare at the mural. With so many other eyes around, Red knew that even if she loved it, she'd have to be pat about it. The ganglord of Paradise Circle couldn't get all poncey over a bit of art, no matter who did it, or why.

Finally, she cleared her throat and looked at him. "I reckon the Circle could use a bit of this right now."

It was, Red realized, the closest she could ever get to saying that she missed him and wished he could stick around. Maybe she hadn't totally been swallowed by her own darkness after all.

"I've got this thing I have to do," he said. "I'm actually looking for Hope and Brigga Lin. You know where they are?"

She grew guardedly more interested. "You need them both? For what?"

"For a job, I guess you could say."

"Must be a big job."

"It is," said Red. "And dangerous. But my employer pays well."

"Judging by that carriage you came in on, and the guns at your hips, I'd say you're speaking crystal on that." She was looking more and more interested now. Not in a friendly way, but in a businessperson sort of way. He realized that this wasn't Nettles he was talking to now. It was truly the Black Rose.

Red gave her a coy smile. "I've done alright."

"Join me at my table," she told him. Then she glanced at Moxy and Hatbox. "Make sure no one comes within earshot."

"Room for him, at least?" Red asked, nodding to Vaderton.

"If you like," said the Black Rose. "He's your responsibility, not mine."

When Moxy Poxy and Mister Hatbox took up positions between the table and the rest of the tavern, all the patrons suddenly found something else to look at.

Once she and Vaderton sat down with Red, the Black Rose said, "So, who's your employer?"

"Her Imperial Majesty, Empress Pysetcha." Red said it with exaggerated casualness.

The Black Rose was too good to let her surprise show. "That so."

Vaderton, however, started choking on his ale. It took him a few moments to catch his breath. "Sorry," he muttered to Red.

Red continued to look at the Black Rose. "Like I said, I made some friends on the inside."

"So you're what, some kind of secret imp now?" asked the Black Rose.

"Things aren't as simple there as we thought. It ain't just us against the lacies and imps. They're all fighting their own battle with the biomancers."

"Thought the biomancers served the emperor," said the Black Rose.

Red shook his head. "It's been the other way around for at least the last twenty years or so. Or it was until Hope and Brigga Lin pissed on their plans at Dawn's Light. Now the biomancers are starting to lose their grip on the emperor, and so the whole empire. The empress wants to take advantage of that weakness and get rid of the biomancers. She's hoping Hope and Brigga Lin will help her do that."

"An empire without biomancers?" asked the Black Rose. "That what your empress is offering?"

"See here," said Vaderton, looking offended. "She's *your* empress t—" He stopped because Red stomped hard on his foot.

"And money, too, of course," Red told the Black Rose. "If you know where they are."

"I'm not sure where Hope is these days, but I *can* tell you exactly where to find Brigga Lin. And she might have a better idea where Hope is, too."

"That's worth something," said Red.

"I don't need money," said the Black Rose. "I want an audience with this empress."

Vaderton looked ready to object, but Red shot him a warning glance and he stayed silent.

"Can't get you that myself," Red told the Black Rose. "But I'll introduce you to someone who can. It'll be up to you to convince her you're worthwhile. Good enough?"

The Black Rose considered it, then nodded. "That'll do."

"Sunny," said Red. "So what do you have for me?"

"Gavish Gray's ship is a smuggling vessel called the *Rolling Lightning*. He's been running various things up and down the eastern side of the empire, but he's based in Vance Post. Last I heard, Brigga Lin and Jilly were on his crew. When they're in Vance Post, they put up at an inn in the Shade District called the Past Is Forgotten."

"What about Alash?" asked Red. "I heard he might be in Vance Post, too."

"Hadn't heard that," said the Black Rose. "But it's a big place. Maybe he is."

"And what about Hope?" pressed Red. "Anything at all you can tell me?"

"Gavish told me that the last he saw of her, she was heading south from Dawn's Light. Alone, and without that sword of hers."

"Well," said Red, thinking about the thirty or so Vinchen that were after her. "*That's* not good."

PART TWO

A "warrior" is one who makes war. It's right there in the name. So can a warrior truly seek peace? I suspect that this paradox within myself, as both warrior and peacemaker, will eventually come to a head, and my resolve will be tested. In many ways, I long for that day. Only then will I know for certain if I have found a new path.

—from the private journal of
Hurlo the Cunning

9

*B*rigga Lin's mentor used to say that a biomancer never stopped learning.

Recently, Brigga Lin had learned that she really liked sex.

She liked pressing her lips to Gavish Gray's prickly mouth. She liked the harsh scrape of his stubble on her cheek. She liked squeezing the lean muscle of his arms under his white sailor's shirt, and she liked tearing the thin cotton material off him to reveal the sweaty slabs of his pectorals. She liked feeling his back muscles tremble with one hand as she drew her nails across them with the other. She liked how he used his large, calloused hands to gently cup her breasts while he kissed the soft skin of her throat and pressed his engorging penis against her bare inner thigh. She liked to smack his penis playfully and watch it bob up and down eagerly while his breath came in harsh grunts.

She liked the feel of their naked bodies pressed against each other, the sweat sealing them together for a moment, then audibly peeling apart as she pushed away. She liked pressing her hands down hard on his chest as she straddled him, feeling him fight for each breath. She liked the heat of his penis as she slid it inside her. She liked how she engulfed him, surrounded him, squeezed him, until she owned him.

She liked how he fought against her strength while she rocked back and forth, sometimes sliding nearly all the way off him, only to plunge back down. She liked arching her back so that she could reach behind and dig her nails into the meat of his inner thighs. But as his movement grew more frantic, she always leaned forward again so she could look at his face. Because the thing she liked best of all was watching the jaded, world-weary pirate grow vulnerable and helpless beneath her as he climaxed. More often than not, that was what brought her to her own climax.

But once her own climax abated, it was her turn to feel vulnerable. Brigga Lin had never before been in the habit of doubt or introspection, but recently those things had begun to creep in. Perhaps this growing insecurity had been caused by Hope's sudden departure and the fracturing of the only group of people she had ever found a sense of community with. Or perhaps it was the unpredictable flashes of foresight that continued to plague her with their hazy possible futures. Whatever it was, it left her at once restless and directionless. It was a feeling that only sex seemed to quell, and then only temporarily.

Now, she and Gavish lay in a narrow bed on a lumpy mattress in a tiny room at a disreputable inn. Moonlight spilled through the open window, the cool night breeze drying the sweat and other fluids on their naked bodies.

"Does it bother you that I once had the body of a man?" she asked quietly.

"Why would it?" he asked. "I've tossed with toms before."

"Really? You like both?"

"You lacies put too much into that sort of thing," he said. "Fun is fun, and us common folk are keen enough to take it wherever we can find it. There ain't a whole lot to go around, after all."

"Am I lacy, by your estimation?"

"You were born into privilege, weren't you? Nice house, education, and the like?"

"I suppose so."

"Then you're a lacy," he said in a matter-of-fact sort of tone. Then he turned his head to look at her and grinned. "Although you're a damn sight more useful than most lacies."

"For *tossing*, as you put it?" she asked. "Or for my assistance in your pirating endeavors?"

"Both, of course. That's what makes you my favorite person in the world."

"Even more than your precious Black Rose?" She said it somewhat teasingly, but with an underlying edge. Brigga Lin was not accustomed to jealousy, either, but it seemed to come with the territory of doubt.

"The Black Rose and I were through when I killed that biomancer. I did that one last thing for her on account of the fondness I once had for her. But she's a different person now, and one I ain't sure I like. A good pirate knows when to cut his losses and look for more pleasant pastures."

"Are you comparing me to a *pasture*?" Brigga Lin ran her nails across his chest.

He laid the flat of his hand on her lower abdomen. "Well, I surely do like plowing your field."

"Pirate humor is so crass," she said.

"It's part of our charm," he said.

"Debatable."

There was a tentative knock at the door.

"This better be good," called Gavish.

"Sorry, Captain," came Fisty's voice outside the door. "You wanted to know as soon as the prize made port."

Gavish Gray sighed. "That I did. We'll be out in a minute."

"Aye, sir," came Fisty's voice.

Gavish slowly sat up and ran his fingers through his prematurely gray hair. "We best get a move on."

"Where are we sailing to now?" Brigga Lin swiveled her body around so that her bare feet touched the chill wooden floorboards.

"Nowhere, actually. A pirate knows that sometimes it's better to let the mark come to you."

"We're going to rob a ship right here in Vance Post? Aren't the local authorities known for their strict peacekeeping?"

"That's only a problem if we get caught." Gavish pulled on his trousers. "And we won't."

"You have a plan, I take it?"

"Naturally." He held up the shreds of his shirt and gave Brigga Lin a hard look. "I don't suppose you could use your biomancery to repair the damage you done to my shirt?"

"Living things only." She pursed her lips. "If you like, I could make your body hair grow to cover you like a shirt."

He shuddered. "No thanks."

"Half your crew are usually shirtless," Brigga Lin pointed out. "Why don't you just do the same?"

He gave her an injured look. "I'm the captain. I have to at least look a *tiny* bit more respectable than the rest."

———

Things were great.

Jilly found she had to remind herself of that a lot. She was crewing a ship with a quality group of true wags, many of them, including the captain, from Paradise Circle. She didn't have to pretend to be a boy anymore. She could drink as often as she liked. She could curse and spit and nobody said a thing against it. What's more, the ship she worked on was one of the most notorious smuggling vessels in the eastern half of the empire. If a person needed cargo moved discreetly anywhere from Vance Post to Pauper's Prayer, the *Rolling Lightning* was the ship to hire. Everyone knew that. Much of that reputation came from the strong leadership of Captain Gavish Gray, who had recognized Jilly's usefulness right away. He never coddled her or tried to protect her like she was some little kid. Respect. That's what he gave her, and so did the rest of the crew.

And it wasn't like she'd completely left everything else behind. She still had Brigga Lin as a master. One of the most powerful women who ever lived was teaching Jilly everything she knew. Or she would. Once she had the time.

Whenever Jilly thought about her life, it was perfectly obvious how great it was. So it was a little strange that it didn't actually *feel* great all that often.

Like many inns in Vance Post's Shade District, the Past Is Forgotten had a tavern on the first floor, and rooms on the second floor. It was a good idea, really. A person could drink themselves cross-eyed and still find their way to bed. Not that Jilly ever drank that much. But some of her fellow crew members did now and then, and with the bed so close, she never had to help any of them find their way, and that was a very good thing. Partly, she just didn't like hauling their smelly, lurching bulk around. But when they got like that, they seemed to think of her less as a fellow crew member and more as a molly nearly old enough to toss. Once or twice, one of them had even made a move. But it was always knives out for Jilly, so they learned real quick that she was not for tossing. Even still, she didn't like cutting on her own crew if she could help it, so she was glad to avoid the whole awkward situation whenever possible.

Now she sat at a table with Slake, a tall thin man

who didn't say much, and Marble Eyes, who talked entirely too much.

Jilly sipped at her ale as she watched Fisty come hurrying down the stairs at the back of the tavern and weave his way through the tables crowded with merchant sailors and pirates alike. Everyone was welcome at the Past Is Forgotten.

"Drain those buckets quick, my wags," said Fisty as he sat down at their table. "The captain and the Lady will be down in a minute."

"She coming along on this?" asked Marble Eyes. He got his name on account of his eyes, which always bulged out in a way that made them look a little like glass orbs had been stuck in his head.

"A'course she is," said Fisty. "The Lady's pulled your cock out of the fire at least as many times as she has mine. We'd all probably be at the Empty Cliffs or dead if it weren't for her."

"I reckon so," admitted Marble Eyes, then took a long gulp of ale. "Still, it gives me the crawlies to work side by side with a biomancer."

"Captain said she ain't a biomancer no more," said Slake. "Got kicked out."

"Aye," said Marble Eyes. "All that says to me is that even regular biomancers are scared of her."

"Something you'll be mighty appreciative of if we ever run into a true biomancer," said Fisty. He glanced at Jilly for a moment, who had been listening to all this in silence, then turned back to Marble Eyes. "Besides, the Lady and Jilly here are a matched set. You wouldn't want to lose our favorite magic thief, would you?" He ruffled Jilly's hair playfully.

She batted his hand away. "Ain't no magic in my thievery," she told him. "Just skill."

"You've got skill to spare," said Marble Eyes. "How's a molly get so lucky? Taught how to steal by Red of Paradise Circle, how to sail by a navy captain, how to magic by a biomancer, and even how to fight by a Vinchen."

"Not near enough." The words popped out of her mouth, bitter and hard, before she'd even considered saying them. She had tried to understand why Captain Bane had abandoned her. She really had. But nothing anyone said lessened the sting. Bane had promised to be Jilly's teacher, but left only a month later. So much for the Vinchen code of honor.

Fisty cleared his throat. "Well, any way you look at it, Jilly here is a great boon to the crew of the *Rolling Lightning*. Ain't that right, wags?"

"Aye," said Marble Eyes.

Slake nodded and raised his tankard.

Jilly could feel herself blushing as she said, "Well, don't get all poncey on me, my wags. We've still got a job to do this night."

"That we do," said Fisty. "Now drink."

They'd finished their tankards by the time Captain Gray and Brigga Lin came down the stairs. Brigga Lin looked as elegant as ever in her white hooded gown with long flowing sleeves. Captain Gray, however, looked a little disheveled, and for some reason, he had no shirt beneath his captain's coat.

"Well, if it ain't the biomancer's own cunt-warmer!"

The man who said that was Clean Kever, so called because he was the most reliable fence on Vance Post. He had a knack for making the taint of suspicion wash away from even the most obviously stolen goods. A short, balding man, and not too impressive, but that worked for him as well. Wouldn't have done to be a fence who stood out. He was well known and admired by many, and not the sort of person you wanted against you. And, like many, he also had an almost religious hatred of biomancers.

Clean Kever now stood at the bar, the bit of hair he still had neatly combed over the bald part. He'd yelled his greeting across the tavern so that everyone could hear it.

"So tell me, Gray," he continued. "As a servant to a biomancer, does that mean you and your crew never have to worry about getting taken? Or is that just so long as you can make her come?"

"I told you before, Kever." Gray's tone was almost friendly. "The Lady ain't a biomancer."

"No?" asked Kever. He gave a skeptical look to the other patrons, most of whom were listening, even if they acted like they weren't. "Then how come I heard she can make a gun explode with just a twitch of her hand?"

"It takes more than a *twitch*, I can assure you," said Brigga Lin, her expression ominous. "Perhaps I should—"

Gavish put his hand on her arm, then turned to smile at Kever. "You got it all wrong, as usual, old pot. Just like that time you tried to sell that crate of pepper as coral spice."

Kever's face flushed. "That was you! You set me up!"

"Of course you say that, old pot," Gavish said lightly. "Of *course* you do."

"We've had our differences, Gray, but coving up to the biomancers is a new low, even for you. You mark me, this will bring trouble for us all."

"Whatever you say, Kever," said Gavish as he nodded to the table where Jilly, Fisty, Marble Eyes, and Slake sat. Then he and Brigga Lin headed for the door.

"That'll be our cue," Fisty said quietly, and they stood up and followed him out of the tavern.

They found Gavish and Brigga Lin waiting for them in front of the tavern. Gavish grinned when he saw Jilly. He leaned in close and whispered, "You get that thing I asked for?"

Jilly returned his smile. "I did, Captain."

"Then hopefully that cock-dribble won't be a problem for too much longer," said Gray. Then he turned to Fisty. "Go fetch the rest of the crew and meet us at the pier. We've work to do."

———

"No pissing way," said Fisty. "With all due respect, I'll follow you into death, Captain, and you know that. But I won't have no part of biomancery."

That night, Brigga Lin, Gavish Gray, Slake, Fisty, Marble Eyes, Jilly, and the rest of the crew huddled in a dock storage building on the northwest pier. Vance Post was a much smaller island than either Stonepeak or New Laven, but it could accommodate just as many ships because of the massive docking system that surrounded it. The piers radiated out from the island in all directions, zigzagging and branching so that it might have looked like a giant snowflake if seen from above. Some piers reached as far as a quarter mile beyond the shore. No one knew exactly how the massive wooden pylons that kept the docks stable had been driven all the way down to the ocean floor. As was often the case, people assumed it was something to do with biomancery and left it at that.

Brigga Lin thought it was interesting that the common people could accept those aspects of biomancery so easily, and yet still revile her. She suspected it had something to do with actually witnessing the biomancery. She couldn't completely blame them for it. Even she had felt that unease the first time she witnessed her master perform it when she was a child. It had been such a simple thing, too. Just a fish being dehydrated. But there was something about the suddenness of it that had made the hairs on her arms stand up. Of course, such reactions were for children, but the majority of people outside of the palace were so un-

familiar with biomancery that they might as well be
children. They certainly acted as unreasonable.

"Come on, my wag," said Gavish. "You've let her
work her biomancery on any number of people."

"Aye, *other* people. Not me. That's where I draw
the line," said Fisty. He glanced around at the rest of
the crew. "And I know I'm not alone in that."

Many of the others nodded vehemently. None
shook their heads.

Gavish looked pained as he assessed the mood of
the crowd. Then he turned back to Fisty. "You trust
Jilly, don't you? She says it's perfectly safe. She's even
had it done to her once before."

"I don't care if my own *mother* says it's safe, I'm
not letting someone put gills on me," Fisty said
adamantly.

"Our mark is all the way at the end of the pier,"
said Gavish. "We can't just walk the whole crew down
there. They'll set an alarm the moment they see us. So
the only way to sneak onto that ship is underwater."

"Then we'll do it with tubes and grease, the way
we've always done it. The *proper* way to do it."

"But, Fisty, my wag, don't you see that this is better? The old way, there's always a chance of getting
spotted."

"That's a risk we're all willing to take, ain't that
right, wags?" Fisty turned to the rest of the crew, and
there was more nodding and murmurs of agreement.

Brigga Lin didn't like letting Gavish Gray—or
anyone for that matter—speak on her behalf. But
she still remembered how poorly her discussion of
biomancery had gone with Nettles, and she worried
that, particularly when speaking to people from the
lower classes, she had a tendency of making things
worse. Even so, she felt Gavish Gray gave in to popular opinion far too quickly.

His eyes swept the crew. Moonlight filtered in

through the narrow windows of the dock house to shine on brown, tattooed skin gleaming with sweat. Serious, furrowed brows looked back at him.

"If that's how it is for all of you, we'll do it the old way." He gave them a tight grin. "Besides, nothing wrong with a little risk now and then, as long as the reward is worth it. And in this case, my wags, it very much is."

They all grinned back at him, relief clearly showing in their eyes. These men loved their captain. Perhaps they were worried that Brigga Lin was too much of an influence on him. That she was *changing* him. If so, they didn't know him as well as she did. Because Gavish Gray would never change for anyone. It was one of the things she liked about him, even if it was frustrating at times.

"Well, then, send someone to fetch some grease from the ship," Gavish said brusquely. "We've much to do, and the moon is already risen."

"Aye, sir." Fisty tapped two sailors to run back to the ship, which was several piers over.

"Marble Eyes, you and Ginty go cut us some reeds along the shore to use as tubes," Gavish said.

"Aye, sir," said Marble Eyes, and the two hurried away.

"Do you still want me to come along?" Brigga Lin asked him.

"You know, Lady Witch, maybe you should sit this one out," he said, not quite able to meet her eyes. "If there were any...unusual-looking corpses found on board, that might run counter to the plan, keen?"

"I see."

Then his face brightened and he looked directly at her. "I tell you what. How about *you* put the finishing touch on it, though."

"And what touch might that be?"

He held out a revolver with a fine rose-quartz-

inlaid handle, the metal polished to a mirror brightness. "Once I give the all clear, we'll slip back into
the water with the loot. You said you can be invisible, right?"

"I can bend the light around me so that people
can't easily see me."

"Right. So you do that...light bending, and leave
this gun in a conspicuous spot on the deck near the
ship."

"Planting false evidence," she said.

He smiled encouragingly. "Right you are. And
of course you were the one who pointed out that
imps at the local garrison have an almost unnatural
obsession with solving crimes. They won't stop until
they find *someone* to put in jail for this, so let's make
certain it's not us. Sunny?"

Did he know how demeaning this all was? Once
she had dreamed of being on the Council of Biomancery. Later she had dreamed of being at the
forefront of a revolution. But now she wasn't even
a proper outlaw. She had been reduced to a pirate's
mistress who planted evidence for him.

And yet, she found herself nodding dully and taking
the gun from him. Because what else was there to do?

———

This was Jilly's first time infiltrating a docked ship
like a proper pirate. There had been some resistance
among the crew about letting her come along, but
Gavish convinced them to go along with it. She had
a feeling he'd probably done it to appease Brigga
Lin, who was clearly pissed and peppered that they
refused to let her use biomancery. But Jilly was so
excited about this job, she did her best not to think
about that too much. She'd *show* those pirates that
she was more than just a lookout and a sneak-thief.

She'd prove to them that she could handle this and any other thing they cared to throw at her.

First was the tub of black grease that Fisty brought from the *Rolling Lightning*. The rest of the crew removed shirts and shoes. Jilly wasn't about to go bare-chested, since she'd just finally started to grow something worth covering. Instead she stripped down to her sleeveless cotton undershirt and gladly removed the pointy boots Brigga Lin made her wear.

She watched carefully as the rest of the crew coated their faces, necks, shoulders, and chests in black grease, then slicked back their hair with it as well. Then Jilly did the same, making sure to even cover the white shoulder straps of her undershirt in grease. Brigga Lin would probably say it was ruined later and make her get a new one, but Jilly wanted to make certain that she did this right. Besides, with the money she made on Gavish's crew, she could afford a new undershirt. Especially after this score.

Marble Eyes brought back a thick bundle of reeds and passed them around. The crew cut them down to foot-length tubes, discarding any sections that couldn't easily pass air through them.

"You ready, my wags?" Gavish asked quietly.

The group of pitch-black faces grinned and nodded. To Jilly it looked like white eyes and teeth bouncing up and down in the darkness. Then, one by one, they slipped off the side of the dock and into the dark water. Just before Jilly slid over the side, she glanced back at Brigga Lin, who still stood next to the storage shed. Jilly felt a pang of guilt at leaving her mentor behind, but she reminded herself that Brigga Lin had just as important a role to play as anyone else.

The crew of the *Rolling Lightning* moved slowly through the water beneath the dock so as not to create much wake. Gavish was in the lead, with Fisty just behind him. From her spot near the back of the group, she could barely make them out in the darkness.

The crew moved carefully and silently under the docks until they reached their mark—a large merchant vessel at the very end of the pier. The hull rose pretty high out of the water, but after all the climbing drills Hope had put Jilly through, she was confident it would be easy to get onto the decks. In fact, she'd probably get there before anyone else.

But first there was a small stretch of open water to clear between the end of the dock and the side of the ship. That's where the reeds came into play. One by one, the pirates dropped below the waterline, put up the reed so they could keep breathing, and made their way slowly to the ship.

Gavish had stayed under the dock cover to watch over his men as they moved to the ship. Finally it was just Jilly and Gavish left. Jilly took a deep breath and sank beneath the surface, but Gavish took hold of her arm and pulled her back up.

"You climb the dock here and keep an eye out for imp patrols," he breathed in her ear.

Her eyes widened. "But, Captain—"

He scowled at her and put a finger to his lips. Then he sank below the surface and made his way across the open water to the boat, leaving Jilly behind to stew. He'd never intended to let her on board. This had been his plan all along. Making her the lookout. Again.

She was so mad that she had to bite her lip to keep from cursing out loud while she shimmied up the dock pylon. She found a crossbeam she could balance on near the top that allowed her to peek over the edge and look down the length of the dock. If a patrol came back, she'd see them long before they saw her or the crew currently scaling the side of the merchant ship.

She glanced back and winced at their clumsy

climbing technique. They were like bears climbing a tree, relying almost entirely on their knives and strength to pull themselves up, rather than using the natural hand- and footholds that were all too easy for Jilly to spot, even at that distance.

She took another quick glance down the dock to make sure it was still clear of patrols, then allowed herself to look back at the merchant ship. The crew had finally made their way up to the decks. Now they were lumbering around, slitting any throat they could find. They didn't seem to have any interest in using the nooks and crannies of the ship to slip up behind their prey unawares. Instead they relied on shock, speed, and crude force. It wasn't the silent, elegantly sinister event she'd envisioned. In fact, it was ugly, brutish, and dull.

Once the merchant crew were all dead, the pirates spread the loot among each other so that no one would be weighed down by too much coin for the return swim. Gavish used a mirror to flash a signal to Brigga Lin at the far end of the pier so she would know it was time to plant the evidence. Then the pirates climbed back into the water and crossed to the cover of the docks again.

Jilly stayed up on the crossbeam and glared down at them as they passed beneath her. She thought the least they could do was give her a nod in thanks for keeping an eye out for them, but most either didn't notice or didn't acknowledge her.

Once the rest of the pirates had continued beneath the docks back to the storage shed where their clothes were kept, Gavish motioned for her to climb down. She kept her angry eyes fixed on him the whole time she made her way back down, not looking at hand- or footholds once. Just to show him how *easy* climbing was for her. The smile he gave her was pained. Maybe even a little apologetic.

"Good work, my wag," he whispered.

"*Easy* work," she said.

"Now, now, don't be like that," he said. "After all, I couldn't have the world's first Vinchen biomancer slinking around a ship cutting throats like some common criminal."

———

The world's first Vinchen biomancer...

What a pissing joke.

Jilly was a smart girl. She had to be, otherwise she wouldn't have lived as long as she had. Maybe she wasn't as clever with words as Red. And she had to admit that she often struggled to understand the books Brigga Lin put in front of her. But she was smart about people. She understood them. Sometimes better than they understood themselves. And now she understood why things didn't feel as great as she thought they should.

It was because she had been let down by everyone she trusted. Bane had abandoned her, of course. But so had everyone else. Sadie and Filler were dead. Finn was God knew where. Vaderton had gone off with Old Yammy. Even Alash had disappeared shortly after Brigga Lin and Captain Gray started tossing. All of that she'd known for a while, and she'd always comforted herself that at least Brigga Lin hadn't abandoned her.

But now, as she sat at a table in the Past Is Forgotten with Gavish Gray and Brigga Lin, she looked at her "master" and understood that a person could abandon you without ever leaving.

"Master, when can we begin actually *doing* things?" she asked.

"Hm?" Brigga Lin had been staring into a glass of wine.

"All I ever do is read," said Jilly. "I was thinking maybe you and me could go off someplace secluded and you could actually show me some things."

"We need to make a run up to Port Blaze soon," said Gray. "We could drop you somewhere on the way and pick you up on our way back. There's many little spits of land coming off Walta, and the mole rats only keep to the largest one."

"Did you finish the last book I gave you?" Brigga Lin asked her.

"Well, no . . . ," admitted Jilly. "But—"

"Then you can occupy yourself with that."

It felt like a load of balls and pricks. She'd finished the *Biomancery Praxis* months ago. Everything since that felt like it was just a waste of time. But Jilly had been with Brigga Lin long enough to know that open disrespect wouldn't get her any closer. So she bowed her head and gave a half-hearted, "Yes, master."

An awkward silence settled at the table, which Brigga Lin seemed not to notice. Captain Gray gave Jilly an apologetic look, which she appreciated, although more and more that seemed the only kind of look he gave her. She sipped moodily at her tankard and stared at a stones game at the next table, not really paying attention to it so much as simply watching hands move stones around.

A short time later, a squad of imps marched through the front door in single file. The tavern fell silent, and the tension was suddenly palpable.

"I think they finally figured it out," Gavish said quietly.

One imp stepped forward, his face hard. The gold epaulets on the shoulders of his white uniform marked him as the squad captain. "I'm looking for a man who goes by the name of Clean Kever."

Every wag in the tavern breathed a quiet sigh of relief. Except, of course, for Kever. He sat at a table near the back and looked up from his tankard to find everyone suddenly staring at him. A moment of panic flashed across his face, but it quickly twisted into an ingratiating smile.

"Uh, what can I do for you, sir? Perhaps you need a sales representative to move some personal items?"

"Hilarious," the squad captain said sourly. "Get him."

Several imps shoved their way through the tables until they reached Kever, then they roughly hauled him to his feet.

"I ain't done nothing!" Kever protested as they clapped irons on his wrists.

The squad captain held out the revolver with the rose quartz handle that Jilly had stolen from Kever the week before. "I have several people who vouch that this one-of-a-kind revolver is yours."

"Now, listen," said Kever. "I know it's frowned upon for a regular wag like me to own a revolver, but there ain't exactly a law against it. And anyway, it was a gift from a valued customer!"

"So you admit that it's yours?" asked the captain.

"Yes, but—"

"It was found at the scene where the esteemed Mr. Mazelton's ship had been infiltrated. The captain and crew had been coldly murdered, and the high-value cargo on board had been stolen."

Kever's eyes went wide. "It must have been *planted*! That gun was stolen from me!"

The squad captain didn't seem interested in anything Kever had to say. He nodded curtly to the imps who held him. "Let's go." Then he turned smartly on his heel and left the tavern.

As the imps hauled Kever past the table where Jilly, Brigga Lin, and Captain Gray sat, he was still shouting.

"It was stolen! I swear to God I was framed!"

"Of course you say that, old pot," Gavish said with a smirk. "Of *course* you do."

Kever went from panic to rage. "You did this! Damn you to every last hell, Gavish Gray. I should have known that the biomancer's cunt-warmer would also be in league with the imps!"

He leapt toward Gavish, but one of the imps struck him on the back of the head with the butt of his revolver and he went limp. They had to carry him the rest of the way out of the tavern.

Once the imps had gone with Kever, and the tavern had settled back down, Gavish turned to Brigga Lin. "Well, I'd say we won."

"Hm?" said Brigga Lin, looking up from her glass of wine as if she hadn't noticed any of it.

"You definitely got the best of him, Captain," said Jilly, forcing a cheer she didn't feel. Stealing the revolver and planting it at the crime had seemed devilishly clever at the time. But there was something about watching the imps do their dirty work that left her unsettled. She couldn't help wonder what Hope would have thought of this plan. She glanced over at Brigga Lin, who had gone back to staring at her wine, and wondered if her master felt the same. But what could they do? Hope was the one who had abandoned them. *Both* of them.

That's when Jilly understood that Brigga Lin might be hurting from that betrayal just as much as Jilly.

She reached out and touched Brigga Lin's hand. Brigga Lin looked sharply at her, a little of the old haughtiness flaring up. Jilly braced for rejection. But then Brigga Lin just sighed, squeezed Jilly's hand, and nodded.

That's when Jilly knew she wasn't completely alone after all.

10

Stephan would not have considered himself *sheltered*. Before today, his concept of that word had meant being shielded from hardship. And certainly as the youngest son of a noble family, he had been sheltered in early childhood. But once he'd been sent to Galemoor at the age of twelve, he had encountered a great deal of hardship. Particularly after Racklock became grandteacher, his life had been mostly about discipline and pain. So if he had been asked, say, *yesterday*, he would have said he was not sheltered.

But as he and Hectory walked the streets of Vance Post's Shade District, Stephan realized he might need to broaden his definition of the word *sheltered*. And perhaps that was not all he needed to broaden.

The Shade District was renowned throughout the empire as a paradise for the merchant class. A place where birth and heritage were unimportant. Anything could be gotten by any person, so long as they had the money. Desire and its fulfillment seemed to be the primary focus of this place. Whether you were a gourmet or a gourmand, high tastes or low, there was a place for you in the Shade District. Fine restaurants were nestled comfortably next to seedy taverns. A shop selling black rose and coral spice could be found next to a shop selling rare herbs and spices from islands at the fringe of the empire. There were "pleasure palaces" filled with orange-powdered women as elegant as any lady of the court just waiting to be your "companion." And across the street, one could find the raunchiest brothel with a haggard topless woman in the window who pressed her bare breasts against the glass, and spewed curses at anyone who passed by without admiring them.

There were even places that catered specifically to men who wanted to have sex with other men.

"Disgusting," declared Hectory as they passed one such place.

Stephan glanced at the front window, where a finely muscled young man dressed only in a loincloth sat delicately eating a tangerine with the help of a small paring knife. There was something about the composition Stephan found particularly compelling.

"Stephan?" prompted Hectory.

Stephan tore his eyes away from the scantily clad man in the window, hoping he hadn't been staring too long. "Yes, disgusting," he murmured.

Stephan knew he was attracted to men. He didn't know *why* that was, but after a lot of internal struggle and meditation, and feeling the embarrassed heat whenever he and the other brothers exercised shirtless on a summer afternoon, he couldn't deny how he felt. Thankfully, since he'd taken the Vinchen vows of chastity, it was an easy secret to keep. It was ironic, actually, that by forcing him to join the Vinchen, his parents had provided him with the perfect excuse to never get married. He knew his mother at least would have pestered him about it endlessly, as she did his older brothers. Now he would never have to break her heart.

While Stephan felt a little uncomfortable amid the decadence of the Shade District, one look at Hectory suggested his friend's reaction was closer to loathing. His eyes darted everywhere, and his hand kept stray-

ing to the pommel of his sword, as if he expected to
be attacked at any moment by a drug-addled man-
whore. "I suppose a place like this is necessary to
sate the appetites of the commoners," he grumbled.
"But do they all have to be so . . . *brazen* about it?"

"Think of it from a business perspective," suggested Stephan. "All of these establishments are
competing for customers." He gestured to a nearby
building that proudly sold coral spice. All of the
buildings in the Shade District were brightly painted,
but that one was a garish purple that Stephan was
certain didn't exist in nature and must be the result
of biomancery. "In a place like this, the one who
shouts the loudest wins."

Hectory grunted and continued his vigilant watch
of the hedonism around him. After a few minutes, he
said, "Well, why are *we* here, then?"

"Because there have been rumors of a female biomancer based in this district," said Stephan.

"But I thought we were going after the blasphemer
first."

"Most likely they'll be traveling together. And
even if they're not, the grandteacher has pledged to
the Council of Biomancery that we would also dispose of Brigga Lin. Since we have a lead on her, we
should follow it."

"But I still don't understand why *we* have to clean
up the biomancer mess."

"I think this is one of those political motiva-
tions that Hurlo was always warning us against,"
said Stephan. "Grandteacher Racklock wants the
Vinchen to resume their proper place at the palace
like the days before Manay the True brought the
order down to Galemoor. The biomancer council has promised that they will help us do that if we
eliminate Brigga Lin."

"Hm," said Hectory. "I guess it's worth it, then."

Stephan wasn't actually sure of that. He agreed with the grandteacher that the Vinchen needed to return to the world. But he secretly agreed with old Hurlo that the order should be above politics and all the petty squabbling of the court. He also had some private concerns about how well the grandteacher, with his rough arrogance, would fit into courtly life. Judging by the way he had been treating people around Vance Post, he feared it would not be a peaceful integration.

"Finally, the police station," said Hectory, sounding relieved. "An island of sanity in this madness. Perhaps they will have some information about the female biomancer. Or maybe even about the blasphemer."

The police station certainly looked like a place of calm order on the outside. It was a large, squat building in a dull gray that put it at odds with the colorful buildings that surrounded it. The few windows that Stephan saw were narrow, making it difficult to see inside. The entire place gave off an air of squinty-eyed sobriety.

But when they walked through the front doors, Stephan had to suppress a smile as he saw Hectory's relief turn to horror. There was nothing orderly, or particularly sober, about the *inside* of the police station.

It was one large, open room with iron, gaslit chandeliers looming overhead. The majority of the space contained a random scattering of desks and chairs where police officers in white and gold uniforms filed reports or questioned people. Holding cells lined the sides and back of the station, and prisoners yelled constantly, so that the officers had to shout to each other or to those they questioned in order to be heard. The range of people they were questioning varied from well-dressed merchants, to greasy pirates, to whores of every type, to people dressed so strangely that Stephan couldn't quite determine who or what they were. All in all, the scene was a chaotic roar that was so disorienting, Stephan could only stand and stare at it with a sort of awe. Hectory looked more like he was in pain.

In the center of the room, there was a desk raised higher than the rest. A hard-faced man with gold epaulets on his white uniform coat wrote in a large notebook, seemingly oblivious to the noise that surrounded him.

"That's probably the captain," shouted Stephan over the din.

Hectory nodded grimly and marched toward the desk.

Despite the frenetic, unfocused activity all around, when the two Vinchen in their black leather armor marched through the room, there was a noticeable dip in the volume. People continued on with their business, but eyes glanced repeatedly at them. Stephan wondered if it was some remnant of respect for the Vinchen order of old, or merely curiosity.

They stopped in front of the captain's desk, but he didn't look up. Instead he continued to write in his small, meticulous script.

Finally, Stephan placed his hand on the desk within the captain's field of view and politely cleared his throat. The captain looked up at them, his expression at first merely irritated, then shifting to mild curiosity when he took in their armor and manner. He placed his pen on the desk and steepled his hands.

"And what can I do for you two gentlemen?" he asked, his voice carrying effortlessly over the shouting that surrounded them.

"I am Stephan of the Vinchen order. This is my warrior brother, Hectory. Our grandteacher commands us to inquire if you have had any reports of a woman posing as a biomancer in the past few months. She would be exceptionally statuesque, and likely dressed in a hooded white gown."

"No one in the cells fits that description as far as I know," said the captain.

"What about a woman of the Southern Isles dressed all in black leather?" pressed Hectory.

"I haven't heard mention of one of those either, but you're welcome to take a look." He waved in the general direction of the holding cells that lined the walls.

"It's unlikely you would have been able to apprehend either of these women," said Stephan. "They both possess formidable abilities not unlike those held by biomancers and Vinchen. We were hoping, however, that you might have heard some intelligence about their whereabouts, possibly from other criminals..."

The captain's face took a distinctly unfriendly expression. Stephan realized belatedly that the man might have taken offense when he suggested the police weren't capable of arresting their quarry.

"So you're chasing after rumors about biomancers," the captain said acidly. "Let me tell you *boys* something. Rumors about biomancers are as common as ghost stories around here, and usually just as fanciful."

"Watch your tone," said Hectory, his hand going to his hilt.

Stephan put a calming hand on his Vinchen brother's shoulder, then turned back to the captain, managing a faint smile. "Perhaps we will do as you suggest and question the prisoners ourselves."

He turned smartly and headed toward the nearest holding cell.

"The disrespect...," muttered Hectory as he followed.

"The Vinchen have been out of the world for centuries, Hectory," said Stephan. "We cannot assume they will treat us as they once did. We must *show* them that we still deserve their respect by acting with honor and decorum at all times."

Hectory grunted but said nothing more.

The two Vinchen went from cell to cell, questioning anyone willing to talk. As the captain had said, most of them had a biomancer tale to tell, and most of those tales were clearly nothing more than legends passed from one person to the next. Stephan treated each respectfully, however, and was generally rewarded with at least an attempt at respect in return. He had to rein in Hectory's temper a few times, but he could hardly blame his Vinchen brother for becoming frustrated. Especially as they continued down the line and the possibility of gaining any real intelligence became less and less likely.

Until they got to a man who called himself Clean Kever. The man seemed to be a fairly well-dressed merchant of some sort, with thinning hair and a sour smile.

"Female biomancer? Yeah, I know her," said Kever as he gave them an appraising look.

Stephan and Hectory exchanged a look of cautious hope.

"What do you know?" asked Stephan.

"Tall, great set of tits, really likes to put on the lords. Mostly folks call her 'the Lady,' but every once in a while I heard one of her wags call her by the name Brigga Lin, which sounds to me like a very biomancer kind of name."

Stephan's heart quickened, but he took a deep, calming breath and was careful not to show an abundance of interest. This man seemed like a savvy opportunist, and it wouldn't do to let him know how much they needed his cooperation.

Unfortunately, Hectory was less restrained.

"That's her! Tell us everything you know!"

Kever sized them up for a moment, then nodded. "Sure, I'll tell you everything I know. Where she hangs out, who her wags are. Everything. Once you get me out of here."

"*What?*" said Hectory.

"Brother..." Stephan again put a calming hand on his shoulder, but this time Hectory shrugged it off.

"You are in no position to make demands!" Hectory shouted through the bars.

Kever stepped farther back into his cell, well out of their reach. "On the contrary, I think I very much am." Then he sat down on the little wooden bench, leaned against the back wall, stretched out his legs like he was getting comfortable, and gave them his sour smile again.

"Fine," snarled Hectory as he spun on his heel and stalked back to the captain's desk.

"Wait...Hectory..." Stephan hurried after him.

"Give us that prisoner," Hectory told the captain, then pointed to the still-smirking Kever.

The captain's expression was cool. "On whose authority?"

Hectory's eyes nearly bulged out of his sockets. "As a brother of the Vinchen order, of course!"

"I am unfamiliar with that rank in the imperial chain of command," said the captain.

Hectory could only make strangled noises, his face turning bright red.

Stephan tried to keep his tone and manner reasonable. "The Vinchen order has been the right hand of the empire since the days of Cremalton."

"Is that so?" asked the captain. "Then it's *strange* that in the many years that *I* have served the empire, I have never seen any of your kind before."

This seemed to enrage Hectory further, but the truth of the comment cut deep into Stephan's heart.

The Vinchen *had* been hiding from the world while simple, honest men like this captain toiled their entire lives to keep some semblance of peace and order in the empire. Really, it was Stephan and Hectory who should be treating this man with more respect. They had no real authority here.

Still, he had a mission, so he gave it one last try.

"We are acting at the behest of the Council of Biomancery. Surely you recognize *their* authority."

"I certainly do," said the captain. "And if a biomancer came in here and asked for one, or even *all* of the prisoners, I would obey without question. But you're wearing the wrong color." He pointedly picked up his pen and returned to his notebook. "Now, if you will excuse me, I have a great deal of work to do."

Stephan took Hectory's arm and pulled him away from the desk. "Come on, there's nothing we can do here."

"That Kever *knows* where she is," said Hectory as he allowed himself to be led to the entrance. "We can't just . . . let it go."

"We'll ask the grandteacher for his wisdom on this," he said.

But Stephan was using the word *wisdom* very loosely. He already had a dark sense of foreboding about what might come next.

———

Stephan and Hectory returned to the Commercial District of Vance Post, where Grandteacher Racklock awaited word of their investigation. The Commercial District was so different from the Shade District that Stephan found it almost unnerving. As one of the most important trading posts in the empire, an enormous amount of money and goods changed hands in the district, and it was all handled with

courteous gravity and a calm efficiency. Stephan
wondered if these were the same people who spent
their leisure time in the taverns and pleasure palaces
of the Shade District. If so, did they recognize their
own duplicity?

The two Vinchen made their report to their
grandteacher in his rooms at the Sleeth Harbor Hotel.
When they finished, he stood up, belted the Song of
Sorrows to his waist and only said, "Take me there."

As Stephan and Hectory led their grandteacher
through the Shade District, they exchanged glances
that were both eager and nervous. Perhaps Hectory
was more eager and Stephan more nervous. They
might well be vindicated, but Grandteacher Racklock
was not known for his restraint in dealing with those
he considered inferior, which was nearly everyone.

It was later in the day, and the chaos of the Shade
District had only increased. Howling, drunken merchants sprawled in doorways, and couples of all
varieties spilled out of various businesses and into
the alleys. Semi- and even full nudity were rapidly
becoming the norm. But Grandteacher Racklock
seemed not to notice any of it. He kept his eyes forward, his stride steady, his face impassive. And
people scurried out of his way.

When they reached the police station, the cacoph-
ony of sound in the enclosed space didn't seem to
affect him either. He didn't slow down in the least as
he made his way to the captain's desk.

"I am Racklock the Just, grandteacher of the
Vinchen order. You will release the prisoner known
as Clean Kever to me immediately."

The captain looked up, and when he saw another
Vinchen in front of him, he didn't even try to hide
his disdain. "As I explained to your underlings, the
Vinchen have no recognized place in the imperial
chain of—"

The Song of Sorrows flashed from its sheath and stabbed through the captain's eye.

There was a moment of absolute silence, except for the lingering hum of the sword. Even the prisoners were quiet as the grandteacher pulled the sword from the captain's head, and the body slumped forward onto the desk, spilling blood across the open notebook ledger.

But the silence broke a moment later when the imperial police began fumbling for their revolvers. Perhaps if they hadn't done so, there would have been no more death. But could Stephan fault these poor, ill-equipped police from merely defending themselves?

Before the first revolver had left its holster, the Song of Sorrows began its eerie drone once again. Racklock leapt through the air, his bulky physique no hindrance to his movements. The first officer lost his gun arm. A second had his belly split open so wide, his guts fell to the floor with a wet slosh. The sword continued to flash back and forth, rending flesh and bone with every blow. The police station was again full of noise, only this time it was with screams of pain, and the terrible hum of that sword.

In mere minutes, there was only one police officer alive. The man lay on the ground, his face pale, his entire body quivering. Racklock was not a tall man, but he loomed large, his massive shoulders slowly rising up and down from his exertion. He pointed the blood-drenched Song of Sorrows at the officer.

"You will give me the prisoner *now*."

The man nodded his head spastically and crawled on hands and knees over to the captain's desk. He reached up with shaking hands, pulled open one of the drawers, and pulled out a ring of keys. Then he crawled back to Racklock and held out the keys. They jingled loudly from the tremors that ran through his hand.

"Stephan," Racklock said tersely.

Stephan had been suffused in a numb shock while he watched his grandteacher slaughter unprepared and unarmed people, many of them innocents. His mind rebelled at the possibility of such wanton and pointless violence wrought by Vinchen hands. Still feeling that great dissonance within himself, he hurried over to Racklock's side and took the keys from the lone surviving police officer. Then he quickly unlocked Kever's door and moved aside.

Racklock stepped into the small cell and pointed the bloody sword at Kever, who had pressed himself back into the corner.

"I am Racklock the Just, grandteacher of the Vinchen. You will tell me everything you know about the woman called Brigga Lin."

And Kever did. In a desperate torrent of words, he told them the name of the ship she sailed on, the names and descriptions of her companions, and the name and location of the inn she frequented.

"Was she ever accompanied by a blond woman of the Southern Isles?" pressed Racklock. "Perhaps wearing black armor similar to mine?"

Kever shook his head jerkily. "N-n-no, sir, Lord Grandteacher, sir. I never seen nobody like that."

Racklock nodded and sheathed the still-bloody sword. "Perhaps it's for the best that we deal with them one at a time."

Racklock took the keys from Stephan and tossed them to the surviving officer. He left Kever's cell door open and, ignoring the carnage he had caused, walked calmly out of the station, with Stephan and Hectory scurrying after him.

11

*H*e did *what*?" demanded Lady Merivale Hemp-ist. Her voice was like two blocks of ice scraping against each other.

Captain Murkton gave her an apprehensive glance, then went back to staring at the gold imperial helmet in his hands.

"That Vinchen chief killed 'em all, your ladyship. Everyone except Furnyum, who sent word as soon as he could. They need a full battalion, as soon as we can mobilize one."

"Policing the Shade District after an event like that, they could probably use two," said Merivale. "Although I don't think we could actually spare that many right now."

"No, your ladyship," agreed Murkton.

Murkton was a new recruit to Merivale's organization. She didn't usually trust common soldiers to be able to handle the nuanced layers of loyalty required of them as servant to both military and espionage wings of the government, which didn't always agree on the best way of doing things. But the former Lord Pastinas had recommended him highly, and while Red was not really much of a spy, Merivale felt that his judgment of character was more reliable than most.

Merivale turned away from the captain and stared out the window at the bright blue sky beyond. It was so often a sunny, cloudless day on Stonepeak that Merivale had long ago decided the monotony was nearly as bad as the endless gray skies of New Laven. Still, staring at such a blank space always gave her a sense of calm clarity.

"I suspect something is coming to a head on Vance Post. And soon," she said. "I need you in that battalion. I realize this takes you away from your family for the time being, but rest assured I will make certain they are looked after, and I will have you recalled as soon as the current threat is past."

"Thank you, my lady," said Murkton.

"I will go see Archlord Tramasta this afternoon to make the arrangements. I recommend you go home to inform your family and pack at once. As you suggest, that battalion is needed in Vance Post to restore order as soon as possible."

"As you wish, my lady." Captain Murkton bowed crisply and left.

Merivale's eyes swept the clean lines of her sparsely decorated parlor for a moment, then she went to her study. She sat down at her desk and stared at the open letter in front of her, which had arrived yesterday from New Laven.

My dear Lady Hempist,

I would like to introduce you to a friend I have known since my youth. The Black Rose is the current reigning ganglord of Paradise Circle, and very sympathetic to our cause. She has expressed an interest in taking a more direct role in events and believes that she and the resources at her command would be of enormous help to us. It should be noted that she played a key support role in recent events on Dawn's Light. The Black Rose is prepared to offer even more extensive service to

> us. *All that she asks in return is the opportunity to speak directly to Her Imperial Majesty Empress Pysetcha on behalf of the good people of Paradise Circle. If this is an alliance that interests you, please send your reply care of Mister Hatbox at the Drowned Rat tavern in Paradise Circle, New Laven.*
>
> *As for me, I continue to follow the trail, which seems to lead next to Vance Post.*
>
> *With fondest regards,*
>
> *Red*

Merivale folded the letter and slid it into the desk drawer. While she trusted Red's judgment, she wasn't sure she trusted it enough to enlist the aid of a ganglord. The fact that this Black Rose didn't want money made Merivale all the more uneasy. And yet, if this woman was partly responsible for the damage done to the biomancers on Dawn's Light, it was an alliance she couldn't dismiss out of hand. She would need to consider this carefully, and since it involved the empress directly, perhaps even consult with her on the matter.

And then of course there was Red's comment about going to Vance Post, where the Vinchen were also on the hunt. Something was definitely brewing there, which was why she needed more of her people there. To ensure that, she would have to call on the newly appointed chief of military, Archlord Tramasta. The previous chief, Lord Gelmat, had been a cantankerous old man who had served the office since before Merivale was born. He hadn't been particularly pleasant to work with, but as long as it didn't inconvenience him too much, he'd allowed Merivale to place her people where she needed them. In return, she had passed along a judicious amount of information to him that made running the massive operation of imperial police, soldiers, and navy slightly less arduous.

She hoped she could reach a similar understanding with Tramasta. They got along fairly well in social situations, and while she found his arrogance and penchant for indulging in cloud glass tiresome, she considered him a fairly intelligent and capable man. She would, of course, have to reveal her true role in politics to him, but that couldn't be helped.

———

It was still only mid-morning, and Merivale knew the archlord habitually rose around noon, so she decided to check in on the ambassador first. It had been a couple of weeks since she'd paid a visit to Nea Omnipora of Aukbontar and in the interim had heard rumors of strange noises coming from her apartments.

When she knocked, the door was answered by Catim Miffety, the ambassador's bodyguard. Catim was a large man, easily six and a half feet tall and with the muscle mass to complement his height. Like all Aukbontarens, he had dark brown skin and dense, curly black hair. Catim tended to keep his hair cut extremely short, which accentuated the hard, chiseled lines of his face. All told, he was a fine specimen of manhood, and if Merivale had thought it would grant her any leverage, she would have gladly seduced him long ago. Sadly, Catim's other most defining trait was his unwavering loyalty to duty.

That didn't mean she couldn't still have a little fun with him, of course. Aukbontarens were an oddly puritanical bunch, and it gave her some pleasure to embarrass the large man.

"Catim, a delight to see you as always," she purred as she pressed her hand against one of his massive pectoral muscles.

"Welcome, my lady," he said, trying to cover his discomfort. "I assume you have come to call on the ambassador?"

She sighed dramatically. "I *suppose* if you're busy with your duties, I will see what Nea's been up to."

"Very good, my lady." He turned stiffly. "Follow me, please."

Catim's command of the imperial language had improved greatly in the months since their arrival. He was now nearly as adept as the ambassador. Most of the Aukbontarens had also taken to dressing in the imperial fashion of straight-legged trousers, linen shirt, and longer jackets. Merivale appreciated that this showed off Catim's physique to greater advantage than his native, more loose-fitting garb, but she did find she missed touching the light, airy fabrics of Aukbontaren fashion.

Merivale followed Catim through the spacious apartments that Prince Leston had set aside for the ambassador and her retinue. As they passed the kitchen, she saw Etcher Kato hunched over the counter, exerting his small frame on something she couldn't see.

"Whatever are you doing, Etcher?" she asked teasingly. She had long ago identified the excitable scientist as perhaps the weakest link in the ambassador's retinue and had been working on him steadily since. She was fairly certain that sexual seduction would not get her very far, but had realized that merely displaying keen interest in his work was all the seduction she needed to gain his affection.

He turned from the counter, a triumphant smile on his expressive face. Although not nearly as handsome as Catim, there was something indefinably charming about the eccentric little man. His hair was longer than Catim's, twisted up into little clumps that stuck out in all directions. He also tried to follow the imperial fashions, but the details seemed to escape him. As usual, his sleeves and shirttails were out and flapping around.

"Lady Hempist, I've made the most delightful discovery!" He held half of a crushed orange in one hand and a glass of orange juice in the other. "In addition to eating the pulp of an orange, one can *squeeze* the juice into a cup to make an exceptionally refreshing beverage!"

"Yes, Etcher," she agreed.

His face fell. "Your people already discovered this, haven't they."

"Centuries ago," said Merivale.

He winced. "In my defense, we have no *squeezable* fruit in Aukbontar."

"I understand perfectly. Come. Why don't you present your findings to the ambassador and I won't say a word."

He gave her an unsure look "She'll figure it out soon enough."

"No doubt," said Merivale. "But we take our praise where and when we can get it. After all, for humble servants such as ourselves, it is our greatest reward."

"As long as you know I'm not really trying to deceive the ambassador." Etcher's eyes flickered momentarily to Catim, who stood impassively in the doorway.

"I suspect neither of us will succeed in the attempt, but it will be fun to try, won't it?"

His smile returned. "I suppose it will. Okay, then." He tossed the orange peel into the basin and hurried forward, leading the way with his glass of orange juice.

Merivale placidly followed the two men down the hall to the room at the back of the apartments. The room should have been a servants' quarters, but the ambassador never treated her people as servants, and insisted they each have their own room. As far as Merivale knew, the servants' quarters was not in use.

But as they approached the room, Merivale's nose detected a number of unfamiliar smells. The closest thing she could liken it to was gun oil. There were also a lot of clanking sounds coming from the room, like metal striking metal. These were the same sounds described by the nosey lords and ladies who lived on this floor.

When Merivale entered the servants' quarters, she saw that the bunks had all been pushed to the walls to make space for the enormous mechanical device that lay in the center of the room. The device was comprised of a bewilderingly complex array of rods, levers, pipes, and gears. Sitting astride it was Drissa, the machinist. Drissa was still somewhat of an enigma to Merivale. The short, stocky woman's command of the imperial langue was limited to only a few haltingly spoken words. She was the only member of the ambassador's retinue who continued to wear Aukbontaren fashion, including a scarf that covered her hair, something none of the other Aukbontarens wore even when they first arrived. Normally, Drissa wore a short, loose-fitting dark blue jacket and baggy green pants that tapered at the ankle. But now she wore a large beige smock made of canvas, and thick leather gloves. The smock, gloves, and even her face were all streaked with black smudges. She also wore goggles with curved lenses that appeared to magnify whatever she was looking at. In her hand she held a large wrench.

"So, this is one of those *machines* I've been hearing about?" asked Merivale.

It was well known that Aukbontar was decades beyond the empire in the mechanical sciences. Their knowledge in this field was part of the proposed alliance between Aukbontar and the Empire of Storms.

In exchange for that knowledge, the empire would offer Aukbontar in-depth knowledge of biomancery. As a show of good faith, the ambassador had set her machinist, Drissa, to adapting the machine they brought with them for an imperial warship. So far, she hadn't asked for reciprocation, which was just as well, since Merivale had neglected to tell her that it was extremely unlikely the biomancers would give their knowledge to anyone outside their order, much less someone from Aukbontar. It was not, after all, Merivale's job to negotiate treaties.

"Yes, Lady Hempist. This is a machine," said the ambassador.

Except for the empress herself, Ambassador Nea Omnipora was the most regal person Merivale had ever met. This was curious, since Aukbontar didn't actually have a monarchy. But perhaps her Great Congress, knowing the empire's deference to nobility, had specifically chosen a representative with a noble bearing. Even now, in a grimy canvas smock and leather gloves similar to Drissa's, no one could mistake Nea for a commoner. Her dark brown skin was smooth and without blemish. The curves of her forehead, cheekbones, and chin were so elegant, they could have been made by a sculptor. Her full lips and bright eyes were so beguiling, it was no wonder Prince Leston had fallen for her at first sight.

But Merivale had come to see that beauty and poise were not the ambassador's greatest gifts. In fact, Merivale had begrudgingly come to realize that Nea possessed a cleverness, resourcefulness, and intelligence that equaled her own. What's more, now that Nea knew Merivale was chief spy to Her Imperial Majesty, a careful guardedness had risen up between them that lent an edge to even the most casual conversations.

Merivale surveyed the machine with fascination. "It looks terribly complex."

"By necessity," said Nea as she removed her gloves. "Drissa, why don't we take a break."

Drissa nodded, then slid off the machine and moved quickly past Merivale toward the kitchen.

"Ambassador, perhaps this most refreshing beverage will quench your thirst after all that work." Etcher eagerly thrust the glass of orange juice toward her.

"What is it?" she asked as she accepted the glass.

"I have squeezed the juice from an orange."

Her eyebrows rose. "Very clever of you." She took the offered glass and sipped demurely. She closed her eyes as she swallowed, and a small smile came to her lips. "Quite delicious. Thank you, Etcher."

"My pleasure, Ambassador." Etcher beamed.

Nea turned back to Merivale. "And to what do I owe the pleasure of your visit, Lady Hempist?"

"I've been hearing reports of strange noises coming from your apartments, so I came to discover the source." She gestured to the machine. "And so I have, apparently."

"I hope we have not been disturbing our neighbors," said Nea.

"Hardly," said Merivale. "More than likely, several bored lords and ladies have been pressing their ears to the door in hopes of hearing something scandalous. There are all sorts of curious rumors beginning to surface about the liberal politics of Aukbontar. I suspect a good number of the nobility are intrigued."

"Better intrigued than hostile," said Nea, then took another sip of her juice.

"Quite so," said Merivale, deciding not to add that there was probably an equal amount of both.

"Perhaps her ladyship would like to try this juice that Etcher has discovered," said Catim with a slight smirk.

"How thoughtless of me," said Nea. "My lady, shall I have him make some for you? Or did you already have some earlier today? I understand this beverage is typically enjoyed at breakfast."

"Ambassador!" Etcher looked crestfallen.

"Now, Citizen Kato," chided Nea playfully. "Did you really think you could swoop in on another culture and invent something to improve their lives so quickly?"

"It's my fault entirely," admitted Merivale. "I put him up to it, terrible person that I am."

Nea smiled as warm as ever, but Merivale spotted the momentary flicker in her eyes that showed a glimpse of annoyance at one of her people being manipulated. "All in good fun, then."

"Nothing more, I assure you," said Merivale, which of course was not true at all. She was testing the limits of her current influence on the ambassador's retinue, and she was fairly confident Nea knew that.

Merivale stepped closer to the machine to examine it more carefully. It was actually quite fascinating. Given enough time, she thought she could at least glean some rudimentary understanding of its workings.

"I don't suppose, my lady, that you would be able to share any news concerning the status or whereabouts of my friend Red," Nea said lightly, as if she were not asking for government secrets.

"Last I heard, he was still very much alive and on the move," said Merivale. "I'm afraid I can't tell you more than that."

"I'm grateful to hear even that much. You know he is dear to me."

Merivale nodded, her eyes still tracing the lines of the machine. "If it gives you some comfort, I will pass along additional assurances of his continued survival as I receive them."

"Thank you, my lady. I would very much appreciate that." There was a pause. "His Highness has also been quite distraught about it."

"Naturally," said Merivale. "Do you...see him often?"

Nea smiled again and Merivale caught the flicker of weariness in her eyes. "His Highness is ever attentive to my needs."

"No doubt it is because of his fervent desire to see this treaty signed," Merivale said lightly.

"No doubt." Nea held firm to her smile.

Merivale knew that Red had given the prince a stern talking-to about pressuring Nea regarding his affections. For a time, it seemed to work, but now that Red was gone, the prince had started backsliding. Perhaps it was merely that with Red gone, there was no one else that Leston felt close to. But even if that were true, Merivale was somewhat concerned that the heir to the throne was unable to attach his affections to anyone other than a criminal and a foreigner. It did not give her a great deal of confidence for his forthcoming reign. She had any number of ideas on how to correct this flaw in his personality, but the empress had explicitly forbade her from meddling with the prince's personal life. So they would all just have to wait and see how he turned out. He certainly couldn't be worse than the current emperor.

———

Merivale took her leave of the ambassador a short time later. As she exited the apartments, waving a flirty farewell to Catim, she wasn't particularly surprised to see Prince Leston coming toward her. The prince wasn't as late a riser as Tramasta, but he tended to linger over his breakfast, so visiting Nea was most likely his first outing for the day.

As the prince drew near, Merivale stopped and curtsied. "Good morning, Your Highness."

"Ah, Lady Hempist. I've actually been looking for you. May I have a moment of your time?"

"I am happy to serve in whatever capacity I am able, Your Highness."

His eyes narrowed. "Provided it doesn't contradict whatever it is my mother has instructed you to keep from me."

Merivale smiled graciously. "Exactly so, Your Highness. I'm glad we have an understanding."

The prince had always possessed an air of ease, as if the world were there to support him. No doubt this was due to a pampered childhood, a lax father, and, in Merivale's private opinion, an overly protective mother. But since Red's absence, a change seemed to have come over Leston. Increasingly, he appeared as if he dressed each morning with a hurried impatience. His hair and clothes had become uncharacteristically untidy, and he seemed to eschew the orange skin powder popular among nobles altogether. Even more striking was the keen sense of loss that haunted his eyes now. His friend had been taken from him abruptly, and with almost no explanation. Merivale suspected it was the prince's first real experience of just how capricious the world could be.

"Where is Rixidenteron?" He said it more like a demand than a question.

"At the moment? I genuinely don't know," said Merivale.

"But you know where he's going?"

"I know his current intended destination."

"He's doing something for *you*, isn't he?"

"With respect, Your Highness, he's doing something for the *empire*."

"But you picked *him* to do it." The prince's frustration was already turning to anger.

"Again with respect, no, he volunteered when it

became clear to both of us that he was the ideal candidate for this mission."

"But it cost him his lordship! His reputation!"

Merivale gave him a cool gaze. "Really, Your Highness. If you think either of those things matter to him, you don't know your friend as well as I thought you did."

That brought the prince up short for a moment, his face flushing. But then he rallied. "Fine. But you can't tell me he did it out of some sense of patriotism or loyalty to the throne either."

"You're quite right about that, Your Highness. Those are *my* motives. His are far more personal."

Leston thought about that for a moment, then his eyes widened. "It's that Vinchen woman of his, isn't it? That Bleak Hope."

She smiled fondly and touched the prince's cheek. "Excellently deduced, Your Highness."

"What is so special about that woman it warrants such risks?"

"She and her companion, Brigga Lin, have the most powerful men in the empire so terrified that they're taking the most desperate measures they can think of. Don't those sound like women we want on our side, Your Highness?"

"I've heard they're not overly fond of imperial authority. Do you think they'll join us?"

"I don't know," admitted Merivale. "But if anyone can talk them into it, it's your good friend Rixidenteron. Wouldn't you agree?"

He smiled wryly. "I suppose that's true."

She curtsied to him. "Now, if you'll excuse me, Your Highness, there is a pressing issue related to the former Lord Pastinas's safety that I must attend to. I trust you appreciate the importance of that as much as I do?"

Leston sighed. "I would not dream of keeping you

from something that vital, Lady Hempist. But we will talk more on this topic at a later time."

"I look forward to it, Your Highness," said Merivale, then took her leave.

———

Archlord Tramasta's apartments were on the forty-sixth floor. There was no official decree that the higher you were, the more power and influence you possessed, but since the prince lived on the forty-ninth floor and the emperor lived at the top on the fiftieth floor, that was how the nobility viewed it. Merivale's apartments were on the far more humble thirty-second floor, several levels below the former Lord Pastinas. After all, being a lord of even a section of New Laven was more impressive than being the lady of a small island known only for lumber. Of course, this also aided in the deception that Merivale had been cultivating for years that she was merely another inconsequential, marriage-hungry lady of the court. It was a guise that allowed her to roam relatively unnoticed through the ranks of the nobility. There were those who knew her true status. The empress, of course, and the emperor, if he had any interest in knowing. Those who worked in her employ, such as Hume, Murkton, and Red. It had also been necessary to reveal her true purpose to Prince Leston, and even more inconveniently, to the ambassador. But beyond that, the only other person authorized to know her role in the government was the current chief of military.

Merivale gave a light, cheerful knock on the door to Archlord Tramasta's apartments. A few moments later, a young serving woman opened the door. Merivale had been to his apartments many times, and she did not recognize this particular servant. But that was hardly unusual. Tramasta went through serving women with voracious rapidity. The way he treated them, she was amazed one of them hadn't stabbed him in his sleep yet.

"Lady Hempist to see Archlord Tramasta on a topic of some urgency," she told the woman.

"Yes, my lady." The woman curtsied awkwardly in the impractically tight and revealing gown Tramasta made her wear. "Won't you come in while I check if the archlord is able to see you?"

"Thank you." Merivale followed the woman into a sumptuous parlor with lush fur rugs, overstuffed furniture, and several paintings of nude women. She strongly believed that the atmosphere of one's home reflected one's mental state. She had often wondered what this over-cluttered and hedonistic setting said about Tramasta. Nothing good, she was sure.

"Feel free to make yourself comfortable while I check with the archlord," said the servant woman, gesturing to the doughy red sofa, which had several stains of highly questionable origin.

"Thanks, but I think I'll stand," Merivale said, and gave her a sly grin.

The woman seemed taken aback for a moment, then returned the smile. "As you wish, my lady." Then she hurried off to rouse the archlord from his chambers.

Archlord Tramasta didn't come hurrying out, of course. He made Merivale wait, as he always did. But finally, he came strolling into the parlor wearing a long silk dressing gown. She might have thought he'd just gotten out of bed, except his hair was neatly combed and styled. Tramasta had many faults. Rudeness, arrogance, addiction to gambling and cloud glass, and nail biting, just to name a few. But he was not a stupid man, so while he might not know the full extent of Merivale's authority, he certainly suspected her of being more than she seemed.

"Ah, Lady Hempist." He flopped down on the thick sofa and reached for the wooden box of cloud glass he kept on the small side table. "To what do I owe the pleasure of your always alluring presence?"

"I'm afraid certain recent events prevent me from indulging in our usual games, my lord," Merivale said crisply.

"And what events are those?" he asked as he took a tiny spoon and carefully scooped a small amount of clear powder from the box.

"Why, the massacre of an entire station of your troops on Vance Post, of course," Merivale said, not without some edge in her voice.

"Oh, that," he said blandly. Then he brought the tiny spoon to his nose, pressed one nostril closed, and snorted the clear powder into the other nostril.

"Yes, that," said Merivale evenly. "When you send the new battalion, I need to have one of my people in it."

"One of *your* people?" He carefully wiped at his nose with a silk handkerchief.

"Yes, my lord. Hopefully it has not escaped someone of your intelligence that I am more than just a frivolous lady of the court. Now that you have been named chief of military, I am at liberty to reveal to you that I am chief of espionage. I believe it is in the best interest of the empire that our two offices work together as cooperatively as possible, just as your predecessor and I did."

"Is that it?" he said with an amused delight. His eyes had already begun to get glassy, and the pupils were dilated. "I knew there was a chief of espionage, and I knew you were up to more than you let on, but to be honest, I never made the connection between those two things." He gave a little laugh. "Really, it explains so much."

Merivale regarded him carefully as he examined his ragged fingernails. Tramasta generally only admitted ignorance like that when he felt secure in his position. Perhaps the cloud glass had given him a false sense of confidence. Or perhaps he knew something she didn't.

"Yes, well, I fear the biomancers have let something—or rather, someone—loose on Vance Post that they can't control," she said finally. "I would like to place one of my people in the new battalion to gather more information."

"Oh, you mean the Vinchen, I suppose," Tramasta said calmly. "I shouldn't worry too much about them. I've been assured it was unfortunate, but necessary, and that it's being contained. Think of it as a bit of controlled chaos to deal with the recent rise in seditionist activity."

"I see," said Merivale. "So you consider the loss of forty imperial troops at the hands of this *controlled chaos* to be an acceptable loss?"

"Every soldier enlists knowing he may have to lay down his life for the good of the empire," said Tramasta, as if that explained everything.

Merivale was rarely caught by surprise. It was possible that her confidence in her ability to accurately assess people and situations bordered on presumption. But if that was one of her weaknesses, then one of her strengths was the ability to quickly adjust her understanding of the situation the moment she detected that her assessment was inaccurate. Now she looked at Tramasta in a different light. Less as a tiresome colleague and more as an adversary.

"That sounds a lot like something a biomancer might say," she said, keeping her tone light.

"They're not bad, once you get to know them," he said.

"And I take it you've gotten to know them quite well?"

"The chief of military must work closely with the head of the order of biomancery," said Tramasta, then chuckled. "The *last* thing the empire needs is for us to be working at cross-purposes with them."

"The very last thing," Merivale said mildly. "I understand perfectly, my lord. If you think further investigation is unnecessary, I will of course defer to your judgment."

"Naturally," said Tramasta. Then realizing he had perhaps gone a bit too far, he quickly added, "If this were concerning *your* people, I would do the same."

"I appreciate that, my lord," said Merivale. "Now, if you'll excuse me, I have other matters to attend to."

"Of course. I'll let you get back to creeping in the shadows, my lady," he said good-naturedly. "Shelby will see you out." He lifted his head and shouted, "*Shelby!*"

Merivale watched thoughtfully as the serving woman from before came scurrying into the room and gave another awkward curtsy. Then Merivale turned back to Tramasta. "A pleasure as always, my lord. And if you ever have need of my services, please don't hesitate to ask."

"Hopefully not, but I suppose you never know," said Tramasta, then he reached again for the small wooden box of cloud glass and the tiny spoon.

"If... you'll follow me, my lady," Shelby said haltingly.

"By all means, lead the way, my dear," said Merivale.

When they reached the front door of the apartments, Merivale turned to the serving woman. "Shelby, is it?"

"Yes, my lady."

"How would you like to play an important role in the preservation of the empire and get paid handsomely for it?"

12

*H*ope and Uter sailed west-northwest for the better part of a week, then turned due north up through the large expanse of sea between Vance Post to the west and the Breaks to the east. Their vessel was a far cry from the relative comfort of the *Kraken Hunter*. The unnamed boat had only one mast, a small mainsail, and a jib. The single cabin was too low to even sit up in, and barely wide enough to fit the two occupants. Its only purpose was to keep them sheltered from the elements while they slept. Sailing one-handed, even on such a tiny boat, was difficult in the less predictable waters north of the Isles, but Hope had taught Uter the basics, and he was even more helpful than she'd anticipated. In fact, the most trying part of the long voyage to Walta was keeping Uter from getting bored.

Hope continued to work with him on reading. She hadn't thought to pack anything specifically for him, but fortunately, she always had Hurlo's journal with her, so she set him to work reading that. She was surprised to discover that hearing someone else read it out loud brought new insights to a text she had already read countless times. As she squinted into the sun, her hand on the tiller and her hood thrown back to let the sea breeze pull at her hair, she listened to Uter's halting, boyish voice talk of dreaming about a better future, and it made sense in a context she hadn't understood before.

But Uter couldn't read all day, and there were still many hours of watching the endless ocean slide past as they made their slow way north. Uter would get fidgety, and on such a small boat, that could easily lead to capsizing. Hope was not completely unfamiliar with the way young boys worked. As a girl, she'd watched how Hurlo and Wentu dealt with the new, undisciplined arrivals to Galemoor. Little boys needed to move around. So even though it slowed their journey, she would drop anchor every afternoon and give him swimming lessons. Once she was confident in his ability to swim alone, she would have him swim laps around the boat until he was panting and barely able to pull himself back on board. It probably added a day or two to the voyage, but she was certain that it made for a much more pleasant trip.

Even after making a point of exercising both his mind and body every day, it was often difficult to get him to settle down at night. Wentu had been in the habit of telling him bedtime stories, but Hope didn't really know any stories. So instead, she told him the story of her life. Without consciously making the decision to do so, she began by describing in vivid detail the massacre of her village. It was something she had sworn she would never speak aloud again, but she couldn't remember why she had even made that pledge. Perhaps she had been eager to rid herself of it and thought that if it went unspoken, the horror of the details would fade from her memory. It hadn't, of course. And now, many years later, she was grateful for that. People should know what had happened. It should be in a history book somewhere, even if only as a footnote. And of course, once she finished telling him about that terrible period on Bleak Hope, she told him of how she came to Galemoor, then about her time on the *Lady's Gambit*, and finally to New Laven.

As she told Uter about Sadie, Hope couldn't help thinking that the old woman would have done a much better job raising Uter than she was doing. But she had grown increasingly tired of chastising herself about every little thing. She wasn't particularly maternal, so she would just do the best she could. And of course make sure her charge didn't kill anyone else.

———

Hope lost count of exactly how many days had passed by the time the southernmost islet off of Walta came into view. It was larger than what she would have considered a standard islet, spanning the equivalent of several city blocks. But all four trailing islets were considered part of Walta, and all four had the sign of the biomancers planted firmly in view to warn people away. In fact, they were planted along the shore at regular intervals so that no matter what direction you approached from, you would see them. Hope had never seen such a conscious effort on the part of the biomancers to keep people away. Perhaps it was merely because it was farther north than most quarantined islands. Or perhaps there was something on Walta they didn't want discovered.

"What do those signs mean?" asked Uter as they sailed past the first islet.

"That the biomancers have done experiments on these lands which make it no longer safe for people to live on them."

"Like they did on your island?" asked Uter.

"Yes. One of those signs is still there, in fact."

"It looks like a picture of a squid," he said. "The one we read about that squirts ink."

"I think it's supposed to represent the kraken,

which some would call their greatest—or most terrible—achievement."

"What's a kraken?"

"I've only heard stories," admitted Hope. "Sailors do like a good sea monster story, so it's difficult to say how much is true. But the way it's been told to me, the biomancers created a giant squid or octopus. They named it the Guardian because they set it to protect the northern border of the empire from invasion. Supposedly, it's as big as one of those islets."

"That big?" Uter's eyes widened as he stared at the second islet, which was now off the starboard bow.

"So they say," said Hope. "But even if it were possible to create such a large creature, the stories around it date back nearly a century, so it seems unlikely that it still lives."

Uter seemed disappointed by that. "Oh. Okay."

She gave him a lopsided smile. "You were hoping to see one, were you?"

Uter nodded firmly. "I would make it my friend."

Hope allowed herself to imagine just for a moment how much destruction might come from Uter controlling something like a kraken, and shuddered. "Well, I'm afraid you probably won't get the chance."

They continued past the third and fourth islets. Hope still couldn't see why they were quarantined. There were small clusters of trees and swaths of grass that suggested a fairly healthy ecosystem. Perhaps it was like her own village, which had likely been quarantined merely because of the chance some of the larvae had escaped. But blocking off an island down in the Southern Isles was one thing. Walta was at a prime latitude and too valuable to simply block off as a precaution. Again, Hope felt a strange nagging suspicion that there was more going on here than it seemed.

It was early afternoon when they finally reached

the shores of the main island of Walta itself. Unlike the smaller islets, it was immediately clear that something on the island was deeply wrong. There were no trees and very little vegetation. In that respect, it was much like Dawn's Light. But where Dawn's Light had been mostly flat, Walta looked as if God had lifted the island up to a great height and then let it drop so that it shattered when it hit the surface of the water.

"Whoa," said Uter as he peeked over the gunwale at the fractured landscape.

"Not very welcoming, is it?" said Hope as she steered their tiny craft toward the shore.

Once they reached land, Hope was able to make out more details. Massive mounds of dirt were scattered across the broken surface of the island. There was a hole in the center of each mound roughly two to three feet in diameter.

"Those must be mole rat tunnels," she said quietly.

"What are mole rats?" asked Uter.

"Don't you remember? We read about them back on Galemoor. Or do you only pay attention to the slimy sea creatures, like squids?"

He grinned. "I like those better."

She couldn't help smiling back. "Well, as the name suggests, mole rats look sort of like a combination of a rat and a mole, with long, sharp front teeth. They lack any fur and they're nearly blind."

"That doesn't sound very scary," said Uter.

"They probably wouldn't be, except that the biomancers decided to make them bigger. So instead of being only a few inches long and weighing only an ounce, they're about seven feet long and weigh over two hundred pounds. Supposedly, their jaws are strong enough to bite off a person's hand in one snap."

"We'd get you another metal one," he said reassuringly.

"I think I'd like to keep the regular one."

"Why?" He looked confused. "I love your metal hand!"

"But then *you'd* have to do all the sailing for me," she told him. "And the cooking. *And* cleaning."

He made a face. "You can keep your regular hand, then."

"Thanks," she said dryly. "Let's try to stay quiet now and give the tunnels a wide berth. Supposedly, mole rats don't come aboveground very often, especially during the day. With any luck, we can find Alash and be on our way without seeing one."

"That doesn't sound very lucky to me," grumbled Uter.

They made their way carefully across the crumbling landscape toward the center of the island. After they'd been walking for a while, Hope spotted a wooden-frame tower in the distance about twenty feet high. There was a platform at the top that was sheltered by a perforated canvas roof. She could see movement on the platform, but it was too far away to make out any details.

"I want to get a closer look at that tower," she said quietly.

She was surprised to find that even the potential of seeing Alash had quickened her pulse. She'd missed him more than she realized. She wished she could walk faster, but the ground grew increasingly more broken and treacherous the closer they got to the tower.

As they drew near, she could tell that the movement was coming from a person, most likely male, but the canvas roof made it difficult to see more detail, so she still couldn't be certain it was him.

"Do you know that person?" Uter said loudly, forgetting that he was supposed to talk quietly.

The person's head turned toward the sound of

Uter's voice, then moved to the closest edge of the platform and looked out across the broken ground below.

"Captain? Is that you?" came Alash's clear, ringing voice.

"Alash!" Now that she knew it was her friend, she hurried toward him across the broken terrain, with Uter eagerly keeping apace.

"Wait!" he yelled. "You must—"

The rest of the sentence was lost in a thunderous crack as the ground gave way beneath her. The dirt slid under her feet as if someone had unstoppered a drain. Hope had just enough time to pull Uter close before they were both sucked under.

For a single terrifying moment they were completely covered in dirt. No light. No air. But they continued to slide downward with the streaming dirt, and it abruptly opened up beneath them. They dropped into an unlit tunnel or small cavern of some kind, and landed hard on a pile of dirt. More dirt continued to pour down on them, hard enough that it would bury them in seconds. Still holding Uter to her chest, Hope rolled to the side. It got them out from under the waterfall of dirt, but in the absolute darkness, she hadn't realized that the tunnel continued from there at a sharp drop. They rolled down so fast, it was almost free fall until the tunnel abruptly leveled off and they landed on hard-packed soil.

They lay there in complete blackness, Uter clinging to her robes as he sobbed.

"We're okay," she said, trying to sound more convinced than she felt.

"I d-don't…want t-to…get…b-buried!" he choked between sobs as he squeezed his little hands hard on her upper arm.

Hope had never known him to be frightened like this. She wondered if being buried alive had been some part of the wighting ritual. She wished she had the time to ask him more, but it would have to wait. Right now, she needed to make certain they were safe.

"Uter, I promise we'll get out of here. But since we can't see anything, I need to use my ears to figure out where we are. And to do that, I need you to be as quiet as you can. Keen?"

"I-I'll…t-try…" It took him a few moments, but he was finally able to quiet his sobs. "Sorry," he said in a shaky voice.

She touched his dirt-caked hair. "You're doing great. Now, let's figure out where we are and how to get out of here."

She closed her eyes. There really wasn't any point in doing that since there was no light, but she didn't like the feeling of staring glassy-eyed into the darkness. At first, all she could hear was the sound of falling dirt farther back up the tunnel from where they'd fallen through. But finally that stopped. The receding echoes suggested that the portion of the tunnel they were in now continued quite a while at this level. The entire area had to be riddled with tunnels, if the surface was that unstable.

Perhaps the falling dirt had piled up high enough where they'd fallen through that they could climb it back up to the surface. If so, all they needed to do was get back up there.

"Okay, Uter. Let's get on our feet. Slowly, though. I'm pretty sure the space we're in is high enough for us to stand up, but just to be safe, keep your hand out to protect your head."

They were able to stand up without banging their heads. Hope felt around for the drop in the tunnel they'd fallen down, and soon she found it. But it was so steep that it was nearly vertical, and the dirt was so loose, it would be slippery going without some kind of anchor. They wouldn't be able to simply crawl on their hands and knees up the side to where they'd fallen through.

"What do we do now?" asked Uter, his voice still shaky.

"Quiet." She could hear something farther down the tunnel. A scratching sound. The sort of sound a mole rat might make while digging.

"What is it?" asked Uter, his voice getting louder.

Then the scratching suddenly stopped, and Hope heard the faint sound of clawed feet scurrying away. Perhaps Uter's voice had scared it off. Or sent it to gather reinforcements. That would of course be the worst-case scenario. There was no need to tell the boy about it yet.

"Uter," she said, keeping her voice calm. "Do you have anything sharp in your pocket?"

"You said I'm not supposed to keep stealing—"

"I know what I said. And it's true, you shouldn't keep stealing sharp objects. But if you *had* stolen one at some point and had it with you now, just this once, I wouldn't be mad."

"Well, Hope. You see, there's that knife you use to clean the fish we catch?"

"Uh-huh?"

"And it just looked so pretty, with the little ridges and everything, so—"

"You have it with you right now?"

"Yeah . . ."

He sounded so guilty, and that was good. He *really* needed to stop stealing sharp objects. But right at that moment, Hope had to stop herself from crying out with relief.

"Give it to me," she said instead.

"What for?"

"I'm going to use it to carve some hand- and foot-holds up the side of this tunnel so we can climb out of here."

The small serrated knife was not an ideal tool for digging handholds in soil. That, and working solely by touch, made for slow progress. The progress slowed even further once they had gone beyond what either of them could reach while standing on level ground. After some fumbling in the darkness, they managed to get Uter on Hope's shoulders, which gave them a few more feet. But then they reached the point where the only way they could progress was to dig while climbing.

"Let's take a short break before we start climbing," said Hope as she helped Uter off her shoulders.

"Sure," said Uter, sounding as tired as she felt.

The two of them dropped to the dirt and rested. Hope's eyes still couldn't pick up anything. There weren't even trace amounts of light this far down. That meant she had to rely even more on her other senses. Her sense of smell was dominated by the close reek of sweat and surrounded by the heavy scent of earth. Touch only found the thin, quivering boy next to her and the endless grainy dirt. Sound was only her and Uter's breath. Until...

"Do you hear something?" Uter's voice sounded even higher than usual.

The last time she'd heard the scrabble of clawed feet farther down the tunnel, it had clearly been only one animal. But now she could hear several sets, and they were getting closer.

Hope stood up, pulling Uter with her. She carefully placed the knife in his hand. "Get on my shoulders, then climb onto the highest handholds we've made."

"O-okay."

"Once you get there, you need to continue carving out hand- and footholds just like we've been doing, except you need to keep climbing up on your own as you do it."

"What are *you* going to do?" asked Uter.

"Try not to get my other hand bitten off," she said grimly.

Once she'd gotten Uter digging and climbing, she stood in the darkness and waited. Behind her, she could hear the boy working at the soil with the knife as he made his way slowly up the tunnel. In front of her, she heard mole rats scrambling toward her with surprising speed.

Vinchen trained in blindfolded combat, of course. But they did so with the idea of killing their assailants as quickly as possible, and that was not something she wished to do. She wasn't certain that her vow not to kill extended to animals in every circumstance, but in this particular instance, she knew that, intentionally or not, she was the offending party here. They were merely defending their territory. Hopefully she could buy Uter enough time to finish their escape route without resorting to killing these creatures.

As she heard them draw near, she tried to tease out the sounds so that she could differentiate them from each other. But they were coming in such a mad rush, and the sounds were so unfamiliar to her, she couldn't even be certain how many there were. Three? Perhaps four? Or even more?

"Hope! Something is coming down!" shouted Uter above her.

Dread shot into the pit of her stomach. Was another group of mole rats coming from the upper end of the tunnel to trap them?

"Can you see anything?" she shouted to Uter.

"No!" His voice was ragged with the panic that had been just below the surface since they'd been underground. "I just hear *digging*!"

If it *was* more mole rats, he should move away from the digging. But to where? Certainly not down with her, because the mole rats were nearly upon her.

"Just...stay where you are!" she told him.

Then the mole rats launched themselves at her so fast, she felt the wind of their approach. She instinctively held up her clamp to block, and heard the screech of breaking metal.

Sparks flared up to show a pale rodent face with wrinkled skin and beady little black eyes. Its teeth, roughly a foot long each, were in the process of biting off the metal clamp of her prosthesis.

This was her window. In this compressed second of time while the spark was still live, she could see everything around her. Five mole rats were clambering over one another to get to her. The two on the bottom were reaching for her ankles. The two on the sides were trying to circle around her, using their long claws to climb the sides of the tunnel. The one directly in front of her currently had its teeth halfway through her clamp.

It was still difficult to move in this space of compressed time, but the months of training had made it feel less like moving through mud, and more like moving through water. There was still resistance, but significantly less.

The teeth on her clamp had already bitten halfway through. There was no way to salvage it. Instead, she moved her free arm so that her fist was aimed toward its lower jaw.

She pivoted her trapped arm slightly to change its trajectory when it came free of the mole rat's bite.

Sweat beaded on her brow. She was already feeling the strain of compressing time. Her muscles throbbed with effort at even the simplest movement.

She bent her knees, lifted both feet, and aimed her heels at an angle down and forward. With the air resisting like water, she wouldn't be able to stay up long, but it would be enough.

Every muscle in her body shook with effort as she angled the top of her head so that it tilted to the left.

That was as long as she could hold it. Time
snapped back into place.

Her fist connected with the front mole rat's jaw,
forcing it to close its mouth on the shrapnel of her
prosthesis. As her other arm ripped free, the jagged,
ruined remainder of the prosthesis slashed across the
face of the mole rat to her right. Her heels slammed
down hard on the heads of the mole rats on the bottom, launching her so that her head rammed into the
windpipe of the mole rat on her left.

Then the spark of light was gone and there was
total darkness again.

Hope could hear the mole rats squealing with
pain and surprise, but it didn't take long for them
to recover. She heard them shift and move as they
grouped back together and prepared for a second
assault. She steeled herself for another time com-
pression, knowing that this one would be in the dark,
and that there would be more luck than skill in it.

"Something's breaking through up here!" Uter
screamed above her.

The ceiling split apart and a shaft of sunlight
spilled down into the tunnel. Hope had to shield
her eyes against the brightness, but the effect on the
mole rats was even more intense. They let out piercing squeals and shifted backward as a group until
they were out of direct light.

"I say, fronzies! Look out below!" Alash called
down. Then a rope ladder dropped down into the
hole.

"Uter, climb up that ladder now!" Hope yelled.

"But who—"

"Do it!"

Uter scampered up the ladder and Hope followed
behind. It was awkward trying to climb the rope ladder with one hand, especially when the end of her
prosthesis was a mess of ragged steel potentially ca-

pable of severing one of the ropes. It became even more difficult as she neared the blinding sunlight above her. By the time she reached the top, she had to close her eyes entirely.

A strong hand grabbed her arm and hauled her up onto some sort of flat wooden plank.

"Are you injured, Miss Hope?" asked Alash.

She sat there for a moment, catching her breath. Then she slowly opened her eyes, letting them adjust to the bright afternoon sun until she could examine her surroundings. She sat on a wooden platform with a large square hole in the center. The platform lay on the ground with the square over the opening Alash had dug down to rescue them.

Alash knelt next to her, looking at her with concern. Oddly, the first thought that entered her mind was how good he looked. His long hair was pulled back in a ponytail, and beneath the beginnings of a beard, his skin was dark from the sun. Instead of his habitual lacy jacket and cravat, he wore a simple linen shirt open at the throat. He also had a lot more muscle tone than she remembered. But he still had that same sweet, earnest look on his face.

"Miss Hope?"

She smiled tiredly. "I'm fine. Well, except for this." She showed him the mangled remains of her clamp.

He frowned as he examined it. "Drown it all, but they do have impressive jaw strength, don't they?" Then he returned her smile. "Still, nothing we can't fix, right?"

"That's why we're here, actually," said Hope.

"Oh?"

"We'll talk about it more later. Uter, are you okay?"

The boy sat crouched on the edge of the platform, looking uncharacteristically meek and wary. Their brief time in the mole rat tunnels had really rattled him.

She inched over to him. "It's okay now. This is my friend Alash. He's your friend, too."

"A friend?" he asked cautiously, looking up at Alash. "Are you sure?"

After such exuberant attempts to make friends in the past, she was surprised to see him so reluctant now.

"Of course I'm sure," she said gently, brushing some of the dirt from his white mop of hair. "He just saved our lives, didn't he?"

His expression softened a little. "That's true..."

"I tell you what," said Alash. "Uter, is it?"

"Yeah."

"Why don't we head back to shelter, where it's much safer. And after a little while, you can let me know if you want to be friends or not. Sound good?"

"Okay," said Uter.

"Wonderful." Alash turned to Hope. "I'm afraid I only have one pair of shoes, so the two of you will have to ride on the platform."

"What do you mean, shoes?" asked Hope.

"Oh, these." Alash sat down on the edge of the wooden platform. He held up two much smaller, thinner pieces of wood with thick hemp ropes on them. "You see, the largest mole rat colony on the island is directly beneath us, and it's so riddled with tunnels that the surface is extremely fragile." He began to tie the thin wood planks to the bottoms of his feet. "In order to reduce the risk of cave-ins like the one you and Uter just experienced, I use these to distribute my weight across the widest area possible."

"That's what this platform is for as well?" Hope patted the wood beneath her.

"Exactly. This is how I've been able to study the mole rats so closely without getting dismembered or buried alive."

"How do you move it around?" she asked. "I know this wasn't here earlier."

"Oh, moving it is actually quite simple." He stepped onto the bare ground with his wide wooden shoes. Then he bent over and picked two thick loops of rope that were attached to the platform and slipped his arms through them. Once they were positioned on his shoulders, he turned back to her. "My apologies. I'm afraid it won't be a particularly smooth ride."

Then he began to haul the platform across the broken ground with Uter and Hope still on it.

"Wow, he's strong," Uter said as he moved closer to Hope.

"Yes," said Hope. "Alash, when did you get so... strapping?"

Alash gave a nervous laugh. "Well, I've been out here on my own for quite a while, hauling this thing around. It's often loaded down with gear, so I suppose it just happened gradually."

It felt strange to sit back and let Alash do all the work. And yet, she was tired from her brief but intense fight with the mole rats, and there wasn't much she could do anyway with only one working hand and no special shoes. So she leaned back and tried to make herself comfortable. It was funny, really. Her intention had been to save Alash from the mole rats, not the other way around. Funny, and oddly thrilling, to see evidence that he—that any person, really—could change and grow so much in such a relatively short amount of time.

———

The way Alash pulled them almost felt like sailing across the fractured earth. That feeling grew even more pronounced when they reached the observation tower and he tied the platform up to one of the tower struts, held out his hand, and said, "Welcome aboard, Captain."

They ascended a ladder fixed to the side of the tower. When they reached the top, Hope was surprised to find how homey it was. There was a sleeping mat off in the corner like the kind the Vinchen used. There was a small writing desk piled with notebooks, parchment, and odd little tools and devices that reminded her of his workshop back at Pastinas Manor. There was also an intricate series of funnels that ran along the canvas roof and converged over a large barrel filled with what was most likely rainwater. The fourth corner was a metal pot suspended over a small pile of black rocks.

"Is that coal?" she asked.

"Yes," he said. "There's not much wood on the island, obviously. All the lumber you see here I had to bring up from Vance Post. At first, I wasn't sure I'd be able to cook anything, and had more or less resigned myself to a life of cold rations. But it turns out there's a large coal deposit somewhere in the colony, and the mole rats are constantly pushing bits of it to the surface to make room for themselves."

Hope knelt down and looked at it more carefully. "I've never seen it before. I've only read about it."

"Likewise," said Alash. "It took me a little while to figure out how best to use it as a fuel source. Frankly, even now I feel like I'm only just beginning to grasp its full potential. The energy output is significantly higher than that of wood. It's quite astonishing, really."

Uter was still being cautious, but his curiosity got the better of him, and he gradually drifted away from Hope's side to the desk with its many strange little tools.

"Care for a drink?" asked Alash. He held up a small earthen jug. "It's a fermented drink I've been developing from the tubers that the mole rats eat."

"Thanks." Hope accepted the jug and took a sip. It was surprisingly sweet. "Not bad."

"It's an acquired taste, but I've grown to like it."
He poured himself a cup and took a slow swallow.

"Why did you come here, Alash?" she asked.

He gave her a wry smile. "I could tell you about
my rekindled interest in the natural sciences. Or
perhaps you'd like to hear about my theory that the
biomancers have been cultivating giant mole rats
because their physiology is potentially the key to
granting humans a longer life span."

"Those both sound...plausible," said Hope.

"It's true those are the reasons I chose specifically
to come to Walta. But the reason I left Vance Post...
well, it was mostly because I couldn't bear to see her
with that pirate."

"Ah," said Hope.

The "her" was obviously Brigga Lin, whom Alash had
been in love with for about as long as he'd known her.
She suspected "that pirate" was probably Gavish Gray,
captain of the *Rolling Lightning*. Hope remembered
seeing him supporting Brigga Lin during the attack on
Dawn's Light. The smuggler did have a certain smarmy,
arrogant charm about him. And as Nettles might have
said, wasn't bad on the gander. He also seemed to lack
Alash's sensitive nature, which was a quality that
Brigga Lin had always seemed to find irksome.

"So why did *you* come here?" he asked.

She laughed. "Honestly, I thought I'd be rescuing
you from the dread mole rats."

"You know, all those terrible rumors are wrong,"
he said defensively. "They're not at all bloodthirsty or
aggressive. They aren't even carnivores. The only time
they attack is when someone threatens their colony."

"Which I did spectacularly today." She held up her
mangled prosthesis. "I also wanted your help rework-
ing this."

"I can see why." He lifted it up and gave it a more
careful look.

"Even before it was damaged, actually," said Hope.

"Oh? I thought you were happy with it."

"I was. But my … priorities have changed. I want something more suitable to general everyday use."

"I'm sure we can come up with something," said Alash as he scrutinized the mechanics more closely. "Although taking the design in that direction will most likely impact sword handling."

"That's fine," she said. "Because I don't intend to ever pick up a sword again."

He tore his eyes away from the prosthesis to stare at her. "Not … *ever*?"

"That's right."

"Okay. I …" He scratched his scruffy cheek, looking mystified. "I just think of the Song of Sorrows almost as a part of your body, so it's difficult for me to grasp this …"

She waited for the inevitable protestation that renouncing swordsmanship was not only impractical, but dangerous. In a world where some of the most powerful people alive wanted her dead, how could she discard the one sure way to defend herself? She'd asked herself that question many times. She always came back to the idea that if she was going to fulfill her teacher's last wish and find a better path for the Vinchen, she must accept that most wild dreams were built upon dangerous, impractical choices. No, not accept it. *Embrace* it. Even if no one else did. Still, this was the moment she dreaded the most. Her absurd ideals running headlong into the cold logic that Wentu and Yammy had been kind enough to keep to themselves.

"How do I put this …" Alash struggled for a moment, then he suddenly smiled. "I think it's marvelous."

"You … do?"

"Of course. I've told you many times that I abhor violence."

"That's true." She'd always shrugged off his declarations as naive. But now here she was, bent on proving it was possible.

"Not such a crazy idea after all, is it?" he asked, as if he knew what she'd always been thinking. Then he went back to studying her prosthesis. "Obviously, we'll need to discuss the design in detail, but regardless of how we decide to go, I'm quite sure we won't be able to do anything with it here on Walta. Fortunately, there's a blacksmith on Vance Post that owes me a favor."

"And you don't mind going back there?" asked Hope.

"More than likely she won't even be there." Tension crept into Alash's face. "They spend a lot of time at sea, doing God knows what. But even if they are on Vance Post, they keep to the Shade District. My blacksmith is in the Commercial District, an area far too industrious and respectable for the likes of that pirate."

"If you're certain," said Hope. "We could try somewhere else if you prefer."

He shook his head. "Think nothing of it, Miss Hope." Then he turned to Uter, who was now fiddling with some sort of sliding ruler. "And you, Mr. Uter."

Uter hastily put the ruler back on the table.

"Have you decided if we are to be friends?" asked Alash.

Uter considered him a moment. "You're awfully nice to Hope," he said. "And you're going to fix her metal hand. So I guess we can be friends."

———

Alash filed away all the jagged bits of metal that made Hope a danger to herself and others. It was near sunset, so they decided not to head for Vance Post until the next morning. There wasn't a lot of room up on the tower for the three of them, but Alash insisted that Hope use the bed.

"It would pain me to think of you sleeping on the bare floor so much that I wouldn't be able to sleep anyway," he declared.

When Hope lay down on the bedroll, Uter snuggled in close. He was still uncharacteristically timid and pensive. Clingy, even. As they lay there staring up through holes in the canvas at the starry sky, she decided to ask him about it.

"Uter, you've been acting strangely today."

"Strangely?"

"Not like how you usually act. Normally you're so cheerful and energetic."

"Oh."

"Do you not like Alash? Does he frighten you for some reason?"

"No, he seems okay."

"Was it the tunnel?"

There was a long silence. Then, in a quivering voice, Uter said, "I don't like being buried. I don't like it."

"Have you been buried before?"

"Yes."

"Who buried you?"

"My lord."

"Why did Vikma Bruea bury you?"

"That's what they do when you get wighted. They make you drink these awful-tasting things. Then they put these smelly oils on your skin. Then they... Then they..."

Hope could feel him shaking next to her. She wanted to ask him how long he had been buried. But she suspected the boy probably didn't know and would find it painful to think about it. Hours? Perhaps even days? All the while struggling with whatever potions the necromancer had given him that kept him teetering on the edge of death. *They suffer for days in more pain and torment than you or I could imagine. Most of them eventually die. Their bodies just can't take the suffering, and give out.* That's what Maltch, the elder on Gull's Cry, had said. How could a young mind process such torment? Perhaps it couldn't.

Hope put her arm around the boy and pulled him close to her so that he shivered against her. She held up her broken prosthesis and stared at it in the faint moonlight.

"Some things that are broken can never be returned to the way they were," she said. "But perhaps they can be made whole, in a new way."

She said it to comfort him, but she knew she was expressing a hope for both of them.

Gradually, Uter stopped shaking and drifted off to sleep, and sometime later, so did she.

13

*B*rigga Lin used to find sailing so thrilling. The sight of the open sea used to make her chest surge with an exuberance she could barely articulate. Release? Freedom? Possibility? One of those. Or perhaps all of them. She used to stand silently for hours on the forecastle of the *Kraken Hunter* with Hope. Words had been unnecessary because they'd both known what they were looking at as they gazed out at the ocean: a better tomorrow.

But now she was alone, and she no longer knew what she was looking at, other than a lot of salty water. It stirred nothing within her.

As she stared at the lead-colored sea beneath slate-gray skies, she was distantly aware that some kind of argument was taking place back on the quarterdeck. The *Rolling Lightning* was a fairly small ship, but even so, they must be raising their voices pretty loudly for the sound to reach her at the bow over the crash of the waves. Not loud enough for her to hear what they were saying. But then, she wasn't trying to hear anyway.

A few minutes later, Gavish Gray appeared next to her, looking quietly furious in that way he had. His eyes would get a hard set, his cheeks would flush, and his nostrils would flare. As often as Brigga Lin saw that look, he rarely communicated to her what caused it. She rarely asked.

After he'd had a few minutes to calm down, he spoke in a light, conversational tone that sounded slightly forced. "I fear you've upset Jilly."

"Oh?"

"Aye. She was hoping for some biomancer training. Just the two of you on a small island."

"She still has plenty of reading to do before we need to start any practical application," said Brigga Lin.

"So you said." Gray was quiet for a moment. "Still, it's been a hard couple of months. Wouldn't hurt to give her a bit of special attention, would it? I think it's that, more than the learning, she craves."

"If you're seeking to appeal to my maternal instincts, you'd have better luck with some of your crew. They're far more attentive to Jilly than I am."

"That's what troubles me," Gray said.

"Attempting to make me feel guilty for my inattentiveness is equally futile," said Brigga Lin.

"No, it's not that." Gray's nostrils and cheeks flared up again. "I just..." He pressed his lips together for a moment. "Never mind. You're right. I've no business telling you how to school your own pupil. I won't trouble you about it again."

Then he turned and walked across the deck back to his cabin, closing the door behind him.

As Brigga Lin continued to stare dully out at the water, a thought slowly rose up in her mind like an air bubble in a pool of oil. Perhaps something else was troubling Gray. Something he couldn't articulate. And he'd been awkwardly trying to find a way to talk it out with her. She supposed that, as his lover, she was expected to attempt to coax it out of him.

She sighed and headed across the deck toward his cabin. It was beginning to rain anyway.

As she passed the hatchway down to the galley, she heard something that made her pause. She stopped

and stood for a moment, trying to think what it had
been. Words. A phrase. A few of the crew speaking.
What did they say? She wasn't sure. It was odd that
she'd heard it and yet not heard it, all at once. But
there had been a coarse laugh and the name Jilly.

She looked up into the sails. As usual, Jilly
lounged in the rigging, one bare foot idly dangling.
How did that girl lose shoes so quickly?

But if Jilly was up among the sails, that meant the
men below weren't talking to her. They were talking
about her.

Brigga Lin remained standing next to the hatchway. She became aware of an unpleasant tightness in
her chest as she strained to hear what the men below
deck were saying.

"Well, I can certainly understand the tempta-
tion," came Fisty's voice, his tone agreeable. "But
you know it would anger the Lady, and that would
anger the captain, and we don't want that."

"I don't give a piss about what upsets the *Lady*,"
said Slake, a sour contempt in his tone. "The captain
should never have let her on board. He can claim all
he likes that she's not a biomancer. She's got that
attitude all them biomancers got. Like none of us are
worth a cup of piss."

"You *know* I'm with you on this," said Marble
Eyes. "The Lady has too much sway over the captain. She has to go."

"So you want the captain should get rid of the
Lady but keep Jilly?" asked Fisty. "How you going to
convince him of *that* one?"

"We'll just tell him how useful she is," said Marble
Eyes.

Slake laughed. Brigga Lin had never heard him
laugh before. It was an ugly, convulsive sound. "And
with the Lady out of the way, she'll be *twice* as useful."

"That baby slice is so fresh, I can almost smell

it," said Marble Eyes, his voice dreamy. Then more firmly, "But don't forget she's got knives. My leg still ain't healed from when I made a grab before."

"The knives just make it more fun," said Slake. "Between the two of us, I'm sure we could handle her. I go first, though. I've been wanting to toss that little slice ever since I laid eyes on her."

Brigga Lin stood above the hatch, motionless. Thunder rumbled in the distance as the rain began to fall harder.

Drowning was usually something that happened fast. A person fell in the water and, within a few minutes, they ran out of air, their lungs filled with water, and they died. But there was a disease called Swimmer's Lung. No one knew exactly how a person got it, but once they had it, their lungs gradually filled up with fluid over the course of many weeks. It was a slow drowning.

The curious thing was that most people who had Swimmer's Lung didn't realize something was wrong until their lungs were mostly full. It was such a drawn-out process that they grew accustomed to the progressive shortening of their breath without even noticing it. At such a late stage, drastic measures were needed to save the victim, such as piercing the chest with a hollow needle to drain it.

Brigga Lin had been slowly drowning for months. Except instead of fluid, she was drowning in time. Old Yammy had warned her this might happen. In her arrogance, Brigga Lin thought she could handle it. After all, she'd spent years growing accustomed to the sense of all the living things around her. But she had not truly appreciated how intense it would be to feel not just what *was*, but also what had been, and what might be. She'd fought to stay afloat for a while, then somewhere along the line, after Hope had left and most of the crew went their separate ways, she'd slowly dropped beneath the waves of time without even noticing.

Now something had yanked her back to the surface. Something hard, and sharp, and clear. Something that brought the painful focus she needed to clear her head, as a victim of Swimmer's Lung cleared their lungs. Something that forced her to finally *wake up*. It was the pure, hot rush of wrath.

She pulled her hood up and walked slowly down the narrow steps to the galley. Fisty, Marble Eyes, and Slake lounged around a small table, each with a cup of grog. When they saw Brigga Lin, their expressions grew uneasy and they stood up, as if attempting some sort of awkward gentlemanly behavior.

"My lady...," said Fisty uneasily. "Is there something we can help you with?"

Brigga Lin smiled as she walked toward them. She lifted her arms so that her sleeves fell back to reveal her elegant, long-fingered hands. Most of the time she cast from afar. But every so often, it was good to get her hands dirty.

"M-my lady?" asked Fisty as he sidled away. The other two were trapped in the corner, their eyes both belligerent and a little frightened.

Not nearly frightened enough.

Brigga Lin decided it was convenient that most pirates went shirtless. Her hands shot out, her left hand against Marble Eyes's bare chest, and her right hand against Slake's. As she touched them, their skin, muscle, and bone in that area softened to the consistency of thick custard. They flailed and struggled to free themselves as she pressed her hands into their chest cavities. Slake even managed to yank out a bit of her hair, which was impressive given the amount of mind-numbing agony they were both experiencing.

Then she tore out their lungs, and they collapsed to the floor.

She turned, a pair of dripping sacks in each hand. Fisty stared at her, his mouth open, his face drained of color. He flinched as she walked past him and back up the wooden steps to the deck.

She continued at that slow, deliberate pace until she reached the captain's cabin. The rain was coming down harder now, and lightning arced across the sky, casting her shadow on the door for a moment.

"Captain Gray." She didn't shout, but her voice rang like a bell.

Gavish Gray opened the door. His eyes grew wide with horror when Brigga Lin dropped the lungs of his crew members at his feet. They landed on the wooden deck with a wet slap, blood mixing with the rain that came down in hard sheets.

"Thank you for your hospitality, but it's time for Jilly and me to move on," Brigga Lin told him. "Once we return to Vance Post, we'll be going our separate ways. Until then, if I see any of the crew go near Jilly, these deaths will seem gentle in comparison."

She turned away, but then stopped. She looked over her shoulder at him, her face half-hidden by her hood.

"Be grateful that I now realize you were trying to express your concerns about Jilly's safety to me earlier. Otherwise, I would have you begging for your own death right now."

———

The rain was coming down hard, but Jilly didn't mind. She sat up in her usual perch, closed her eyes, and turned her face to the sky. When she'd first started sailing years ago, and had her first time up in the shrouds during a storm, it had been miserable. That was back when she'd gone by the name of Jillen, posing as a boy. One of the old salts had taken pity on her and told her the secret. Don't flinch against the rain. Don't tense against it as if you could fight it. Because you could never fight a storm. Instead you had to learn to embrace it, and all the chaos that came with it. Ever since then, she'd done just that. Forced herself to stay up there in the worst weather a storm could throw. It hadn't always been easy, but it was a lesson that had served her well. How to embrace the storm.

She sighed and felt the rain patter on her face, dripping from her chin.

Then her solitude was broken when she felt the presence of someone else. She opened her eyes and saw Brigga Lin. There were flecks of blood on her master's white gown, fading in the rain, but still visible.

"Master?" She sat up straight, as if even up here Brigga Lin would criticize her posture.

"Hello, Jilly." Brigga Lin settled in on the yard beside her.

"I don't think I've ever seen you up here before, master," she said. "I mean...I wasn't sure you could *get* up here."

"It isn't easy in a dress," admitted her master. "But the reason I've never come up here was because I didn't *want* to. Frankly, I think it's unladylike."

Jilly waited for her to say more, but Brigga Lin only sat there and gazed out at the choppy gray sea speckled with rain. Water dripped steadily from the rim of her hood.

"It's not like you to stay out in a storm, either," said Jilly, becoming increasingly uneasy. "Not without an umbrella, at least."

"It's gratifying that you know me so well," said Brigga Lin. "The fact is, I am up here in this storm for you."

"For *me*?"

"I have to tell you something you won't want to hear, so I thought it best to tell you in a place you prefer. I wish I could wait until the weather was more pleasant, but I'm afraid I can't."

"I see..." Thick, cold dread filled the pit of Jilly's stomach. Was Brigga Lin about to tell her that she no longer wanted to train her? Maybe she'd realized that Jilly wasn't book smart enough. Maybe she'd decided Jilly was probably hopeless. That could be why she'd been putting off proper training.

Jilly steeled herself for the worst. She would take it like she'd taken every other bad turn. After all, you can't fight the storm.

"Once we return to Vance Post," said Brigga Lin, "we will be leaving the crew of the *Rolling Lightning*. Until then, you are not to speak to or go anywhere near any members of this crew. Do you understand?"

Jilly stared at her. "N-no, master. I don't understand at all."

"I know you are fond of the men on this ship, but they are not your friends."

"Well, maybe not *friends*, exactly. But we're all wags."

"No, Jilly. You're not. They were planning to *rape* you."

Jilly stared at her master for a moment. She knew Brigga Lin wouldn't lie, so it had to be something else. "I think there's maybe been a...a *misunderstanding*. There was one night when one of them got grabby while he was drunk, and I stabbed him. So it's taken care of. We're all chum and larder now."

"You thought that would be the end of it?" There was pity in Brigga Lin's eyes. Like she was talking to a naive child. "That their idiotic pride could suffer such a setback? Jilly, I heard them, today, plotting what to do to you."

"But..." Jilly wasn't sure why it hurt so much to

hear this. Why it felt like such a betrayal. It was all twisted up in her chest.

Brigga Lin reached out and gently put her hand on Jilly's rain-soaked shoulder. It was, Jilly realized, the first time her master had ever touched her. "There are good men in the world. But the men on this ship are not among them."

"Not even Captain Gray?"

Brigga Lin gave her a weary, bittersweet smile. "Not good enough for us."

Red had always assumed that no neighborhood could equal Paradise Circle in its ardent embrace of sex, drugs, and violence. But as he walked through the streets of Vance Post's Shade District with Vaderton, he couldn't help but feel that his old neighborhood had been nothing but part-timers and hobbyists. At least as far as the sex and drugs went. Perhaps the Circle still had more acts of violence being perpetrated per block, but the sheer number of whorehouses and drug dens packed into each square mile of the Shade District was staggering. And they weren't shy about the nature of their business either. Brightly painted signs hung in front of every door, sometimes even with illustrations.

He gazed at a sign that read A GOOD PLACE FOR BAD ENDS, which included a simple illustration of what appeared to be a female demon sticking her tail up a male angel's ass. Next door was another whorehouse with a sign that read PISS ON US ALL and included a picture of a nude woman squatting. The building after that had a sign that read DUELING COCKS. Whether it was a whorehouse exclusively for toms or a place that bet on rooster fights was unclear, since there was no illustration and either seemed likely.

"How do they all stay in business?" he asked Vaderton.

"The Shade District is known throughout the empire for offering anything one might desire to anyone who can pay the price," said Vaderton.

"I'm fairly sure you can get anything you want in Paradise Circle as well," protested Red.

"Ah, but not with the same level of sophistication," said Vaderton. "The Shade District is where merchants come to pretend they are decadent nobility."

"*Are* there decadent nobility?" asked Red. "The ones I encountered barely even wanted to talk about sex."

"Certainly. They just tend to keep it away from the palace. Now, come on, I think the inn is this way." He turned down a side street.

"You've been there before?" asked Red as he followed.

Vaderton shook his head. "I just know it by reputation. The Past Is Forgotten is the most infamous smugglers' den on Vance Post, making it one of the most well known in the empire. At least, it's known to those of us who spent a sizable portion of our naval career running down smugglers."

"Why'd you leave the navy, anyway?" asked Red.

"I didn't," said Vaderton. "They left me. Specifically, they left me for dead on the Empty Cliffs so that I wouldn't spread the word that Captain Bane— I mean, that *Hope* was taking a sizable bite out of our fleet."

"Why would they want to keep that a secret?" asked Red.

"I can't say for sure, but my guess is simply pride. Both the navy and the biomancers like to maintain an image of invincibility. To admit weakness, especially at the hands of a woman…and going by the name Dire Bane?" He shook his head. "It's the sort of thing that could either start a panic, or else get some bolder folks thinking about rebellions of their own. I don't think the navy has their heads so far up their asses that they don't realize how little they are loved by the common folk."

"You'd think that would give them some pause to reconsider how they handle the common folk," said Red.

"You think the people in power got there by worrying about what other people think of them?" asked Vaderton.

"Leston worries about it a lot," said Red.

Vaderton gave him an amused look. "And just how much power do you suppose the prince actually has?"

"Good point," said Red. "But he will one day."

"Let's hope so," said Vaderton. "Here's the place."

In a neighborhood where businesses competed to be the most eye-catching, the Past Is Forgotten Inn and Tavern was notably subdued. Red imagined that such a notorious place probably didn't need to advertise.

The inside wasn't particularly remarkable either. It could have been like any other tavern full of wags. But there was an ominous tension in the air that Red could almost taste. Like just before a storm.

"I'll handle this," he told Vaderton.

He walked up to the bartender, a pat old wrink who still had a hard gleam to his eye, like running the bar of a smugglers' den was his idea of retirement. Red placed his hand on the counter and splayed his fingers to show coins between each one.

"Hey, old pot." He kept his tone relaxed. "You see a molly around here lately who's a bit taller than most? Maybe wearing a white hooded gown?"

The bartender looked down at the coins, then back up at Red, squinting at his smoked lenses like he was trying to gauge the eyes beneath.

"Maybe."

The old wrink clearly didn't trust him. It made sense in a place like this. Some things, like reputation, were more important than a bit of coin. If he thought Red was here to make trouble for the inn, he wouldn't be much help.

Red remembered that Nettles said Jilly was sailing with them. Perhaps if he showed he knew more about them, he'd convince this bartender he was a friend. "She would have had a little girl with her. Maybe eight years old?"

"Twelve," corrected Vaderton. "Jilly's twelve now."

Red's eyes widened. "That old already?"

"You wags know Jilly, then?" asked the bartender, looking a little more friendly.

"Know her?" asked Red. "I taught her everything she knows."

"Not everything," protested Vaderton. "I taught her how to sail."

"Well..." The bartender scrutinized them for another moment, then shrugged. "I reckon a friend of Jilly's is a friend of mine. She and that Lady Witch sailed out on the *Rolling Lightning* about ten days ago."

"Any idea when they'll be back?" asked Red.

He pursed his lips. "Gavish said it would be a short run. So could be back any day now."

"I guess we'll get a room and stay until they show up, then," said Red.

"You should know you ain't the only ones waiting," said the bartender.

"Oh?" asked Red.

"A gaf come in the other day. He was only asking about the Lady Witch, not Jilly. But he didn't set right with me at all. I told 'em I didn't know nothing, but I could tell right away he didn't believe me. He's been coming in regular every day since then. Just sits in the back, taking up table space and not even drinking."

Red felt a tickle of unease. As far as he knew, there was only one other group looking for Brigga Lin. "This gaf…anything unusual about him? Like maybe some strange black armor?"

The bartender looked surprised. "Yeah. Like he was pretending to be Vinchen or something."

"Piss'ell," muttered Red, giving Vaderton a look of concern. Then he turned back to the bartender. "He wasn't pretending."

"What, you mean *real* Vinchen? Here on Vance Post?" The bartender didn't look so much surprised as alarmed. "I reckon the rumor is true, then."

"What rumor?" asked Red.

"Wags been talking that a Vinchen chopped up the imp headquarters. But I figured it was balls and pricks."

"What do you mean *chopped up*?" asked Red.

"I mean like he killed all the imps in the place. Had some magic sword that hums a bone-chilling tune while he swings it."

"Wait, he had the pissing *Song of Sorrows*?" demanded Red.

"The what now?" asked the bartender.

Red shook his head. "Never mind. We'll take a room. But first, I reckon a couple pints of dark."

As they watched the bartender pour the ale, Vaderton asked quietly, "Do you honestly think you can take on the Vinchen?"

Red grinned and rested his hands on his pistols. "Hadn't you heard, old pot? I'm the Shadow of Death."

For a neighborhood that had recently been rid of all law enforcement, the Shade District was surprisingly orderly. Of course sex, drugs, drunkenness, and violence abounded. But it was all conducted with a businesslike lack of fuss, because for the most part, that was the business of the Shade District.

Still, there were signs that something was amiss. A bit more violence than sex on the streets. A few shop fronts broken into. And, of course, there were the Vinchen. There'd been sightings all over the Shade District, and reports of seeing them in the Commercial District as well. It made wags uneasy, suddenly having these figures of legend roaming around. Especially after the rumors of the attack on the imp headquarters had been confirmed.

Red watched as a tom in gleaming black armor walked in with that telltale smooth confidence. Like liquid lightning, he'd thought when he'd first seen Hope. It was far less appealing in this context.

"Red," Vaderton muttered into his tankard.

"I see him."

It had been a few days like this now. It wasn't always the same person, but it was always a young Vinchen, and he always came in early in the morning and stayed until well past sunset when the tavern was closing. And no matter which one it was, he always went to the same table in the back, and he was always either oblivious or indifferent to the stares of the patrons. He never ordered anything or spoke to anyone.

There was a kind of arrogance that radiated from this one. As if he could barely stand to be in such a disreputable place. Red wondered if Hope had been like that once. Perhaps. But by the time he'd met her, she'd already been seasoned by several years aboard a merchant vessel among regular folk. Even then he'd found her a bit aloof at first. But that had been nothing compared to what he witnessed with this Vinchen. If Red was being totally honest with himself, he was itching to take a shot at him. And taking him out preemptively would be the most efficient strategy. Hit him fast before he was ready. A shot to the head when he was looking the other way. That's all it would take, and then there'd be one less Vinchen to worry about and a little less heat on Brigga Lin. He'd be stupid not to take this opportunity. Because that's exactly what it was. An opportunity...

"Red?" murmured Vaderton.

Red froze, realizing his hands had been curling around his guns. The Shadow Demon had slipped right into his head and he hadn't even noticed that time.

"A little premature, don't you think?" Vaderton said quietly. "The Vinchen don't know that we're looking for Brigga Lin, too. Don't want to lose that element of surprise."

Red nodded. "Good call."

And so they sat through another day. Other tables emptied and filled again as people came in and out for lunch, then drinks, then dinner. But Red, Vaderton, and the Vinchen didn't move. Two tables coiled and ready to explode into violence the moment someone fitting Brigga Lin's description walked into the tavern.

Except that wouldn't be how it went at all. Because Red had one great advantage. The Vinchen knew Brigga Lin only by physical description. Red knew what she sounded like. What's more, he knew Jilly's voice so well, he could have picked it out of a chorus, even if he didn't have enhanced hearing. And that night, as he sat there nursing the same tankard of ale he'd had for the last hour, he heard a smart little voice just outside the front door say:

"Did you see how I hit that, master? Thirty paces, must have been!"

"It was a very nice throw, Jilly," came Brigga Lin's ringing voice, sounding a little weary.

Without thinking, Red fired a shot, and the Vinchen dropped dead onto his table.

There was a momentary pause as everyone in the tavern stared at the dead Vinchen, then at Red and Vaderton.

"What did—" began Vaderton.

"Come on."

Red grabbed Vaderton and headed for the door. A moment later, Brigga Lin and Jilly appeared in the doorway. They stared at Red for a moment. Then a big grin broke on Jilly's face.

"Red! It's you!"

Red turned them around and pushed them back toward the door. "We have to get out of here. *Now!*"

Brigga Lin looked over her shoulder and frowned. "Is there a dead Vinchen on that table?"

"Yep, and that's why we have to go," said Red.

As he shuffled them back onto the street, Brigga Lin gave him a strange look. "Red, it's good to see you, but what's going on?"

"Long story short, the biomancers have set the Vinchen after you. They must have found out where you've been staying, because they had one staked out for you at that tavern. I killed him, but there are many more nearby I'm sure."

Her eyes widened. "Vinchen? Working with the biomancers?"

"It's as crazy as it sounds, but I'll have to explain later," said Red. "Now we need to be somewhere else. *Anywhere* else would do, really."

"My ship," said Vaderton. "Southeast docks, pier forty-two. Let's move."

As they hurried down the street, Jilly craned her head back to look at Vaderton. "Captain? You're with Red now?"

He smiled. "I'm wherever Yammy tells me to be."

"How is she?" asked Brigga Lin.

"Wouldn't say. You know how she can be," said Vaderton.

Brigga Lin nodded. "I suppose I understand it better now."

They turned down a side street, but Brigga Lin jerked to a stop. "Not this way."

"But this is—" began Vaderton.

"Trust me," said Brigga Lin.

Vaderton seemed to recognize the look in her eyes and nodded. "We'll find another route."

They stepped back into the main street and hurried on. That's when Red caught flickers of black up on the rooftops of the alley they'd just avoided.

"Vinchen! They've spotted us!" he said.

They ran faster. Out of the corner of his eye, Red could see more black shapes along the rooftops following after them.

"They must have had an ambush back in that alley," he said. "How did you know?"

"I had some…instruction from Yammy," said Brigga Lin as they ran.

Red found that both terrifying and astonishing. Most importantly, he realized it might have just saved their lives. One or two Vinchen he could handle. But not all of them ambushing him at once. As he and his friends sprinted down the street, weaving past market stalls, carts, and pedestrians, he kept seeing more black shapes on the rooftops, and they were getting closer.

He didn't like open violence in the streets with so many people around, but it looked like there wasn't much choice. He pulled out one of his revolvers and fired up at the nearest Vinchen. Thankfully, the gaf didn't slap the bullet out of the air, but he easily dodged behind an outcropping along the roof. Red hoped it might have been luck, but after missing a few more times, he was forced to admit that they were too fast and there was too much cover for him to hit one.

"We're not going to reach the ship before they

catch us," he said, shoving through a milling crowd of people who were now starting to panic because of the gunfire. "We need a new plan."

"Stop running and kill them all?" suggested Brigga Lin.

"I like the way you think, my wag, but for me to contribute as much as I possibly can to the death-bringing, I'm going to need an open space so I can get a clear shot at them."

"I know a place nearby," she said. "Follow me."

14

$\mathcal{H}$ope stared down at her new hand. The broken clamp had been replaced by three prongs that curved inward so that their points met in the center. Rotation had been greatly restricted, with most of the wires that were attached to her tendons redirected to control the prongs. Each one could be articulated separately.

She opened and closed the prongs experimentally. They made a faint, odd clicking sound.

"I tried to map the mechanism so that it approximated the same muscle groups you would have used to control your original flesh hand," said Alash as they sat at a large worktable in the room adjacent to the smithy's forge. Even though there was a wall separating them from the forge, heat emanated through the thick leather curtain that covered the doorway. "It still might take some time for you to adjust, though."

"It's so light," said Hope, hefting it up and down experimentally.

"The prongs aren't solid metal," said Alash. "Beneath the metal shell, it's actually whalebone, which is still structurally sound, but significantly lighter."

"Metal *and* bone?" asked Uter, his eyes wide as he leaned across the table to get a closer look. His impulsive enthusiasm had returned. He was no longer shy toward Alash either. Instead he had become awed as he watched Alash sketch designs for the new hand and then make them real with the help of Garett the blacksmith.

"You won't be able to stop a bullet with it," Alash told Hope. "But you could parry a few blows from a sword without any trouble."

"You've done a magnificent job," said Hope. "I owe you a great deal. And I promise, we'll get you back to your research on Walta. Then Uter and I will return to Galemoor."

Alash looked surprised. "Why?"

"What do you mean?" asked Hope uneasily.

"I may be avoiding Brigga Lin, but that's because she more or less told me to go away. But *you* should at least go see her while you're here. And Jilly, too. When you left...I think it hit them hardest."

The sudden sadness in Alash's eyes was more than Hope could stand to see. Instead she went back to examining her new hand.

Then it struck her. She had always made a point of not looking away from terrible things. Perhaps it had even been a point of pride that she would witness even the worst that life brought. But here she was, unable to meet Alash's gaze.

"I suppose I've been hiding from that," she admitted quietly. "And from them. I just didn't..." She trailed off. Even after all this time, it was difficult to express in words the awful clash of feelings in her chest. Guilt, remorse, shame, disgust, confusion, embarrassment...

Alash put his hand on her new one, so that it was in front of her eyes. A hand that had grown strong from labor and brown from the sun. But his voice was gentle. "They don't care if you're Dire Bane, champion of the people, or Bleak Hope, outlaw Vinchen, or someone else entirely. They just miss *you*."

Hope forced herself to look back into his eyes this

time. He was smiling. And somehow that smile made its way onto her face.

Garett the blacksmith stuck his head around the leather curtain. His face and bald scalp were red and gleamed with sweat. In many ways, he looked like a typical blacksmith. But he was the most cheerful blacksmith Hope had ever met.

"Hello, my wag," he said to Alash. "Someone at the door to see you."

"Oh?" said Alash.

"That pirate friend of yours," replied Garett.

Alash glanced over at Hope. "Pirate friend?"

Garett shrugged. "I remember seeing him before is all. You want me to tell him to piss on his way?"

Alash shook his head. "No. I'll go see who it is." He gave a little forlorn smile. "Who would have thought someday 'pirate friend' wouldn't be specific enough to describe one of my acquaintances." He turned to Hope. "I'm sure this won't take long."

Alash got up and followed Garett into the smithy.

"What do you think—" began Uter, but Hope held up her hand to silence him and listened carefully.

She heard Alash's voice, sounding both displeased and a little curious. "Oh. Gavish."

"Thank God you're still here, my wag," came Gavish Gray's voice, sounding more desperate than Hope had ever heard him.

"Well, I actually just got back a few days ago," Alash corrected primly. "But what's the trouble?"

"Look, you and I don't get along, but I need you to set that aside because our lady is in the worst sort of trouble, and nobody will lift a finger to help her!"

Hope was through the curtain so fast, she must have compressed time without meaning to, because Alash, Gavish, and Garett all jumped when they saw her, as if she'd appeared out of nowhere.

"Brigga Lin is in danger?" she demanded.

Relief washed across Gavish's broad face as he looked at Hope. "Captain? You're *back*? Then she might actually survive this mess after all!"

"Where is she?" Hope's claw hand clacked opened and closed eagerly. "And who's after her?"

———

Stephan thought that if Vance Post's Shade District was a maelstrom of decadence and hedonism, then Visionary Square must be its eye. Ringing the outside of the square were the largest and most opulent whorehouses and drug dens in the Shade District, not to mention shops offering oddly vague wares such as "rare animal goods" or "exotic mechanical devices." But in the square itself, there was a strange sort of tranquility.

It was an open public space paved with cobblestones, but there were small sections of grass interspersed throughout. In the center was a statue of a man by the unlikely name of Fulton Brash, who had conceived of the legalized vice district over a century ago. If one could say that the people of the Shade District had a creed of sorts, Brash was its originator. Stephan had expected the man to look as depraved as his ideals: corpulent, with large cheeks, beady eyes, and a smile that was more of a leer. But the statue depicted a graceful man, almost delicate in features, with long wavy hair and a wistful, dreamy air about him as his giant stone form lay stretched out on an oversized stone bench. Children scrambled up and down the statue playfully, while people sat on regular benches nearby, drinking, playing stones, or simply talking. There were also a few artists working on standing easels, and off to one side, a fiddle player performing a light, mournful tune. All told, there had to be close to fifty people in the square. And right in the middle of them was the female biomancer.

The Vinchen had grouped on a nearby rooftop around Grandteacher Racklock to assess the situation. Brigga Lin sat almost casually on a bench. Next to her was someone dressed in the fine clothes of a Stonepeak lord, but he was a much better shot with those revolvers than any noble Stephan had ever seen.

"Grandteacher, that man with the dark glasses seems unusually skilled," said Malveu.

"He's the one who killed Frache," Hectory said grimly. "No normal man could do such a thing."

The grandteacher nodded. "He's an assassin trained by the Council of Biomancery. I recently received word from Ammon Set that he has turned on them."

"You…knew that when you sent Frache in there?" asked Hectory.

"Of course," said Racklock, his eyes still focused on their quarry below.

Hectory didn't say anything more, but Stephan could see his friend struggle with the realization that their grandteacher had thrown away the life of one of their brothers so callously.

"What of the other two?" asked Ravento. "The older man and the girl?"

"I don't know anything about them," said Racklock. "But neither seem much of a threat."

"Why do you think they've taken a position in the middle of the square?" asked Stephan.

"Obviously so we can't attack directly from the rooftops," said Racklock, starting to show impatience at all the questions. "That way the assassin can get a clear shot, and the female biomancer will be able to see any attackers before they strike. The primary target remains the female biomancer. Since she can cast from afar, you will all have to continue to remain just out of her sight until I dispose of her. Until then, you must contain this square. Make sure none escape."

"The old man and the girl as well?" asked Malveu.

"Everyone," Racklock snapped. "There's no telling how she might infect or control these people with her biomancery."

"What should we do if innocent bystanders attempt to escape the perimeter?" asked Stephan.

"Kill them, of course!" growled Racklock.

"But, Grandteacher!" Hectory's eyes went wide. "You can't mean—"

The Song of Sorrows flashed from its sheath, bringing its unearthly hum as it severed Hectory's head from his body. The body flopped down on the roof. The head fell over the edge and landed on the cobblestones far below with a sickening squelch. There was a ten-second pause before someone walked past it and screamed.

Racklock's hard eyes swept the remaining Vinchen.

"Any other objections? Or are you ready to complete your mission?"

Stephan stared at the man he had called *grandteacher* for the last few years. He stared at the Song of Sorrows, which still dripped with the blood of his warrior brother. No, Hectory had been much more than that to Stephan. And as he continued to stare at his beloved's blood, and hear the shouts of panic from the innocents down below who had stumbled across his beloved's head, Stephan felt that deep within him, something profound had been lost, and he didn't know if he would ever get it back.

———

Jilly perched on the edge of the bench next to Red and stared at the Vinchen who had gathered on the rooftop at the border of Visionary Square.

"Why don't they just come at us?" she asked.

"Because they're not bludgeon," said Red. "In an open space like this, Brigga Lin and I have the advantage. If we can pick them off before they can get close, the fight's over. I've got twelve bullets loaded and there are only fifteen Vinchen." He grinned at Brigga Lin, who sat on his other side. "I feel confident in saying you could easily take out the other three."

She gave him a cool look. "As well as any you miss."

He looked hurt. "Miss? Me?"

"You did miss several shots on the way here," pointed out Vaderton, who stood behind them. Of course the old naval officer wouldn't feel comfortable lounging before a fight.

"That was while they were under cover, old pot," Red said airily. "Nothing between them and my bullets now."

The Vinchen seemed to be arguing among each other. Then suddenly one of them drew his sword and cut off another one's head. Jilly watched in amazement as the head fell over the side and landed with a splat on the street below.

"Did he just..."

"He certainly did, my wag," said Red.

A young woman in a long robe hurried by a moment later and let out a yelp when she saw the head. She glanced fearfully around, but when she didn't see any sign of imminent danger, she simply hurried on her way. This continued to happen over and over again. Jilly found it fascinating how everyone in the Shade District acted the same way. Old men and little boys, merchants, drug dealers, and whores all reacted with shock when they saw it. But nobody called the imps. Nobody chose to investigate further. Once they ascertained that it posed no direct threat to them, they decided it wasn't their business and continued on their way.

"They're moving," said Red.

Jilly tore her eyes away from the head-discovery parade and looked back up at the Vinchen. They were spreading out along the rooftops until they encircled the entire square.

"They're not just going to rush us, then?" asked Jilly.

"Not all clumped together, anyway," said Vaderton. "It makes more sense for them to come at us from different sides at once because they're not using firearms and don't need to worry about crossfire."

They all dropped down to ground level.

"Get ready," Red said tersely as he got to his feet and drew his revolvers.

But instead of coming at them, the Vinchen swiftly moved behind the cover of market stalls, alleys, or doorway alcoves.

"What are they playing at...," muttered Vaderton.

Jilly's eyes scanned the square and saw that one Vinchen was coming toward them. He was short, but broadly shouldered. It was the one who'd chopped off the other's head. He held a familiar-looking sword in his hand.

"Look!" she said.

Red turned and grimaced when he saw him. "Racklock."

"Is that the Song of Sorrows?" asked Brigga Lin, her voice suddenly threaded with concern.

"Looks like it," Red said grimly.

"Damn it," Brigga Lin said. Jilly had never heard her curse before. "I knew we shouldn't have left that sword behind on Dawn's Light."

"It seemed the right thing to do at the time," Vaderton said placatingly.

Brigga Lin only grunted.

"That going to be a problem for you?" asked Red.

"The wielder of that sword is immune to all biomancery."

"Even yours?"

"Even mine."

"Piss'ell."

"Exactly."

"Guess it's up to me to take down the leader," said Red as he pulled the hammers back on his revolvers. "Don't worry. I'll let you have more of the lackeys to even it out."

Then he fired at Racklock.

But the grandteacher slapped the bullet aside.

"Oh, right. There's that . . . ," murmured Red.

The gunshot spooked the people in the square. They began to flee as Racklock continued slowly forward, his eyes never leaving Brigga Lin. He struck down anyone unlucky enough to get in his path.

"Well, he can't block them all," said Red. "Right?"

He fired several shots in succession. Racklock not only blocked them all, but sent the ricocheting bullets into the nearby escaping crowds. Several people cried out or fell to the cobblestones.

"Vaderton, get Jilly out of here," said Brigga Lin. "We'll meet up with you later."

Vaderton nodded and grabbed Jilly's arm.

"Wait a minute!" she protested, but Vaderton hauled her toward the nearest side street while Brigga Lin and Red prepared to meet Racklock head-on.

"You think you're ready to go up against *that*?" Vaderton demanded as he pulled her along. "Brigga Lin wants you alive, and that's how I'm going to keep you. Now, come on. Let's get out of sight so you're not dividing her attention anymore."

He was right. She was more of a hindrance than a help fighting opponents of this caliber. Jilly allowed herself to be yanked toward the alley, cursing herself for being so useless. They were joined by several other panicked bystanders, all looking to get away from the flying bullets and flashing sword.

Then a young Vinchen warrior appeared out of nowhere to block the alley. His stance was strong, and the grip on his sword was firm. But his eyes were red and puffy, as if he had just been crying.

"No one leaves," he said hoarsely.

The anger and frustration Jilly had just been feeling toward her own helplessness channeled itself toward this stupid Vinchen. She didn't even pause to consider her actions. She just grabbed her knife and lunged at him.

The Vinchen neatly parried her thrust with his sword, then grabbed her wrist with his free hand and yanked her off balance. He swept her legs and she was on the floor in a heap, her knife clattering away out of reach.

The Vinchen placed the tip of his sword almost gently at her throat. "Please. Don't make me kill you."

She closed her eyes, feeling the shame burn in her stomach even as the heat of her tears escaped down the sides of her face. She was so useless.

"Okay, you've made your point," Vaderton said. "Now let her up. I'll make sure she doesn't give you any more trouble."

Jilly felt the tip of the sword leave her throat. She opened her eyes and saw that Vaderton was holding out his hand to her.

"That was dumb," he told her as he pulled her to her feet.

She nodded and wiped her eyes as she turned to look back at the square. Red and Brigga Lin were facing off against Racklock alone. The other Vinchen were preventing anyone from leaving the square. It looked like they'd even killed a few people trying to flee. But they didn't move to help their grandteacher in any way.

The majority of Racklock's focus was on Brigga

Lin. It was clear that only he, as wielder of the Song of Sorrows, was a match against her. So of course she would need to be taken out before the other Vinchen could join the fight. But while Brigga Lin couldn't attack directly, she was far from defenseless. Since she couldn't use biomancery on him, she used it on herself. She hardened her arms so they were like steel, which allowed her to fend off the flurry of vicious blows from Racklock, and strike at him as if she wielded a sword herself. But as a swordsman, she was no match for the Vinchen.

There was something so wrong about hearing the hum of the Song of Sorrows coming from someone other than Hope. Maybe it was Jilly's imagination, but the tone of it seemed darker and colder. His blows were almost inhuman in their ferocity. As thickset as he was, he moved with an almost animal grace. If it weren't for Red, Jilly was certain that Brigga Lin would already be dead.

But thankfully Red was there, constantly harrying the grandteacher with gunfire, and when he ran out of bullets, with throwing blades. Jilly didn't know what had happened to him up there on Stonepeak, but he moved differently. His old swagger and showmanship were gone, replaced by a cold, calculating efficiency. It was almost frightening to watch. The Vinchen was able to ward off the attacks, but every time he was forced to do so, it gave Brigga Lin a moment of respite.

Unfortunately, Red had only so many knives, so finally he was forced into close quarters with his last two knives. The three spun in a flurry of violence. The Vinchen was in the center, pivoting and spinning in his gleaming black armor while Brigga Lin in her flowing white gown and Red in his sleek gray suit both danced around him, never quite connecting, but never quite losing, either. At least, not for a little while.

Then Racklock got past Brigga Lin's defenses. A bright red line welled up along her white sleeve, and her arm went limp. Brigga Lin's face creased in pain and she began to falter. Red lunged in more boldly than he should have. It got Racklock's attention, but left him open as well. Racklock parried the thrust, similar to the way the other Vinchen had done to Jilly. But then his sword continued in the same arc so that the fist holding the sword was past Red's guard. His knuckles smashed into Red's face.

Red stumbled back, his eyes glazed and his nose gushing blood, but Racklock didn't press his advantage. He immediately turned and renewed his attack on the weakening Brigga Lin. She'd managed to heal her arm in the pause, but the blood loss was still taking its toll.

"They can't last much longer," Vaderton said quietly.

Jilly glanced at him, wanting to object, but knowing he was right. So she pressed her lips together, and looked back to the battle. That was when her eyes caught movement on the rooftop on the far side of the square. She saw a figure that hadn't been up there a moment ago, who now stood gazing down at the battle in Visionary Square.

Jilly smiled. "I don't think they need to."

The figure on the roof didn't wear the black leather of a Vinchen warrior, or the dashing coat and hat of a pirate captain, but it was unmistakably Hope. She wore a simple black robe, like some strange inverse of a biomancer, with the hood thrown back, and her blond hair gleamed in the afternoon sun. She didn't appear to be armed in any way, but the look on her face was more fearsome than any Jilly had seen before.

"Racklock!" she called down to him.

Racklock froze, allowing both Brigga Lin and Red

to stumble back to a safe distance. He snapped the
Song of Swords so that the blood from Brigga Lin's
arm splashed across the cobblestones.

"Bleak Hope." He spat it out like it was a curse.

"You sully the honor of the Vinchen order beyond
bearing, just as Hurlo said you would." Hope's
voice rang through the square. "Though I am no
true Vinchen, it seems you insist that I be the one to
stop you."

"At last!" Racklock held out his arms as if to
embrace her. "Come and fight me, you blasphem-
ing peasant whore. It is my fate to take the Vinchen
order in a glorious new direction. Your friends are
all but dead. You are the only thing that stands in my
way. So come! Show me you are at least capable of an
honorable death!"

15

*H*ope leapt down from the roof, her black robes billowing around her as she landed before the current grandteacher of the Vinchen order. Innocent bystanders gathered fearfully along the edges of the square, prevented from escaping by the Vinchen. Hope didn't understand why they were being kept prisoner until she saw Jilly and Vaderton among them on the far side. Racklock would not want anyone associated with Brigga Lin to escape.

Brigga Lin looked wounded and exhausted, but still alive. Hope hadn't expected Red to be with her. When she first saw him, she'd lost her composure for a moment. She'd had to push him completely from her mind before she could act. Now she allowed herself only a quick glance to make certain he wasn't mortally wounded. Then she gave her complete attention to Racklock.

The memory of when he had beaten her within an inch of her life came quickly and vividly to mind. She had only been a little girl then, but there were many nights after when she'd woken in a cold sweat, haunted by the combination of recollection and nightmare.

Yet she was even more surprised that such an intense memory no longer kindled any fear within her. As terrible as that moment had been, it had also been her first step down the path of the warrior. Even more than the pain of that beating, she remembered the surge of relief she'd felt when Hurlo had challenged her not to be a victim to her own suffering, but to use it for her betterment. That had been his greatest lesson. And she *had* become better. Time and again, with each new challenge, she had forced herself not to flinch or look away. She had allowed herself to grow. She did not fear this man any longer.

She felt doubt, of course. It had become her ever-present companion since she'd left the battlefield of Dawn's Light and renounced the sword. But she didn't try to banish that doubt. It was her reminder to never again fall sway to the vainglory that had consumed her as Dire Bane. This doubt told her that her chances of success were low. After all, Racklock wielded the Song of Sorrows, and she had no weapon at all. But she accepted that without fear. She would find a better way. Or she would die trying, just as Hurlo had.

And so she stood before him, alone, no sword in her hand, nothing but a smile on her lips.

Her smile seemed to enrage him. His thick, broad shoulders heaved up and down. "I will kill you, blasphemer!"

"You are welcome to try," she said.

His style was aggressive. Swift and fierce. One blow, particularly from the Song of Sorrows, would mean death. He was so fast that even with her new ability to compress her time, she might not have been able to avoid him.

But as he swung the blade, something happened that she didn't expect. When the sword came rushing toward her with its fateful hum, she understood the song.

Perhaps it was because of those many months of having the sword connected directly to her nervous system, but its song was not just in her ear. It also hummed in her veins. Her forearm tingled just as it used to. The song told her not only where the blade was, but also where it was about to be, as if it wished to warn her.

So she dodged the blow with a casual grace.

He stood there stupidly for a moment, the sword extended, as if he could not conceive of having missed an unarmed target so completely. There were several gasps from the Vinchen observing nearby. When he heard those, his eyes narrowed down to wrathful slits, and the fight began in earnest.

He was a formidable opponent. Even with the constant whispered warnings of the sword, she was hard-pressed to avoid his blows. In truth, she was awed by his unique combination of precise form and brutal savagery. No movement was wasted. Every strike was a death blow. He unleashed them in a flurry of flashing steel that continually pushed her back as she dodged, ducked, or leapt to avoid his attacks.

But he had already been a grown man when she was a girl of eight. She didn't know how old he was now, but she could tell that his stamina was not what it once had been. He didn't seem to be aware of it, but as he pushed her back and forth across the square, he was gradually slowing down. Soon, his face was flushed and sweaty, and his blows were not only slower, but ever so slightly clumsy. That was when she made her move.

As the sword swung toward her in a wide arc, she waited until it was close, then she compressed her time. In the single moment of a breath, she stepped backward out of the sword's path, then reached forward with her new metal hand and took hold of the tip of the Song of Sorrows between the three curved prongs. She nudged it ever so slightly in the opposite direction to stop its momentum.

Then time snapped back into place, and the sword's hum stopped. Hope stood holding the tip of the Song of Sorrows, her eyes gazing intently into Racklock's.

He stared down at the greatest sword ever forged as if it had betrayed him. And perhaps it had. Or perhaps he had betrayed it.

Still holding the tip of the blade, Hope delivered a roundhouse kick that broke his forearm.

She released the blade and it nearly fell to the ground. But Racklock caught the handle with his other hand.

"I don't need both hands to defeat you, peasant whore!" he screamed, the balance of precision and rage shifting strongly toward the latter. That made him careless and sloppy.

She avoided a few more blows, watching as his technique continued to degrade. Then she caught the blade again, and broke his other arm the same way.

This time, the Song of Sorrows clattered to the cobblestones. Racklock stood before her, his arms hanging useless at his sides. His face was a twisted, inhuman mask of rage as he screamed incoherently at her.

She could kill him. A swift blow to the throat would crush his windpipe, especially if she used her claw. But killing was not what she did anymore. Instead she swept his feet out from under him. Judging by the sharp crack, she may have broken one of his ankles while doing so.

He lay there, howling in pain and anger and shame. Then he rolled onto his side like a beached seal, and glared at the other Vinchen. By this time, they had abandoned their posts, letting the bystanders escape, and moved in to gather around this battle, such as it was.

"What are you waiting for?" he screamed. "Kill her!"

The Vinchen who had been guarding Jilly and Vaderton had been the only one hanging back. Perhaps because he knew his wards were friends of Brigga Lin's. Perhaps he even knew they were friends of Hope's. He put his hand on the hilt of his sword. Hope knew that she couldn't get through all the other Vinchen and reach him before he drew his sword and struck Jilly, even if she compressed time. But that didn't mean she wouldn't try.

Then the young Vinchen said, "This was an honorable battle between two renowned warriors. To step in now would dishonor you, and us, even beyond the dishonor you have already brought to the order." He gripped the handle of his sword firmly, as if preparing to draw it. "But if you would prefer death over living with a defeat at the hands of your sworn enemy, I will gladly grant you that wish."

He kept his hand on his sword, and waited for an answer.

"Traitors...," moaned Racklock. "Betrayers... You have doomed the order!"

Hope walked slowly toward the young brother. The other Vinchen shuffled uneasily out of her path like errant schoolchildren, none of them meeting her gaze.

When she reached the Vinchen who had spoken, she put her hand on his sword arm.

"What is your name, young brother?"

"Stephan," he said, his eyes guarded.

"Regardless of what the code says, Stephan, it has been my experience that there is never honor in needless death."

"Though they trouble me, your words ring true," he said stiffly and released his sword.

She smiled gently at him. Had she sounded that formal once? She supposed so. Now she looked at the rest of them, these fresh, inexperienced, and troubled young warriors who, despite their tough demeanor and extensive training, clearly needed some words of comfort. They must all feel the dishonor their grandteacher had brought them.

"I don't think you have doomed the order," she told them. "Perhaps, like me, you will find a new path." She gestured to the dead bodies of innocents lying nearby. "One that will allow you to redeem the dishonor that has been brought to the Vinchen name."

"Well, now. When did you get so pat at making speeches?"

Hope felt a wrenching in her heart as a voice reached her that she had not heard in over a year, and yet recognized instantly. A voice that kindled both a deep longing, and an icy dread.

She turned and saw him standing there. He wore a lacy coat and shirt. His hair was longer, his posture more wary. His nose was a little swollen, possibly broken. But there was no mistaking those twinkling crimson eyes or that mischievous grin.

It was Red.

Or was it? Progul Bon said he had changed him, and she was painfully aware that biomancers didn't lie. Brigga Lin had explained the reason to her once. It wasn't that they *couldn't* lie, but that falsehoods and broken vows degraded the power their will held over life. And if there was one thing about biomancers you could count on, it was that they never willingly gave up power.

So who was she looking at now? The man she had longed to see for the past year? Or some biomancer demon in the shape of him?

———

There wasn't a doubt in Red's mind. It was Hope.

To be sure, she looked different from the last time he'd seen her stumbling out of the palace with Brigga

Lin on that terrible night more than a year ago. She'd traded her black leather armor for a black hooded robe. Her lost hand had been replaced with some sort of fancy mechanical contraption that had probably been built by Alash. And there was something different about those dark blue eyes. They were just as deep and fathomless as ever, but they were not so hard. There was a generosity to them. An empathy that was usually born from a great deal of suffering. His heart ached to think of how it might have come about, and that he hadn't been by her side when it happened.

Despite those changes, it was still her, and he couldn't help but grin stupidly as he looked at her.

But she didn't return his smile. Instead, she gazed at him with those blue eyes, her yellow hair whipping in the breeze. She looked apprehensive. Fearful, even.

"Hope…it's me." His voice faltered. It was a stupid thing to say. Who else would he be?

But she asked, "Is it?"

"What do you mean? Of *course* it is!" He took a step toward her, but when he saw her stiffen, he stopped.

Brigga Lin spoke up. "Progul Bon led us to believe that you had been…altered. That you were no longer the man we knew." Her hands were poised, probably ready to turn him inside out with a flick of her wrist.

Red looked back and forth helplessly between them. This was not how he had expected it to go at all. Damn Progul Bon. Even in death he could mess things up.

"You're both full of balls and pricks." Jilly stepped over to stand protectively next to him. "He's the same Red as ever. He fought by Brigga Lin's side and everything. Saved her life, I'd say."

"Jilly, you know that biomancers do not lie," Brigga Lin said. "Perhaps this new Red seeks to gain our confidence until he can carry out orders to kill us." Her eyes turned back to Red. "Perhaps he himself is not even aware of his orders. It would not be beyond Progul Bon's ability to create such a split within a person's mind."

Red had hoped to put the whole Shadow Demon thing behind him. Maybe it was dishonest, but he hadn't wanted Hope to know that he'd been a puppet of the biomancers, doing their dirty work. After all, it wasn't like it mattered now. The Shadow Demon was gone. Well, maybe not gone, but under control. Regardless, it looked like the only way he was going to convince them that he was himself again was if he told them the whole pissing thing.

"Progul Bon wasn't lying when he told you that," Red said quietly. "I *was* under their control."

"Red?" Jilly looked up at him, leaning away, perhaps unconsciously.

"It was just like you said," he told Brigga Lin. "I was one person during the day, and a different person at night." He shook his head. "Not even a person. A...monster. And I did a lot of terrible things as that monster. I don't know for how long. Weeks, months. It's hard to say for sure, since I don't remember it. I only know what other people told me."

Hope's face was tense, haunted. Her arms wrapped around her torso like her insides ached. He'd forgotten how beautiful she was, even without smiling. The hard, sleek lines of her alabaster face balanced with the velvet pink of her lips. Her long, elegant eyelashes balanced with the light, rugged spatter of freckles across her nose. He'd just seen her take out one of the most fearsome warriors in the empire, unarmed. And now, seeing her like this, unsure and conflicted... made him want to rush over to her and pull her to him. Although he knew that was probably the worst thing he could do right now.

"But I got free of their control," he said instead. "That monster is gone. I swear."

"How did you get free?" asked Brigga Lin, her tone strangely neutral. "Overlaying a secondary mind needs to be carefully woven into the host mind. It's not something one simply discards like a piece of clothing."

"I don't really understand how it happened," confessed Red. "A friend of mine took me to this… wisewoman on Lesser Basheta. Sort of like Old Yammy, but not as nice. She had me do some stuff, and I think she was also doing something? Although honestly it looked like she was just sitting there. Eventually I passed out, and when I woke up, I was fine. Even when I got back to Stonepeak, and the biomancers tried to command me again, it didn't work. I'm free. I don't know how I can prove that, but it's true."

He looked pleadingly at Hope. "You have to believe me."

———

Hope felt like her heart was being slowly turned in her chest, like the winch on a ship that raises the anchor. She knew that Brigga Lin's caution was the most logical and pragmatic approach. But when she looked at Red, all she saw was Red. Even in his current fear and frustration, his voice was like cool water on her burning skin. There was so much she wanted to tell him. So much she *needed* to tell him. And there he was, after all this time, right in front of her. And he looked completely brokenhearted in a way she'd never seen before.

Of course, that could merely be an act. He was, according to Broom, a fine actor. Perhaps that's what Brigga Lin was thinking.

But if he wasn't faking it, then she was now bringing new and completely unnecessary suffering into his life. She was *hurting* him, and that was one thing she never wanted to do.

How could she tell if he was being truthful or dishonest? Trust him, and potentially welcome a cold-hearted biomancer assassin? Or distrust him, and potentially break the heart of the person she cared about more than anyone? It hardly seemed fair that after everything else they'd gone through, both together and apart, it now came down to this simple, unsolvable riddle.

Experience had taught her that the world wasn't always the way we wanted it to be, and it sure as piss was rarely fair. But wisdom had taught her that sometimes the world was how we chose to see it. And if there was no "solution" to this riddle, perhaps the only choice to make was the one she felt in her gut was right.

Hope walked slowly over to Red. She noticed a tremor beneath his eye she'd never seen before. A strange twitch brought on by fear of discovery? Or the pain she had caused him by not rushing immediately into his arms? She didn't know. Maybe she would find out.

She laid her one good hand gently on his cheek. He hadn't shaved recently, and his stubble felt rough against her palm. He closed his eyes when she touched him, and she felt a shudder run through him as he leaned into her hand.

"I believe you," she said quietly. "Not because you have somehow convinced me, or that you have charmed me into thinking there is no risk. I believe you because having you back in my life is worth the risk."

His eyes remained closed, but his mouth parted slightly, and his warm breath escaped against the inside of her wrist. His lips were large for a man's—sensual and expressive. It was what made his grin look so pronounced. But when he wasn't smiling, his lips did something else. They invited her in. When she saw his mouth was soft and open like this, something caught in her chest, and she felt the short space between the two of them as if it was something warm and alive.

She had never kissed anyone before. It honestly hadn't even occurred to her to do so. She'd felt affectionate impulses, of course. Grasping a hand, patting a shoulder. The rough fondness of comrades-in-arms. The rowdy bonds of friendship. Those she knew very well. But this was a gentler, more vulnerable impulse. And yet, there was also an intense heat to it that kindled deep within her. She had no guard against it. No countermeasure to put in place to protect herself. A warrior should always be aware of her surroundings, and yet, everything around her slid away until there was nothing but the pull she felt toward him. It was a longing that had stretched across the empire and over a year without breaking, and yet now seemed unwilling to bear even a moment with a few inches of distance. There was, she decided, no need to be strong *all* the time.

So she pulled him to her. She felt the heat of his stomach and chest against her as she pressed her lips onto his. She felt his own doubt and fear be replaced with an intense hunger that matched her own. The smell of him, earthy and spicy, was heady this close, and she could not quite clear her mind. Soft sighs escaped his mouth in the moments when his lips weren't pressed against hers, and his hands clutched desperately against her back as she held him closer than she'd ever held anyone in her life.

Hope knew something about the elasticity of time, of course. That it was subjective and strange, and not altogether accountable. But she had never before felt it rendered completely meaningless. Somehow beyond words and expression, she and Red were reconnecting, reaching through time with all the joy and suffering it had brought each of them. Hope was always Hope, and so even in this moment of passion, there was a small part in the back of her head that said, *Aha! This is something new to understand!* But that didn't take away from the way it felt to have him back, to have him *more* than back. And if there was still some sort of biomancer control, she would find a way to tear its grasp from him. She would burn it with the white flame of her own passion, if that's what it took. Because she was not letting him go again. Not ever.

But just as time can be forgiving and elastic, it inevitably reasserts itself. And so after an unclear number of minutes, Hope gradually became aware that she and Red were kissing in public in front of a bunch of people, including a group of fully armed and perhaps not entirely friendly Vinchen warriors, and a few dead bodies. She might have felt the sting of shame or embarrassment at the inappropriateness of it, if this kiss hadn't felt so long in coming and, frankly, so well earned. So instead she just gently disengaged, and smiled at him.

"I should have known you'd be able to free yourself from the biomancers."

"I'm a bit offended, really," he said. "I hope you weren't fretting about it too much while you were off having adventures."

"It may have caused some worry now and then," she admitted.

Then a sharp pang of guilt hit her in the gut like a rock. She grabbed his hand and squeezed. "Red, I'm so sorry. Sadie, and Filler—"

"It's okay," he said quickly, wrapping both his hands around hers. "I know all about it. Nettles told me everything."

Another pang of guilt. "Nettles…"

"That's not on you. None of it is on you, keen? We each make our choices, and we have to respect the choices others make. Besides, I wouldn't give up on the old *Black Rose* quite yet. She might still surprise us all." He smiled happily. "Someday I want to show you the mural I made for Filler and Sadie. I think it'll help."

"Mural?" asked Hope.

The old rakish twinkle returned to his eyes. "I might have taken up painting again. Art is good for the soul, it seems. Those doing it as well as those viewing it."

"I look forward to seeing it." Hope turned to the others, who all looked uncomfortable to varying degrees, but were either kind enough or courteous enough, or perhaps simply too shocked to have interrupted.

"Sorry, everyone," she said.

"Is the kissing over?" Jilly asked sourly.

"I owe you another apology as well, Jilly," said Hope. "You and Brigga Lin. The three of us made a commitment to each other, and in my doubt and fear, I broke that commitment."

Brigga Lin shook her head. "Even though I was physically present, I also broke my promise to Jilly. The two of us have proved to be unworthy teachers."

Jilly's eyes flashed warily back and forth between them. It was in moments like this that Hope remembered Jilly had grown up on the hard streets of downtown New Laven. That she was someone used to getting let down. It made Hope sick to think she'd only confirmed that worldview.

"Yeah, well," Jilly said finally. "I've messed up a time or two. Seeing as how this was your first try at being teachers, I reckon I'll give you another chance. If you want it. I still want to be the world's first biomancer Vinchen, after all."

"I'm sorry, *what*?" said Stephan.

"It's nothing you need to concern yourself with,

boy," Brigga Lin told him in a tone that bordered on contempt.

"I plan to pass on everything I have learned, which includes the Vinchen arts passed down to me by Hurlo the Cunning," Hope told him with what she hoped was a much more cordial tone. "But of course she won't be an actual Vinchen."

"That's right," said Brigga Lin. "She won't be encumbered by your order's misogynistic and myopic attitudes."

To Hope's surprise, Stephan seemed more hurt than offended, and didn't try to defend himself or his order. The other Vinchen seemed to look to him, and so they followed his lead, saying nothing. They all seemed so young and unsure of themselves.

"What happened to the older brothers?" she asked. "Brother Yeta? Brother Kentish? I know there was more than this when I left." She may not have been friends with any of them, but she remembered them well. After all, she had watched them, cooked and cleaned for them for years.

"They left Galemoor with us," said Stephan.

"Except old Brother Wentu," said a different Vinchen.

Stephan nodded. "That's right. He remained behind. In retrospect, he must have seen, even then, that Racklock was becoming mad with power. The older brothers you name left us later, when Racklock decided to form an alliance with the biomancers. I'm not sure where they went, although I doubt they went back to Galemoor. I'm ashamed to say we destroyed it when we left. It...seemed an important gesture at the time. We were so caught up in Racklock's fervor."

"Manay the True built the temple well," said Hope. "You didn't destroy it completely. Brother Wentu and I did some work to restore it. The rest of the repairs may take some time, but with enough willing hands, it could be accomplished."

"Even in this you prove yourself a better Vinchen," said Stephan.

"Stephan, that's…blasphemy," said a third Vinchen.

"Is it, Malveu?" he asked, turning on his brother. "To commend someone, man or woman, for restoring the rightful home and temple of the Vinchen order? You call *that* blasphemy?"

Malveu was silent.

"I'm sure this is a very important discussion," said Vaderton. "But perhaps we could do it somewhere other than in the middle of a square strewn with dead bodies?"

"It's not like the imps are likely to cause much problem," said Red. "Since thanks to your man over there"—he nodded to the now-unconscious form of Racklock—"there aren't any. But we've probably drawn more than enough attention to ourselves already today."

"We will need to bury our dead first," said Stephan quietly.

Hope noted that there were four townspeople who had been killed during the fight before she had arrived. "It's commendable to care for these innocents."

Stephan looked at her steadily. "I meant *our* people as well."

"*Your* people?" she asked.

"Oh, uh…" Red looked suddenly sheepish. "I *may* have killed one of them when we were making our escape from the Past Is Forgotten."

"That was Frache," said Stephan. "There is also Hectory."

He pointed to a small pile of pulp beneath one of the buildings. It took Hope a moment to realize it was a head.

"Where is…the rest of him?" she said.

He pointed wordlessly to a headless corpse on the roof of the building.

"Who did that?" Hope looked at Brigga Lin and

Red, but it didn't seem like the sort of thing either of them was likely to do.

"*He* did." Stephan looked at Racklock, and the fury on his face was unmistakable.

"He...killed one of his own students?" she asked, not quite able to believe it. A teacher could be hard. Cruel, even. But the punishment of death was only for the very worst crimes, such as Hurlo's heresy when he trained Hope. "What could he have possibly done to warrant that?"

"He objected to the slaughter of innocents." Stephan's voice was bitter, but he seemed more angry with himself now than anything else. Perhaps he regretted not speaking up as well.

"Right." Red rubbed his hands briskly together. "So, four townsfolk and two Vinchen. Plus, we'll have to lug around old broken bones here if you're not going to kill him. Jilly? Vaderton? Let's go get a wagon. We're going to need it."

As the three of them trooped off, the Vinchen whispered quietly among one another, probably trying to decide what they should do with Racklock, and how much they could trust Hope. It must all be very confusing for them.

While they discussed among themselves, Hope knelt down next to the Song of Sorrows. Ignoring the unconscious Racklock, she gently wiped the sticky, drying blood from the blade. She pulled the sheath from Racklock's belt and slid the sword home.

"I'm sorry, old friend," she whispered. "Perhaps you can finally rest now."

She stood back up and handed the sheathed sword to Stephan.

"I would ask you not to ever use this sword lightly, or without honor. It suffers greatly when you do."

"How can a sword suffer?"

She shook her head. "I don't know, really. But this

sword and I have been through a great deal together, and I can tell you that the Song of Sorrows is not just a name."

"And you're simply . . . giving it to me?"

She nodded. "I love this blade, and it has taught me much. But I can't walk its path any longer."

He bowed and took the sword from her, although he suddenly looked a little apprehensive in holding it.

As he should be, she thought.

While they waited for Red to return, Hope learned the names of the other Vinchen and a little bit about them. Just as she suspected, they were all young and inexperienced. Stephan seemed to have emerged as their leader, although more from the conviction of his fury over the loss of his fellow brothers than from any actual leadership ability. That would come in time, of course. It was odd, though. Hope felt strangely protective of them, as if she could somehow steer them on a better path than the one Racklock had taken them.

"Well, this should be big enough," said Red as he pulled a wagon into the square. He sat in the front, holding the reins, a big grin on his face. Jilly sat next to him, looking very pleased with herself as well. Hope thought it was pretty likely they hadn't gotten the wagon or the horse by honest means, but she knew that asking Red not to steal was like asking Brigga Lin not to gruesomely murder people who angered her. And really, when seen in that light, stealing didn't seem so bad.

"Wonderful," she said instead. "Now all we need is a boat."

Vaderton's hand rose slowly from the back of the otherwise empty wagon. "I suppose that's where I come in."

16

*R*ed knew that lacies often buried their dead in the ground, but that had always seemed a little unsettling to him. Maybe he just wasn't used to the idea, since he'd never lived anywhere where there was enough dirt to do something like that. But the thought of taking the body of someone you loved and sticking it in the filth and muck of the earth, with bugs and worms and the like . . . it made his stomach squirm just to think about it.

Nea had told him once that there was a region of Aukbontar where people held air burials. Apparently, the trees were so big and so dense in that part of the country that it would have been impossible to dig a proper hole among all the overlapping roots. What's more, there wasn't a body of water large enough for a sea burial within twenty miles. So instead they climbed as high as they could on the tallest tree they could find, and they laid their loved one's body so that it was cradled in the branches, and after saying some suitable words, simply climbed back down. Apparently the birds and insects up there took care of the rest. An air burial didn't sit too bad with Red. In fact, there was a strange sort of loveliness about it, being left up there high above the world.

But like any proper wag of the Circle, it was a burial at sea that seemed best to him. To be slipped gently back into the place where all life began. The place where storms come from. A place that was slow, and dark, and quiet. That's where Red wanted his body to end up when he died.

As he drove the wagon of dead bodies through the streets of the Shade District, he was glad everyone else agreed that a burial at sea was best. Of course, they couldn't exactly ask the family or friends of the dead townspeople, since they'd very understandably fled in terror as soon as they were able. Anyway, there weren't really any other options. Vance Post was more dock than actual land, and there wasn't a tree higher than ten feet in the whole place.

In Paradise Circle, as often as not, a person was simply tossed off a pier. But a proper burial at sea should be done far from land. Partly this was to reduce the risk of a bloated corpse showing up a day or two later a few miles down the coast. It was also because, in a true burial at sea, the body should sink forever into the watery blue, gone completely before it ever touched the ocean floor. Unless there were sharks or seals nearby, it needed to be deep enough to give the smaller sea creatures time to completely decompose the body on its way down.

It hadn't been a pleasant task to gather the bodies and pile them in the wagon. It hadn't been easy to lower the headless one down from the roof on a rope, either, but simply tossing it over the side seemed far too disrespectful. The barkeep at the Past Is Forgotten had been very grateful that they'd taken the dead Vinchen off his hands. As they loaded up the wagon, they didn't bother to keep Racklock separate from the dead. They just tied him up and tossed him back there, broken bones and all. The endless, agonizing pain was keeping him mostly unconscious, but they'd remember not to toss him overboard with the rest. Probably.

Now Red steered the wagon slowly toward the pier where Vaderton's ship was docked, and most of the company walked alongside. The wagon couldn't have gone fast anyway, what with one horse hauling seven bodies, plus Red and Jilly.

The main docks were wide enough and sturdy enough to allow the horse-drawn wagon through. But then they had to turn off into one of the smaller branches to reach Vaderton's ship. And that's when the real work began. Red was able to convince the dockhands to lend them a couple of wheelbarrows, neglecting to mention what would be put inside them, of course. But even so, the wheelbarrows would hold only two bodies at a time, so it took a few trips down the rickety side dock before they were all loaded onto Vaderton's ship. And then there was another complication.

"You call this a ship?" Hope asked plaintively as they stared at the tiny, one-masted vessel. "I would call this a *boat*."

"Don't be so fussy," Vaderton advised. "We'll fit."

"Not comfortably," said Brigga Lin.

They couldn't just pile all the bodies in the stern, of course. On such a small vessel, the weight needed to be distributed as evenly as possible to minimize the danger of capsizing it. So the bodies were spread out around the ship, from bow to stern. And that meant the passengers were forced to spread out among the dead. Thankfully, they had been dead for only a couple of hours, so decomposition was still in its early stages and the smell wasn't too terrible. Even so, the bodies, both living and dead, weighed down the small ship, so it was slow going out of the piers and into open waters.

Spending that much time with corpses in close quarters was more unsettling than Red had expected. But finally, when Vance Post was only a smudge on the horizon, Hope decided they were far enough out to cast the dead back into the sea.

Red truly had no idea what to make of Hope. She was just as he remembered her in so many ways. Her seriousness, her compassion, her dedication and honor. If anything, another year of life had only added to her beauty. But there were some things about her he found surprising, such as her refusal to use a sword and her reluctance to kill. He didn't know where these new resolutions came from, but he figured she'd tell him when she was ready. The other thing that had changed was her ease with command. She ordered everyone around, friends and Vinchen alike, as if she'd grown up in Stonepeak. Even Brigga Lin deferred to her. And yet, there was never a sense that she was looking down on any of them. She treated everyone with sensitivity and respect. Red had to admit it was damn sexy to watch.

"What?" said Hope when she caught him staring at her.

He just smiled and shook his head. She squinted at him for a moment, then returned his smile with one of her own.

That was another thing different about her. She was, in her own understated way, *flirting* with him. Not that he was complaining at all. In fact, as he began to untie the corpses and get them ready to meet their end, he realized he was happier than he'd ever been. Maybe that was selfish and wrong, considering the circumstances. Flirting over a bunch of dead bodies was more than a little grotesque, really. But he couldn't help it. After losing so many other people, he was finally with the person he'd been afraid he'd never see again.

"Someone should probably say something." Hope looked around, but no one seemed particularly eager. Finally her eyes settled on Red. "Well?"

"I suppose I could speak a little something." He climbed up onto the gunwale and held on to one of the shrouds. He looked around at the strange gathering, some of whom he didn't know and didn't trust in the slightest, others he'd recently gotten to know, and a couple he'd known for a while.

"*The Book of Storms* says that many thousands of years ago, we all lived under the ocean. But since it was impossible to talk underwater, we didn't have language, and that meant we didn't have a proper civilization. Then God made the first storm, and it was so powerful, it brought many islands to the surface, and us with it. Only then, when we came to live above the water, were we able to form words, and language, and culture, and ships, and everything that we think defines us. And that's all real sunny. But with the good came the bad. With civilization came cruelty and injustice. So to my mind, there's a certain rightness that when we die, we're allowed to leave all that behind. To go back to the sea, and a simpler time, when people were just people. Who knows? Maybe that's what Heaven is like."

There was a moment of silence. Some looked down at their feet, some looked at the dead, and some looked out at the rolling sea all around them.

Finally Hope said, "Thank you, Red. Now, let's see this through."

And so, one by one, they carefully and respectfully returned each of the dead to the sea, where there were no power-hungry swordsmen or biomancers or trigger-happy assassins to make them suffer anymore. When it was finished, there was much more room on the boat and everyone took their space, each lost in their own thoughts. Without a word, Vaderton turned the boat and headed back toward Vance Post, which was now just a silhouette in the purple and red sky of sunset.

It was near dark when they reached the docks.

"What will you do with Racklock?" Hope asked Stephan.

"Set his bones, of course. But beyond that, I'm not sure."

"Once he's had a few days to heal, I'd like to talk to him," she said. "Would that be okay?"

"Of course," he said. "Where are you staying?"

"The Broadside Inn on Salt Road," said Hope.

"I'll send word once he's stable," Stephan promised.

Red watched the Vinchen march off down the dock, carrying Racklock in a makeshift stretcher made from two old oars and a bit of sailcloth. Even then they moved in perfect formation. He wondered if they were aware of how silly they looked trooping down the street like that. Probably not.

Hope turned to him. "We should probably head back to my lodgings and make sure your cousin is doing okay alone with Uter."

"Uter?" he asked.

"Have you picked up another stray?" asked Brigga Lin.

"Are you saying *I* was a stray?" asked Jilly.

"I *know* I was a stray," said Vaderton.

Hope smiled. "It's a long story. I'll fill you all in on the way."

————

Once Hope had told them about Uter, Brigga Lin had a lot of follow-up questions for her about wighting, the necromancers, and the Jackal Lords. Red felt a little left out, and not just because he'd missed their confrontation with a real Jackal Lord. The way Hope and Brigga Lin talked to each other made it clear that they had a close and easy friendship. It was a sharp reminder to Red that Brigga Lin and Alash had actually spent more time with Hope than he had.

He felt the ugly stirrings of jealousy, and he didn't like that at all, so to take his mind off of it, he turned to Jilly and Vaderton. "So how do you two know each other? Through Hope?"

Vaderton shook his head. "Jilly sailed under me when I was the captain of an imperial frigate."

"I didn't think they let girls sail on imperial naval ships."

Jilly gave him a satisfied smirk. "They don't. I pretended to be a boy."

"Really?"

"Had *me* fooled," admitted Vaderton. "Although I'm not sure you could pull it off anymore. You've grown quite a lot in the last year."

"I could still pull it off," Jilly asserted. "I can do pretty much anything if I set my mind to it."

Red laughed. "That's my Little Bee."

She grinned up at him for a moment. But then the smile faded away. "You hear about Filler and Sadie?"

Red nodded. "Nettles told me."

"Is...*she* okay?"

"Hard to say. I'm not sure how much of herself she's given up to become the Black Rose of Paradise Circle."

"Sometimes letting go of who you were is a good thing," said Vaderton. "I like to think I'm a far better man now than I was when I captained the *Guardian*."

"Nicer, anyway," said Jilly.

"Maybe the same will be true of the Black Rose," said Red. "Better at least. Probably not nicer."

"Nettles being nice would be kind of creepy," agreed Jilly.

A short time later, they arrived at an inn in the Commercial District called the Broadside. It was small, but neat and clean. Exactly the sort of place he would expect Hope to pick.

It occurred to him that he kept grabbing eagerly at any sign that he still knew her. He wasn't sure why he needed that comfort, and he didn't like the fear it implied. Hope had said things were all chum and larder between them. Hells, he'd even gotten a kiss as proof. What was he worried about?

When they entered the lobby, Hope glanced at the innkeeper, who sat behind a desk, then at the older couple sitting and talking quietly at a small table.

"Let's all go up to the room rather than calling them down," she said. "It'll be a little cramped with all of us in there at once, but if Uter is feeling overly...friendly, I'd rather not risk any bystanders getting hurt."

"You're worried he might try to kill someone?" asked Brigga Lin. "A little boy?"

"I think I've trained it out of him," said Hope. "Mostly."

"Maybe if you didn't give him weapons?" suggested Vaderton.

"I *don't*!" Hope said a little defensively. "Somehow he keeps finding them on his own. No matter where we are, he's always able to get his little hands on something sharp. Last night he snatched a corkscrew from the serving woman at dinner and tried to make her his 'friend' so she'd give him another dessert."

"Sounds like a wag with his priorities in line. I can't wait to meet him," said Red.

"Do *not* encourage it," she told him sternly.

They followed her up the stairs and down the hall to a well-scrubbed wooden door. Hope rapped on the door with her knuckles.

"Alash, Uter, I'm back."

"Everything okay?" Alash called through the door.

"Yes. Uter, I'm bringing a few new people in with me. They're already friends, so you don't need to *do* anything except say hello. Understand?"

"You *sure* they're already friends?" came a piping little voice.

"Positive," Hope said firmly. "We're all coming in now."

She opened the door. Inside was a small room with two beds and a mat laid out on the floor with a pillow. Alash sat on one of the beds with a book in his hands. He looked very different from the last time Red had seen him. Healthy and strong, like he'd done a great deal of honest labor. Next to him was a small, wiry boy with bone-white skin and hair, just as Hope had described him. He wore a plain beige smock and big black boots that clunked loudly on the floor when he jumped to his feet and hurried over to them.

"That's a lot of friends!" he chirped.

"Why don't you move aside so we can all come in," suggested Hope.

As he stepped to one side, Uter gaped up at Brigga Lin. "Are you a *queen*?"

She let out a rich, throaty laugh. "No, I'm not a queen, little boy. But I like you already."

"This is our friend Brigga Lin," said Hope. Then she turned to Red. "And this is our friend Red."

"You have fun eyes," Uter told him.

"Thanks," said Red.

"This is Captain Vaderton," Hope told Uter.

"Not really much of a captain these days," said Vaderton, "but pleased to make your acquaintance." He held out his hand to the boy.

The boy looked at it strangely, like he didn't know what to do with it. But then his eyes strayed to Jilly, and suddenly it was like the rest of the room ceased to matter.

"Who are *you*?" he asked her.

"I'm Jilly," she said guardedly.

"Are we friends?" he asked.

"I guess," she told him. "But I'm older than you, so you have to do what I say."

"Okay!" he said happily. "What do you want me to do?"

"Uhh..." Jilly looked taken aback. "Well, nothing

right now. But just, you better mind me when I tell you something."

"Sure," he agreed. "You ever seen a whale? I did, and it was very big. At first, I thought it was an *island*, that's how big it was!"

As Uter continued his attempt to impress Jilly with his knowledge of whales and other sea creatures, Red turned back to look at Alash. There was clearly something going on between his cousin and Brigga Lin. A thick, palpable tension.

"Ms. Lin." Alash had risen from the bed, and now he bowed stiffly to her.

"Alash..." She seemed to weigh something in her mind. "I'm sorry—"

"It is *I* who should apologize," he said quickly. "For putting you in such an awkward position. I promise, I will never do so again."

She gave him a strange look, then nodded. "Thank you."

Hope looked around at everyone pressed in together in the small space and smiled ruefully. "I suppose we'll need to let a few more rooms. It won't be cheap, but we'll need somewhere to stay until we decide on our next move."

"Don't worry about money for the rooms," said Red. "I'll take care of that."

"Oh?" asked Hope. "I take it you liberated it from some lacy before you left Stonepeak?"

"Actually, I earned it honestly," Red said.

"*You* got a *job*?" asked Jilly. "Doing what?"

This would be a tricky topic to introduce, and he was well aware there was a lot riding on how well they received it. So he would ease them in slowly. "Okay, so you know that friend who helped me shake the biomancer control?"

"The one who took you to this 'wisewoman,'" said Brigga Lin.

Red nodded. "I guess you could say that I felt I owed her for that."

"Certainly," said Hope.

"So when she asked me to come work for her, it seemed like the right thing to do."

Hope's eyes narrowed. "And…where does she work?"

"She's the imperial chief of espionage."

Hope stared at him for a moment. "The what?"

"Chief of espionage?" asked Vaderton. "I'd always thought that was a myth."

"I did, too," admitted Brigga Lin.

"Wait. You've both heard of this person?" Hope asked them.

"In a manner of speaking," said Brigga Lin. "There was always talk, even amongst the biomancers, of a shadowy, mysterious figure who scurried around in the background, enacting various schemes, but it all seemed a bit unlikely to me."

"Whenever Lord Gelmat handed down an unpopular order to the admirals, there were always rumors of him being pressured by some network of imperial spies. But like Brigga Lin, I thought it was just long talk among the captains."

Hope turned back to Red. "But this person is real, and you went to work for her as a spy?"

"At first," said Red. "But it turns out that secrecy and subtlety don't exactly play to my strengths."

Hope's eyebrow raised. "I never would have guessed."

"Are you *teasing* me?"

She smiled and shrugged. "So, once you realized you were no good at spying? What then?"

"She asked me to come find you and Brigga Lin."

Hope's expression suddenly cooled. "Why?"

Red already knew she'd be a little uncomfortable with the idea of working within the imperial power structure. After all, she didn't know the full picture like he did yet. But he knew she'd like the goal. "To ask you to help us get rid of the biomancers once and for all."

"Us?" She didn't seem to immediately grasp what he was saying. "So you've already allied yourself with this...chief of spies?"

"Like I said, she's been a true friend. Helped me out of a situation I don't think I could have gotten out of otherwise. But I think you're missing the point here."

"Oh?" Her blue eyes were now as cold and hard as ice. That had definitely not been the best way to phrase it. "What is it you think I'm missing?"

"That we're working to take care of the biomancer problem *for good*."

"No, I heard that part," said Hope. "It sounds like the emperor has lost control of his favorite toys and wants us to come in and clean up his mess for him."

"It's not like that," said Red, although even as he said it, he had to admit to himself it was a bit like that. The emperor *had* lost control, just decades ago, rather than recently. But saying that probably wouldn't help his case any. "Look, the emperor doesn't even really matter anymore. He's old and bedridden and doesn't do much of anything. It's the empress who's pushing for this."

"A *woman* allowed the biomancers to run amok?" asked Hope. "That's even worse."

This was not going Red's way at all. He suddenly flashed back to that tavern when he'd tried to convince Hope not to storm the palace. He'd known even as he argued that he was failing. It couldn't be like that again. He wouldn't let it. He would convince her somehow.

"I thought this was what you wanted. To get rid of the biomancers."

"I *do* want to stop their abuse of power," said Hope. "But allying myself with a different abusive power to do so doesn't make sense to me. Especially since Brigga Lin and I were already fighting the biomancers on our own."

"And with some measure of success," said Brigga Lin.

Red nodded agreeably. "Sure, but think how much faster you could get it done if you worked with the empress."

"At what cost?" asked Hope. "What would we have to concede in order to bring about such an alliance?"

"Nothing!" said Red. "The empress just wants your help. If anything, *you* could demand some kind of payment or boon from *her*."

"As long as we do it *her* way," said Hope. "The imperial way, which has never shown itself to care even the slightest about the needs of the common people." She shook her head. "I don't understand how you, of all people, could be okay with this."

"Because I *know* these people. They aren't faceless symbols of power to me. They're real people who are genuinely trying to do the best they can with a difficult situation that they inherited from someone else."

Hope turned to Brigga Lin. "You've been invited to this...coalition, too. What are your thoughts?"

"You've more or less said what I was going to say," Brigga Lin told her. "Except you were nicer about it."

"You're both looking at this all wrong." said Red, trying to keep his voice calm, but knowing there was an edge of desperation coming to it. It was like that pissing tavern all over again.

"Oh, our feelings on the matter are *wrong*?" asked Brigga Lin, sounding almost amused. "How kind of you to tell us."

"I didn't mean it like that..." Why was he messing this up so badly?

Hope looked around the small room. Everyone was jammed in there so tight, there was no way any of them could avoid this conversation. "What about the rest of you?"

"I don't know, cousin." Alash looked at Red apologetically. "Sending *you* of all people to parlay seems a little...manipulative on their part."

"I've been betrayed once by the empire," Vaderton declared. "I'm not inclined to allow that to happen again."

Jilly looked guiltily at Red. "I mean, come on, Red. Joining with the imps? Don't seem right, does it?"

Red looked around the room. *All* of them? Everyone except the crazy white-haired boy, who probably had no idea what was even going on, was against this?

"I can't believe it," he said quietly.

Hope turned back to Red. Her eyes were sorrowful, but firm.

"I'm sorry, Red. I'm glad the empire is finally taking a firm hand against the biomancers, but that doesn't exonerate them from decades of gross misuse of power. We will see the end of the biomancers, but we will do it our way, not theirs."

17

*L*ady Merivale Hempist loved listening to music.
Well, perhaps *listening* wasn't the right word.
More precisely, she loved being in the room while
music was being played.

With Red gone, Prince Leston had poured a lot of
his energy into forcing his fellow nobles to appreciate
the fine arts as much as his friend did. He had been
inspired to take this more active role in the artistic
community by Ambassador Omnipora when she
remarked on the lack of concerts being performed at
the palace. Apparently, the Great Congress of Aukbontar not only invited musicians to play for them on
a regular basis, but also funded a number of artists,
performers, and musicians. Her Congress espoused
the idea that culture was the true measure of a soci-
ety. Naturally, Leston had picked up on Nea's sug-
gestion immediately. He had sponsored several art
showings at various galleries in the city, including
one with the rather lurid work Red had done in the
few months before his departure. The prince also
began to invite small orchestras to perform at the
palace. Attendance by the nobility was not manda-
tory, but anyone who hoped to curry favor with the
future ruler of the empire made a point of showing
up, so they were generally well attended.

Merivale was not particularly knowledgeable

about music, nor had it ever held a great deal of interest for her. But she attended the first concert out of curiosity, as much to see who was trying to please the prince as anything else. Unexpectedly, she found she quite enjoyed herself. She wasn't really aware of paying attention to the music, but each week, as she sat in the ballroom with twenty to thirty other lords and ladies and listened to the light, yet complicated weave of melodies coming from violins, violas, and cellos, she was able to allow her mind to wander in ways that were both unexpected and highly rewarding. For some reason, music allowed her to temporarily shake off her habitual pragmatism and consider more unconventional ideas.

For example, that night, as the orchestra crescendoed with the last strains of their final piece for the evening, Merivale was pondering the true nature of governance and thinking she would like to have a long conversation with the ambassador on how, exactly, a representative democracy worked.

As she slowly filed out of the ballroom with the other attendees, the prince walked up beside her. "Lady Hempist." He offered her his arm.

She slipped her arm through his and said, "Good evening, Your Highness. Another lovely concert."

"I'm surprised you've taken such an interest," he said.

"I delight in surprising people," she said.

"Any word from Rixidenteron?"

"Not since you and I spoke."

"Do you think they're searching for him? The uh..." He glanced around, trying to look unobtrusive and failing. Then he whispered, "The *biomancers*?"

"I knew who you meant, Your Highness," said Merivale. "And no, I don't think they are actively searching for him."

"Well, that's good, isn't it?"

"Not if the reason is because they have something even worse planned," she said, thinking of their new military command puppet, Archlord Tramasta.

"What else could they be planning?"

"I'll let you know when I find out," she told him. He looked surprised. "Will you?"

"Tell you? Eventually."

His eyes went flat. "When I become emperor?"

"Something like that."

"Will you at least keep me up to date on how Rixidenteron is doing?"

"As much as I am permitted to do so," said Merivale.

"I suppose that's the best I can ask for."

"It is from me," she told him. "You could always ask your mother."

"I think she'd be even less inclined to tell me anything substantive."

"Probably," Merivale agreed cheerfully. "I suppose you'll have to rely on me, then, Your Highness. Now, if you'll excuse me, I have some work to attend to." She curtsied deeply to him and turned to leave.

"Lady Hempist." He gave her an uncharacteristically grave look. "Do you ever wonder if by supposedly protecting me, you are putting the empire at even more risk?"

Up until that moment, she had not. But when he asked that question, she decided she should consider it.

When she returned to her apartments, she intended to go through the most recent reports from her spy network. There was a great deal of chatter across the empire regarding the return of the Vinchen. Word of Racklock's decimation of the Shade District police force had spread, and many, particularly in the lower classes, were construing it as some sort of anti-imperial statement. That the Vinchen were even encouraging open rebellion against the emperor. Given what Merivale knew of Racklock and his current allegiance with the biomancers, this seemed highly unlikely. But even if it wasn't an intentional rallying cry, it could still be an effective one. And the last thing the throne needed in this perilous time was riots in the streets. Unless...

She opened the door to her apartments and found Hume standing just inside. It might not have been obvious to most people, but with the creased brow and firm set at the corners of his mouth, she could tell he was terribly agitated.

"Good evening, Hume." She handed him her shawl. "Is everything all right?"

"A...guest is waiting for you in the parlor, my lady," he told her. "I suggested he return later when you were present, as I did not know precisely when you would be home, but he insisted on remaining."

"My, my," said Merivale. "And who is this guest?"

"He introduced himself as Ammon Set, chief of the Council of Biomancery."

"I see," said Merivale. "Naturally, you've already offered him a drink?"

"He declined, my lady."

"Well, I would very much like a drink. Please fetch me a glass of wine while I see to our guest."

"Right away, my lady."

When Merivale entered her parlor, she found the presence of the biomancer almost laughably incongruous. While it was true she favored a minimal, almost austere decor, the furniture and the few pieces she had on the walls were exquisite works of beauty. They clashed terribly with Ammon Set, who was neither exquisite nor beautiful.

The chief of the Council of Biomancery sat in a high-backed chair made of fine Lesser Basheta wood with his dry, cracked hands on the lap of his dusty white robes. His hood was pushed back to reveal his rough-hewn, hairless head. The more powerful a biomancer became, the more their work altered their appearance. And as far as Merivale knew, Ammon Set was the most powerful biomancer in the world. When she'd first come to the palace during her teenage years, his skin had still looked somewhat like flesh. Now it looked like sandstone that had been chiseled into an approximation of a human being. His face looked like crude sculpture, his eyes like chunks of stained glass, his teeth like flecks of mica, his tongue a slab of quartz. She hadn't seen him show a facial expression in years, and wasn't sure he still could. His jaw moved up and down as if on a hinge. Merivale had always wondered if he'd had to split it at one point so that he could continue to talk. It seemed like the sort of thing he would do.

In all the years she had observed the chief of the order of biomancery, she had learned that there was nothing he wouldn't do to accomplish his goals. He was, she had to admit, a formidable adversary. Up until now she had enjoyed the luxury that he was unaware they were adversaries. Now, she suspected, that was no longer the case.

"Lady Hempist," he said in his dusty voice. He didn't bother to rise from his chair.

"Ammon Set." She gave him a light curtsy. "To what do I owe the pleasure?"

"Pleasure? I doubt it," he said. "Still, it appears that I and the Council of Biomancery have greatly underestimated you."

"Everyone does. I wouldn't beat yourself up about it," she told him as she accepted a glass of wine from Hume. "Thank you, Hume. That will be all."

Hume nodded and quickly left, though of course, just to the next room where he could still hear everything. One of the nice things about working with someone for such a long time was that Merivale and Hume really didn't need to communicate a great deal to each other anymore. If Set was here to kill her, there probably wasn't much either of them could do about it. However, Hume would immediately ride for Sunset Point to inform the empress so that she could plan accordingly.

"I suppose that's the point," said Ammon Set. "Your ruse as a shallow, fashion-obsessed, marriage-hungry noble."

"The fashion-obsessed part is actually true," said Merivale. "We must all have our weaknesses."

There was a quiet grinding sound, and Set's rocky lips tilted slightly. Merivale wondered if that was his version of a smile.

"I must say," he said, "I am disappointed that neither I, nor anyone on the council, was informed of your important role in the government."

She gave him a full, dazzling smile. Tramasta had revealed her position to the biomancers, but perhaps they didn't suspect her of having an agenda counter to their wishes yet. Maybe there was a way to wiggle out of this.

"Progul Bon was quite aware of my activities," she said.

She didn't actually know if Bon had known she was chief of espionage, but she was fairly certain that if he *had* known, he would have kept it to himself. Like her, Bon had been a schemer. And schemers never gave up any information freely, even to supposed allies. What's more, she guessed Ammon Set was also aware Bon possessed those qualities.

"I see," he said, giving her all the confirmation she needed.

"I always wondered if he kept the rest of the council in the loop," she said. "But of course it was none of my business. I do try to keep clear of the affairs of your council as much as possible."

"Which may explain why we have never had the chance to work together," said Ammon Set. "I confess I find it frustrating. The council could have made great use of an imperial spy network."

"I hadn't realized I could be of use to you," said Merivale. "In the future, simply put in a formal request to His Majesty, and I will be happy to consider it."

"Naturally, you are aware that the emperor is bedridden and unable to speak."

"Yes, I'd heard as much," said Merivale. "But surely he'll rally, as he always does."

"Perhaps not this time," said Set.

"Ah," said Merivale. She wondered if this meant they were finally going to let the poor old man die. But if that was so, they must have another plan in place that would allow them to maintain power. Something to do with that "ultimate sacrifice" Chiffet Mek had spoken of.

Ammon Set still hadn't said anything that indicated he suspected her of working against him. Perhaps she could take that even further...

She gave a resigned sigh and dropped down into the chair opposite Ammon Set. Then she gave him a knowing smile. "Well, it was good while it lasted, wasn't it? I suppose I'd better get used to someone telling me what to do again."

He paused for a long moment, his stony face and glassy eyes unreadable. Did he buy her overture?

Finally, he said, "It *has* been nice to have so much autonomy, hasn't it?"

"I'm so glad you agree! Why, I haven't received a direct order from the emperor in years. And the empress...well, I'm sure you know, the jewel of the empire is a lovely, but exceedingly delicate creature."

She leaned in conspiratorially. "And to be perfectly honest, I feel I've accomplished far more for the empire without their meddling."

"It may be that we won't have to give up all we've managed to accomplish, Lady Hempist," said Ammon Set.

"Oh?"

"I have studied the history of mankind in great detail. And the one thing you can be certain of is that nothing lasts forever. Change is imminent."

"Are you speaking of Aukbontar's recent diplomatic attempts?"

"In a sense," he said carefully.

She leaned over and patted his rough, craggy hand. There was no warmth or humanity in it. "I don't think you need to worry a great deal about that," she assured him.

"How so?"

"Well, this sort of thing *does* fall into my jurisdiction, after all. I and several of my people have inserted ourselves into their confidences. Everything about them, from their true political and economic motives, to more... personal information, is known to me."

"Is that so?" Ammon Set's head tilted to one side, which seemed to indicate increased interest.

"They must be handled delicately, of course." She smiled. "After all, we wouldn't want to start an international incident, would we?"

"Of course not," he said.

"Can you believe some imbecile tried to assassinate the ambassador? Twice?" She shook her head. "Really, if I ever find out which party is responsible for such a fiasco, I'll have strong words with them, I can assure you. International relations cannot be handled with such brute-force tactics. They require finesse, artfulness, and a great deal of deception."

He paused again. "I had heard that you spend a great deal of time with the ambassador. I was concerned about that when I learned of your true role as chief of espionage because it appeared your sympathies might be in her favor."

"Naturally it *seems* that way," said Merivale. "Because I am very good at my job." The best kind of lies were ones that aligned very closely with the truth. The fact was, she actually did consider the ambassador another potential adversary, once she managed to settle the current domestic conflict. "One thing you can count on when dealing with spies: Nothing is ever what it seems."

"So I am starting to understand," said Ammon Set. "Perhaps...you and I could work together toward a mutually beneficial future."

"I am fond of building alliances," said Merivale. "But you will find when dealing with me that everything is an exchange. If the ambassador is a concern of yours, I can provide you with a wealth of information about her and her people. For example, her supposed motives, as well as her *true* motives. But I will expect something in return of equal value."

"No wonder you and Progul Bon got along," said Ammon Set. "Very well, what would you consider to be of equal value? Are you still troubled by that incident concerning the Vinchen on Vance Post, as Tramasta informed me?"

She waved her hand dismissively. "Ultimately, that's his jurisdiction. My interest was only in offering my services to him and initiating a positive professional relationship with the new chief of military."

"You truly are a political animal, aren't you, Lady Hempist," said Ammon Set.

"It's gratifying to be appreciated, Ammon Set." She leaned in toward him and smiled. "Now, what I *really* want to know is how you plan to make certain we retain our autonomy in what I presume to be the forthcoming transition from Emperor Martarkis to his son, Leston."

———

Merivale listened to Ammon Set's plan with her usual cool detachment. Once he left, she allowed herself to truly feel some measure of shock and dismay at the sheer scope and boldness of what he intended to do. But only for a few minutes. If the empire was to be saved, she would have to take countermeasures immediately. It began with writing a letter:

To the Black Rose of Paradise Circle,

Our mutual friend, Red, suggested I get in touch with you regarding a possible alliance. First let me express my heartfelt thanks regarding your contribution to the events on Dawn's Light. Months later, I am still discovering new opportunities that would not have been possible without the death of Progul Bon, lead biomancer on that most odious project.

I am also gratified to hear that a respected leader of the community such as yourself wishes to take an even more direct role in making our empire safe and secure against the tyranny of the biomancers. I understand that in return you ask for an audience with the empress. Based on some initial reports regarding your history and general practice, I have some idea what it is you plan to discuss with her. As luck would have it, my thoughts have been leaning in that direction myself. So be assured that I will support your cause in whatever way I can.

I invite you to come directly and with all due haste to Sunset Point on the north-west peninsula of Stonepeak, where the empress spends the majority of her time. Events are unfolding which concern all of us, and time is of the essence. I would also ask that you bring as many of what Red would call "true wags" on your ship as you can fit. I will explain the reason for this when you arrive, but know that it will benefit both of us greatly. Also bring guns. Lots of guns.

If this is agreeable to you, please indicate as much to the person bearing this message, as well as an approximate date for your arrival at Sunset Point.

Most sincerely,
Lady Merivale Hempist

Merivale looked over the letter, rereading it several times. So much for her reluctance to align herself with ganglords. She would have to smooth it over with the empress, especially if she was right about what the Black Rose wanted in exchange for her services. But this was not a time to shy away from bold measures.

A swift messenger on a fast ship could reach Paradise Circle in a few days, but Merivale had no idea how long it would take the Black Rose to marshal a small force and sail up to Stonepeak. A week? Two? Entirely too close to Ammon Set's timetable for her liking. Still, there wasn't much to be done about that.

She sealed the letter, then rang the small bell on her desk.

Hume appeared in the doorway. "My lady?"

"See that this gets to Paradise Circle and directly into the hands of the Black Rose as quickly as possible. The messenger will need to return immediately with a reply."

"I will enlist our most reliable courier, my lady," said Hume as he gravely took the envelope. He looked at it, then back at her. "Is that the *only* message to deliver?"

Hume had heard the entirety of Ammon Set's plans along with her. She knew what he was asking. Really, it was quite lovely the way that Hume had taken to the former Lord Pastinas. His concern was touching.

"I'm afraid Red didn't indicate any way to reach him once he arrived on Vance Post," she told him. "I'm not sure a warning would do much good, anyway. I fear that what's heading toward Vance Post is beyond even his abilities. At this point, I don't think we can count on him, or his promised reinforcements, being any help in the coming conflict, even if they somehow survive."

18

The Painted Caves of Pauper's Prayer were said to be one of the great wonders of the empire. The island itself wasn't much to look at. A squat, mountainous lump dotted with scrawny trees and brush. It was only when you entered the bay on the southern side of the island and saw the entrance to the caverns that you began to realize that what you were seeing was only the outer shell of the true island.

Entoch the Hermit was the lone inhabitant of Pauper's Prayer. Bream didn't know a great deal about where Entoch had come from, other than that he was of noble birth and he'd studied art at the imperial academy. Many thought he was insane. Bream felt there was some truth to that, although not as much as people claimed. Most folks couldn't understand why someone would choose to live out their life in seclusion, all alone. But Bream had dealt with enough awful people in the world that he could see how the idea might hold some appeal.

Bream had come to the island for the first time some five years earlier. He was a merchant, and it had been a slow summer. On a lark, he decided to bring the wife and kids aboard his fastest ship and treat them to a trip to the famed Painted Caves. It wasn't an easy voyage. The waters in that part of the empire where the currents of the Dark and Dawn Seas clashed were unpredictable, raked by sudden storms or suffused with inexplicable calms, depending on the time of year. If Bream was being honest, he hadn't had much interest in seeing the caves himself. But he had figured, correctly, that the beauty of it would set his wife and kids in a good mood for months to come. What he hadn't figured on was stumbling across the most lucrative trading pact of his life while he was there.

Even someone like Bream had been awed by the caverns the first time he saw them. As his helmsman steered their ship through the narrow bay, he and his family had stood at the bow and watched the massive cave entrance draw near. It was big enough to allow their sloop to enter, mast and all. It would have been difficult to get it back out again, though, so instead they anchored just outside the entrance.

Bream had rowed his family the rest of the way in the jolly boat through the entrance to the rocky, interior shore. Most of his men stayed behind to watch the entrance. There were rumors that pirates sometimes used the caves as a hideout, and Bream was taking no chances with the fastest ship in his humble little merchant fleet. He also wasn't taking chances with his family's lives, or his own, so along with his wife, son, and daughter, he brought his first mate, Bilge Joe, and enough rifles for all of them. Just in case they stumbled across pirates during their explorations.

But they quickly forgot about rifles once they were in the caverns. It wasn't dark, like he'd thought. In fact, some rooms were so bright that he had to squint. Many of the walls were covered in giant slabs of crystal, which amplified even the tiniest bit of light that snuck in from cracks in the cave ceiling. Most of the crystal was colorless, but here and there were outcroppings of red, blue, green, and even the occasional purple. That, of course, was where the name Painted Caves came from. In some rooms, it was a dazzling display of brilliant, ever-changing color more won- drous than the temple on Stonepeak.

Bream and his family wandered the caverns aim- lessly for hours until they turned a sharp corner and were surprised to find a man in a ragged robe sitting in a small emerald-colored cave. His back was to them, and he appeared to be working intently on a painting.

"Hello there, good sir!" Bream called good-naturedly, which sent the artist into a near panic. When Bream finally calmed the man down, he learned that his name was Entoch, and that he'd come the year before to escape the world and only make art.

"I thought I'd have enough paint and canvas for several years at least," Entoch said, his eyes sparkling ruefully from his thick beard and long hair. "But this place is so drownedly beautiful, I haven't been able to pace myself. I'm already down to but a few canvases, and half the colors in my palette."

"I'm sure you're ready to get back to civilization, anyway," said Bream.

Entoch shook his shaggy head. "I would give any- thing to be able to just stay here and paint for the rest of my life."

Bream looked at the small painting on his easel. He was no art critic, but it seemed impressively done, somehow managing not only to capture the colors, but the light as well, as perfect as if he were looking at the thing itself.

"You must have a lot of paintings by now," Bream said. "Are the rest this good?"

Entoch jumped eagerly to his feet. "Come! I'll show you!" Then he hurried down a small passageway.

Bream and his family followed after the strange

artist, and soon they came to a large room that was only dimly lit. Paintings were stacked all along the walls. Some were realistic renderings of the caverns, like he'd seen in the emerald room. Others had people or animals in them.

"A lot of other people come here?" he asked, pointing to a painting of a rose-colored room he'd passed earlier. A family appeared to be having a picnic by the small pool of water in the center of the room.

"None," Entoch said. "That's why you surprised me." He nodded to the painting. "That was a dream I had. I suppose even I get lonely now and then, but then I dream of some people, and paint them, and I don't feel lonely for a while."

Bream's eyes were next drawn to a dramatic painting of a room filled with reds, blues, and purples. It appeared to be two men in a sword fight. "What about this one?"

"Ah! That one is from history!" Entoch said. "I stumbled across the room where Dire Bane made his last stand against Hurlo the Cunning. It was like I could almost see them both there, so I had to paint it."

Bream picked it up and examined it more carefully in the dim light. Dire Bane loomed over the lean, black-clad Vinchen, but he looked gray and weary—a jarring sight among the rainbow colors that surrounded him.

"It's good," he told Entoch. "I bet I could sell these back on Stonepeak for you."

"Money has no interest for me."

"Ah, but it interests *me* a great deal. I could sell these, and use the money to buy you more paints and supplies, minus, of course, my commission and expenses incurred in bringing the supplies to you."

Entoch's eyes lit up then. "You mean, I could stay

here and you would come and go, bringing me paints and canvases at regular intervals?"

"As long as you keep providing me with art to make it worth my while, we can do this as long as you like," Bream said.

Entoch grinned wide, showing surprisingly white teeth in his dense beard. "I accept your kind offer!"

Bream had known the paintings would sell. But he'd underestimated how well. Entoch's work became some of the most sought-after art in Stonepeak. He'd asked Entoch if he wanted a cut of the profit. After all, there was only so many paints and canvases a man could buy, and Bream prided himself on being an honest merchant that his children could look up to. But Entoch had politely declined. And so over the last five years, Bream had slowly amassed a fortune. Other merchants had tried to cut in on his business and buy paintings from Entoch, but the hermit always refused. They didn't understand how to talk to him. They didn't understand that for a man like Entoch, it was all about the art. While Bream didn't understand art, he had a broad mind and a willingness to grasp viewpoints that had nothing to do with his own. It was odd to think that such a quality was ultimately responsible for his becoming the most successful art dealer in the empire.

Bream arrived on Pauper's Pray at his usual interval. Along with the paints and canvases, he brought a bottle of whiskey. Not for Entoch, who seemed content to live on nothing but rainwater, lichen, and fish. But over the five years he'd been working with Entoch, Bream had gotten into the habit of spending one night in the caves with him whenever he visited. The hermit's conversation topics were often bizarre, but Bream found that a strong dose of whiskey made them quite enjoyable.

That night, the two men lay on soft beds of moss

Entoch had been patiently cultivating as sleeping mats in the room where the paintings were stored. A tiny sliver of moonlight slipped in through a crack in the ceiling to illuminate the newest painting, still drying on the easel.

"One of your dream paintings?" Bream pointed his bottle at the canvas, then took a sip.

Entoch smiled his usual, serene smile and shook his head. "No, that's something I actually saw the other day."

Bream choked on his whiskey, coughing for several moments before he could wheeze out, *"What?"*

"Magnificent, isn't it?" Entoch said dreamily.

Bream crawled on hands and knees over to the painting so he could get a better look. Instead of an interior, this was a painting of the coast as seen from the entrance of the caverns. The rocky shore of the bay stretched out on either side, with the wide-open sea in the distance. And rising from the sea was something so big, at first glance, it looked like a new islet had suddenly formed. But it wasn't a land mass. It was a massive, bulbous head half submerged in the sea. Just above the water level, a dark orange orb housing a thin black rectangle glared balefully out of the painting. Behind it, a few thick trunks that looked very likely to be giant tentacles rose from the water.

"Is that…a *kraken*?" asked Bream.

"I don't know what else it could be," said Entoch. "I'm so lucky to have caught a glimpse of it."

Bream shivered. "Wherever it's heading…those people are definitely *not* lucky."

PART THREE

In the end, I see now that my gravest mistake was in thinking that I must carry the burden on my own. But progress is never borne on the shoulders of one person. Instead it happens when many people come together with a unity of purpose.

Unfortunately, I cannot imagine a situation so dire that it would unite the people of this fractured empire. What a glorious and terrible day that would be...

—from the private journal of
Hurlo the Cunning

19

*H*ope had never thought a great deal about kissing before she kissed Red. Perhaps her overriding obsession with revenge throughout her girlhood had squelched such romantic inclinations. Even when the idea had occurred to her, it always seemed so trivial as to be hardly worth pursuing.

Yet now that she'd done it, she thought about kissing Red quite a lot. His firm, soft lips, the way that his hands had gripped her, the heat and closeness of him…if she let herself linger on the memories too long, she began to feel a little light-headed. It left her with a vague, gnawing hunger for more of him. Almost like a physical need.

But it seemed unlikely such a longing would be fulfilled now. He had clearly been hurt by her refusal to join his alliance with the empress. He wasn't brooding, exactly, but his cheerfulness seemed forced, and there was now a wall just behind his eyes.

She understood that it was personal for him. He cared about these people deeply. That was no surprise, because he was an extremely caring person, despite his attempts to appear otherwise, and he had spent about as much time with this Lady Hempist and Prince Leston as Hope had spent with Brigga Lin and Alash. What Hope didn't understand was why he ever thought she would join such an alliance in the first place. Did he know her so poorly? Or maybe it was that his own perspective had changed so much, it was hard for him to remember how he had once viewed the world. From the bottom up.

Well, one way or another, he *had* changed. Even more than she'd first thought. There was a focus to him that she'd never seen before, like he'd finally found a purpose to life other than chasing girls, winning games, and robbing the rich. And he didn't try so hard to seem pat all the time. Hope found both of these new qualities admirable. *Attractive*, even. And yet somehow they also came with a newfound loyalty to the throne, something she could hardly even comprehend, much less relate to. But, maddeningly, that did not lessen the attraction.

She'd worried that he might leave after she turned down his request. It made a certain amount of sense. He'd been tasked with recruiting them. He had failed. He should return to his chief of spies and report back. The fact that he decided to stay was both a relief and a concern. On one hand, she didn't know if she could bear to part with him again so soon. On the other hand, she worried that the reason he had decided to stay was because he believed there was still a chance he could convince her to join the empire.

As she sat in the lobby of the Broadside Inn, she glanced over to Red as he played a game of stones with Jilly at a nearby table. She'd never seen this nurturing side of him before either. She was grateful he was finally allowing her to see these depths to his personality. And yet...

She sighed. This push-pull of longing and distrust was expending far too much energy. She just didn't know how to stop.

She looked down at the folded sheet of paper that had been delivered that morning. It was written in a careful, yet still somehow messy script:

Dear Hope,

You mentioned that you would like to speak with Racklock when he had recovered enough to receive visitors. Although he is still in a great deal of pain, and will likely not be moving around for a while, I believe he is coherent enough to speak with you. I expect we will not stay on Vance Post much longer, so if you still wish to talk to him, I suggest you come as quickly as is convenient for you.

—Stephan

Hope folded the letter and put it in one of the deep pockets of her robe. Then she walked over to where Red and Jilly were playing stones.

"Where is everyone else?" she asked.

"Alash and Vaderton are working on the boat," said Jilly. "Brigga Lin is in our room, trying to teach Uter how to meditate or something."

"Go ask Brigga Lin to come down," said Hope. "And then I need you to look after Uter while we're gone."

"Me?" Jilly looked crestfallen. "I want to come with you!"

"We're going to pay a visit to the Vinchen. Things will be tense enough without someone like Uter around. So I need you to keep him here." She gave her a teasing smile. "Besides, he thinks of you as the big sister he never had."

She groaned. "The little brother I never wanted."

"Go," she told her.

"Yes, teacher." She rose from the table, and hurried up the stairs.

Hope stood there, and Red sat at the table fiddling with the numbered stones. It was these awkward silences that she hated most.

"Do you want me along?" he asked finally.

She looked at him. "I always want you along."

———

Sleeth Harbor Hotel, where the Vinchen were staying, was not what Hope had expected. It appeared to be the most opulent lodgings in all of Vance Post. It was six stories high and took most of the city block, with more columns, trellises, and balconies than many of the manor houses she had seen in Hollow Falls. It looked like the sort of place rich merchants went to be treated like nobility.

Hope stopped and stared at the building for a moment.

"Aren't Vinchen supposed to be ascetics?" murmured Red.

"Yes," said Hope.

"Do I…misunderstand the meaning of that word?"

"No. You don't." She shook her head in disgust. "I suppose there's no point in standing out here. Let's go in."

The interior was even more luxurious than the exterior. The fine furniture, crystal chandeliers, and lush tapestries rivaled the Hotel Sunset, where Thoriston and his wife had stayed in Silverback.

"Why didn't *we* stay here?" asked Brigga Lin.

Hope gave her a disapproving look.

"What?" Brigga Lin asked innocently. "The Vinchen may take vows of poverty and celibacy, but trust me, biomancers do not."

Hope walked across the lobby to a desk where a lacy old man in a jacket and cravat was looking at them in a very unwelcoming manner. Hope supposed she and her friends didn't look like the sort of people who could afford such opulence. Or perhaps he looked at everyone that way.

"Excuse me, perhaps you've lost your way," he told them pointedly.

"No," muttered Hope. "But it appears others may have."

"I'm not sure I understand, madam, but if you seek lodging, I will need to verify—"

"We've been invited by the Vinchen," Hope cut in. "Where are they staying?"

"Oh. Them," the old man said sourly. "Of *course* it would be them." He shook his head wearily and pointed to the last of three staircases. "Take those up to the top floor."

"Well, that's *some* show of frugality," said Brigga Lin. "The top floor is generally considered the least desirable."

"Say, maybe that's why they picked this hotel," said Red. "It's the tallest building in the district. I reckon climbing all those stairs is good exercise."

Hope rolled her eyes. "I suppose we're about to find out. Come on."

Six flights of evenly spaced, plushly carpeted stairs did *not* seem like much of a workout to Hope. Certainly not enough to justify selecting such an opulent hotel. At the very top of the stairs was a short landing, and a large, ornately carved wooden door. Hope banged loudly on it with her metal claw, not caring if it scuffed the wood.

The door opened a moment later, and one of the Vinchen opened the door. Hope wasn't sure of his name. He was stripped down to the waist, wearing only his leather pants and boots.

"Oh my," said Brigga Lin, eyeing his sleekly muscled torso appreciatively.

"We have been invited as guests," Hope told the Vinchen.

"Yes, you have," he said, and stepped aside.

Hope walked into the room, with Red and Brigga

Lin behind her. The narrow foyer opened into a
large, lavishly decorated living room. It was odd to
see the grim, hardened Vinchen warriors scattered
around such a place, some sharpening swords or
knives, others polishing their armor.

"Ah, you've come," said Stephan as he stood up
and pulled his leather jacket on over a thin linen
shirt and began to buckle it. He nodded to the shirtless Vinchen who had let them in. "Thank you,
Ravento." Then he turned back to Hope. "I wasn't
sure you still wanted to come."

"Yes..." Hope's eyes scanned the room. "Very
fine furnishings you've found for yourselves."

"Oh." Stephan looked away, and a faint blush
crept onto his cheeks. "Racklock chose it. He said...
well, it seems a bit silly now, but he said that before
Manay the True, there was no vow of poverty, and
we should just go back the way things were then. It,
uh, seemed persuasive at the time."

"I'll bet," said Hope. But the lengthy lecture she'd
been storing up dissolved in the face of his earnest
shame.

"Is it true?" Red asked curiously. "That Vinchen
lived in luxury before Manay the True?"

"Yes, back when they lived at the palace," said
Hope. "I suspect that Manay brought them down to
Stonepeak to escape the luxury as much as to escape
the politics. Both distract from the true focus of the
Vinchen."

Stephan smiled sadly. "Your words remind me of
when Hurlo was still living."

"Hurlo the *Cunning*," said Malveu, sitting nearby.
He was still in his linen undershirt, working black
polish into his armor. "We should return to calling
him by his proper name, as it will be remembered in
the history of the order."

Hope looked questioningly at Stephan. He again

looked embarrassed. "Racklock sought to discredit Hurlo the Cunning and remove him from the records."

"*Remove* him?" All gentleness left her. "After everything he did for the order? For the empire? For all of us?"

They remained silent. Each and every one of them. She looked around, daring one to meet her furious gaze. They knew it had been wrong. But they had been so cowed by Racklock that none of them had spoken up.

"Is your *grandteacher* able to talk to me?" she asked finally.

"We no longer recognize Racklock the Cruel as grandteacher," said Ravento as he sat down and began to work a nick out of his sword with a whetstone.

"We put it to a vote," Malveu said quickly. "As dictated by the code."

"He's awake," said Stephan, finally answering her question. "I will take you to him."

"Thank you," said Hope.

Stephan led them to one of the bedrooms. Inside, Racklock lay on top of a large four-poster bed. His arms and leg had been splinted, and he was chained to the bed. He looked up at them with haggard eyes when they entered, but didn't seem surprised.

"Come to gloat, blasphemer?" he growled.

Hope walked past him to the window. She kept her back to him as she picked at the lace curtain. "Curious choice of insult, given your own attitude toward the basic tenets of the order."

"We should be treated with the honor befitting our rank, not groveling like southern peasants," he said.

She was silent for a moment as she continued to examine the intricate design of the lace. Then she said, "I used to wonder whether it was my peasant background or my gender you hate most." She turned to face him. "Now, I simply don't care. I didn't come to gloat. I came seeking information."

He gave a short grunt. Or maybe it was a laugh. "And you think I will provide you with that information?"

"If you have any desire to see the order survive beyond your own ambition, then yes, I think you will."

"And you imagine yourself the savior of the order?" he asked mockingly.

"You know," she said as if she hadn't heard him. "In at least one respect, you and I actually agree."

His eyes narrowed. "Oh?"

"Just like you, I believe the Vinchen order should end its seclusion and return to the world."

"Really?" Racklock seemed genuinely surprised.

"While I understand Manay the True's reasoning in sequestering the Vinchen down in Galemoor, far away from the corrupting influence of the palace, it has allowed the order to become stagnant and rigid."

"Yes!" He struggled to rise, forgetting both the chains and broken bones in his sudden enthusiasm. He winced in pain and fell back on the bed, but his eyes still blazed. "We cannot continue as we are! Only obsolescence and death await us in the Southern Isles!"

Hope nodded. "But that isn't my only reason for wanting to leave Galemoor. The absence of the Vinchen these last few centuries has allowed the biomancers to go unchecked. They prey upon the good citizens of this empire like livestock. The Vinchen must once again become the protectors they were meant to be."

Racklock's body suddenly went lax, and his excitement was replaced with a bitter sneer. "I see. So it's coddling the weak you long for. I take back whatever I may have said in the past about your abilities as a student. You are Hurlo's perfect pupil, aren't you?"

Hope smiled. "Whether you meant that as a compliment or an insult, you're only partly right. I left Hurlo's instruction years ago. And while it's true he taught me many things, my view of the world is informed at least as much by what I have experienced since leaving Galemoor." She gave the broken old Vinchen a pitying look. "A world which you have only just begun to comprehend."

He closed his eyes. "I grow weary of your presence. Get out."

"I want to help the Vinchen adjust to this world. To *flourish* in it," said Hope. "Tell me what alliances or pledges you have committed them to, so I at least know what I'm working with."

He didn't open his eyes, but the bitter smile returned to his lips. "We pledged to kill you and your biomancer witch, for which service we would be welcomed back as the right hand of the emperor. So by all means, retain the honor of the order and fulfill that pledge."

"You swore this to the emperor?" she demanded.

He remained silent, a mocking smile on his bruised lips.

"He didn't swear it to the emperor, just the biomancers," said Red. "I was there when he spoke to the council."

"That's somewhat less problematic," said Hope.

"See?" Red's smile was a little tighter than usual. "Sometimes it's helpful to have someone on the inside."

Was he trying to convince her to join the "inside" again? Or was he just trying to prove to her that he wasn't bad for being on the inside? Hope didn't know. She wanted to ask, but not here in front of Racklock.

"You're *always* helpful, Red," she told him instead. "I'm done with this bitter old man. Let's talk to the other Vinchen and see what they intend to do next."

When they returned to the living room, Hope noticed that the Vinchen had all made themselves presentable. Armor was on and buckled, weapons had been sheathed and properly stored.

"Well?" she said. "What do you plan to do now?"

They looked uncertainly at each other.

"I suppose we should return to Galemoor?" said Malveu.

"I'm sure Brother Wentu would be eager to welcome you all back," said Hope. "But have you considered staying?"

"What do you mean?" asked Ravento.

"I know you don't recognize me as a true Vinchen, and I don't hold that against you. But if you will allow me to offer you some advice, I believe the time for hiding in Galemoor is over. For you, the younger generation of Vinchen, this is your opportunity to make a difference in the empire. To earn back the respect the order once held."

Stephan shook his head. "It's too late for that. Those who know us, resent us. And the rest simply don't care. Perhaps Racklock is right and the order is doomed. Perhaps it *should* be. Are we really anything more than a relic of a bygone romantic age?"

"That is just pathetic," said Brigga Lin. "I thought Vinchen were supposed to be resolute. Implacable. *She* certainly is." Brigga Lin gestured to Hope. "Are you telling me she's the only one? That the rest of you are merely petulant little children who now wish to run home at the first sign of failure?"

"Brigga Lin...," said Hope.

"No, no," said Brigga Lin. "It's this, or I literally vomit on them. Because I am *sick* of these—"

Hope put her hand on Brigga Lin's arm. "I know you're trying to help, but this isn't the way right now. Trust me."

Brigga Lin rolled her eyes but said nothing else.

"Just think about staying," Hope told the young men. "You could do a lot of good in the empire. Even if you never earn back the respect that the Vinchen of old enjoyed, isn't that enough?"

She didn't wait for their answer, but instead turned toward the door.

"That's it?" Red asked quietly. "We're leaving?"

"They'll need time to deliberate," she told him.

Ravento stood up from his chair and hurried to open the door in a sudden and unexpected show of courtesy.

But before Hope could leave, a great rending sound filled the air. It was like a thunderclap that went on too long, vibrating the glass in the windows for several seconds.

Once it subsided, Red said, "What in all hells was *that*?"

There was another sound, so loud it shook the floor beneath their feet. It was followed by the distant screams of people frightened or in pain.

"It's coming from east of here," said Hope.

They hurried over to the balcony door. Red yanked it open and Hope stepped out onto the open platform. Everyone else crowded after her into the small space. For a moment, Hope considered telling them to step back a little. But then she looked toward the coast of the Shade District, amid the extensive network of docks that splayed out like veins in a leaf, and saw something that took every other thought out of her head.

The kraken.

"Oh, God," she whispered.

The Guardian's bulbous head, which towered over even the tallest buildings, was speckled with barnacles. Caught in the rough exterior were rusted objects such as spears and anchors that would have pierced a grown man through, but seemed as negligible as splinters to the great sea monster. Eight arms, each longer than a city block and nearly as thick around as a sloop's waist, swept across the intricate network of docks that comprised a large portion of Vance Post, pulling up clusters of pylons like they were clumps of grass. It hurled the thick wooden poles into the city, where they took the roofs off buildings or crushed swaths of panicked bystanders in the streets.

"I'd heard about it, of course," Red said, his voice awed, "but I honestly wasn't sure if it was even real."

"I can't believe the Council of Biomancery sent the Guardian into such a heavily populated area," said Brigga Lin. "This...This is unprecedented. There's no research value in this. I can't think of any reason for this other than sheer wanton destruction."

"Perhaps the biomancers learned that we have abandoned our mission and seek to destroy you themselves," said Stephan.

"Surely if their only goal was our deaths, they could have found a more efficient means to do it," said Hope.

"Especially since we just have to sit tight here," said Red. "We're near the center of the island, and not even the kraken can throw *that* far."

"Alash!" Brigga Lin grabbed Hope's arm. "He and Vaderton are tinkering with that stupid boat! They're right in the middle of it!"

She shoved her way through the pack of Vinchen and hurried toward the door.

"Brigga Lin, wait! We need a *plan*!" called Hope.

But Brigga Lin either didn't hear or didn't care to make any plans, and kept moving.

Hope turned to Red. "Go with her. Keep her from getting herself killed."

Red nodded grimly, then followed after.

Hope turned to the Vinchen who still crowded around her. "Will you help?"

"What could swords possibly do against such a creature?" asked Ravento.

"There are hundreds of people hurt or dying right now, with many more to come. You could help them. This was what every Vinchen swore to do in the days of Selk the Brave," she said.

They looked uneasily at one another.

"Go to the Shade District," she urged them. "Rescue as many as you can. *Earn* the trust of the people. Show them the Vinchen are an ally, not another enemy."

As if to drive home what Hope was saying, another crash thundered outside. It sounded like an entire building had caved in. Screams of pain and fear filtered in through the louder sounds of destruction.

Finally, it was Stephan who said, "If you lead us, I will go." Then he dropped to one knee.

"As will I," said Ravento.

"As will I," said Malveu.

One by one, the Vinchen all dropped to one knee and asked her to lead them.

Hope would have been lying to herself if she tried to pretend she didn't feel a surge of satisfaction. Perhaps even triumph. All those years of being told she was not, and could never be, as good as them. And now it was they who declared her the most worthy.

But this was far too reminiscent of her recruitment on the Empty Cliffs for her to be comfortable with it. So next to that feeling of triumph, she carefully nestled the dark pearl of doubt and humility she had gained on Dawn's Light. She would keep it there to remind herself that leadership was not glory, but responsibility to the people she commanded.

"Very well," she said quietly. "I will lead you until this threat is past. Now, let us remind the world that the Vinchen can save as well as kill."

20

I'm sorry your negotiations with the emperor have stalled again."

Lady Merivale Hempist sat in a high-backed chair, her hands moving swiftly and efficiently as she knitted a long maroon scarf that was unlikely to ever be worn.

Ambassador Nea Omnipora sat opposite her in a matching chair, her guitar in her lap.

The ambassador inclined her head as she quietly picked out a melody on the strings. "It's frustrating. But the health of the emperor must come first. Is he likely to recover soon, do you think?"

"I'd say he's not likely to recover at all," said Merivale.

Nea paused in her strumming. "Oh?"

"He is nearly a hundred and fifty, after all," said Merivale pleasantly. "Not even biomancers can work miracles forever."

"I suppose," Nea said carefully.

Merivale smiled at her. "Don't worry, Ambassador. If all goes according to my designs, the next time you begin negotiations, the tone will be much more progressive."

"That is…encouraging," said Nea.

"I should probably mention, however, that it will absolutely get worse before it gets better." Merivale kept her tone light. Almost playful. "But that is the way of things, I suppose. Nothing we can do except our duty, isn't that right?"

"I strive always to do just that," agreed Nea.

It was clear the ambassador wanted to press Merivale further, but she was holding back. Perhaps out of a misplaced courtesy? Or fear of what she might learn? Or perhaps she was as crafty as Merivale suspected and knew that to ask outright would be to show weakness. A dependence on Merivale's intelligence-gathering. And yet, to *not* take advantage of that intelligence would be foolish. Such a conundrum for the poor ambassador. Merivale thought it best to throw her worthy adversary a bone. After all, their particular conflict would likely not come to fruition for several years yet. And in this current conflict, she hoped the ambassador might prove to be an invaluable ally.

"I go to speak to the empress this afternoon," she told Nea. "Alone, on a swift horse."

"I take it on a matter of some urgency."

"The utmost urgency," agreed Merivale.

"It is unlikely you'll share the specifics with me at present," said Nea.

"It is."

"So why tell me at all?"

"While I'm gone, you may wish to make certain all your people remain in your apartments. Just in case."

"Oh?"

"And if you have any...fortifications you could employ, I would utilize them."

"Fortifications?"

"Yes," said Merivale. "And weapons. If you don't *have* any weapons, speak with Hume on your way out. He'll furnish you with some. Just in case."

"Merivale, just what do you suspect is going to happen?"

Merivale pretended to think for a moment. "And

provisions. Yes, I would definitely set in some provisions. A week's worth perhaps?"

Nea gave her a hard look. "Just in case?"

Merivale smiled. "Exactly. One never knows when or where violence might erupt, and believe it or not, in my own way, I've grown rather fond of you, Ambassador."

Nea's eyes widened. "My lady, are you suggesting—"

"That you make it an early night? Absolutely," said Merivale. Then she put down her knitting and let the chipper artifice slip away. "You must hold out for three days. By then I will have returned with assistance."

"And to what do I owe this generosity?" asked Nea, still looking alarmed.

"Well, now that you mention it, I'd appreciate it if you would keep the prince with you. I'd hate for him to be captured by the opposing faction, and he's ever so fond of you, so I know he'll come quietly."

"*Opposing faction?*" Nea looked to be on the verge of panic now.

"Yes, Ambassador. Biomancers, to be precise. Perhaps you've heard of them? And possibly a large portion of the imperial military."

It was so rare that Merivale was able to rattle her, and she could not help but savor the look of astonishment on Nea's face. Then she smiled.

"Now, if you'll excuse me, I need to pack for my trip."

———

Merivale was grateful for the brisk ride through the countryside of western Stonepeak. It gave her time to think, and while she had always disliked sailing, she was rather fond of riding. As she rode west across the open grasslands, and then north along the coast, the sound of the horse's hooves thundered beneath her. Her hair was not done up as it usually was, but instead had been pulled back in a loose ponytail. She had also left behind her gowns in favor of the more practical riding jacket, pants, and boots. Thankfully, she happened to know she looked quite fetching in riding clothes.

Things had unraveled more quickly than she would have liked. She'd hoped to already have the Black Rose in place before the biomancers made their move. Instead, she had to set things in place as carefully as she could and hope that her people and the ambassador could handle the follow-through while she made haste out to Sunset Point to begin negotiating under the worst possible condition: weak bargaining leverage. If the Black Rose was as emotional and impulsive as Red, it would turn out fine. But if she was more calculating... well, things could get complicated.

As Merivale neared Sunset Point, she was relieved to see that the small dock remained empty. She'd been concerned that the Black Rose would arrive before her, and that the empress would begin the negotiations without her. Merivale had tremendous respect for the empress, of course. But royalty had little understanding of the true cost of things, and generally made terrible negotiators. Also, there was the small but pivotal matter of class separation between the two sides. Some sort of intermediary would be absolutely essential. And with Red on Vance Post, hopefully not being eaten by the kraken, Merivale would have to do the best she could on her own. Certainly, three intelligent women could sort out even a situation as dire as this.

Her horse clattered through the courtyard of the empress's home and skidded to a halt.

"My lady." Kurdem, head of the household ser-

vants, stood in his impeccable white uniform at the
front door. "Please go immediately to Her Majesty's
chambers. I will see that your horse is taken care of."

"I'm sorry to say I pushed him rather hard. Please
take special care," she told him.

"Yes, my lady."

Merivale handed Kurdem the reins, then hurried
inside.

The empress's interior design had been the primary inspiration for Merivale's own. Both women
appreciated an uncluttered, minimalist aesthetic.
But the empress's decorations were primarily muted
pastels in curved, flowing shapes, which gave visitors
a sense of calmness and tranquility. Merivale had
instead opted for hard geometric shapes and stark
color contrasts, mostly because she preferred to give
her guests a vague sense of unease.

Lady Hempist strode through the house, her riding boots clacking on the polished wood floors. She
paused at the door to the empress's chambers for a
moment and gathered herself together. It had been
a long ride, after all. She smoothed her hair and
clothes, and dusted off her boots with a handkerchief. Then she quietly knocked.

"Lady Hempist?" came the empress's calm voice.

"Yes, Your Majesty."

"Excellent. Do come in."

The empress was already in a formal gown to
receive guests. She stood at a window that overlooked
the Dusk Sea, which was just visible in the last rays
of the sun. She looked as inspiring as ever. A perfect
picture of mature grace, intellect, and femininity.

"What do you suppose is beyond that horizon?"
the empress asked quietly, her eyes still out to sea.

"Perhaps that mystery will be solved before the
end of our lifetimes," said Merivale.

"Yours, at least," said the empress darkly.

"Now, now, Your Majesty," Merivale said gently. "That's hardly the proper attitude."

Pysetcha sighed. "I suppose you're right. It's not like I can leave everything to Leston yet."

"Perhaps not everything quite yet, Your Majesty," agreed Merivale. "Although I'm happy to report that he seems to have matured somewhat during the last few months."

"Thank goodness for small miracles." The empress turned away from the darkening sea and looked at Merivale. "Now, to the matter at hand. Is everything ready?"

"As it can be, Your Majesty."

"And you really think the biomancers' response will be that swift and drastic?"

"I fear we've pushed them into a corner, and now they are desperate," said Merivale.

"But it seems so..." The empress shook her head. "It's hard to believe they would go so far."

"I have learned through experience never to doubt the length to which the biomancers will go to further their cause."

"But saving something by destroying it?" said Pysetcha. "It hardly makes sense."

"I have also learned never to count on the actions of biomancers to be particularly sane," said Merivale. "Although in their defense, it does have a kind of internal logic. If one begins with the premise that—"

There was a knock on the door.

"Sorry to interrupt, Your Majesty." Kurdem's voice sounded uncharacteristically shaky. "But there is a, uh, Black Rose and... *companions* here to see you."

"Thank you, Kurdem. Please send them in."

"Are you certain, Your Majesty? They are somewhat—"

"Kurdem?" A slight edge came to the empress's voice.

"Yes, Your Majesty. Right away," Kurdem replied
hastily.

The door opened. Kurdem looked pale and wor-
ried, but he quickly stepped aside and bowed low.
"The Black Rose of Paradise Circle to see Her
Imperial Majesty and Jewel of the Empire, Empress
Pysetcha."

The woman who stood in the doorway was short,
busty, and entirely inelegant, but she had a certain
coarse beauty that made the name "Black Rose"
oddly appropriate. She wore clothing similar to
Merivale's riding ensemble, although less well made,
and probably not just for riding. She also had a thin
metal chain coiled up at her hip, although Merivale
couldn't determine if it was an attempt at jewelry, or
a weapon of some kind.

Behind her stood two of the most unsettling
people Merivale had ever seen. One was what Merivale guessed to be a woman, although she couldn't
be certain, due to the ragged, shapeless clothes and
the matted, filthy hair that covered most of her face.
The other was a man in stark black-and-white formal wear, including a top hat, that might have been
in fashion half a century ago, but certainly no more
recently.

There was a moment of tense silence while the
empress waited for the Black Rose to make some sort
of curtsy or sign of respect, and the Black Rose waited
for God knew what.

This was why Merivale had nearly killed her favorite horse to get here in time. The empress had been
the most powerful woman in the empire for most of
her life, and in previous discussions with Merivale,
she'd had a difficult time comprehending that she
couldn't treat someone like the Black Rose as simply one of her subjects. But if Merivale had learned
anything from Red about the underclasses and the

folk culture of New Laven, it was that someone of the Black Rose's stature should be treated more like a visiting dignitary. Merivale had attempted to explain this at length to the empress, but here it was, the moment of truth, and it seemed all her careful coaching had fled from the empress's mind in the tension of this historic visit. So it would be up to Merivale. As usual.

"Welcome, Black Rose," Merivale said, giving her a completely unnecessary curtsy. "We are very glad you came."

"Yes, I am delighted to meet such a respected leader of the community," the empress said, always quick to recover.

"I thought you'd be a rotted old wrink," said the Black Rose in a hard, quiet voice. "But to speak true, you ain't bad on the gander."

Another pause.

Merivale turned to the empress. "The Black Rose has just praised your beauty."

The empress smiled warmly at the Black Rose. "You are very kind. But while my beauty is carefully cultured, yours is true and untamed."

Merivale inwardly winced at the word *untamed*, but if the Black Rose was offended, she gave no indication of it.

"And who are your companions?" continued the empress.

The Black Rose glanced back at the two odd people lurking silently behind her. "These two? They work for me."

"Ah, your bodyguards?" asked the empress.

The Black Rose's face hardened. "I don't need nobody to protect me."

"Naturally not," Merivale said quickly.

"It's for other people's protection I keep these two close," continued the Black Rose. "If I didn't have a hand on them, they'd murder everyone they come across."

"You hear the truth of that, Mister H?" asked the woman in a voice as ragged as she looked.

"It is a joy to be so well understood," said Mister H in a voice as ghostly as he looked.

"We appreciate your restraint," Merivale told the Black Rose. "There will be a time for murder, but this is not it."

The Black Rose narrowed her eyes. "Yeah, I was a little surprised when you asked me to come up with a big group of solid wags and a pile of guns."

"Our mutual friend has indicated that there is something you wish to ask of the empress. If she finds your request amenable, perhaps there is something you can do for her in return."

The Black Rose nodded. "Now you're speaking crystal. Something for something. I like it."

"So what is it you want, my dear?" asked the empress, her voice defaulting into the stately, regal tone that the lords and ladies loved, but Merivale had expressly urged her not to use with the Black Rose, since it sounded terribly condescending. Lords and ladies expected to be condescended to by their empress, but Merivale was fairly certain that ganglords did not.

The Black Rose looked at the empress for an uncomfortably long time. It occurred to Merivale that she might be doing it less from awkwardness, and more as a way to deliberately unnerve them. Merivale knew she could not make the mistake of underestimating this woman. Despite the Black Rose's lack of education, she was a tiny woman with a lot of power. Such things did not happen without a great deal of tenacity, ferocity, and cleverness.

Finally, the Black Rose broke eye contact with the empress and looked down at the thin metal chain coiled at her hip. She patted it fondly.

"One of the truest wags in the world made this for me some years back. He was real sunny, keen? Without even realizing, I used to bask in that brightness. But when he was murdered, I was left alone in the dark. And my vengeance was so cruel that even *wearing* this thing he made seemed an affront to his memory. So I put it aside, determined to make peace living without the light."

She looked suddenly at the empress, her eyes hard. "Because that's how it is in the Circle. It's something most of us have to do sooner or later."

The empress opened her mouth to speak, but it was clear she was struggling on how best to respond. Truthfully, Merivale wasn't sure there *was* a proper response to such a statement.

After a few moments, the Black Rose nodded and released the empress's gaze, as if satisfied with her speechlessness. Then she turned to look out the window. The sun had set, and only a glimmer of water could be seen in the moonlight.

The empress looked questioningly at Merivale, but Merivale continued to watch the Black Rose. Patience and caution were the best choices at present.

Then, to Merivale's surprise, a smile slowly grew on the Black Rose's dark, full lips.

"It's funny." The ganglord's voice softened slightly. "I guess Hope and them rubbed off on me more than I thought. Because to speak true, no matter how hard I tried, I *couldn't* make peace with the darkness. I wanted to hold this chain in my hands again with pride, the way he would have wanted." Her hand closed around the chain tightly so that her raw, scuffed knuckles whitened. "But to do that, I knew I had to earn it back." She looked back at the empress. "And that's where you come in."

"I'm not sure I understand," admitted the empress.

"I aim to make Paradise Circle better than it's ever

been before. Not just with dance halls and whore-houses and all that. I want to make it a *healthy* sort of place, where even the weak can prosper and feel safe. And to do that, the people of Paradise Circle need a real, proper say-so on what happens to their neighborhood. Not just me, but *everyone*. It needs to be something that can't be taken away after I'm dead."

The empress kept her calm demeanor, but clearly she had no idea what the Black Rose was proposing. That was probably for the best.

In truth, the idea was even more bold than Merivale anticipated. She had suspected that the Black Rose sought legitimacy. It was the most likely reason someone like her, who already had wealth and power, would want to meet with someone like the empress. But even then, Merivale had thought the Black Rose would be looking for a lordship and some property. Merivale had even begun considering whether to give her Pastinas Manor. She was certain Red would approve. But this... This was more than just a lordship. It was, in a sense, a revolution. Common people having a direct voice in their own governance. It made Merivale think back on that night at the orchestra when she'd begun to seriously consider the advantages of a representative government. Ever since then, she'd studied various methods of such government with increasing fascination. So this proposal, at this time, was quite thrilling to her.

But she kept her expression neutral as she turned to the empress. "The Black Rose seeks representation for the people of Paradise Circle at the palace."

"Yeah," said the Black Rose. "No special treatment. Just a seat at the table."

The empress's eyes slowly grew as she considered the full ramifications of the idea. At last she said, "That is simply—"

"An astonishing and profound request." Merivale

smoothly interrupted what she suspected would have been an outright rejection. She turned to the Black Rose and gave her most winning smile. "Would you be so kind as to let Kurdem see to your food and lodgings while the empress and I discuss the matter at length?"

Another smile flickered on the Black Rose's lips. "I keen. Sure, we can be distracted with a bit of food and drink. I know it's no small thing I'm asking, so I'll give you tonight to think on it."

"Very generous of you," said Merivale. "Kurdem?"

The serving man appeared immediately in the doorway, not even attempting to hide the fact that he'd been lurking nearby in case the Black Rose became unfriendly.

"Right away, my lady," he told Merivale. Then he turned to the Black Rose. "If you will follow me."

The Black Rose gave Merivale another knowing look. Perhaps she suspected the general tone of the conversation that was about to take place. Perhaps it didn't matter to her, as long as the answer was one she liked. Then she let Kurdem lead her and her companions out of the room.

Merivale closed the door, then braced herself as she turned to face the empress.

"Really, Merivale," the empress said coldly. Her eyes were beautiful balls of righteous indignation. "I'm trying to determine which of your many impertinences I find the worst."

"I suspect that interrupting you in front of guests tops the list," Merivale said calmly.

"You do understand the full significance of what she is asking for, don't you?" demanded the empress.

"Of course."

"And you honestly believe that the threat to the empire is so dire that we should restructure the very seat of its power simply to enlist the aid of this... *criminal*?"

"Do you recall our previous conversation concerning the biomancers and how they believe that they must tear down this empire to save it?"

"That's precisely what *you* are proposing!" The empress rarely lost her poise. In fact, Merivale couldn't recall ever seeing her so furious.

"Yes, I am," said Merivale, matching the empress's anger with cool detachment. "I realize you cannot see these things for yourself. So it apparently falls to me to be the one to tell you that the empire as it currently exists is already fracturing. The nobility hide in their sheltered little lives, but the majority of your citizens are impoverished and desperate. The only thing that keeps them from open rebellion is their dread of the biomancers. If we remove the biomancer threat completely, things *will* spiral out of control."

"And so you propose that we placate the rabble by giving them, what... political representation?"

"A slice of the pie, if you will," said Merivale. "But a small slice. We could allow the people to choose their own local representatives, each of whom would have as much authority as, say, a lord."

"And what of the lords?"

Merivale shrugged. "What of them?"

"Surely you would not want someone like the Black Rose to take Lesser Basheta from you."

"Frankly, I doubt she'd want it. And I can think of several commoners already on Lesser Basheta that I would be willing to work with on a mutually beneficial platform. But I concede this solution might not be tenable for *all* nobility, and there are a great many details that would need to be worked out in order for it to be acceptable to all parties."

The empress shook her head. "This is starting to sound suspiciously like the Great Congress of Aukbontar. I cannot see how I would be saving the empire by turning my back on half a millennia of tradition."

"It is a weighty decision, to be sure," said Merivale. "We have until tomorrow morning to reply to the Black Rose. Why not sleep on it?"

Empress Pysetcha narrowed her eyes. "Playing for time, Lady Hempist?"

"We shall know soon if I'm correct in my predictions," said Merivale. "I pray that I am wrong. But sadly, I rarely am."

Captain Murkton arrived in the predawn light. He'd taken two horses, switching back and forth to keep them from total collapse. Even so, they were lathered and swaying, their glossy brown coats steaming in the chilly air, when he cantered into the courtyard.

Merivale caught a glimpse of the horses out the window as she walked from her room to the empress's chambers. She'd slept a few hours, but had already been awake and sipping a cup of tea when one of the household servants knocked on her door, apologizing for the hour and informing her that the empress had requested her presence immediately.

When Merivale entered the room, the empress sat in her nightgown, slumped into a high-backed chair. Merivale had never seen the empress slump before. Her head was bowed, and she massaged her temples with the thumb and finger of one elegant hand. Next to her stood Murkton, his white and gold uniform caked with dirt and spattered with blood.

"Your Majesty," Merivale said, and curtsied.

"Tell her," the empress said tersely, not looking up.

Murkton turned to Merivale. "My lady, it is as you feared. Emperor Martarkis passed away late last night. Immediately upon his death, Archlord Tramasta ignored the laws of succession and seized power, declaring Ammon Set the new emperor."

"Ah." Merivale's insides twisted into something cold and hard. As much as she'd been trying to prepare herself for this event, she still felt the full weight of it as if it were a surprise.

"But he hasn't completely solidified his control yet," continued Murkton. "When I left Stonepeak a few hours ago, there was open fighting between soldiers, both in the palace and on the streets of the city. So far, the other biomancers haven't acted to support either side."

"Simply allowing Ammon Set to assume control is all the declaration of support they need," said Merivale.

"How…" The empress looked up at Merivale. "How is this even *possible*? The biomancers have sworn an oath—"

"The ultimate sacrifice," said Merivale. "When Red interrogated Chiffet Mek, that's what he called it. Red mistakenly assumed it meant death. But I have never met a biomancer who truly feared death. It's an ever-present risk in their work. No, what they fear is powerlessness. By breaking his oath and wresting the throne, Ammon Set has sacrificed his ability to use biomancery. Now he's just a man."

"A man with the might of the imperial navy at his back," Pysetcha said bitterly.

"Not entirely," said Merivale. "I have been working to shore up support for Prince Leston within the military. Despite his immaturity, or perhaps even because of it, many of your subjects are fond of him. Certainly *some* soldiers will blindly follow Tramasta, but others will defect to us once we arrive at the palace."

"And how on earth do you plan to reach the palace alive?" the empress asked.

"With the help of the Black Rose and her people, naturally," said Merivale. "That's why I invited them."

The empress stared at her. "Help which she will only offer when we agree to give her political representation."

"Just so, Your Majesty," said Merivale. "Imagine how motivated she'll be when it's not just *our* cause, but hers as well that she fights for. And if the stories I've heard have any basis in fact, she and her 'wags' are some of the most deadly people in the empire. I doubt we'll find a better ally in this conflict."

Pysetcha's head dropped back down in defeat. It pained Merivale to see the empress like that. Doubly so, since it was her doing. But the empire must stand, in one form or another. There was a great deal more at stake here than the pride of a few nobles.

"Fine," said the empress bitterly. "Can...Can you work out the details with our new allies? I...I didn't sleep last night and I find it difficult to focus at present."

"You may rely on me to take care of everything, Your Majesty," said Merivale.

21

*B*rigga Lin generally prided herself on maintaining a certain level of grace and poise. She wouldn't have admitted it to anyone, probably not even Hope, but it was something else she had worked hard to perfect during those years when she had been developing her mastery of the lost biomancery art of casting from afar. But just as there were times to eschew casting and get her hands dirty, there were also times when she needed to abandon decorum, hike up her skirts, and run like all hells.

As she ran toward the Shade District, she told herself that the primal panic she felt regarding the possibility of Alash getting flattened by a kraken was due to an understandable but entirely unromantic fondness for the man. During their time aboard the *Kraken Hunter*, they had become kindred spirits of a sort. As the two "lacies" among a crew of pirates and ruffians, it had only been natural. Neither had wanted to draw attention to the disparity they sometimes felt with the rest of the crew, so they had often quietly confessed their unease and bewilderment to each other. Even Hope had trouble grasping many of the niceties of civilized culture. While Brigga Lin's best friend was vastly more educated than most people in matters of war and philosophy, she seemed to have no idea that soup should be eaten with a spoon rather

than slurped directly from the bowl. Only Alash had
understood how it made Brigga Lin cringe inwardly
every time she witnessed one of the crew pick their
nose or scratch their bottom. Especially in those
early months, when Brigga Lin had struggled to find
her place among her new companions, Alash's kind
patience had been essential in helping her adjust.

So it was no wonder she felt a certain affection for
the man. An affection that had obviously not dimin-
ished even after his embarrassing and bumbling declaration of love. A declaration she conceded that perhaps
she had not responded to as kindly as she could have,
given his gentle nature. It wasn't as though she had
enjoyed laughing in his face, or watching him break
into tears after. But his stuttering, hand-wringing proposal had been so absurd, she wasn't able to help herself. It had just come bubbling out of her.

But he was back and hadn't made any further
overtures or pressured her in any way. In fact, he had
been a complete gentleman. Of course he had *always*
been a complete gentleman, but her time with Gavish
Gray had taught her to appreciate such a quality in
a way she hadn't before. There was also the muscles.
She appreciated those as well. Perhaps it was shallow
of her, but his newly honed physique did make the
possibility of having sex with him more appealing.
Not that she would, because she knew it would be terribly confusing for such a sentimental, romantic man
like Alash. He would no doubt jump to the conclu-
sion that she loved him. Which she obviously didn't.
Because biomancers absolutely did not fall in love.

Reaching Vaderton's ship turned out to be more
difficult than Brigga Lin had anticipated, in large
part because while she ran toward the docks, nearly
everyone else was running in the opposite direction.
As she pushed her way through the crowds of wild-
eyed people, she was tempted to simply melt anyone

in her path. She resisted the impulse, however. She
was rescuing Alash, after all, and killing a bunch of
people in the process of doing so was exactly the sort
of thing that would upset him.

But her resolve not to kill, or at least severely
maim, began to weaken when she hit a large intersection within sight of the entrance to the docks.
She stared in fury at the pack of people who milled
shoulder to shoulder in front of her. Some were going
north, others south, and still others west, and all of
them seemed to be trying to do so at this particular
intersection all at once.

"Well, this isn't good," observed Red.

Brigga Lin hadn't realized he was following her.
"What are you doing here?"

"Hope asked me to help. And don't forget, Alash
is my cousin."

"Would it be terrible if I just melted a few?" Brigga
Lin gestured to the knot of people in front of her.

"I think I have a less murderous solution." He
drew a revolver and fired a few shots into the air.
"Clear the way for imperial business!" Then he fired
a few more shots for good measure.

People turned and looked at Brigga Lin standing
there in a white hood, and suddenly there was hardly
anyone in the intersection.

"Not bad," she conceded.

Red grinned. "After you, then, my lady."

———

When the noise first started, Jilly knew it had to be
an attack of some kind. No way were those biomancers going to let Hope and Brigga Lin go that easy. So
she and Uter climbed up onto the roof of the Broadside Inn to get a better look at what was coming.

It wasn't hard to see.

"Piss'ell," she whispered as she stared across the rooftops at the massive sea creature laying waste to the Shade District.

"What is *that*?" asked Uter, his eyes wide.

"That, my wag, is a kraken."

"Hope told me about those! Have you seen one before?"

She shook her head. "Captain Vaderton told me about it once. The deadliest thing in the sea, he said. He told me it was big, but..." She stared at the massive hulking thing as it smashed through piers like they were reeds. "The mind can hardly hold such a thing."

"Do you think it will be our friend?" Uter asked.

"Don't be bludgeon. Of course it won't be our friend."

"It will if we kill it!"

Hope had told Jilly about Uter's strange and creepy ability. She looked over at the ghostly boy as he looked longingly at the kraken, his little hands opening and closing like he couldn't wait to find something sharp.

"And how are you going to kill something like that? I mean, except maybe making it laugh itself to death."

"You can die from laughing?" asked Uter.

Jilly sighed and turned back to watch as the kraken tore up a section of the docks and tossed it several blocks. "I'll bet Hope and Brigga Lin are going after it right now. They'll know a way to kill it."

"I wish we could ask them," said Uter.

Jilly smiled. "Now that I think on it, we *can*. I may not know a lot about biomancery yet, but I know how to do that."

She sat cross-legged on the rough slates of the roof, aware that Uter was mimicking her. She closed her eyes so she wouldn't be distracted by it.

"Master! Where are you?"

Ouch. Don't shout. I'm at the docks, came Brigga Lin's thoughts.

"I knew it! You're going to kill the kraken, aren't you?"

Don't be absurd.

"Wait, so you're not going to kill it?"

There was a pause before Brigga Lin replied.

To be honest, I'm not sure what we're going to do yet. Right now, I need to make sure Alash and Vaderton are safe. Then we'll worry about what happens after that.

"Can I come help you?"

You need to stay with Uter where it's safe.

"I'm not a kid anymore, you know."

Brigga Lin's thought came hard and unyielding. *Are you talking back to me?*

"No, master! I just . . . I want to help."

Very well. Establish a connection with Hope so we can coordinate our efforts.

Jilly groaned. "This again?"

So you don't want to help after all?

"No, I do, master," she said quickly. "I'll start building the connection now."

Thank you, Jilly.

Jilly opened her eyes and turned to Uter. "Okay, we've got a job."

"We do?"

Uter looked very impressed, so Jilly decided to go with that.

"Yeah, it's really important, so we can't mess it up."

Uter leaned in eagerly. "What do we do?"

"I have to use biomancery to make sure Hope and Brigga Lin can talk to each other even if they're on opposite sides of the city."

"You can *do* that?"

"It's easy," said Jilly, affecting a careless tone.

"So what do *I* do?"

"This takes a lot of concentration, so you'll have to get stuff for me. Like if I get hungry or thirsty."

"I can do that!" said Uter.

"Great." Jilly shifted her butt on the cold, hard shingles. "Start by going down to our room and getting me a pillow to sit on."

———

The intricate snowflake design of the docks on the eastern side of Vance Post was in ruins. Miles of wooden planks had been torn apart. Some now lay floating in ragged clutches along the coast, but most appeared to have been hurled into the city. When Brigga Lin arrived, she was relieved to see that the kraken hadn't worked its way down to the southeastern portion of the docks where Vaderton's boat was kept. But she was infuriated to see that both men were still on the boat, with no sign of leaving, and the kraken now less than a quarter mile up the coast from them.

She shoved her way through the panicked crowds that were carrying whatever they could as far inland as they could go, like intelligent people. Finally she reached the boat and climbed aboard without permission.

"What are you two still doing here?"

"Would you have been *less* angry if we'd come all this way and they weren't here?" muttered Red as he climbed aboard behind her. "Or *more* angry?"

Brigga Lin ignored him and continued to glare at Alash and Vaderton, who sat on the boat huddled over a parchment as if there wasn't a giant sea monster heading directly toward them.

"It won't let any ships escape," said Vaderton, not looking up from the parchment, "and there didn't seem much point in joining the panicked throngs." He waved his hand vaguely. "So we're more or less stuck."

They both seemed so intent that she finally gave in to curiosity. She moved closer so that she could look over their shoulders at the parchment, which was covered with odd diagrams, scribbles, and mathematical equations. "What is this you're working on?"

Alash glanced up, appearing to notice her for the first time. "Ah, hello, Miss Lin. A delight to see you as ever. Frightful situation, isn't it?" He then went back to the parchment and frowned, making a few marks on it with a charcoal pencil.

Vaderton squinted at the calculation he'd just written. "Really? That much?"

"If we want to be certain it will work," said Alash. "Although that doesn't solve the delivery problem."

"Alash," Brigga Lin said, the frustration in her voice returning. "Catch me up."

"Oh, sorry, Miss Lin!" said Alash. "Vaderton and I have been trying to determine if there is a way to use explosives to either deter or kill the kraken, and if so, approximately how much gunpowder it would take."

"The idea," said Vaderton, "would be to pack a ship full of gunpowder, get the Guardian to eat it, then somehow ignite the explosives."

"How much gunpowder would you need?" asked Red.

"Roughly thirty barrels," said Alash.

"Is there even that much gunpowder on Vance Post?" he asked.

"Possibly at the police station," said Vaderton.

"Regardless, I'm not convinced we'd even be able to get the kraken to eat it," said Alash. "Observe."

He pointed to where the kraken loomed, now less than a quarter of a mile away. They watched as it picked up a ship in its tentacles and cracked it in half like a nut. It then used a third tentacle to reach in and get the people who had been hiding inside.

"The ship might not even stay intact long enough to deliver the full payload of gunpowder," said Red.

"Exactly! I'd say the chances are extremely slim! And sometimes, the kraken simply chucks the ship into the city, and that would be even worse! Why, that much gunpowder could level a city block!" Alash beamed at them. As usual, when consumed with a technical problem, he seemed to lose sight of the dark reality it represented.

"So what you're saying is that after all your calculations, you've determined it's a terrible idea," said Red.

"Oh, well, yes, I suppose. But, see, now we know—"

"What about biomancery?" interrupted Vaderton as he turned to Brigga Lin. "Could you take control of this beast?"

"Most likely there is a biomancer on Vance Post controlling it as we speak," said Brigga Lin. "My understanding is that the kraken has always required a 'keeper' to assure its obedience. It might be possible for me to wrest control from that biomancer. But to do that, I would have to figure out which of many possible techniques the biomancer is using, and that would be merely a process of trial and error until I found the right combination. It could take several hours. Perhaps longer."

They watched the kraken decimate yet another pier as it worked its way down the coast.

"Not sure we have that long," said Red. "What if we found this... keeper?"

"Most likely that would still be Fitmol Bet," said Vaderton.

Hearing her old master's name so suddenly jarred Brigga Lin more than she would have expected. "You know Fitmol Bet?"

"I served under him in the navy until he was assigned as the Guardian's keeper."

"When did that happen?" Brigga Lin didn't know much about the details of the keeper position, but it seemed an odd fit for him.

"About two years ago, I suppose," said Vaderton.

"While I was secluded on Wake Landing, then," said Brigga Lin.

"So you just need this Fitmol Bet taken out of the picture. Sounds easy enough," said Red. "Leave it to me."

"How could you possibly find one man amongst all this?" Alash waved his hand at the general chaos on the streets nearby.

Red gave them that rakish grin he was so fond of and said, "Trust me, my wags. I'll get him."

"We'll need him alive," said Brigga Lin. "If you kill him before I've taken control, the shock might drive the kraken mad, and then we'll be in even worse shape than before."

Alash stared up at the kraken as it ripped another pylon out of the water and hurled it like a spear into the top floor of a building ten blocks in from the coast. As the wall of the building began to crumble, screaming people spilled out and fell to their deaths on the street below.

"It can get worse?" he asked.

"Mr. Havolon, it can always get worse," Brigga Lin said grimly.

———

Sheltered though he realized he was, Stephan was grateful for the few hardships he'd endured in his life. He suspected it had given him the humility to be the first among his brothers to shrug off the arrogance instilled by Racklock and recognize what a truly remarkable person they now had in their midst.

"Don't you think so?" he pressed Malveu. The two of them were leading a group of children out of some sort of workshop that had sustained enough damage from the debris being tossed by the kraken that the structure had become unstable. Stephan didn't know why there hadn't been an adult in the building with them. He could only guess that he or she had fled in the first panicked wave of people heading toward the safety of the Commercial District, abandoning the poor children. It had taken Stephan, Malveu, and Ravento a lot of time and a considerable amount of patience to coax the children out of the building. They were so young that it was difficult to even get them to understand that their hiding place was less safe than being out on the street.

Ravento was now leading the majority of the children to the makeshift shelter they had set up in the center of the island, while Stephan and Malveu herded the more reluctant ones from behind.

Malveu glanced uneasily at Ravento, who was not within earshot, then back at Stephan.

"She bested Racklock in combat. There's no denying that."

"Without even using a sword!" said Stephan. "That is remarkable, but what I'm talking about is more than just her skills in combat."

"I know." Malveu seemed uneasy about it.

"She is more Vinchen than any Vinchen I have ever known since Hurlo the Cunning."

"We were only boys when Hurlo the Cunning died," said Malveu. "How much could you possibly remember?"

"I remember enough to know that *she* is his greatest pupil. And I think she has a great deal to teach us. *All* of us."

Malveu glanced again at Ravento at the front of the line. "Be careful how you talk, Stephan."

"I don't care who hears it," said Stephan. "Do you know why? Because if she had been leading us instead of Racklock the Cruel, Frache and Hectory would still be alive."

"Breaking a law of the Vinchen code that was established centuries ago by Selk the Brave won't bring them back."

"But it might keep you or Ravento or one of the others from also dying in a dishonorable or needless way. That alone is reason enough for me to consider it."

The sullen little boy whom he had been pushing along was beginning to slow down again.

"I don't want to go that way," he told Stephan. "I'm not supposed to cross the river."

"It's the safest place for you right now. You can come back here later. Let's hurry along now."

The boy glared up at him. "Who are you gafs, anyway?"

"We are the Vinchen," Stephan told him.

"The *who*?"

"The people saving your life right now," said Malveu. "So move, unless you want a spanking."

"Okay, okay!" The boy hurried up toward the front of the line.

"We should have tried that from the beginning," mused Malveu.

"Did you hear him, though?" said Stephan. "The younger generations haven't heard of us. Even our legends are fading. This is the perfect time to redefine ourselves. To find new relevance in this world, just as Hope has suggested."

Malveu looked like he was going to respond, but as they crossed an intersection, they saw her in front of a building. She waved to them.

"Stephan! And Malveu, isn't it? Can you help me with this?"

The two young men looked at each other silently. Then Stephan turned and shouted, "Of course."

Without waiting to see if Malveu was following, he crossed the intersection. A moment later, he heard his warrior brother's footsteps following behind him.

"Thanks," said Hope when they reached her. "There's a group of people trapped in this building, and it sounds like the roof might give way soon." She gestured to the rubble that blocked the door, and held up the strange mechanical claw she had instead of a hand. "I'm afraid this isn't particularly good at lifting large, heavy objects, so it might take too long for me to clear it out on my own."

"Lucky for you, I won the strength competition on Galemoor three years in a row," said Malveu.

Hope gave him an amused look. "Let's pray your time away from Galemoor hasn't let your muscles atrophy as greatly as your humility."

Malveu looked so crestfallen that Stephan had to laugh, despite the grave situation. Malveu scowled at him, but Stephan continued to smile as the two set to work clearing the rubble that blocked the door.

"Can you still hear me?" Hope called through the door.

"I don't think we've got long before the ceiling falls on our heads!" came a muffled voice from inside.

"We're nearly through, so get everyone by the door," said Hope.

The three of them hurried to remove the remaining debris, which mostly consisted of bricks and broken wooden beams that had been knocked clean out of the side of the neighboring building by a wooden dock pylon as thick around as Stephan's torso.

"Aren't doors supposed to open inward to prevent just such a situation?" Malveu grunted as he tossed aside a thick piece of splintered pylon.

"I don't think the Shade District was constructed

with a great deal of care," said Hope. "You will find negligence toward the poor a common occurrence in the empire. I doubt Racklock spoke of this, but Hurlo felt that the code's words concerning charity and compassion for the poor to be among its most important tenets."

"Compassion for the poor? But we have no money ourselves," said Stephan.

"True, but the wealth of your education and training offers advantages others may never even know exist. And if I am not mistaken, you come from a noble background, making you doubly blessed."

Stephan felt the sting of those words even though they were gently spoken. Pushing himself harder to remove the debris helped to lessen that feeling somewhat.

Finally, the way was clear and Stephan yanked the door open. He knew the people trapped inside were just on the other side and would be eager to escape. But he was not quite prepared for them to be mostly naked.

He stood there stupidly as a man dressed only in a thong embraced him, letting out a relieved sob. "Bless you, sir! Bless you!"

"There now, you're okay," soothed Hope as she gently disengaged the man from Stephan's shoulders. "Keep moving so everyone can get out. The old temple on the corner of Gale Street and Imperial Way is open as a shelter to all who need it."

The man nodded and hurried on.

Stephan watched, his eyes wide, as the rest of the people, all with little to no clothing, hurried past. He could feel his face burning from the lingering memory of the touch from the man who had embraced him.

He glanced over at Hope, and she gave him an inquiring look that only made him blush more.

Then suddenly she burst out into that strange, raucous pirate-like laugh of hers and slapped him on the shoulder.

"We'll make you a man of the world yet, Stephan," she told him.

———

Red knew it wouldn't be easy to locate one man in the general panic that had enveloped the Shade District. Brigga Lin had asked several times how he planned to go about it, most likely concerned that his boasts were nothing but balls and pricks. That was fine by him. Let her think what she wanted. He liked having a few secrets. It wasn't that he didn't trust her, but, well, it didn't hurt to have the advantage, just in case he should ever need to use it against her.

The thing was, Red could hear when biomancery was being used. Or maybe "feel" was a more accurate word. It wasn't a *sound* exactly, more like an ache in the back of his teeth. In fact, it was so subtle that it had taken him months to become conscious of it, and several months after that before he figured out the source. Interestingly, the sensation was stronger when Brigga Lin used biomancery than when any of the others did. Maybe because it traveled through the air? He didn't really understand it, but it would be very handy if Hope and Brigga Lin ever had a falling-out.

For now, this ability was helping Red locate Fitmol Bet. He walked at a measured pace, his eyes half-closed to reduce the amount of visual distraction coming from the people running by and buildings crumbling around him. He probably looked bizarre. Everyone else was sprinting to get away from the carnage, eyes wide with terror, while he stumbled along, barely looking where he was going, as if sleepwalking.

He crisscrossed through the neighborhood, guided by the subaudible pulse that echoed through his jaw. He lost the trail several times, and each time would have to stop, close his eyes completely, and regain his bearings. But, slowly, he drew near his prey.

When he reached a building along the northeast entrance to the piers, he hesitated. The feeling seemed to come from within the building, but when he peeked through the windows, there was no one inside. He knew some biomancers could bend light to make themselves effectively invisible. But would a biomancer be able to maintain something like that while also controlling a kraken? He didn't know for sure, but it seemed unlikely.

Then a much simpler explanation occurred to him. He climbed carefully up the side of the building, wishing he had the soft gray shoes from his Shadow Demon clothes. It was much more treacherous going up a wall when wearing stiff-soled lacy boots, even if they did look pat.

Finally, he reached the roof. It was quieter up there, away from the screaming and panic below. Off in the distance, he could see the kraken on its rampage. It had cleared most of the eastern pier by then and was working its way south. As he watched, several ships on the north side of the island tried to head out into open water. The kraken shot up the coast faster than any ship, and grabbed them all. It didn't take the time to eat the passengers in those ships, however. Instead, it just hurled them into the city. Then the kraken slid back down and resumed slowly dismantling the southeastern portion of the dock. Despite the chaos, there was something oddly methodical about it all.

And the method was most likely coming from the figure in a hooded white robe who stood about thirty paces away on the roof. The biomancer's back was to

Red, and his arms moved with the kraken's two long front tentacles, as if the great beast was simply mirroring him. He seemed completely unaware of Red's presence.

Red had the sudden, powerful urge to just shoot him and be done with it. But he knew that was the Shadow Demon talking. Brigga Lin had warned him that simply killing the biomancer like that could be disastrous. Still, the urge of the Shadow Demon was so strong, it took a huge amount of effort to stop himself. It was like turning down a molly that he was leaky for, or refusing a fresh tankard of ale. But he gritted his teeth and rode out the desire to kill like a wave.

Once he felt he could trust himself, Red climbed quietly onto the roof, drew his revolvers, and slowly crept toward the biomancer. He might not plan on shooting the biomancer, but he'd noticed that people generally became more cooperative the closer they were to the end of a gun barrel.

"I know you're there, creature," said Fitmol Bet without turning around.

Red went perfectly still.

"Whatever you are, I can feel the alterations done to you, nearly as keenly as my own," said Fitmol Bet. "Has Ammon Set sent you to destroy me once my task is complete?"

Red slowly circled the biomancer in a wide arc. "I'm not sure what you're talking about, old pot, but I'm not in the habit of taking orders from Ammon Set anymore. In fact, I . . ."

Red trailed off when he got a good look at Fitmol Bet. The man's eyes were completely white, and an unpleasant pinkish ooze seeped from them. His robes were open in the front to reveal his bare, emaciated chest. The skin was almost translucent so that Red could see the veins, muscles, and sinews outlined beneath. There were six little tentacles attached to his torso, three on either side. They undulated as if they had minds of their own.

"Piss'ell."

"Do I truly look so grotesque?" asked Fitmol Bet, his voice distant and unconcerned. "Perhaps it is for the best I lost my own sight. It may surprise you that I was once an attractive man. Perhaps my vanity was one of the reasons I was chosen for the *honor* of keeping the Guardian." Only the word *honor* held any emotion, and Bet ground it out flavored with years of anger and resentment.

"I take it they did this to you so you could control the kraken?" asked Red.

"Can you believe that at first, I honestly thought I was being rewarded? Recognized at last for my work in synthesizing the longevity traits in mole rats?" He smiled faintly. "Of course, I have no interest in availing myself of such treatments anymore. This life has become a burden, and I look forward to the moment when you end it."

"I hate to disappoint, but I'm really not here from Ammon Set, and your death isn't what I'm after."

Fitmol Bet frowned. "Who sent you, then? Has Chiffet Mek finally grown a backbone? Or one of the others from the council? I thought they had long ago sublimated their wills to Ammon Set. All except Progul Bon, of course, and now that he's dead, Set is free to do the thing he's desired for so long."

"Oh? And what's that?"

"Depose Martarkis and ordain himself emperor. He believes it's the only way to avert the predictions of the Dark Mage and save the empire. Very convenient for him, isn't it?"

"Depose the emperor? When?"

"Perhaps it's already begun. They don't always bother to tell me things anymore. They all believe my mind is too connected to the Guardian and that

I don't think completely like a man anymore." He paused for a moment, as if pondering the idea. "They're not wrong."

"So what happens to Leston, then?"

"The prince? I should think allowing the former heir to continue living would be ill advised," said Fitmol Bet. "From a practical standpoint, that is. And if Ammon Set has any feelings of sentimentality, I am unaware of them."

"Look." Red glanced at the kraken, which continued to follow Fitmol Bet's gestures as it ravaged the coast. "Can you just…stop destroying Vance Post for a bit so we can talk about this?"

"I wish I could, but I am under compulsion, directly from Ammon Set, to prevent anyone from leaving this island. Apparently there are people here he fears might interfere with his plans."

"True enough," admitted Red. "Hells, I reckon even Racklock would have objected to Ammon Set making himself emperor. Look…could we, I don't know…get rid of the compulsion somehow?" asked Red. "Someone did it for me once."

"I suppose, but it would require a very powerful biomancer indeed. And even then, I'm not certain it would work."

"Well, sunny for you, I know just about the most powerful biomancer who ever lived. So why don't I introduce you?"

"I wish I could accept such hopeful words, but the compulsion will not allow me to stop what I am doing until I'm dead."

"I see. And hypothetically speaking," Red said, "if you were to lose consciousness for a short while, what would the kraken do?"

"Most likely take the brief respite to sink below the water and recover. We had a long journey here, and there hasn't been a moment of rest."

"Well, then." Red nodded casually. "Keep with the death and destruction, then. I'll just be going now."

As Red walked past Fitmol Bet, the biomancer continued to undulate his two arms and six tentacles. Then, once Red was directly behind him, he slammed the butt of his gun into the back of the biomancer's head. He watched Fitmol Bet drop to the rough slate roof.

A moment later, the kraken paused in its carnage, then slowly withdrew, sinking back into the water and out of sight.

Red looked down at the biomancer's slimy, tentacled, unconscious form. He winced at the foul odor that seemed to be some combination of stagnant water and rotting fish. "It's going to be a long, unpleasant walk back to the docks, I reckon."

22

*C*hiffet Mek stared down at the corpse of the emperor and was surprised by how sad he felt. He hadn't known the man well, and what little he'd known, he hadn't liked. But still, as he looked down at the gaunt, wasted body with papery skin that was laid atop the lushly embroidered coverlet, he felt a weight in his chest. What was it Pastinas had said to him? *Better to be among ordinary men, than a dog to the exalted ones.* This "emperor" had truly been a dog among the exalted. A puppet for decades, little more than a meat sack propped up now and then to make an official declaration. The very idea always seemed rather distasteful to Mek, but it had been one of the few things Ammon Set and Progul Bon ever agreed on.

And that's how it had always been. Ammon Set and Progul Bon, constantly clashing, fighting for dominance while still somehow trying to work together toward the common goal of protecting the empire. Chiffet Mek had been there through all that time, quietly observing, obeying as necessary, but careful never to side with one over the other.

But those days were over now. Bon was dead. Ammon Set had broken one of the most sacred vows and wrested power from the imperial family. One could not be so forsworn and still expect life to heed your

commands, so Set had lost his formidable powers as a
biomancer. Chiffet Mek had told Pastinas that it was
the ultimate sacrifice, and that Ammon Set would be
forever revered for it. In that moment, he had believed
it. Now, as he looked down at the dead body of the
emperor, he wondered if he had been mistaken. Would
Set be revered? *Should* he be?

It occurred to Chiffet Mek then that, as newly
appointed head of the Council of Biomancery, his
own opinions actually mattered. If he disagreed
with Ammon Set's strategy, he had the power and
authority to contest it. After so many years of defer-
ring to him and Progul Bon without question, it was
a strange thing to consider. But it would now be up
to Chiffet Mek to determine the shape of the order in
the years to come.

He brushed a stray strand of white hair back from
the dead emperor's forehead as he considered this.
What did *he* want for the order, and for the empire?

"Mek!" Ammon Set's voice rang from the next
room. "What are you still doing in there? We don't
have time for sentimentality!"

That was very true, thought Chiffet Mek. Sentimentality and old attachments would not be of much
use to him in the future.

"The *future*..."

Chiffet Mek liked the sound of that word as it slid
from his throat. After all, it was progress, above all
else, that he valued most.

———

The Black Rose of Paradise Circle sat alone in her
cabin and polished her chainblade. It didn't need to
be polished, because she hadn't used it in months.
But it made her happy to do so. It was an odd feeling, really. Doing something just because she en-

joyed it. That was something she hadn't done in months either.

The last half year or so had been lost to the darkness. She'd succumbed to it so fully, she'd even begun to forget there was anything else. But then Red had shown up and shaken things loose like he always did. It was that pissing mural of his, more than anything else. It had been like a lantern lighting up everything so it became crystal, and she could suddenly see for miles.

Which wasn't to say she'd gone back to being Nettles. Those days were over forever. But now at least she could look beyond the day-to-day survival. She could see something bigger and better out there. She could find a way for every wag of the Circle to not just be true and loyal, but also *happy*. Thanks to the odd friendships she'd made over the years—people who had challenged her and expanded her view of the world—she had something none of the previous ganglords did. She had vision. So she had resolved to drag not just herself out of the darkness, but all of downtown New Laven with her.

There was a knock on the door.

"Nearly there, Rose," said Ruby Raw, a mousy little thing who'd been with Hope at Dawn's Light.

The Black Rose planned to thank Hope for that one of these days. Not many of her wags had come back from that crusade. But those that did had steel in their bones, salt water in their veins, and were worth five regular wags.

"Thanks," she told Ruby.

She coiled her chainblade and headed up the narrow stairs to the deck. The *Never You Mind* was a fine vessel, bigger than the *Kraken Hunter* and faster than the *Glorybound*. It had a full three masts—the only one in the Black Rose's small fleet. It didn't have a great deal of firepower, since it was a merchant ship

rather than a military vessel, but as the Black Rose
understood it, this would be more of a land fight anyway, and a merchant ship's hold could fit a lot of wags.

Most of those wags were gathered on the deck
now. The Black Rose walked through them, feeling their tense eagerness. They'd come to fight some
imps, and they were hungry for it. But even wound as
tight as they were, they all moved aside respectfully
to let the Black Rose pass.

The quarterdeck was much less crowded. Crate
Allen was at the helm, and Captain Strongjaw stood
next to him. They were both big, solid wags, and yet
they looked uneasy, perhaps even a little fearful, in
the presence of their guest, Lady Merivale Hempist.

The Black Rose found Merivale to be a real
puzzle. On the outside, she seemed the laciest lacy
who'd ever dabbed her nose with orange powder. But
the Black Rose had caught glimpses of something
harder than steel underneath. She didn't know how
a person could be both those things at once, but she
was fascinated, and more than a little leaky for her.

She didn't trust Merivale, of course. The lacy
molly had a disinterested air about her that some
might confuse for indifference, but the Black Rose
suspected was because she was already ten steps
ahead of everyone else. A schemer to her core. Not
that there was anything wrong with that. Initially,
the Black Rose had been surprised and a little
uneasy that Merivale had been so eager to support
her cause before the empress. But after she'd spoken
to her awhile, she realized it wasn't out of some fickle
pity, but because it coincided with one of Merivale's
own schemes. And that was exactly the sort of reasoning the Black Rose could rely on. At least for as
long as their two schemes worked together.

"We should be coming in sight of the outer docks
in a few minutes," Strongjaw told her.

"I doubt we'll see any resistance there," said Merivale. "But once we reach the inner docks near the Thunder Gate, we should expect a strong show of force."

"My wags will be ready," said the Black Rose. "You're sure there will be some imps who join our side once we make land? I don't relish taking on the entire island."

"Some will defect to us the moment they see me," Merivale said. "And once we secure the prince, I expect the majority will rally behind him."

"Assuming he's still alive," said the Black Rose.

"I have another ally on the inside who is keeping him safe."

"What if she can't?" asked the Black Rose.

"In the unlikely event that the prince is killed, we'd either have to stage a coup of our own or else seek asylum in Aukbontar. Because trust me, an empire ruled by Ammon Set isn't a place either of us want to live."

"So getting to the prince will be our priority, then," said the Black Rose. "Instead of trying to hold any ground we take, we'll just batter through until we get to the palace and hope to God your ally still has him safe."

"A sound plan," said Merivale. "And I shouldn't worry too much about my ally. The ambassador of Aukbontar has proven in many ways to be as formidable as myself."

The Black Rose grinned at her. "I reckon coming from you that's the highest compliment someone can get."

"True," admitted Merivale.

They watched quietly as the coast slid by along the port side. Finally they reached the opening of the bay, which was lined on either side with thick, sturdy docks that could withstand the harder currents out here. The last time the Black Rose had sailed past them, they'd been crowded with masts, but now there wasn't a single ship to be seen. Most likely, the merchants and traders had seen what was coming and fled to friendlier islands. Friendly for now, anyway.

As the *Never You Mind* neared the inner docks and the city beyond, the Black Rose saw puffs of smoke and flashes of gunfire. She took Strongjaw's spyglass to have a look.

"Two groups of imps are fighting each other along the dock," she said. "I reckon one of them is on our side?"

"Presumably," sad Merivale. "I have men planted in several squads and told them to urge their fellows to meet us down here."

"We don't want to kill them if we can help it, then," said the Black Rose. She turned to Strongjaw. "Fire a warning shot. The ones with us will hopefully be smart enough to scatter. Once they do, send mortars up along that main street as far as they'll reach to clear us a path."

"Aye, Black Rose." Then Strongjaw began shouting brisk orders to his crew.

A few minutes later, the *Never You Mind* sent a cannonball skipping up the bay to smash loudly into a piece of unoccupied dock. The soldiers all paused for a moment and looked at the incoming ship. The ones on the left side suddenly disbursed, melting into the nearby buildings.

"Okay, they're clear," said the Black Rose. "Shell the rest into whatever hell awaits them."

Strongjaw gave the order, and there was a string of blasts. For a moment, the sky looked like it had caught on fire. Then it all came crashing down on the horrified soldiers. The mortars cut their numbers in half, but the rest stood their ground and readied themselves to repel the invading ship.

"This is it, my wags!" the Black Rose yelled to the toms and mollies on the main deck. "You all know what we're doing here and why. This isn't just for us, but for our children, and our children's children. This is for all the true wags now and in the future. So hold nothing back!"

A line of wags along the gunwale fired rifles to lay down some cover fire. In the cloud of smoke that followed, the whole ship emptied out. Wags spilled over the side and onto the dock, charging headlong into the soldiers.

The toms and mollies had been cooped up on a ship for far too long, and the sudden release was like an explosion. The orderly ranks of soldiers faltered when they saw the howling wave of chaos descending on them. That moment of hesitation was their undoing, and those true wags of the Circle shredded that line of imps like a cheese grater. And in the thickest part was the Black Rose, urging them all on as she whipped her chainblade at anything dressed in white and gold.

It didn't take long before the remaining imps broke and ran. That was when Merivale, who had hung back until then, came forward and spoke into a silver bullhorn that amplified her voice.

"All those still loyal to Prince Leston, join us against the biomancers!"

The imps who had been hiding in nearby buildings along the edge of the docks began to emerge.

"Now is the time for all people, rich and poor, soldier and worker, to come together to save their empire from the biomancers," Merivale shouted through the bullhorn. "Follow us to free Prince Leston, rightful emperor of the Storm!"

The imps cheered and came closer as if drawn to Merivale like some spell.

The Black Rose could feel her people getting nervous.

"Easy, my wags," she told them. "It's like the lady says. We work together on this one. The biomancers have gone so far this time, even the imps are on our side."

She'd told them all this before, of course, but now that it came to the reality, she could see them struggling to accept it.

"Don't you remember how crazy it sounded, us working with Hammer Point?" she pressed. "But we did it, and we didn't lose nothing of ourselves in the process. I promise you this will be the same, except this time, it'll be the imps owing us one. And won't that be sunny? Now, follow me."

It wasn't long before the Black Rose found herself at the head of another mob, this one even more conflicted, but with a purpose so clear and true, nobody could doubt it.

"Save the prince!" shouted Merivale into her bullhorn.

"Death to the biomancers!" the Black Rose shouted.

"Save the prince and death to the biomancers!" was the reply.

———

Of all the roles that Lady Merivale Hempist had played over the years, commanding soldiers had never been one of them. But soldiers needed direction and purpose, and she had plenty of that. Combined with the Black Rose's natural, earthy charisma, it was easy enough to bring soldiers and criminals together.

As the strange army continued up the street toward the palace, they encountered pockets of soldiers loyal to Tramasta. Each time, she would step back and let the fighters fight, and when they were victorious, she would praise them and urge them on again toward the palace. She noticed their army continued

to grow as they went. A few of Tramasta's soldiers
had a change of heart, or perhaps merely saw the
inevitable turn of the tide. But she was surprised to
see regular townsfolk also take up arms. Maybe it
was the already motley appearance of their army that
made them feel welcome to join. And, of course, the
people of Stonepeak had always had a soft spot for
their earnest young prince. At this point, Merivale felt
that training and skill were less important than sheer
numbers, so the bigger her army, the better.

"I didn't expect quite so many of the townspeople
to join us," she confessed to the Black Rose as they
continued their march toward the palace.

"Look around us, Merivale." The Black Rose had
made it clear at the very beginning that she had no
patience for titles and would only refer to Merivale
by her first name. "All these broken windows and
charred stones. Ammon Set already sent imps in
here to scare 'em and I reckon it worked well enough.
But he also gave them more reason to side with us.
As far as some of these folks are concerned, they're
simply defending their homes."

The town of Stonepeak had always seemed a little
shabby and squalid to Merivale, so she hadn't noticed
the difference, but now that it had been pointed out to
her, the recent damage was obvious. Merivale decided
she could gain a great deal of valuable perspective
from this vulgar little woman. It was downright hum-
bling. Fortunately, Merivale's ego was not so delicate
that it couldn't withstand some additional tempering.

"An excellent point," she said.

The Black Rose nodded. "What *I* don't understand
is why the biomancers haven't joined the fight. Even
with these numbers, we'd be hurting bad if they did."

"First, there aren't nearly as many as there used to
be, thanks to the culling your friends Bleak Hope and
Brigga Lin did last year. And second, the biomancers

have all sworn to serve the emperor. So until Ammon
Set is legitimized, they have to stay out of it or risk
breaking their oath."

"So what do they need to do to legitimize Ammon
Set?"

"There will need to be a coronation ceremony. But
before that, all other contenders for the title must be
eliminated."

"Which means killing the prince."

"Precisely."

The Black Rose nodded. "We better go rescue
him, then." She turned back to her men. "All right,
wags! Let's hurry to the palace! And let no one stand
in our way!"

———

As Merivale had expected, the majority of Tramasta's forces were still concentrated in the palace. He
and Ammon Set would want to secure their base
completely before making a concentrated effort to
expand. Once they held the palace and Leston was
dead, they could perform the coronation ceremony.
With the addition of the biomancers, they would easily dominate the rest of Stonepeak and beyond.

"I take it you have a plan to get us inside," the
Black Rose observed when they reached the closed
iron gates of the palace.

"Naturally," said Merivale.

No doubt the soldiers at the Lightning Gate had
orders not to let anyone through. Fortunately, those
soldiers were fiercely loyal to Captain Murkton,
and he'd given them instructions to open the gate to
Merivale before he left for Sunset Point.

When she and the Black Rose arrived with the
motley army at their back, the soldier on watch
waved down to them.

"How does the captain fare, my lady?"

"Alive and well," she called up to him. "For his valor, I have given him the honor of keeping Her Majesty safe during this time of conflict."

"It's always heartening to hear a great man recognized," said the soldier. Then he signaled down to the gatekeepers, and the iron lattice slowly lifted.

"That was easy enough," said the Black Rose.

"That wasn't the hard part." Merivale pointed to the large battalion of soldiers hurrying out from deeper in the courtyard, shouting curses as they pulled on their coats and hastily loaded their rifles.

"Let's get to it, my wags!" the Black Rose shouted to the crowds behind her. "This is the one that counts!"

They rushed through the gates and soon the courtyard was filled with the sounds of gunfire. Both sides scattered, seeking cover behind wagons, carriages, and anything else that might stop a bullet. But there wasn't nearly enough to hide even half the people in the courtyard, and soon people were dropping on both sides. The soldiers were better organized, but Merivale thought she could sense their doubt and confusion. Who, exactly, were they fighting for if the emperor was dead? Perhaps they had been told they were protecting Leston? Or perhaps they had been told nothing at all and were merely reacting to armed aggression. In either case, they did not seem confident.

The Black Rose's people, on the other hand, were filled with a confidence that bordered on madness. She had convinced her people that this was the key to a better life not just for them, but for their family and loved ones. That they were reshaping the very landscape of the empire. And she wasn't wrong.

As the battle raged on, the soldiers began to fall back. The Black Rose's people were more than just ferocious fighters. It was becoming increasingly clear that they were just as skilled in the use of firearms as the imperial troops. What sort of place must Paradise Circle be, if everyone there knew how to properly shoot a gun? Merivale wondered. And what sort of place might those people make the empire into if they had a say in its government? It was a fascinating question to ponder, but unfortunately, there were a great many things that needed to be taken care of first.

"You and I will take a small group around to a side entrance," Merivale told the Black Rose. "We must secure the prince as quickly as possible. We might even be able to stop this battle before everyone's dead."

The Black Rose nodded. "Moxy Poxy, Mister Hatbox. With me."

"That's all we're taking?" asked Merivale.

"If we're going in quiet, we want to keep our numbers down. And when it comes to being deadly, this is all we need."

Merivale eyed the ragged woman and the ghostly man, then inclined her head to the Black Rose. "I defer to your judgment on this. Let's go."

The four of them skirted the mass of fighting that sprawled across the courtyard. One of the imperial captains had arrived, and was shouting the soldiers back into a wedge formation, intent on splitting the invading forces into two groups. It worried Merivale to see them rallying like this, but she didn't have time to do anything about it. The priority had to be the prince. Without a legitimate heir, they were done.

"The groom's entrance is over here." She led the other three into the stables along the side of the courtyard. The smell of horse manure was still strong, even though the stables had been emptied. She led them to the very back, where there was a plain, unmarked door. They hurried through the door and up a narrow, curved stair until they reached the wide, open hallway of the first floor of the palace. Normally it would be bustling with servants in the middle of the afternoon, but Merivale was pleased to see it was empty and silent. The night she left for Sunset Point, she'd told Hester what was likely to come and had asked her to spread the word to the servants as much as she could. Hopefully, most of them had stayed home today.

"Where to now?" the Black Rose whispered.

Merivale pointed to the lift in the center of the main hallway. "There's the lift."

It was guarded by a small squad of soldiers, but they were facing toward the front entrance. None of them were expecting to be attacked from the stables.

"Quick and easy," muttered the Black Rose. Then she and her two murderers launched themselves at the unsuspecting soldiers. Merivale almost pitied the soldiers. She watched Mister Hatbox puncture the eyes and ears of one soldier, then move on to slit a second one's throat before coming back to finish the first one off. And Moxy Poxy apparently felt the need to stop and cut off a finger from every soldier she killed. They weren't very efficient, Merivale decided, but they got the job done, and that was the important thing. Soon all the soldiers were dead and the lift was free.

Once they reached the thirtieth floor, Merivale could hear a sound like metal crashing into thick wood coming from down the hallway. It came again a moment later, and repeated at regular intervals. When they arrived at the main hallway intersection, Merivale had her group hang back, then peered carefully around the corner.

There was a squad of soldiers about thirty yards down the hallway attempting to batter down the ambassador's door. Judging by the gold and red epaulets on their shoulders, they were Tramasta's personal guard. Naturally, he would have given them the mission of finding and killing the prince. They had served him even before he became chief of military, and were loyal to the death.

"That's where we have to go, ain't it?" murmured the Black Rose next to her.

Merivale nodded.

"This hallway's like a shooting gallery," said the Black Rose. "The moment they see us coming, they'll gun us down, simple as sideways."

"The only alternative I can think of is waiting until they break through the door," said Merivale. "Once they've gone inside, we could come up behind them."

"But they'll also be gunning for your prince at the same time. Will we reach them in time?"

"I don't know," admitted Merivale. "It's too much of a risk. If the prince dies, we've lost our primary advantage."

The Black Rose stared at the soldiers as they continued to hammer at the ambassador's door. "I reckon we better make a go of it, then, and hope they're as bad at shooting as they are at knocking doors down. If we're lucky, we'll be halfway down the hall before they see us."

They geared themselves up for what could very well be a suicidal charge. Merivale even accepted a gun from the Black Rose. Resorting to physical violence always meant she'd miscalculated in some way, but if she was to die in this hallway, she'd at least want to kill as many of Tramasta's men as she could, with the admittedly thin hope that the remaining soldiers would be too few to break into the apartments.

But as they prepared for their charge, Moxy Poxy cocked her head to one side. "You hear something strange?"

"Yeah," said the Black Rose. "Sounds like... thunder? Coming from inside?"

Then the ambassador's door blew apart and what appeared to be a giant metal insect burst through, smashing headlong into the stunned soldiers.

"What *is* it?" asked Mister Hatbox, showing the first genuine interest Merivale had ever seen him exhibit.

"It's our chance," said the Black Rose. "Move in while they're distracted."

As Merivale and the others charged down the hallway, the massive metal insect lurched across the floor, crushing soldiers beneath its long steel legs. The thing roared and smoked and hissed in a way that wasn't natural at all. As they got closer, Merivale saw that it wasn't actually an insect, but a machine. The body of it was composed of the Aukbontaren engine. The legs appeared to be broken pieces of bed frames lashed together. Drissa the machinist sat astride the engine, her grin bright beneath thick goggles as she pulled levers and turned cranks. Catim sat behind her, using a rifle to pick off any soldiers who made it past the massive steel legs. By the time Merivale and her companions reached the shattered remains of the door, all the soldiers were either unconscious or dead.

"Truly a thing of beauty," breathed Mister Hatbox as they drew near the smoking, grinding machine. He took off his hat and held it to his chest respectfully.

"Lady Hempist!" boomed Catim as he climbed down from the machine. "You made it just in time to see Drissa's handiwork up close!"

"Very impressive," agreed Merivale, trying her absolute best to appear calm and in control, even though her heart was hammering in her chest. "I assume by your lighthearted tone that the prince is safe inside?"

"Of course! You asked us to look after him, didn't you?" Catim turned to Drissa. "You better shut her down for now. We don't have a lot of fuel."

Drissa muttered something sulkily in Aukbontaren that made Catim laugh, then nodded. She pulled a few levers and twisted a few knobs, and the great metal insect stopped smoking and fell silent.

"This way, my lady," Catim told Merivale, then stepped carefully over the wreckage of the door and into the apartments.

"All clear!" Catim bellowed.

A moment later, Etcher, Nea, and Leston peered cautiously from the kitchen.

"Lady Hempist!" said the prince as he hurried over to her. "It's just awful! Ammon Set has gone mad! He's killed my father and declared himself emperor!"

"Yes, Your Highness," said Merivale. "My condolences on the loss of your father."

"This that prince, then?" asked the Black Rose. "He don't look like much."

Leston's eyes widened. "Excuse me?"

"This is Rixidenteron's friend," Merivale told the prince. "The Black Rose of Paradise Circle."

Leston gave the Black Rose a lofty look. "I don't think he's ever mentioned you."

"He probably would have called me by the name Nettles," she told him.

For some reason, the prince suddenly began to blush. "Oh, uh, yes, well…he may have told me about…that is, the name sounds familiar."

The Black Rose laughed coarsely. "I see the length of it." Then she nudged him in the side with her elbow. "All true, by the way." As the prince's blush deepened, the Black Rose turned to Nea. "You all from Aukbontar, then?"

"Yes," said Nea, as calm and regal as ever. "We are here on a diplomatic mission to promote peace and prosperity between our two peoples."

"How's that going for you?" said the Black Rose.

Nea gave her a pained smile. "Today has not been one of the better days."

"Let's see if we can't turn that around, then," said the Black Rose.

"We need to get everyone in the courtyard to stop fighting long enough for the prince to take command of the soldiers," said Merivale.

"It'll take something pretty impressive to get 'em all to pay attention," said the Black Rose.

"Yes..." Merivale looked through the broken doorway at the giant mechanical spider. "That's what I was thinking, too..."

———

The fighting in the courtyard had not lessened. If anything, it had grown more intense, and more chaotic. The neat lines of battle had dissolved, and now the whole place was just a writhing mass of blood, screams, and people killing and trying desperately not to be killed. The quarters were too close for guns to be very effective, so most of them had switched to swords, spears, axes, clubs, or sometimes just fists, feet, and even teeth. The eyes of the men and women locked in this furious struggle had little thought, or even much emotion beyond terror and rage.

Then the front doors of the palace burst open to reveal a massive mechanical spider. It hissed and clanked, belching thick black smoke as its metal feet pounded down the short flight of stairs onto the courtyard. With the scream of instinct still pounding in their veins, those who had been fighting looked up at this metal beast in awe as it loomed over them like it was a demon of war that had suddenly become manifest before them. It stomped into the center of the courtyard, and both soldiers and criminals shrank away before it.

"You must stop fighting each other!"

A man had suddenly climbed astride this metal demon. A handsome, dashing young man with a serious, earnest face. In his eyes was not the rage of battle, but a deep sorrow.

"I am Leston, prince of the empire, and I beg you to listen to me. Archlord Tramasta and the biomancer Ammon Set have conspired to seize the throne. *They* are the ones who have set you against each other. They would have you kill each other, soldier and civilian, so that they might be rid of you *both*."

As the madness of battle began to recede, the soldiers and criminals looked at one another with both hope and distrust. Nobody wanted to keep fighting and dying. But could they really trust the other wouldn't suddenly turn on them?

"I know this is difficult to accept," said Leston. "But surely the idea of the powerful and the nobility using commoners such as you for their own vile ploys is not new to any of you."

There were gasps and murmurs among the crowd. Hadn't this man just said he was the *prince*? So why was he talking against the nobility?

He smiled sadly at them then, and nodded in acknowledgment of their whispers. "I know this because my best friend is a commoner. I have learned of your plight thanks to him. I don't honestly know what I can do to ease those problems when I become emperor, but I *do* know that allowing a coldhearted biomancer like Ammon Set to become emperor will only multiply them. Now, I beg of you, instead of using your weapons against each other, join me in protecting the empire that includes *all* of us."

Merivale and the Black Rose watched from the doorway, as Leston slowly talked the people in the courtyard back to sanity. It was going surprisingly well. Once Drissa got their attention, the prince seemed to know just how to speak to them. It was,

Merivale decided, an excellent precedent to set for the future emperor. Assuming they all lived that long.

She leaned in close to the Black Rose.

"Keep the prince safe," she breathed into her ear. "Once he's finished speaking, close the front gates and get ready to repel reinforcements from Ammon Set from either outside the walls, or from inside the palace."

"You think there's more coming?"

Merivale nodded. "This isn't over yet. I'm going to go see if I can learn exactly what to expect."

"You want me to come along?"

"Your people are loyal to you, but perhaps not quite yet to the prince. I'd rather have you stay here to keep them in check. Besides, I'm quite capable of handling things myself, if it comes to that."

The Black Rose grinned. "I reckon you are."

As Merivale slipped back into the palace, she decided that she was looking forward to working with the Black Rose beyond this crisis.

She tried the lift, but the gears only gave a sad little whimper, and it didn't move. They had brought Drissa's metal spider down to the ground floor with it, but the weight of the machine had apparently done more damage than she'd realized.

So Merivale began the long climb up the palace stairs to the forty-sixth floor. Again she was thankful she had opted to wear her riding clothes for this operation. Handling this many stairs in a gown and heels would have been torturous. Perhaps even impossible. As it was, she was breathing hard by the time she reached the floor where Tramasta's apartments were located.

A man like Tramasta would want to be present for his "victory," but not so close that his life would be in danger, so this seemed the logical place. Besides, she'd heard from Shelby that Tramasta's dependence on cloud glass had grown to the point that he rarely left his apartments.

Merivale knocked on the door, and Shelby answered a few moments later, looking tense and exhausted.

"Is he here?" Merivale asked.

Shelby nodded.

"The prince has secured the front gate, but I'm not sure how long the palace will remain stable. I suggest you head home while you can. I can see myself in."

"Thank you, my lady," said Shelby, and hurried away.

Merivale found the archlord of Fashlament and chief of military in his bedroom. He sat on the floor with a box of cloud glass open in front of him. He wore a red silk robe that was open in front to reveal that he was completely naked underneath. His eyes were glazed over and he was grinning like an idiot.

Merivale looked at him with something very close to sadness. Tramasta had once been a worthy adversary. Under different circumstance, sparring with him as chief of military would have proven immensely satisfying. But seeing him reduced to this hollow shell was not.

"Perhaps you have been overdoing it a bit, my lord?" she suggested.

"Lovely Lady Hempist!" he said, not bothering to cover his nakedness. "So good of you to come congratulate me on my victory!"

"Victory?" asked Merivale. "Perhaps you have not been keeping up with current events. I have rescued the prince and he has just brought your poor, misguided soldiers back to his side."

"Is that so?" he asked, not seeming very troubled. He took a pinch of cloud glass from the box and sniffed it, then licked his fingers. "Well, well, well, I *knew* it would come to this!"

He jumped to his feet and began pacing. His expression grew almost feral as he rubbed his hands together.

"Ammon Set thought you were only a greedy opportunist and that we could use you," said Tramasta. "But I told him you were not to be trifled with! I *knew* you would be trouble!"

"Your appraisal of my abilities is flattering," she said. "If only he had listened to you."

He barked a laugh. "Oh, but he *did* listen! Did you think this was the extent of our plan?"

"No, but I'm not sure what might come next. After all, he can't use his biomancers until he's coronated."

"Ah, not directly! But he can use the weapons they've been slowly amassing over the last decade!"

Merivale considered that. "Which are all kept in the sublevels of the palace."

"Just so!"

"It's inconvenient, but we'll have to evacuate the palace for the time being."

"Then what will protect you from the bombardment?" His eyes gleamed with delight.

"Bombardment?"

"See for yourself!" He gestured to the window.

Merivale forced herself to walk at a calm pace to his bedroom window. In the distance she could see a fleet of ships to the southwest.

"They should be here by nightfall," said Tramasta.

"Ammon Set plans to raze the entire island?"

"Sacrifice one island to save the empire. Seems a worthy trade," said Tramasta.

He came up behind her so that she could feel his breath on her neck. It smelled foul, as if the cloud glass was making his body rot from the inside.

"It's not too late to change sides." His hands gripped her waist. "If you please me, I'll make certain Ammon Set overlooks the trouble you've brought."

For the second time today, Merivale was forced to resort to violence. Really, it was quite vexing. But she couldn't see any other way out of this situation, and she doubted there would be any mechanical spiders leaping out to save her this time.

"Can I tell you a secret, my lord?" she asked as she began to slowly unbutton her blouse. "Something not a single living soul knows?"

"Oh yes, my lady," he murmured, pressing closer to her.

"My breasts are not as large as they appear. I wear a harness that pushes them up to create the alluring cleavage you and many others find so enjoyable to gaze upon."

"W-w-what?"

"It's terribly uncomfortable," she admitted. "But it does make room for the small, snub-nosed, single-shot pistol I keep holstered there at all times. An advantage that has saved both my pride and my life several times now."

Then she turned and shot him in the chest.

He stared at her, his mouth opening and closing for a moment before he dropped to the ground. She allowed herself the small satisfaction of watching him die. Then she turned back to the window.

Remain in the palace and brave the horrors of biomancery, or escape into the streets and the inevitable rain of fire that was to come. Merivale was not accustomed to having such limited options to work with. Nor was she used to having such a low chance of success.

"Very well played, my lord," she told the corpse of Tramasta. "I suppose it's possible I'll be joining you in some hell or other shortly. You'll forgive me if I don't give up quite yet, though."

23

Jilly thought she might be the worst student of biomancery ever. Theoretically, once a mental link
with someone had been established by direct contact,
it should be easy to reestablish at any time. That's
what Brigga Lin had told her when they'd first set
things up with Hope before the attack on Dawn's
Light. And it was pretty clear that Brigga Lin expected her to be able to reestablish it now while she
sat in the inn with Uter, far from the dangers currently plaguing the Shade District. But for some reason, it hadn't worked. She couldn't connect to Hope
at all.

Of course, she could have contacted Brigga Lin
again and asked for help. But she knew Brigga Lin
was dealing with the kraken and didn't need to be
bothered with Jilly's pathetic and probably unimportant failure. So she would have to fix this the only
way she knew how. By direct physical contact with
Hope. And that meant heading for the chaos of the
Shade District. Possibly this was an excuse to get
into the action. But she was pretty sure it was a convincing excuse.

She and Uter ran through the crowded streets.
Being smaller, it was easy for them to slip through
the knots of people that milled around.

"Hey, Jilly, you look grumpy. You should cheer up!"

Uter held out a dead mouse in his hand and made
it do a little dance.

"That's disgusting!" She smacked it out of his hands.

"Sorry." He glanced over his shoulder as they ran
on, leaving the dancing mouse behind.

Jilly knew she was more frustrated with her own
pathetic failure and general uselessness than she was
with his weird wighting power. Still, it wasn't right to
turn the dead into jokes. Not even animals.

"Why in all hells do you do stuff like that?" she
demanded. "What is *wrong* with you?"

He stopped running and just stood in the middle
of the busy street. His head bowed and his arms
hung limp at his sides.

"Uter, what are you…" She stopped and stared
at him. She couldn't see his face beneath his mop of
spooky white hair, but when she saw his shoulders
start to shake, she realized he was crying.

"Piss'ell. Come on, Uter…"

"S-s-sorry," he said. He looked up at her, his pale
face wet and blotched with red. "I d-d-don't know."

She sighed. "Don't know what, Uter?"

His lips puckered for a moment, and his forehead
creased like he was in pain. "I don't know what's
wrong with me."

Now she felt bad. "Ah, listen, Uter. I didn't mean it
like that. We're *all* messed up in one way or another.
I mean, look at me, I make little boys cry for no good
reason."

"You don't *like* me."

"That's not true, Uter. I just…" What could she
say? She resented being burdened with him? That
probably wouldn't make him feel any better. And she
didn't have time to explain it all to him anyway. She
had to find Hope.

"Look, I like you fine. I just don't like it when you
bring dead things back to life. So don't do it. Okay?"

He sniffled loudly and swallowed what was probably a huge glob of snot. "Promise? You like me?"

"Sure I do, old pot. Now come on, we have to find Hope, remember?"

He sniffled again and nodded.

"Sunny." Jilly scanned the street ahead. The crowds in front of them were getting even thicker. She wasn't sure they'd be able to weave their way through as easily as before.

"It'll take forever getting through those people," she told Uter. "Come on. We'll go around."

They made a wide sweep around the mass of people. It forced them close to the docks, but it was the southern piers, which were still pretty far from the kraken. Even so, in the distance, she could hear the kraken continue to lay waste to everything in reach.

"Those ships are huge!" said Uter as they ran along the pier. Trust him to be distracted from a giant monster attack by something silly like that.

"Those ships aren't even that big," she told him, glancing at the ships briefly as they hurried past. "When I was in the navy, I sailed on much bigger ships than that."

"With cannons and everything?" asked Uter.

"Of course with cannons," said Jilly. "What kind of navy vessel doesn't have cannons?"

"I don't know, what kind?" he asked earnestly.

She sighed. "You're hopeless, you know that?"

"Well, that's why we're going to find her!" he said.

"What?" she asked.

He smiled like he'd just said something very clever. "*Hope*. We're going to find her because we don't have her right now. We're *hope-less*, right?"

Jilly groaned. "I can't believe I got stuck with you."

His smile suddenly vanished. "I'm sorry, Jilly."

She felt awful immediately. Right after she'd just cheered him up, too. "You just don't know any better, and that's not your fault. Honestly, babysitting you is probably what I deserve. I can't even follow through with my master's command."

She glanced over at him as they ran, and saw that wasn't really cheering him up.

"Listen," she said. "When I was your age, I was the same way."

"Really?" He looked doubtful.

"Sure. I was always bothering Red about something. I thought he was the most pat wag who ever lived and I wanted to be just like him. So I was always asking him for advice." She thought about it for a moment. "He was always pretty nice about it, too. Nicer than I'm being, anyway. So, I'm sorry, too, I guess."

Then she jerked to a stop.

"Do you still hear it?" she asked Uter.

"Hear what?"

"The kraken. Can you hear it anymore?"

He shook his head.

"Come on, we've got to get a better look!"

"Okay," said Uter agreeably.

"Try to keep up," she told him. Then she started climbing up the fire escape of a nearby building. The buildings on Vance Post weren't as easy to climb as the ones on New Laven. There were fewer broken bricks or cracks to utilize. It took some pretty creative zig-zagging to make her way up. As she neared the roof, she half expected to see Uter still down at the bottom. But when she turned, he was right beneath her.

"Are we almost there?" he asked.

"Almost. You're doing great."

His eyes lit up. "I *am*?"

"Yeah." She had reached the roof by then. She leaned over and held out her hand. "Here."

He grabbed her hand and she hauled him up to stand next to her. Then she scanned the eastern skyline.

"I don't see it," she said. "The kraken is gone..."

"Did they kill it?" Uter looked eager.

"I don't know," said Jilly. "Maybe they just drove it away or something. Sure did do a lot of damage before they got it, though." She shook her head as she surveyed the shattered buildings and rubble-strewn streets. From this vantage, it looked even worse than she'd thought. The city looked...broken. She wondered, could a city ever sustain so much damage that it just...died?

"Why's that man over there waving to you?" asked Uter.

"Huh? What man?"

Uter pointed to a two-masted brig that was tied up at a nearby pier. The cut of it looked awfully familiar. And standing on the quarterdeck was someone she recognized immediately.

———

"Where'd it go?" asked Vaderton.

Brigga Lin shook her head. The kraken had been moving slowly but steadily closer. They were preparing to abandon Vaderton's small craft. But then it seemed to abruptly lose interest in its rampage. It had loomed over them, motionless for a few moments. And then it withdrew, sliding back out to sea and into deeper waters. That had been roughly a half hour ago, and the kraken hadn't returned. People were even starting to ease back toward the wreckage of the docks from wherever they had been hiding.

"Perhaps my cousin found Fitmol Bet and persuaded him to stop the attack," said Alash.

"I'm not sure 'persuaded' is the right word," said Brigga Lin. "Look."

She pointed down the dock. Red was walking slowly toward them. In his arms, he held the limp body of someone in the white robes of a biomancer.

"Did he kill him after all?" asked Vaderton.

"No, this one is still very much alive," said Brigga Lin. "I have a feeling Red has only earned us a brief respite."

Red continued unhurriedly toward them, a cheerful smile on his face.

"Well?" Brigga Lin had to make an effort not to sound impatient when he finally climbed aboard with the biomancer slung over his shoulder.

"He's actually pretty light," said Red. "I don't think he's been eating enough. Can't be healthy."

"She means, did you resolve the issue with the kraken," said Alash.

"I know what she meant," Red told his cousin, then turned back to Brigga Lin. "And sadly, no. But that's your job, isn't it? I was just supposed to bring him here alive."

"Yes," said Brigga Lin.

"Look at this." He laid Fitmol Bet on the deck with unexpected gentleness. "I feel kind of bad for the gaf, really."

He opened the biomancer's robes, and Brigga Lin saw what he meant. She stared at the vestigial tentacles fused onto her old master's sides, then sighed. "That's one way to do it, I suppose. Unfortunately, it's not something I could replicate without the proper materials. And even then, I doubt we'd find a willing volunteer to replace him."

"That's just it. I don't think we need to," said Red. "Bet's been compelled to attack Vance Post. If you could remove that compulsion, I think it's likely he'd stop."

"As I said before, and as I'm sure you're aware, compulsions can be extremely tricky. If this one was done by Progul Bon before he died—"

"He said it was done by Ammon Set."

"Really? How strange." Brigga Lin hadn't known Set to be particularly skilled in that area. "I'll take a look."

She placed her hand on Fitmol Bet's head and closed her eyes.

"Dear God," she whispered. Because what she found inside her old master's head was not so much a compulsion as it was endlessly repeating mental assault.

"Is it bad?" asked Red.

"It's...," she began. Fitmol Bet had not been a kind or warm master, but he had always been conscientious in his responsibilities, even in training such a frankly mediocre student as she had been. She was surprised to find herself hurting for him more deeply than she'd expected. But she was unwilling to show such weakness to Red.

"I can see how this is the work of Ammon Set," she said finally.

Fitmol Bet's eyes fluttered for a moment, then opened.

"Be still," she advised him.

"I cannot," he told her calmly. His arms, legs, and vestigial tentacles began to undulate gently.

"You're bringing the Guardian back," she said.

"I must."

"Ammon Set has torn out so much of...*you* to make room for his compulsion, that I fear there isn't really enough left to stand on its own. The only reason you're able to function right now is because you are bonded to the Guardian. In essence, you are using its cognitive abilities to supplement your own."

"I understand."

"If I remove the compulsion, what's left of your independent consciousness will be subsumed by the Guardian's. You will, in essence, switch roles, with it controlling you."

"Could you join us completely, then?"

Brigga Lin's eyebrow shot up. "That's what you want?"

"It seems the best possible outcome, given the options," he said. "And in a sense, I am already lost anyway."

"True," admitted Brigga Lin. "If I do this, what assurance do I have that the Guardian will cease its attack on us?"

"I can't say for certain, but it seems likely that another target will replace you."

"Ammon Set," she said.

"Hurry, I'm nearly here," he said.

"Ms. Lin, I see it out there," said Alash. "Coming in quite fast."

"I suppose we'll have to chance it, then," said Brigga Lin. She laid her hand on Fitmol Bet's forehead. "You deserved better than this."

"Did I?" he asked dreamily. Perhaps he no longer remembered. Or cared.

"Yes," she told him. "I was a student of yours once, and I admired you greatly."

He smiled. "Were you? That's nice to hear. You've turned out so well."

All through her training, Brigga Lin had longed for validation from this man, and he had never given it. She had thought she'd outgrown that longing ages ago. But perhaps some things lingered, no matter how old she got, because hearing those words shattered her usually impenetrable defenses and left her with an aching sadness.

She closed her eyes, and brought her attention inward to the electrical flickers that ran through her mind. That ran through *his* mind. She connected them, feeling just for a moment the great surge of power as she also touched the animal mind of the Guardian. The word *animal* was terribly inadequate. There was something ancient and ageless about its mind. Not subhuman, but merely prehuman. Primal and simple, but not brutish.

Brigga Lin tore out the garbage that Ammon Set had rammed into the elderly biomancer's mind. It was brutal work, but actually quite simple to remove. She let what little remained of Fitmol Bet's mind sink into the Guardian's power.

"Brigga Lin...," she heard Red say. Abstractly she was aware there was panic in his voice, but she was too far into what she was doing to react to it. She had to see this through.

She heard the great kraken breach the surface, the water streaming away as it rose up so close, she could smell the thick, heavy stench of it, like the bottom of an untouched sea dredged up and brought to the air for the first time.

She opened her eyes and saw the kraken looming over her. "Get back. All of you."

The three men obediently scrambled back to the far end of the boat.

Brigga Lin stripped Fitmol Bet's robes off, then carefully picked up the naked body.

"Ms. Lin!" shouted Alash. "Watch out!"

Brigga Lin ignored him and stood her ground as the kraken reached slowly toward her with one long tentacle. It stopped only a few feet from her. The mottled flesh on the thick trunk of it gleamed wetly, and the tip quivered, as if eager. Perhaps it was.

She closed the remaining distance and laid Fitmol Bet's body on the soft flesh of the tentacle.

"Union, at last," she said.

Then she pressed down until Fitmol Bet's body was absorbed into the tentacle.

She stood there for a moment, her hands laid directly on the kraken's flesh, feeling the strength of it up through her palms. She understood why he had wanted this.

"You are free," she told the Guardian. "Live as you see fit."

The tentacle pulled slowly away as the great kraken turned and headed back out to sea.

"Where do you think it's going?" asked Alash quietly as the three men cautiously came back over to her.

"I reckon if there's anything left of Bet in there, it's heading for Stonepeak to settle a score with Ammon Set," said Red.

"I suspect the Guardian may have already had its own score to settle with that man," said Brigga Lin quietly. She sat down and pulled her arms in close.

Alash sat down next to her. "Are you okay?"

Her eyes gazed out to sea at the wake left by the Guardian. "Do you remember some months back, we were sailing to Dawn's Light for the first time, and you were so excited to see those metal ships along the Breaks?"

He nodded.

"You said there were still mysteries in this life worth exploring..." She smiled sadly. "I think I understand now what you meant."

They sat there for a moment in silence.

"Preposterous!" Vaderton shouted at Red. Apparently, they'd been having a quiet discussion of their own while she and Alash had been talking.

"Well, yeah, but that doesn't mean it ain't true," said Red.

"What is it?" asked Brigga Lin, climbing wearily to her feet.

"He claims that Ammon Set is staging a coup to wrest power from the royal family."

"That's what Fitmol Bet told me," said Red.

Vaderton shook his head. "The man was hardly in his right mind."

"Even if he'd decided to degrade his own power by

lying, there wasn't enough of his mind left for him to make something up," Brigga Lin told him.

"Which is *why* we have to get over there and help!" said Red.

"We did just send an angry kraken after Ammon Set," Alash pointed out.

"It won't be enough," said Red. "We need to go, too. We need to go *now*."

"We'll see what Hope says," Brigga Lin told him.

———

It was strange that in the midst of this crisis, Hope felt such peace. Although the situation was dire, she was grateful for the simplicity of it. There was no real question of what to do. A kraken had attacked innocents; those innocents needed help. And even though the kraken appeared to have fled, most likely thanks to Brigga Lin, the people still needed help. That was something she could do without any conflicting emotions.

"Half the district is in ruins," Stephan told her quietly. "But I think we've managed to find all the survivors."

Hope looked around at their makeshift shelter in the old temple, which had been built to straddle the river that marked the boundary between the Commercial and Shade Districts in the center of the island. Like nearly every temple she had seen in the urban areas of the empire, it lay empty and unused. She'd never really thought before on *why* people never came to temples anymore. But now it occurred to her that it was because there was no one to lead them there anymore. There were many stories of the old days where the emperor made tours of his empire, coming to each temple to speak directly to the people. But after the time of the Dark Mage, when the

Vinchen and biomancery orders split, the emperor
stopped coming to the temples. Perhaps the common
people had still used them as community meeting
places for a while. But slowly the temple had fallen
into disuse.

It was, however, an ideal place to house the many
refugees from the Shade District. The open space,
free of clutter and furniture, allowed families and
friends to gather together for comfort. It also provided an area for the Vinchen to treat the injured. As
she had once boasted to Red, the Vinchen could heal
as well as kill.

"We did good work here today," she told Stephan.
"I only wish I knew what the kraken was after."

"Perhaps *they* know the answer to that." Stephan
pointed to the entrance of the temple. Brigga Lin,
Red, Alash, and Vaderton had come in and were
looking around the huge, crowded space.

Hope was not prepared for the sudden spike in
her pulse when she saw Red. Without thinking, she
threw up her arms and waved eagerly.

Red's sharp eyes spotted her first, of course. He
nudged the others, and they hurried over.

"You're alright?" Red asked as soon as he was in
earshot.

"Of course," said Hope. "You?"

"Yeah, I'm fine."

Red jerked to a halt a few feet from her, his arms
tense. It seemed like he'd wanted to embrace her, but
had stopped himself at the last moment. Now they
just stared at each other in silence. Hope hated this
space that was between them, but she didn't know
how to close it.

"Things are more complicated than we'd thought,"
Brigga Lin said.

Hope forced her eyes away from Red to look at
her. "In what way?"

"The kraken had been sent by Ammon Set to prevent anyone from leaving Vance Post while he attempts to seize power from the imperial family and declares himself emperor. That's why the kraken was going after the ships."

"How dare he!" said Stephan, his eyes wide with fury. "We'll eviscerate the traitor!"

"I think that's the exact reaction he wanted to avoid, old pot," Red told the Vinchen.

"Red believes we should go to their rescue." Brigga Lin's voice and expression were carefully neutral. Hope didn't know what to make of that.

"I have to agree with him," said Vaderton. "While I have no love for the navy anymore, this is the *emperor* we're talking about. The symbol of our entire people. I can't imagine someone like Ammon Set, who is capable of causing..." He glanced around at the many wounded and frightened people. "*This*, to represent the entire empire. It's unconscionable."

"You have suggested that we return to the code and the vows of Selk the Brave," Stephan said. "Isn't our most basic vow to save the empire from those who would destroy it? Can you think of a worse fate for our people than someone like Ammon Set wresting power? The Vinchen *must* rally and face this threat."

"Hope..." Red's eyes were wide as he looked at her. The wall behind them had come down, and they shone wetly in the lamplight of the temple. "Piss on duty and vows and the empire itself, for all I care right now. Leston is my *friend*, and they're going to kill him."

Hope stared from one to the next, feeling utterly bewildered. "Why are you all talking like it's up to me? I don't command any of you. I'm not in charge of anything. I don't even have a ship to get us there. Why do you all look to me? You don't need me."

"Ah, but we do, my dearest friend." Brigga Lin reached out her long, slim hand and laid it with unexpected affection on Hope's cheek. "You are our hope, after all. And what bold action could ever be successful—or even begun—without that?"

Hope's chest felt tight. It was difficult to look at them. It was difficult to even speak. "There is no reason—"

"There doesn't have to be one," said Brigga Lin. "We need you with us. It's that simple."

She stared at them a moment longer as she struggled to breathe. To regain some composure.

"Of course I will come," she said finally. "I don't know how I feel about empires or emperors. But you are my friends. If you need me, how can I possibly turn away?"

"Teacher!"

Hope jerked her head back toward the entrance as Jilly and Uter came bursting through, nearly tripping over a family by the door.

"Teacher!" Jilly called again.

"Teacher, teacher!" Uter mimicked gleefully.

"Be careful of the people around you!" Hope scolded automatically.

Jilly slowed down, then grabbed Uter, forcing him to slow down as well. They walked the rest of the way over to Hope at an even pace, although their eyes continued to blaze with excitement.

"You have to come and see this!" Jilly said.

"You have to see the—" Uter began, but Jilly yanked his arm hard.

"You promised you wouldn't spoil it!" she hissed at him.

"I won't spoil it!" He clamped his mouth shut, but it looked like the effort to do so was almost painful.

Jilly squeezed Hope's hand. "Please, teacher. Will you just come and see?"

Hope looked at the others.

"Are you kidding?" said Red. "Anything that's got Jilly this excited has to be worth it."

"It is, Red! I promise!" said Jilly. Then she gave Brigga Lin big pleading eyes. "Master, please!"

Brigga Lin winced. "What a horrible expression. Stop it at once."

"Will you all come?" asked Jilly.

"Hope?" asked Brigga Lin.

"I suppose we will," said Hope, feeling like she had no control over the situation and had no idea why anyone was asking her.

"This way!" Jilly said, and hurried back toward the entrance.

"This way! This way!" said Uter, scampering after her.

———

Jilly led them zigzagging through the streets of the Commercial District in a southwesterly direction until they finally came to the docks. Jilly normally tried so hard to act mature and older than she really was. Hope wondered what could have inspired such childish delight.

But when they reached the docks, she saw exactly what had them so excited.

"Is that...," she whispered.

"Ahoy, Captain!" called a very familiar voice.

Missing Finn, that old, one-eyed sailor from Paradise Circle, stood at the gunwale of the *Kraken Hunter*. Except, no, it looked like Finn had changed the name back to the *Lady's Gambit*.

"I hope you don't mind me bringing back the original name, Captain," said Finn. "I always felt *Kraken Hunter* was something the ship took on just like you took on the name Dire Bane. Now that you're back to being you, so to speak, I reckoned it was time to get her back to her old self as well. Except I kept the cannons, of course."

"How..." Hope's hand trembled slightly as she reached out to touch the rough wooden siding.

"The Black Rose helped me get her seaworthy again," Finn told her. "She's got a soft spot for this old tub, too. Don't ever let her tell you otherwise."

Hope turned to Jilly, who was smiling so fiercely, it looked like her face might split. "You were right, Jilly. This was worth it."

"It's your ship, Hope!" said Uter. "You remember, right? The one where you cut off the head of that oarfish! The one you sailed to that island of owl monsters! The one—"

"Yes, Uter, I remember." She patted his head and he smiled up at her. "And I'm impressed you remember all those stories. Now..." She turned back to look up at Finn. "Permission to come aboard, Captain?"

"She's yours by right," objected Finn.

Hope shook her head. "No, Finn. She's *yours* by right now. You were the one who didn't give up on her."

"Ah, well..." He smiled fondly as he touched the wooden rail with his wrinkled, brown hand. "She's all I got now, I suppose." Then he looked back at them, and his face was suddenly serious. "If you all don't mind coming aboard, we've got a grave matter to discuss."

Hope glanced at the others. "Yes, I think we do."

Finn had a couple of his crew slide out the gangplank. As Hope walked back onto the ship where she had spent so much of her life, she felt all its old memories come back to her, and with it the people she'd known and lost. The original crew, with Carmichael, Ticks, Sankack, Mayfield, and even Ranking. Then later Filler and Sadie. All of those people had a place on this ship once. In a sense, they were all still a part of it.

A new crew was bustling about the deck. Ten or so solid wags from the Circle. Just the right amount of hands. More than was needed on a calm day, but in a real luffer, barely enough to get through. Carmichael would have been pleased.

And in the middle of it all was Missing Fin. His white hair was a little thinner, and his skin a little more weathered. And there was a quiet sadness behind his one eye that spoke of grief that might fade, but would never truly go away. He still had the same old salt-stained black eye patch and white linen shirt.

Hope walked right up to him and gave him a rough embrace.

"Captain, I—"

"It's just Hope now," she told him, squeezing him harder. "And shut up."

"Aye, fair enough," he said, and squeezed her back.

Once Hope finally let him go, he gave her a serious look. "The Black Rose brought this ship we love back to life, and now she needs it. And she needs you."

"Oh?"

"She's cut a deal with the empress."

"She followed through with that?" asked Red, looking delighted.

"Aye," said Finn.

"What kind of deal?" asked Hope.

"We get the empress and her son out of their current mess," said Finn, "and they give us a seat at the table."

"I'm not sure I understand," said Hope.

"Oh, this…." Red ran his hands through his hair, looking thrilled. "This is big. I can't believe Pysetcha agreed to it! They must be desperate." He shook his head. "Merivale must have had a hand in it, too. Maybe even Nea."

"Red, what are you talking about?" asked Hope.

He put his hands on her shoulders. "Don't you see? Nettie's bargained to get representation at the palace. Common people having a voice in the government! This could change everything!"

Hope stared at him. It almost didn't make sense. Normal people making decisions about how the government should be run?

"That's assuming we win, of course," said Brigga Lin calmly.

Hope turned to her, a tight grin on her face. "If this is truly what's at stake, I have nothing but pity for anyone who stands in our way."

24

*T*here was a throne room on the first floor of the palace. Technically speaking, it was the official seat of power, but it had not been used in years. Emperor Martarkis had been too weak to make it all the way down there. It was not just his physical weakness that Ammon Set had loathed about him. The man had been weak of spirit as well, something Set knew better than anyone.

Ammon Set had received his biomancer name the same year that Martarkis had been made emperor. Even at that young age, it had been obvious that the emperor was impulsive and self-indulgent. It was bad enough that he drank and ate to excess. But his lecherousness was so rampant that he never gave any effort to searching for a wife who would bear him a legitimate heir. Then when he finally settled down enough to consider marriage, he became absurdly picky about his mate. By the time Martarkis had chosen the young maiden Pysetcha from Belgranada, he was so old, the act of sexual intercourse had become impossible.

It had been that damned Progul Bon who put the idea in Martarkis's head to order the biomancers to make him young again. Bon convinced the emperor that it was so he could enjoy his beautiful young wife, but Ammon Set knew it was to ensure there would be an heir to the throne. That was a very serious concern, to be sure. But so was extending the rule of a weak man made even weaker by stretching his life out that long and thin. It was the first of many arguments that Ammon Set and Progul Bon had over the next two decades. And, unfortunately, it was not the last that Bon won, much to the detriment of the empire.

"Ridding ourselves of Progul Bon was one good thing to come from all this," Ammon Set said aloud.

He stood with Chiffet Mek in the emperor's apartments. They ignored the plush, sumptuous furniture that Martarkis had insisted on in his later years. Partly because it felt like sitting on a fat woman, and partly because it stank of old age, sickness, and decay. Once Ammon Set was coronated, he would have it all burned.

The two biomancers looked out of the large bay window at the southern wall, which afforded an excellent view of Tramasta's fleet sailing in from Fashlament.

"I consider Progul Bon's loss unfortunate," said Chiffet Mek in his flat, scraping voice. "He was better at keeping you in check than anyone else."

"You think I have crossed a line," said Ammon Set. "But I am trying to save this empire."

"Has it occurred to you that it is *your* actions that will fulfill the Dark Mage's prophecy? A divided empire is no match for Aukbontar."

"We were already divided," said Ammon Set. "So disjointed, one could barely call us an empire at all. Once we eliminate the prince and his little resistance, *I* will make us strong and united."

"Leston has proven a more formidable opponent than you thought."

Ammon Set grunted. "It's that damned Hempist woman. I can't believe she's been scheming under our noses for years. I can't believe Progul Bon never told us!"

"Can't you?" asked Chiffet Mek. "Perhaps she was his safeguard against you all along."

"That would be just like him," Ammon Set said sourly. "And *maybe* if he were still alive, the two of them would have been a serious threat. But she's on her own now, and what can one regular woman do against the raw power at my disposal?"

"You still mean to open the pens, then?" asked Mek.

"It's already been done," said Set.

———

Merivale decided that running down forty-six flights of stairs would take too long. So instead, she took the lift. Or rather, the lift shaft. She found a thick pair of leather gloves in Tramasta's wardrobe, perhaps used for hunting with a falcon. She also found an old sword that was thin enough to slip between the lift doors and sturdy enough to pry them open.

Once the doors were open, she saw the thick metal cables that trailed down into the dark shaft. They seemed to be composed of thin metal strands all woven together to form one thick rope. The gloves would hold, probably. And her riding boots went nearly to her knees, so those would protect her ankles well enough, although she feared they wouldn't survive the descent intact.

Of course, there was also the nagging fear that *she* wouldn't survive the descent. But she certainly couldn't take the time to clamber down one flight at a time when monsters could be spilling out into the courtyard at any moment to gobble up her unsuspecting compatriots.

So she took a deep breath and jumped to the cable. She gripped it hard with her gloved hands until she was able to wrap her leather-sheathed ankles around it. Then she slowly began to loosen her grip so that she slid down.

As she picked up speed, she could feel the leather on her palms and ankles heating up. The air blew up at her face, lashing her ponytail hard enough to free a good portion of her hair. She didn't dare let go of the cable even to brush hair out of her eyes, though. She could smell the leather gloves beginning to singe. She had no way of knowing how fast she was traveling in the dark, so she didn't know how much farther she had to go. It occurred to her that perhaps the leather wouldn't hold after all. And at this speed, the friction would shred her bare hands in seconds...

Then she came to a jarring stop as her feet slammed into something metal. The pain shot up her legs and into her hips. Her breath came out in a whoosh, and it took several moments for her to recover and take stock of her surroundings.

She had landed on top of the lift. She discarded the gloves, which were uncomfortably hot, the leather seared black in places. She knelt down and pulled up the emergency hatch, then climbed down into the lift.

The lift door was open and she could see down the hallway. It appeared to be empty. No monsters in sight. She'd made it in time.

Or else she was far too late.

Preferring to remain optimistic, she hurried out into the hallway and headed for the front door that led to the courtyard. There wasn't much lighting, so when she glanced down a side passage, she thought she saw one of the servants who, like Shelby, hadn't been given permission to flee yet.

She stopped for a moment and waved to the silhouette as it walked slowly toward her. "This way! Hurry! We have to get outside immediately!"

The person didn't reply but continued their slow movement in her direction. She couldn't be certain if it was a man or a woman, but the bald silhouette suggested a man. The way he moved was...strange. There was a limping quality to it. And now that she was looking more closely, she realized he was...dripping.

A few more steps and he passed close enough to a gaslight that it revealed more details. The "person" had no skin. Muscles and sinews gleamed wetly with blood and thick yellow pus as they flexed and contracted. Beneath the taut facial muscles, it appeared the skull had been somehow re-formed so that it had a pointed muzzle instead of a normal nose and mouth. Without the flesh of lips, it was easy to see the long, pointed teeth housed in the muzzle. The hands and feet had been similarly altered so that they had short, curved claws.

"Piss'ell," muttered Merivale. She generally avoided cursing, since she considered it to be unladylike, but there were exceptions to every rule.

She had, of course, reloaded her single-shot pistol. She drew it from the holster beneath her bosom and fired. Snubnoses were not particularly accurate at anything other than close range, but she aimed for the center of the body, and since she was an excellent shot, it struck the creature in the chest.

The creature reeled, and stumbled, but didn't fall. Instead, it stupidly clawed at the bullet in its own chest, causing far more harm to itself than Merivale's tiny gun could have done. The more pain it felt, the more incensed it became, making gargling noises as it dug deeper into its own chest. After a moment, it tore out the bullet, along with a large portion of its own chest cavity. It swayed for a moment, clutching the bullet, muscles, veins, possibly part of a lung, and what appeared to be a chunk of its heart. Then it flopped to the ground with a wet squelch.

"Well...," said Merivale, about to give herself a smug congratulations.

But then another form rounded a corner into the hallway. There was no mistaking this one for a person. It was the size of a horse, and appeared to be some jumbled mix of frog and cat. Another creature quickly followed, this one sliding across the ground like a snake with a human head. And still more came after that. All manner of horrors that the biomancers had apparently been stockpiling for some time now. And they were all coming at her.

Merivale prided herself on keeping a cool head in any situation, but even she felt an icy terror in her stomach at seeing this army of monstrosities coming toward her. For just a moment, her body seized up and she could not move.

But this would not be her end. It *could* not be. She knew that like she knew the sun would rise in the morning, no matter what else happened. So she bit down on her lip until blood flowed to her chin. The spike of pain got her body moving. As the creatures began to howl and hiss and roar, she turned and sprinted for the front door that led to the courtyard.

She could hear them pursuing her. Her flight had piqued their interest, like a cat after a mouse. She heard claws scraping and wet limbs slapping the stone floor. She heard labored breathing and a groan of longing. She did not turn or look back. She just kept running.

She'd never realized how long the distance between the lift and the front door was. And to be perfectly honest, she was not much of a runner. By the time she was in sight of the open door, her chest burned with fatigue. She saw the Black Rose standing at the top of the step where she'd left her, facing out at the courtyard with her arms crossed.

"Get these doors closed!" she shouted. *"Now!"*

The Black Rose turned and saw Merivale pounding toward her, then took in the mass of creatures behind her. And God bless her, she didn't even blink. She turned and bellowed into the courtyard, "We need to get these doors closed and barricaded before all hells come bursting through!"

By the time Merivale reached the doors, soldiers and criminals were working together to get the massive doors closed. She slipped through the narrowing gap and a moment later heard them slam shut behind her.

"Brace the doors!" she shouted, turning to push against them. Those who had closed the doors, including the Black Rose, did the same.

"Get ready!" said Merivale.

A moment later, the creatures on the other side hit the doors, and they buckled.

"Piss'ell, what is on the other side of this?" said one of the soldiers.

"All your nightmares made real," Merivale told him. Then to those soldiers standing stupidly nearby, she said, "Gather things to barricade the doors! Do it now!"

"Yes, my lady!" several shouted and began to look around for anything large and heavy. Several more hurried over and took her place at the door.

As she stepped into the courtyard, she heard the prince's voice.

"Lady Hempist!"

Leston and Ambassador Omnipora rushed over to her.

"Ah, Your Highness," Merivale said breezily as she smoothed back her hair and fixed her ponytail. "Glad to see you've sorted things out here."

"Are you okay, my lady?" asked Nea.

"Well enough for now, but I'm afraid I'm going to need to ask you to lend us Drissa and her astonishing machine for when those creatures inevitably break through."

"What *were* they?" asked Leston. "I only caught a glimpse before the doors closed, but they seemed like beasts of some sort."

"You may not have been aware of this," said Merivale, "but the biomancers maintain several sublevels beneath the palace, most of which contain various experiments they've engaged in over the years."

"How long has that been going on?" he demanded.

"Decades, at least. Probably longer."

"And we never knew?"

"Well, *I* knew, and so did your mother. Of course, Red knew as well. And I'm sure your father did at some point."

"Unbelievable," muttered Leston.

"So now the biomancers have set all their nasties free?" asked the Black Rose.

Merivale nodded.

"Can't we just escape into the city?" asked Nea.

"I'm afraid not, Ambassador. If you'll all kindly follow me."

Leston, Nea, and the Black Rose followed Merivale to the ladder that stretched up the side of the outer wall to the guard station.

"Please watch your step," she told them as she began to ascend.

Once they reached the guard platform, Merivale pointed south across the rooftops to the sea that lay behind. In the gathering dusk, she could see the approaching fleet of ships.

"That's almost the entire imperial fleet!" said Leston.

"Yes," agreed Merivale. "And they have orders from Tramasta to raze the city, killing everyone in it."

They all stared silently at the distant ships.

"We should be out of mortar range here," said Merivale. "Unfortunately, the resulting fires that will no doubt spread throughout the city are another mat-

ter. But, regardless, we have more pressing concerns."
She gestured back to the courtyard behind them. Soldiers had piled everything they could find in front of the door. An old wagon, crates, barrels, and bales of hay from the stables. They'd even piled the corpses from the previous battle in the wagon to give it more weight. But Merivale knew better than any of them what lay beyond the door, and felt certain the barricade wouldn't hold long.

"The choices are burn to death or get eaten alive," the Black Rose said quietly.

"Surely there's something we can do!" said Leston.

Merivale shook her head. "Survive as long as we can. If we outlast the bombing, we might be able to sneak through the rubble and escape. Once we're outside the city walls, we can regroup at Sunset Point and come up with our next plan of action. That is, assuming Tramasta didn't have the foresight to bomb the empress's home out of existence as well."

"Actually," said the Black Rose, and there was an unexpected twinkle in her eyes. "I took the liberty of calling in a few favors."

"Oh?" asked Merivale.

"If we can hold until sunrise, I reckon we should be getting some serious reinforcements."

"What kind of reinforcements?" asked Merivale.

"The kind you've been trying to get for months."
The Black Rose grinned. "If only you'd come to me from the start, instead of sending that saltheaded red-eyed thief on such a delicate mission alone."

Merivale stared at her for a moment. She debated whether to make an issue out of the fact that the Black Rose hadn't bothered to tell her any of this until now. But she thought better of it.

Instead she said, "Even I make mistakes from time to time."

Lady Merivale Hempist prided herself on her lack of
sentimentality. She'd never been particularly sentimental, and as she'd worked her way rapidly through
the government to the position of chief of espionage,
she had willfully dismantled every instance of it
within herself that she could find.

But as Tramasta's fleet began to shell the city of
Stonepeak, even she felt the sting of tears in her eyes.

Strangely enough, it was the thought of Hooper,
her dressmaker, and his beautiful shop being reduced
to rubble that caught her unprepared. Such a small
thing. In the scope of an empire's past, present, and
future, one dressmaker hardly seemed a great loss.
And yet, he had been an *exceptional* dressmaker.
An artist, really. His work had given her more pleasure than could ever be paid back in something as
banal as money. And now, as screaming arcs of fire
rained down on the city again and again, she knew
that shop was more than likely gone, along with the
owner and his charming lover.

"My lady..." Leston handed her a handkerchief.

"My sincerest apologies, Your Highness." Her
voice was thick as she took the offered handkerchief
and dabbed at her eyes. "This is most unprofes-
sional, not to mention unbecoming of me. It is a side
of me you should never have to witness."

"And yet I'm grateful for it," he said quietly.
"Because sharing this grief with you makes it more
bearable."

They watched as death rained down and the
explosions erupted through the city. Lives, culture,
history, all lost forever.

"Here now," the Black Rose growled nearby.
"Those poncey looks won't do. I need anger right
now, my wags, not tears."

Merivale sniffed and wiped her eyes one last time, then turned to the ganglord. "You're quite right. Let's go check on the palace doors. As terrible as the shelling is, it is not our most immediate concern."

"Well put," the Black Rose said approvingly.

The two women climbed back down the ladder to the courtyard. Merivale spotted Drissa and Catim working feverishly on the machine near the stables.

"Is everything functional?" she asked them.

"It's all pretty makeshift," said Catim. "If we'd had better material to work with, I'd be a lot less concerned."

"I'm afraid you'll just have to make do with what you have," said Merivale.

"That's what I figured," Catim said grimly. "Don't worry. We'll do our part to keep the prince and ambassador safe."

"How much time you reckon we have before those things break through?" asked the Black Rose.

"See for yourself." Catim nodded to the entrance.

The door already had several large cracks in it, and one of the hinges was coming off. Every few seconds, something smashed up against it on the inside and their makeshift barricade shuddered.

"Not long," said the Black Rose.

As the two women stared at the shaking door, Merivale said, "May I ask you a question?"

"Of course. Don't mean I'll answer, though."

"The reason you didn't tell me that Bleak Hope and Brigga Lin were coming...Did you truly enlist them as reinforcements for us? Or was your original intention to bring them as a means to guarantee that the empress would comply with her end of your deal?"

The Black Rose grinned. "Pick whichever one you like, Merivale."

Merivale was silent for a moment. "This Paradise

Circle of yours must be quite a place to produce such remarkable people as you and Red."

The Black Rose's smile faded away. Then in a singsong voice, she said:

> *Where it's cold, and it's wet,*
> *And the sun never gets.*
> *But still it's my home.*
> *Bless the Circle.*

A loud crack echoed across the courtyard as another split appeared in the doors.

"What do you think, twenty minutes?" asked the Black Rose.

"Less," said Merivale.

"Lady Hempist!" Nea waved down at them from the guard tower. "You must see this!"

"Back up we go," said Merivale as she and the Black Rose hurried over to the ladder.

"Has something changed?" asked Merivale once they reached the top. "Have our reinforcements arrived?"

"I'm not sure!" said Leston. "Look!"

Merivale scanned the dark southern edge of the island. Now that the sun had set, the only times she could make out any details were when mortars were fired. After a few moments, one flared up, and she was able to see what had Nea and Leston so worked up.

"That's..."

"The kraken!" said the prince. "It's tearing the fleet apart!"

She couldn't make out much of it. A large round head loomed over the highest mast. A long, thick tentacle lifted a massive, three-masted war frigate into the air and slammed it back into the sea with enough force to split the hull. Another tentacle lifted a

smaller two-masted brig and tossed it almost negligently into the city streets, where it burst as it was
dashed across the cobblestones.

"Is this...*their* doing?" Merivale asked the Black
Rose.

"No idea," she replied. "But I wouldn't put it
past them. They're not known for their subtlety or
restraint, keen?"

"Your Highness!" one of the soldiers called up
to them from the courtyard. "The door is about to
give way!"

25

$\mathcal{H}$ope and Red stood on the quarterdeck of the *Lady's Gambit* and gazed out at the carnage along the southern coast of Stonepeak.

Red grinned. "Looks like the Guardian beat us here."

"It had a head start," said Hope. Then she gave Missing Finn a sideways glance. "And there was some fuss at the beginning of the voyage."

Finn gripped the helm and rolled his eyes heavenward. "*Horses*, Miss Hope. Having horses on board just ain't natural."

"Nonsense," said Vaderton, who stood next to him. "The navy brings horses aboard all the time."

"They make such a mess, though!" said Finn.

"They do," Vaderton agreed. "But that's the job you give to the crew member who hasn't been pulling his fair share of work."

"Ain't nobody on my ship like that," Finn said loftily.

"There's *always* someone like that," said Vaderton.

"Regardless," said Hope. "Once we land, we've got twenty-five people to transport from the docks to the palace as quickly as possible. A wagon and team of horses was the obvious solution."

"Ooooh," said Red, wincing as he continued to watch the kraken. "It's cracking frigates like eggs. At this rate, we should have no problem getting to the docks."

"Unless it decides to crack *us* like an egg," said Vaderton.

"It wouldn't do that, right?" Missing Finn asked nervously. "Ain't it melted with Miss Lin's old master or something?"

"It is," said Red. "But I wonder how much of Fitmol Bet is actually still in there."

"Jilly!" called Hope.

"Right here, teacher!" Jilly called down from her perch in the foremast.

"Me, too!" called Uter, who was nestled into the crook between the mast and the yard beside her.

"She can *see* that," Jilly told him.

"Go get Brigga Lin," said Hope. "She'll want to see this anyway."

"Right away, teacher!" Jilly gave her a sharp salute.

"Right away!" Uter mimicked the salute.

Jilly glared at him, then began climbing down the rigging to go find Brigga Lin, with Uter following close behind.

Missing Finn grinned at Hope. "That boy is a trial for her."

Hope nodded. "She could stand to cultivate a little more patience anyway."

As they waited for Brigga Lin to arrive, Hope glanced over at Stephan. He and the other Vinchen stood nearby, silently observing the chaos wrought by the kraken. She knew she'd need to count on them in the coming battle, so she decided to assess their mood.

"I'm surprised you chose not to carry the Song of Sorrows," she told Stephan as she walked over to him.

He patted the sword at his waist. "This one will serve me fine. And to be honest, I don't feel ready to wield such a mighty blade."

"I was your age when I took it up," she told him.
"Do you think *I* was ready?"

"But you said Grandteacher Hurlo commanded
you to take it."

"True," she admitted. "I wouldn't have been bold
enough to do it on my own."

"Then you understand."

She smiled. "I suppose I do."

Brigga Lin hurried over, eyeing the kraken in the
distance as it tossed naval warships around like toys.
"Well, that worked out better than expected."

"Will it attack us as well?" asked Hope.

"Probably," said Brigga Lin. "I may be able to get
through to the part of Fitmol Bet that's still in there,
but not until we're close."

"By which point, if it doesn't work, there'll be nothing to do but greet Death in his cups," said Missing
Finn.

"Let's try to avoid the kraken, then," said Hope.
"And only use Brigga Lin's plan as a last resort if we
get caught."

Missing Finn nodded and swung the *Lady's Gambit* wide around the battle.

But Hope could see that it would be tricky to keep
clear. The kraken was so massive, its movements created
their own eddies and currents. One tentacle lifted a ship
into the air while its cannons continued to fire wildly. It
slammed the ship back down against the surface, and
the impact not only destroyed the ship, but knocked the
Lady's Gambit back, only to pull it even closer as the
water filled back into the momentary vacuum.

She glanced over at Finn, whose face was red with
exertion from spinning the large wheel back and forth
as he tried desperately to compensate for the shifting
forces and keep them headed toward Stonepeak while
maintaining as much distance from the kraken as
possible.

Hope's wasn't the only ship trying to skirt around the kraken. Several of the naval frigates at the back of the fleet were doing the same thing. But then the kraken noticed them. It spun in a circle, its tentacles reaching out in all directions so that water began to form a whirlpool that sucked them all back in, including the *Lady's Gambit*.

"Pretty smart strategy," admitted Hope as the ship began circling closer to the kraken.

"Hopefully that's an indication that I'll be able to reason with it," said Brigga Lin.

No matter how Finn fought against the wheel, the *Lady's Gambit* drew closer to the kraken. Hope saw a thick tentacle shoot toward them, then slide underneath the port side. The deck beneath her feet shuddered as the tentacle struck the rudder and the whole ship tilted hard to one side.

"Grab on to something!" roared Missing Finn.

Hope grabbed on to one of the mainmast sheets. Others caught hold of pieces of rigging, the gunwale, or whatever else was in reach. Most things on the deck had been secured, of course, but as the ship continued to lean, Hope could hear things shifting in the cabins below and the whinnies of frightened horses.

Then the tip of the tentacle rose up the starboard side of the ship and curled over the deck back toward the port side so that it circled the ship completely around the waist.

"It's got us!" said Finn as he clung to the wheel. "Hope, whatever you're going to do, you better do it!"

Hope's stomach lurched as the *Lady's Gambit* rose quickly into the air.

"Brigga Lin!" she shouted.

"Right here!" said her friend. "I need to touch it directly!"

Hope snapped her claw on the sheet she'd been

holding hard enough to cut cleanly through the line. She grabbed the line with her flesh hand, then hooked her other arm around Brigga Lin's waist.

"Stephan!" she shouted. "Get ready!"

"For what?" he shouted back.

"You'll know!" Then she turned back to Brigga Lin. "Hold on tight."

Brigga Lin nodded and put her arms around Hope's shoulders.

Hope pulled hard on the line to make sure it was still firmly attached to the top of the mast. Then, carrying Brigga Lin in one arm, she ran down the sloping deck toward the stern until the sheet pulled taut. She jumped, letting the line swing her and Brigga Lin through the air in an arc around the stern and back toward starboard. Once they were at the right trajectory, Hope let go of the line, and the two women flew the short distance into the side of the tentacle. Then they both scrambled up so they sat precariously astride it.

Brigga Lin put both hands on the slippery surface of the tentacle.

"Grant us mercy from your wrath, my old master. We are not your enemy."

There was a deep, bellowing groan that came from the half-submerged head of the kraken off the port side of the ship. It shifted so that one of its rect-angular orange eyes could see them.

"Get us back down to the deck. *Now!*" shouted Brigga Lin.

Hope nodded, grabbed Brigga Lin around the waist with both arms, and pulled them both over the side. They fell to the deck, where the Vinchen were waiting to catch them.

"Hold on, everyone!" shouted Brigga Lin as she stumbled to her feet.

The kraken threw their ship toward Stonepeak,

skipping it across the water like a stone. Its aim was perfect, sending them right into the bay toward the inner docks. Each time they hit the water, the ship slowed somewhat, but it wasn't enough for Finn to regain control. The *Lady's Gambit* slammed headlong into the docks. There was a heavy wooden groan, followed immediately by a sharp crack.

"The hull's been breached!" shouted Missing Finn. "Grab the horses and get to the docks! Abandon ship!"

Hope turned to see his face screwed up with the agony of losing his ship again so soon.

"I swear we'll do everything we can to get her back!" she told Finn.

He bit his lip and nodded.

———

The Black Rose managed to reach the front of the line by the time the monsters broke through the doors. The moment one of the soldiers called up to them on their safe perch at the gate, she knew she had to get down there and show her wags what it looked like to face nightmares and not flinch. She'd heard Merivale call to her as she vaulted over the side and slid down the ladder. Probably some poncey nonsense about hanging back to observe and make strategic decisions. She'd let Merivale do that. The Black Rose knew where she belonged.

The doors didn't blow apart in a big explosion like she'd expected. It was the hinges that gave way first. The doors shuddered for a moment, then just toppled forward.

There was a strange moment when the Black Rose, her wags, and the soldiers stared at the mass of bizarre creatures all pressed together in the hallway on the other side. A single breath of surprise and si-

lence as the two groups sized each other up. And then
every hell that had ever been imagined broke loose,
and the courtyard was awash in screams, roars, and
blood.

The Black Rose quickly abandoned trying to
mentally catalogue all the horrors that the biomancers had created. Reptile things and insect things and
furry things. Some were massive and lumbering,
others were small and sneaky. Some might have been
humans once, others probably never were. None of
them seemed evil, really. Just crazed and hungry.
But that's how it was, not just in the Circle, but all
over. Everybody wanted to live, and sometimes that
meant killing others to do so. It wasn't good or bad.
It just was. There wasn't any point in getting upset
about it. But she did try to make her kills as clean as
possible.

Once the monsters poured into the courtyard, the
Black Rose never stopped moving. Her chainblade
gleamed red as she whipped it one way, then the other,
spreading flecks of blood in all directions. It had been
a very long time since she'd had to fight this hard. A
long time since she'd truly not known if she was going
to live another minute. But at least she wasn't alone.
She had her wags, all of them knowing how grave this
was. And she had Moxy Poxy and Mister Hatbox,
who were often as not insufferable, but in a pinch like
this, the most welcome sight a wag could have. Those
two swam through the worst of the carnage as if it
were water and they were fish. Fighting monsters with
monsters made a certain kind of sense.

And then there was the Aukbontarens and their
crazy machine. That tiny molly, Drissa, with the
headwrap and goggles, was going toe-to-toe with the
biggest, scariest creatures, and she was *winning*. She
might not have her own strength, but she'd built that
mechanical beast and she sure as piss knew how to

use it. Its metal legs slammed and smashed continuously, sometimes so hard that the smaller creatures went flying through the air. It was a glorious sight to behold, and the Black Rose decided that if she lived through this, she wanted a giant metal spider machine of her own. Maybe she'd give it to Tosh as a present.

But the Black Rose couldn't be thinking too long about Tosh's soft, creamy thighs at a time like this, other than as another reason to stay alive past today. Because the monsters just kept coming. Ten years' worth of biomancery came spilling out of the palace, pissed and peppered, and out for blood.

The fight wore on interminably. The Black Rose didn't know exactly how long, but her arms were aching and her breath was coming out in a harsh whistle. The others weren't looking any better. Soldiers lay dead on the cobblestones. Moxy Poxy was slumped against a barrel, and the Black Rose couldn't tell if the woman was alive or dead. Mister Hatbox continued on his monster murder spree, a truly slippy look in his eye, but his white shirt was torn and he seemed to be spraying as much of his own blood now as anyone else's. Drissa had managed to kill the biggest brute, a strange, long-nosed, big-eared house of a creature with leathery gray skin, but her machine was all out of fuel now, so she'd had to abandon it in the middle of the courtyard and run to the safety of Catim, the tall Aukbontaren tom with the quickfire rifle. She noticed that even he was getting careful about his shots, probably down to the end of his ammo. But there were still more monsters spilling out of the palace, fresh and eager for blood.

So this was how it would be? Eaten by monsters while fighting alongside wags and imps and foreigners? There were worse ways to die, she supposed. She'd witnessed a few of them. And it wasn't like she was some innocent molly. She'd done things. Terrible things. She'd killed and tortured and maimed. She'd hoped to make up for all that before she died, but she knew better than most, you didn't always get what you wanted.

Then, out of the corner of her eye, the Black Rose saw Merivale gesturing wildly over by the gate. She was shouting urgently at one of the soldiers, but he had a streak of blood across his face, and his hands shook violently. He looked so dazed and horror stricken, he probably didn't understand a word she was saying.

"Piss'ell." The Black Rose kicked away the skeletal bird creature she'd been fighting, and ran as fast as her exhausted legs would allow over to them. "What is it?"

"We need to get the gate open!" Merivale yelled. She had a revolver in her hands now, and fired a shot at an approaching wolf-ant creature, hitting it square between its insect-like eyes.

"Why?" asked the Black Rose as she snapped her chainblade at a wasp thing the size of a bird, sending it careening to the ground.

Merivale gave her a grimly exultant grin. "Reinforcements."

"Say no more."

The Black Rose examined the gate mechanism. It looked chewed up, like it had been struck by stray bullets. She tried the lever, but it broke off in her hand. She grabbed an ax and began hacking at the chain. Sparks flew, but the chain held firm.

Drissa suddenly appeared, holding up her hand for the Black Rose to stop. She examined the gate mechanism carefully for a moment, then pointed to a metal pin that threaded through one of the gear wheels.

"That the weak spot?" asked the Black Rose.

Drissa nodded.

The Black Rose swung the ax down on the pin as hard as she could and the whole thing broke apart, sending gears and other bits of metal flying everywhere. One of the gear wheels struck the side of her head, and she saw more than felt as her body dropped to the ground.

She lay there on the cobblestones, dazed. Then she felt strong hands dragging her to one side.

"I have you," came Catim's deep voice.

The Black Rose turned her head and saw that the gate was now open. A team of horses charged through, pulling a large wagon. She lifted her head, and even with her slightly unfocused vision, she recognized Bleak Hope, Brigga Lin, Red, Jilly, and what looked like an entire gang of Vinchen warriors.

"Is she okay?" Merivale's voice was right next to her ear, sounding genuinely panicked.

"I've stopped the bleeding for now," said the other Aukbontaren tom, Etcher. "But you see how it is…"

Dimly, the Black Rose wondered if they were talking about her. It wasn't just her head that was hurting now. The lower half of her left leg felt hot and heavy and wet inside her boot. But she wasn't paying it much mind, because there was far too much beauty to see.

It was Bleak Hope times twenty. The courtyard was awash with leather-clad bringers of justice and death. It was like all the old stories about Vinchen her mom used to tell her. The ones she'd never believed, even as a little girl. How could something so great and fearsome be on *her* side? *Well, sorry, Mom, you were right and maybe I shouldn't have doubted you. There are some good things in this old world after all.*

"Nettie! Nettie!" Red's face loomed over, looking pale and terrified.

The Black Rose tried to speak, maybe tell him to use her proper pissing name, but the best she could manage was a weak, "'ey."

"I think I've got her stabilized, my lord," Etcher told him. "She's going to live."

"Red, you need to get in there and put an end to this," Merivale told him. "Go now, while the way is open. Ammon Set will likely be in the emperor's apartments on the top floor."

Red looked at her, his eyes hard. Then he nodded.

"You better still be alive when I get back," he told the Black Rose. Then he disappeared from her field of view.

She rolled her eyes up at Merivale and Etcher. Merivale still looked very concerned, and Etcher looked sick.

"Wazziz?" she asked.

"I'm sorry," Etcher said. "The only way I'm going to be able to save your life is if you lose the leg."

He rummaged through a large leather bag and pulled out a bone saw.

Ah, she thought.

What was the word for it...

Oh yeah. *Atonement.*

———

Red took one look at the smashed lift and knew he would need to pace himself if he was going to run up fifty flights of stairs and still be in any shape to deal with whatever would be waiting for him.

"You weren't really thinking of doing this without us, were you?" Hope's voice came from behind him.

He turned around and saw them. Brigga Lin in white and Bleak Hope in black. They were blood-spattered, but firm.

"Naturally not," he said. "But you'll have to keep up."

"Don't flatter yourself," said Hope. "I'll race you to the top."

Brigga Lin glanced at the broken lift, then at the stairwell, and sighed. "This is not my strong suit. You two go on ahead. I'll get there as soon as I can."

Red turned to Hope, and despite how grave the situation was, he couldn't help grinning.

"Ready?" he asked.

She grinned back at him. "For you? Always."

So much for pacing himself.

———

"Where in all hells have they gone?" Jilly demanded, wiping the blood off her knife. The monsters had all been killed, and she finally had a moment to check on her friends. But Hope, Brigga Lin, and Red were gone.

"Who?" asked Uter, still stuck to her side like always. He smiled in a way that might have looked sweet, if his white hair and face hadn't been spattered with blood.

She ignored him and started searching around. She saw Stephan helping a wounded soldier and hurried over to him.

"You know where teacher is?" she asked.

"I saw her, the biomancer, and the assassin go into the palace, but I don't know where they went from there."

"After Ammon Set, I reckon," said Jilly. "Uter, you stay here. I'm going to—"

"They're coming!" A lacy tom up on top of the outer wall shouted down to them. "The Guardian is gone, and two ships made it through!"

"Piss'ell," muttered Jilly. "Uter, stay with Stephan."

"But—"

"Do it!"

"Okay, Jilly, you don't need to shout."

Jilly climbed up the ladder to the lacy. He was looking out at the city, a worried frown on his face, and with good reason. Two naval ships had reached the inner docks. Now there were two battalions of imps marching up the main street toward the palace.

"Can we get the gate closed again, Your Highness?" asked a dark-skinned lacy molly with an accent next to him.

Apparently the lacy tom was a prince.

"I think they had to break the gate lock to let the Vinchen through in time," he said.

"Don't worry, Princey," Jilly told him, patting his arm. "I've got it under control."

"Who are *you*?" he asked.

"Only your lucky break, old pot," she told him. "But you can call me Jilly."

"She's like a tiny Lord Pastinas," said the dark-skinned molly.

"You're talking about Red, aren't you?" asked Jilly. "Just so happens, I learned from the best."

"Well, Jilly," said the prince, "I'm not sure what you have in mind. My soldiers are exhausted and out of ammunition. And while the Vinchen are fearsome warriors, I don't think even *they* can face two battalions of fresh troops alone."

"Like I said, don't worry about it." She turned back to the ladder, then stopped and looked at him over her shoulder in a very pat way. "Oh, and don't go all wobbly if you see some things that ain't exactly...natural."

The prince's eyes went wide. "You mean more so than what I've already seen?"

"You ain't seen nothing yet, Princey," she assured him.

She slid down the ladder and hurried back to where Uter waited dutifully next to Stephan and the wounded soldier.

"You know you're my best wag, right?" she told the boy, squeezing his shoulders.

"I *am*?" he asked, wide-eyed.

"A'course you are! And that's why I believe *you* are going to save the day."

"Really? Me?"

She nodded. "It's time for you to do what you do best."

"What's that?" he asked eagerly.

She gestured to the dead monsters that lay scattered around the courtyard.

"Make some new friends."

———

Hope had told Stephan that the strange little boy Uter had been the product of the Jackal Lords and their necromancy. He knew that the boy could supposedly raise the dead, at least for a short time, with just a drop of his blood. But he'd never seen it before. And of all the things he'd seen since leaving Galemoor, witnessing the boy raise a small army of monsters to do his bidding was the most chilling.

"I'm not sure how this is going to work," he admitted to Ravento as they watched the boy hop from one monstrous corpse to the next. "But we have to repel these soldiers and protect the prince by any means necessary."

Ravento smiled wryly. "By now, I think we've learned the important lesson of flexibility well enough to adapt to just about anything. Even fighting alongside monsters risen from the dead."

"You say that now...," said Stephan.

They watched in sick fascination as the monsters slowly began dragging themselves back up onto their feet.

"I didn't say I was going to feel comfortable with it," said Ravento.

"I suppose we don't need to," Stephan said grimly.

"Let's go. If we can hit them in the street before they reach the palace, that will minimize the risk to the prince."

Ravento nodded.

"I'll see if I can help Uter formulate something that resembles a strategy," said Stephan. "You get the rest of the brothers ready."

———

Merivale spent a few minutes holding the Black Rose's hand, even after she had passed out. She had plans for this woman. This new, strong ally *had* to survive.

"Well?" she asked Etcher.

"As long as she gets the proper treatment, and there's no infection, she'll be fine," said Etcher.

Merivale nodded. "I need to go check on the prince. Will you stay with her? She's done a great deal for all of us."

"Of course," said Etcher.

Merivale climbed back up to the top of the gate. That was when she saw the mass of imperial soldiers marching up the street toward the palace.

"My God, why didn't I know about this?"

"I shouted down to you," said Leston. "But I think you were in the midst of helping the Black Rose through her amputation. Understandably, you didn't hear me, and I thought it best not to—"

"Not to come get me?" Merivale's cold steel turned white hot. "The gates can't close. We can't possibly defend against this with the spent troops we have! Even—"

"It's being taken care of, my lady," said Leston with surprising firmness.

"By whom?"

"A plan is in place. Please, trust someone other

than yourself for once," said the prince. "That's an order, by the way."

For the first time in a very long time, Merivale found that she didn't quite know what to say and was too tired to come up with something, so she simply nodded.

The troops that moved slowly up the street didn't have any cannons or other heavy artillery. That would have slowed down their approach. But two hundred soldiers with rifles was still more than their current forces could handle.

She caught a flicker of movement on one of the rooftops. Just a quick flash of black that let her know the Vinchen were positioning themselves above the soldiers. That was smart, but it still wouldn't be enough. Not against that many troops.

Then a little white-haired boy walked boldly out into the middle of the street.

"What is going on?" hissed Merivale.

"Just watch," advised Leston.

Merivale did not like this feeling of knowing less than other people.

The soldiers came to a halt and looked warily at the boy. He waved cheerfully to them.

"Boy! Clear the way!" shouted one of the soldiers. "Clear out or we'll be forced to shoot you!"

Merivale could just barely hear his high, piping voice as the boy replied. "I want you to meet my new friends!"

Then all the biomancer creatures from before, somehow alive again, came out from the alleys and side streets. Seemingly unhindered by their own fatal injuries, they swarmed the soldiers.

The soldiers were completely unprepared for such a horrific onslaught. Many understandably broke and ran. Those who stayed and fought didn't last long. They were torn apart, eaten, dismembered, or disemboweled. One strange crab-like creature was tearing out whole spines and consuming them. Another small ratlike creature leapt at their faces and greedily ate out their eyes, leaving them alive, but blind and shrieking. There were only a handful of soldiers left when the monsters abruptly collapsed back into death. That was when the Vinchen plunged down from the roof-tops to finish them off.

"Who is that boy?" asked Merivale.

"According to Jilly, he is Bleak Hope's ward," said Leston. "This Hope does have a number of impressive friends. I think a long-term alliance with her would be extremely beneficial to the empire. Don't you agree, Lady Hempist?"

"Without question, Your Highness," she said. Then, "Wait, who's *Jilly*?"

———

Hope and Red reached the imperial apartments at the same time. Both of them were winded, so they took a moment to catch their breath.

"It's probably locked," said Hope. "Should we break it down?"

"Easier to just pick the lock, don't you think?" asked Red.

"Oh sure, if you want to be clever about it," said Hope.

"I mean, if you were just really dying to kick down a door, I don't want to take that away from you," said Red.

"No, no, we'll do it your way this time," said Hope.

"You spoil me," he told her, then knelt down and began working on the lock.

A few moments later, it gave a quiet click, and the door swung open to reveal a large, open room. Hope and Red walked in warily, ready for an attack from any side.

"I wish you would have brought that sword of yours," Red muttered.

"It's no longer my sword," replied Hope. "And I swore never to pick one up again."

"Not even just this once?"

"Not even just this once."

"What if I run out of bullets?"

"What if you don't even need bullets?" asked Hope.

"That seems unlikely," said Red.

At the far end of the room was Ammon Set, sitting on a thick throne made of beige sandstone that blended so well with the biomancer's rocky skin that he almost appeared a part of it. His hood no longer covered his face, and Hope could easily see his stone-like face staring at her. He was flanked on either side by a line of biomancers, all with their hoods drawn low and their faces hidden.

"Well, well," Ammon Set said, his voice like rocks grinding together. "This looks familiar. How long ago was it when we took away your hand and sent you on your way? Clearly we were far too benevolent with you the last time."

"*We?*" asked Hope. "My understanding is that you are no longer a biomancer. Now you just have the disfigurement of one."

"Ouch," muttered Red.

"It was a necessary sacrifice," Ammon Set told her. "To ensure the security of the empire, I had to take hold of it myself. To make it strong."

"That's not what you've done, though," said Red. "You've made it a mess. And if Aukbontar were to sweep in here tomorrow, we'd be doomed."

"I will bring it back together, once I've finished off you and your pathetic resistance."

"Pathetic?" asked Hope. "We've crushed everything you've thrown at us."

"What about the two battalions of soldiers that drove off the kraken and made it to shore?"

"What?" said Hope, her stomach suddenly ice-cold.

There was a crack as Ammon Set's mouth tilted slightly into a slanted half smile. "Your friends below are probably being slaughtered as we speak."

"Actually, no," said the biomancer who stood next to Ammon Set. His voice sounded rusty and grating, and when he pushed back his hood, it revealed a face lined with bits of metal.

"What do you mean?" demanded Ammon Set.

"In addition to uniting Vinchen, nobility, and commoner, the two people who now stand before you have even inspired the loyalty of the Jackal Lords."

"Impossible," said Ammon Set. "The Jackal Lords are all dead."

"Apparently not all. A young boy has allied himself with the prince."

"Just one little boy? He won't be much trouble," said Ammon Set.

"Hmm. Except it seems he's been wighted."

"Nonsense. There hasn't been a successful wighting in over a century," said Ammon Set.

The metal-laced biomancer turned to look at Hope, his cloudy, rust-colored eyes not giving away any emotion. "You ask a good question, Vinchen. What *does* Ammon Set mean by 'we'?"

"What are you talking about, Chiffet Mek?" snapped Ammon Set.

Chiffet Mek ignored him and continued to regard Hope. "I am the current senior member of the order of biomancery, and I speak for the council. We believed, wrongly, that only the might of the bio-mancers would save the empire from Aukbontar. But you have proven that biomancery alone is not enough. Only in unifying *all* elements of the empire

can we hope to survive the storm that will one day
sweep across the world."

"I'm not sure I understand what you're getting at,
Mek," said Red.

"That I was *wrong*, Lord Pastinas," said Chiffet
Mek. "The Council of Biomancery has stood neutral
in this conflict between Ammon Set and the prince
until now. It is time for us to choose a side." He
turned to Ammon Set. "And it is not yours."

"Wait!" shouted Ammon Set.

Chiffet Mek touched Ammon Set's neck, then
stepped away. As Ammon Set stared back at him,
his stone features began to soften so that his face
could express the horror he felt at this betrayal.
He lurched to his feet and stumbled away from the
throne and the biomancers. Hope and Red stepped
nimbly aside, keeping their distance as they watched
him stare down at his hands, which had also become
soft like flesh. But it became apparent that his body
was not turning back to flesh. Not exactly.

"It is time to stop clinging to the traditions of the
past. Instead, we must look toward the future," Chiffet Mek said. "We must have progress above all else.
We must think more efficiently…" He smiled coldly.
"And *cull* the fat."

"No…," said Ammon Set, but his voice sounded
bubbly. His features began to sag. He swayed as his
legs wobbled beneath his robes and his arms became rubbery and limp. Then he began to lose all shape until he
was nothing but a giant mound of jiggling fat in a robe.

Hope looked over at Red. "Is he…dead?"

"I sure hope so," he said.

Chiffet Mek turned to them. "What can we do
to make amends for our cowardice and lack of
foresight?"

"Are you *kidding*—" began Red, but Hope held up
her metal hand and he fell silent.

"You say you were neutral, but we consider your lack of action to defend the prince to be treason. Therefore you will need to surrender to us."

Mek didn't seem surprised. He turned to the other biomancers and they all linked hands. There was a moment of silence, then Mek turned back to Hope.

"Very well. What are your terms?"

Hope looked at Red. "Your turn."

"Me?"

"You know the situation here much better than I do," said Hope.

"Ah, well, yes..." As Red turned to Chiffet Mek, his grin was suddenly so wide, it looked downright sinister. "First, you must accept Leston as emperor and renew your oath to him. Second, you must honor any commitments he or the empress dowager have made during this conflict. Third, you must help facilitate a *peaceful* treaty negotiation with Aukbontar. Fourth, you will cease all involuntary experimentation on people immediately." He paused for a moment, his red eyes sparkling. "You got all that?"

There was a pause, then Chiffet Mek nodded.

"Pretty thorough for coming up with something on the spot," murmured Hope.

"Thank you," said Red.

"So those are your terms?" asked Chiffet Mek.

"One more." Hope could hear the sound of fine shoes clomping up the last set of steps and recognized the footfalls immediately. "When Brigga Lin walks through that door in a few moments, you will invite her onto the council and welcome her as one of your own."

Again there was a momentary pause as the biomancers communicated silently.

Then Chiffet Mek turned back to Hope and Red. "Agreed. We understand the depth of our wrongdoing and thank you for leniency. I swear, on behalf of the entire order of biomancery, that we will abide by your conditions for surrender."

"Sunny," said Red. "Now's your first opportunity to put it into action."

Brigga Lin burst into the room, a flurry of white fabric, her arms waving, her hands poised, her expression fierce and deadly. Then she assessed the mood, and noted the empty throne. Her arms lowered slightly.

"What's going on?"

Chiffet Mek looked at her for a moment, and Hope couldn't detect any resentment or disgust. In fact, he seemed completely indifferent.

"Brigga Lin, we humbly ask you to sit with us on the council as an honored member of the order of biomancery."

"Huh." She thought about it a moment, then dropped her arms completely. "If I accept, I intend to train other women in the arts of biomancery."

"I suspected as much," said Chiffet Mek.

"And you accept that?"

"I am now senior member of the order of biomancery and my will is paramount."

"Progress, above all else," Brigga Lin said quietly. "Wasn't that your focus?"

He nodded. "You remember my instruction well. And if this is how progress must be achieved, I have no choice but to accept it."

"At least you're not trying to pretend you like me," said Brigga Lin. "Fine. I accept your invitation to the council."

"Very well done, my wags," Red told the biomancers. "See, it's not nearly as hard as you thought to be decent, regular people. Now, for the finale, how about you all go down to the courtyard and present yourselves to your new emperor-to-be?"

Jilly sat next to Nettles. Or the Black Rose. Or whatever she wanted to be called. Jilly didn't really much care, as long as the ornery slice didn't die.

"She'll be fine," the skinny Aukbontaren named Etcher assured her. "She just needs to rest and heal."

"We'll have Alash make her something just as great as Hope's hand," she told him.

He was kind enough to smile and nod reassuringly, even though he likely had no idea what she was talking about. That was when Jilly decided she liked him.

"Watch out!" The shout came from a soldier who lay bandaged and exhausted near the door. He struggled to rise. "The biomancers are coming!"

Everyone in the courtyard tensed up. They were all exhausted, even the Vinchen. Now they would have to face the worst foe of all?

They appeared in the doorway. Fifteen men in white hooded robes, looming like some childhood nightmare. Even Jilly felt her defiance crystalize in fear.

"Whoa, whoa, whoa, let's not get the wrong idea here, my wags! It's all chum and larder!"

Red pushed his way through the line of biomancers and stood there smiling at the people in the courtyard for a moment. Then he shooed the biomancers to either side. "Make room, make room."

Hope and Brigga Lin emerged from the palace and stood in the middle of the line of biomancers. It was a sight Jilly would never forget, no matter how long she lived. She would cherish that memory almost like a talisman whenever anything seemed impossible.

"Your Highness?" Red called as he looked around the courtyard.

"Rixidenteron, you're okay!"

The prince ran across the courtyard and, to Jilly's surprise, embraced Red in a firm, brotherly way.

After a moment, Red gently parted them. "There, there, my wag. These gafs got something to say to you."

The biomancers all pushed back their hoods, and then they were suddenly just people. Fairly ugly, what with their biomancer marks. But still just people.

One with metal bits on his face bowed low to the prince, and the rest followed after him.

"We hereby renew our vows to you, the rightful ruler of the empire, that we may serve you and your allies to our last breath."

The prince stared at them in shock, his mouth slightly open. Jilly had to agree, it seemed preposterous. After everything that happened, they were just expecting to be welcomed back?

The lacy woman known as Lady Hempist moved smoothly over to his side.

"As tempting as retribution sounds from the standpoint of personal satisfaction, Your Highness," she told the prince, "I'd advise you to accept this humble plea, so that we can get on with the work of healing our broken empire."

He turned to Lady Hempist, and Jilly saw something sad in his eyes. This, she supposed, was politics, and Jilly wondered if his heart maybe wasn't stern enough for such things.

Finally, he sighed. "Very well." He turned back to the biomancer. "I will accept you again as the left hand of the empire, but only on condition that I have the right hand of the empire to serve as a counterbalance." He turned to the Vinchen. "Will you come out of seclusion to once again serve the people of this empire?"

Stephan gave him a tired smile. "I think we already have, Your Highness."

"It seems, however, you will need to select a new grandteacher," said Merivale. "That is tradition, is it not?"

"It is," said Hope. "And I suggest Stephan. Although he is young, he has shown himself to possess the qualities of leadership and courage that will greatly benefit the Vinchen order."

"I'm afraid I must respectfully decline," said Stephan. "I am not ready for such an honor." Then he drew his sword and held it out so that it pointed skyward. "Instead, I nominate Hope the Defiant as grandteacher of the Vinchen order. Who is with me?"

The other Vinchen followed suit, drawing their swords.

"Hope the Defiant, grandteacher of the Vinchen order," they said in unison.

Hope's expression stayed calm and thoughtful, but Jilly saw her sway ever so slightly. Brigga Lin subtly took her upper arm to steady her. That was the moment Jilly realized she loved these two women more than anything.

"I accept your nomination," she said, her voice remarkably clear, all things considered. "And I swear that I will dedicate my life to the benefit of the empire and the Vinchen order."

The prince smiled. "Well, Grandteacher, will you join us once again at the palace?"

"No," said Hope.

Everyone froze.

Then she continued. "We *will* once again serve the people of this empire and provide a counterbalance to the power of the biomancers. But we will not do so at the palace. Instead we will live among the people we serve."

"Sunny." Red rubbed his hands together. "Well, that's about it, then, isn't it? We've got it all worked out."

"There is one more thing," said the prince.

"Oh?" asked Red.

"I must ask that you take the role as official adviser to the emperor."

Red winced. "Is that an imperial command?"

"It's a pleading request from a *friend*," said the prince. "The empire needs you. And so do I."

Red sighed and smiled ruefully at Hope.

It dawned on Jilly what was really being asked here. If Hope was refusing to stay at the palace, and Red agreed to be at the palace, that meant they couldn't be together. And Jilly felt pretty sure they were *supposed* to be together.

As Jilly watched Hope and Red, somehow something was communicated between them without words or biomancery. Then Red turned back to the prince.

"Of course, Your Highness. I would be honored to accept."

The repairs to Stonepeak began immediately, despite everyone's exhaustion. The kraken had stopped the fleet early on in their bombardment, but even so, more than a quarter of the city had been reduced to smoking rubble, and the number of deaths was incalculable.

At Red's urging, Prince Leston left his jacket and cravat at the palace, rolled up his sleeves, and joined in the rescue effort to find every last survivor and ensure they received medical treatment. Having the soon-to-be emperor there, visible, to encourage the weary soldiers as they pulled people from collapsed buildings, and to comfort those who no longer had a home, was a sight never before seen in the empire. Word quickly spread of the prince's heroism and kindness, as Red knew it would.

The first combined effort of the Vinchen and biomancers was to set up a triage center for the wounded in the large thoroughfare in front of the Lightning Gate. While it seemed many on both sides were open to the theory of this new alliance, putting it in practice was something else entirely. The atmosphere was tense, and if not for the watchful eyes of Grandteacher Hope, Brigga Lin, and Chiffet Mek, open conflict might have erupted at several points throughout the day.

It was not until all the fires had been put out, and every survivor had been treated, that everyone finally rested.

But Red had them all up early the next day. He had been asked to advise the prince, and he knew that the people needed someone to believe in right now, and some assurance that things would get better. So he had soldiers ride through the city, announcing that the prince would address the people at midday, and all were welcome to the courtyard to hear him.

The courtyard filled up well before noon. With the help of Captains Murkton and Vaderton, Red was able to convince the soldiers to allow commoners to sit up on the gates to make more room.

Empress Dowager Pysetcha had traveled from Sunset Point through the night, but there was no hint of exhaustion on her radiant face as she accompanied Leston onto the parapet that overlooked the courtyard from the third floor. They were flanked on either side by Hope and Chiffet Mek, one in black robes, the other in white, their hoods pushed back. Merivale had expressed some concern about allowing people to see the marks of biomancery on Chiffet Mek, but Red had assured her that a hooded biomancer would have been far more frightening to them.

The message Red had Leston deliver was a simple one. His coronation would take place in one week, and it would begin a new era of unity and justice for everyone in the empire. The prince then introduced Chiffet Mek as the new head of the order of biomancery. The crowds got a little nervous, as Red expected, so Leston quickly followed that up with introducing Hope the Defiant, grandteacher of the Vinchen order and hero of Paradise Circle.

Red still got a nice warm glow whenever he heard that title. He'd wanted to add Dire Bane to the list, but decided it was a bit too much. Instead, he'd con-

vinced Merivale to have her spies start spreading the
rumors in the taverns of Hope's time as a pirate and
seditionist, especially those taverns near the docks,
where the stories might spread beyond Stonepeak.
He wanted every commoner in the empire to know
that the Vinchen were back and they were on the side
of the people.

Red and Merivale stood off to one side, watching
the prince finish up his speech with a rousing reaf-
firmation that he would work to heal the wounds not
just of his people, but the empire itself.

"He's a lot better at public speaking than I
expected," Red whispered to Merivale.

"You're a much better statesman than I expected,"
she told him.

He shrugged. "It's kind of like pulling a con,
really. Convincing people to think and feel the way I
want has always been a gift of mine. The only difference is that now there's a chance of actually deliver-
ing on some of the crazy promises I always make."

"Since we've gotten the people more or less
assured that it isn't the end of the world, we need to
start preparing for this coronation," said Merivale.

"Do we really need a whole week to prepare?"
asked Red.

"For the actual coronation? Not really. But we
need that long to prepare for the ball that will take
place after."

"A *ball*?" asked Red. "Stonepeak is a mess. Vance
Post is worse. And you want to have a little lacy
dance?"

"Don't forget that the lords and ladies also need to
be conned," said Merivale. "We are about to propose
some very drastic changes to the power structure of
the empire. We need to assure the nobility that they
won't lose everything they hold dear in the process."

Red sighed. "I suppose you're right."

Merivale gave him one of her rare wolfish grins. "Besides, I am dying to get your beloved Hope into a proper ball gown."

"Well, I'm not sure *beloved* is the right—"

"Don't insult me by claiming it's anything less," Merivale said. "And promise me that the two of you won't let your appallingly principled life choices prevent you from having a torrid love affair, at the very least."

To Red's horror, he found himself actually blushing. "Yeah, well, we'll see. We haven't talked about it yet, and I don't want to assume anything."

She pinched his cheek hard enough for it to hurt. "You really are adorable, aren't you?"

———

Red had been to many balls in the last year and a half, and they had never once made him anxious. Until now. He tugged nervously at his jacket, which had been made from the remains of his old deerskin longcoat that he loved so much. As Lord Chamberlain, he couldn't go sweeping around the palace in a longcoat anymore, so it was comforting to have something he was so fond of from the old days modified to fit his new life. He supposed it was a sort of compromise between Red and Rixidenteron.

"Announcing the Lord Chamberlain, Rixidenteron Pastinas!" intoned the high steward, who had somehow managed to survive through the chaos with his dour, grumpy expression completely intact.

Red didn't give a great deal of thought to pestering the old wrink, or even to leaping out from the curtain in a dramatic fashion as was his usual wont. Instead he shoved the curtain aside, eager to see Hope in her new gown.

But after quickly scanning the crowd, his shoulders sank.

"Of *course* she isn't here yet," he muttered.

"My Lord Chamberlain?" asked the steward.

Red gave a wry smile. "Never mind, old pot." Then he sighed heavily and stepped into the ballroom.

As he made his way to the bar, Red scanned the room again, knowing it was futile, but unable to help himself.

There was a small string orchestra off to one side playing the usual light and tinkling stuff that lacies liked to hear.

He saw Brigga Lin and Alash talking quietly in the corner. Red would have thought they would both be completely at home here at the palace, finally surrounded by the finery they were accustomed to. But they looked just as odd and out of place here as they did anywhere else. Perhaps their time away had changed them too much. Or perhaps they'd never fit in a place like this either. They only ever seemed truly at ease when they were together.

Poor Leston was trapped on his official imperial chair at the far end of the room, while person after person came to greet him. He smiled and nodded to each, but he kept looking longingly over to where Nea and the other Aukbontarens stood and talked quietly with some of Hope's Vinchen. The Vinchen all wore regular lacy clothes tonight, but even if Red hadn't recognized some of them, he could have spotted them by their stance and general bearing.

But no Hope. Or Merivale.

"Piss'ell," he muttered as he accepted a glass of wine from a servant.

"Something troubling you, Lord Chamberlain?" asked Vaderton, who once again wore the imperial white and gold uniform of a naval captain, although he'd apparently decided to keep the beard.

"She's doing this to me on purpose," Red told him.

"Who is?"

"Merivale. She's making Hope late just to draw out the suspense." He took a large gulp of wine. "Some would consider this cruel."

"I'm sure Lady Hempist has your best interests at heart."

"Merivale only has her own interests at heart."

"Ah. There she is now," said Vaderton, looking at the ballroom entrance.

"Announcing Lady Merivale Hempist of Lesser Basheta," intoned the steward.

Red turned just in time to catch the look of blazing triumph that Merivale was throwing in his direction. Then she moved deftly to one side as the steward announced the next arrival.

"Announcing Hope the Defiant, grandteacher of the Vinchen order."

To Red's eye, Hope looked like nothing less than a work of art. She stood framed in the entrance, completely unrecognizable yet utterly familiar. Her blond hair had been carefully piled up on top of her head in an intricate weave. Her tight, streamlined black gown was sleeveless, so that her pale neck and shoulders were completely bare. She wore a long black glove that reached past the elbow on one side. On the other, she wore a modified version that allowed her claw, polished to an almost mirrorlike gleam, to show. Her lips had been painted a delicate pink on her narrow, pale face. Her eyes were as they always were—a fathomless blue in which he felt he could lose his very soul.

When Hope's eyes met his, his knees almost buckled.

"Steady now," Vaderton murmured. "You'll be fine." Then he slipped away to go talk to Brigga Lin and Alash.

Hope gave Red a wry smile as she walked over to him with her usual fluid grace.

"Why are people staring at me?" she whispered to him.

"Because there's suddenly nothing else worth looking at," he told her.

"Don't be ridiculous," she told him.

"Oh great and wise Grandteacher, haven't you learned by now, I'm always ridiculous?"

"I do like that about you," she admitted. Then she sighed. "This place has me completely unnerved. I feel like I've stepped onto a battlefield with no knowledge of what the conflict even is."

"Not to worry, there is one surefire way to stave off the enemy."

"What's that?" she asked.

"Dance with me!"

She laughed and shook her head.

"What, don't Vinchen dance?" he asked.

"No, as a matter of fact, they don't," she told him. "Luckily, Lady Hempist anticipated this and has been teaching me some of the more popular ballroom dancing techniques." She looked over at the empty dance floor in the center of the room. "But no one else is dancing."

"That's because they've been waiting for us to start."

"I doubt that," she said.

"Don't believe me?" He took her hand and led her into the center of the room. "Just wait and see."

He signaled to the orchestra conductor, who gave him an enthusiastic nod, clearly seeing this as their chance to liven things up a bit.

Then, as the music surged, Hope and Red began to dance.

There are some feelings that only words can convey. Some that require paint, or sculpture. There are some that only music can express. And then there are some emotions that can only be communicated through movement. Beyond language or vision or hearing, it was an expression fully inhabited and purely in the moment, without fear, or doubt, or self-consciousness. Hope and Red came together and glided across the ballroom, their eyes locked onto each other. Hope's gown was backless, and Red could feel the warm muscles of her back against his hand. He could also feel the sharp bite of her claw against his own back, but that was fine because it was an indelible reminder of all they had sacrificed for each other.

"Do you remember the day I painted your portrait at Old Yammy's?" he asked her as they continued around the room.

"Of course."

"That was when I fell in love with you."

"All at once?" she asked.

"Pretty much."

"I don't know when I fell in love with you," she admitted. "I think it happened when I wasn't looking. I was so focused on my vengeance that I wasn't paying attention to anything else. Then when the need for vengeance was gone, there it was. As if it has always been there. But in nearly the same moment, I lost you."

"Well, one thing is pretty clear," he said.

"What's that?"

"We're in love."

She smirked. "Yes, I think we both knew that."

"I just wanted to say it out loud," he said.

"Feel better now?"

"I reckon so. But you have to admit, it's all so... complicated."

"It is," she said. "Unlike your clever little stories, things don't fit neatly into a happily ever after. But does it need to?"

"Of course not. I just don't know what we're going to do about it."

"What we *do* is figure things out one day at a time.

It won't always be easy, of course. And there will probably be times when your responsibilities to the emperor will put you at odds with me and my responsibilities to the Vinchen and the people."

She gave him a smile that was very close to a leer.

"But for *tonight* at least, I think the most important thing to worry about is how you're going to help me out of this ridiculous gown."

Hope had agreed to Red's request that she and the Vinchen stay at the palace until after the coronation and ball. So this was her last night before she left to establish a new permanent home for the Vinchen. She had insisted on taking a small one down in the lower levels, of course. There was little more than a bed and a few other small pieces of furniture. But that was absolutely fine with Red.

As they stood facing each other in the small room, it suddenly felt strange being alone with her. Everything was charged and filled with portent. He was aware of every shadow on her face, every whisper of her gown, and every touch of her hand.

They looked at each other for a moment in silence.

"So you like the gown?" she asked.

"It's perfect for you."

She touched her bare shoulder. "You don't think it...shows too much skin?"

He stepped in close, wrapped his arms around her waist, and kissed that shoulder. "It shows exactly the right amount of skin."

"All of my scars, though," she said. "Not very elegant."

"Your scars are pat," he told her as he traced one that ran from her shoulder to her collarbone with his finger.

She pushed his jacket off and let it drop to the floor, then laid her head gently on his shoulder so that her lips tickled his neck as she spoke. "At one point, I was worried you'd find me...too damaged."

"Molly of my heart," he whispered. "I have a demon living in my head now. So I'm not sure who's more damaged."

"Does it trouble you?" she asked. "The demon they put in there?"

"Only when I'm not looking at you," he said.

He could feel her smile against the crook of his neck.

He let his hands slide from her shoulder down her arms, slowly pulled off her gloves. One got snagged for a moment on her claw, but he quickly freed it.

"Sorry," she muttered. "This thing..."

"Don't be." He took her claw and pressed it to his chest. "And it's not a thing. It's a part of you. So I love it, too."

She lifted her head and looked at him, one eyebrow arched skeptically. "I suppose you love all my scars, too?"

He grinned. "Well, I don't know. I haven't seen *all* of them yet."

She returned his grin. "You want to see *all* of them?"

"Yes, please."

"Some of them are difficult to find."

"I promise to be thorough."

"You better see to this gown, then."

He reached behind her and unhooked the clasps on the back of her gown. The whole thing slid off in one smooth, satisfying sigh of velvet so that she stood gloriously naked in front of him.

"My turn." She reached up with her claw and carefully sliced down his shirt and then his trousers so that they fell away in tatters.

"Thanks for taking off the jacket first," he told her.
"You're welcome."

Then they stepped in close and pressed their bodies together. The heat and electricity, the hard muscle under soft skin, their lips touching, their breath mingling. They tumbled into the bed together without letting go and melted into each other completely. For now, at least, they were united. And that was enough.

DEATH *or* GLORY

A Dramatic Musical Epic Adventure in Three Acts
Being an account of how the illustrious Lord Rixiden-
teron Pastinas and the radiant Grandteacher Hope the
Defiant did save the empire from certain collapse.
Written and directed by the great theater master
Broomefedies who knows them both personally.

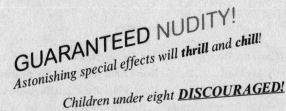

GUARANTEED NUDITY!
Astonishing special effects will *thrill* and *chill!*

*Children under eight **DISCOURAGED!***

Dramatis Personae

Grandteacher Hope the Defiant .... The Luscious Lymestria

Lord Rixidenteron Pastinas, aka Red .... Varaton Baggelworthy

Filler/Emperor Leston .... Misandry Andy

Racklock/Missing Finn .... Rock Craig

The Black Rose .... The Tantalizing Tosh

Brigga Lin/Lady Hempist .... Madgie the Hatchet

Hurlo the Cunning/Ammon Set .... Avery Birdhouse

Sadie the Goat/Empress Pysetcha .... Jagged Jenny

Soldiers/Vinchen/Biomancers/Wags, etc .... Mollie Marbles,
.... Bill the Bold,
.... Leaky Lucy,
.... Wallace and His Ass

And the great theater master Broomefedies as himself!

Musical Numbers

ACT ONE

Death or Glory for Me (and Me!) .... Hope, Red, Company
A Girl Can't Be a Vinchen! .... Hurlo, Racklock, Hope
That Red-Eyed Son of a Whore .... Sadie, Red, Wags
A Lonely Life at Sea .... Hope, Sailors
Angel in Black Leather .... Red, Filler, Hope
Riot in the Circle .... Hope, Red, Black Rose, Wags
Hunt for the Biomancer .... Hope, Red, Biomancers
Who Needs a Penis? .... Brigga Lin, Biomancers
Attack on Stonepeak! .... Hope, Red, Lin, Set, Biomancers
I'll Wait for You .... Hope, Red

ACT TWO

All Hail Dire Bane! ..... Hope, Lin, Sadie, Finn, Black Rose, Filler
Lordy, My Lord .... Red, Leston, Hempist, Set, Soldiers
Curse of the Jackal Lord .... Hope, Black Rose, Lin, Biomancers
Who Is the Shadow Demon? ..... Red, Hempist, Leston, Set, Wags
Bless the Circle .... Black Rose, Filler, Wags
Wisdom of the Theater .... Hope, Broomefedies
Jewel of the Empire .... Red, Leston, Hempist, Pysetcha, Nobles
Prisoners No More! .... Hope, Lin, Black Rose, Wags
Am I a Man or a Monster? .... Red, Hempist, Leston, Pysetcha
The Horror of Dawn's Light .... Hope, Lin, Sadie, Finn, Wags
Love Alone Can Save Me .... Hope, Red

ACT THREE

The Death of Love .... Racklock, Set, Biomancers
How Can I Face Him Again? .... Hope
I Will Find You .... Red, Hempist, Black Rose, Wags
Savagery of the Mole Rats .... Hope, Finn, Mole Rats
Here in Visionary Square ..... Red, Lin, Racklock, Hope, Vinchen
Love Alone Can Save Me (Refrain) .... Hope, Red

Interview with a Theatrical Genius
By Thoriston Baggelworthy

Reprinted with kind permission from the Hollow
Falls Gentleman's Quarterly.

At this point, it is unlikely I need to inform any of
my readers of my passion for the arts and culture of
downtown New Laven. The popularity of my articles
has been extremely gratifying, and I thank you all
most sincerely for your enthusiasm and interest.
What's more, the prestige of becoming a man known
as a champion of folk culture has granted me additional access to people and places throughout Silverback, Hammer Point, and Paradise Circle that I might
not otherwise have achieved. A perfect example is the
following candid—and exclusive—interview I conducted with the great theater master Broomefedies
shortly after the triumphant opening of his most
recent theatrical masterwork, *Death or Glory.*

*Thoriston Baggleworthy: I'll get straight to the point, as
I know you're a busy man. I thoroughly enjoyed* Death or
Glory *and am desperate to learn how you accomplished
such a feat of theatrical genius that is both immensely
profound yet also wildly accessible and popular.*

The great theater master Broomefedies: I'm so glad
you enjoyed it, Thoriston, my wag, considering
you financed a great deal of it.

TB: Be that as it may, it far exceeded even my expectations.

TGTMB: It's all about balance, old pot. You take a song like "Hunt for the Biomancer," which is a real pensive, thoughtful number about that fear of biomancers we all live with each day.

TB: *Dear me, yes! What was the line,* Each of us a victim, just waiting for our turn. Each of us in terror to freeze or melt or burn. *Evocative stuff!*

TGTMB: Right. And you follow up such a serious thing with that first Brigga Lin song, "Who Needs a Penis?"

TB: *Indeed! My wife isn't as acclimated to the earthy folk humor of downtown New Laven as I am, and she was utterly scandalized.*

TGTMB: [*laughs*] I have to admit that the brilliant piece of stage business was Madgie's notion. She comes in one day holding a cucumber and says, "Broom, I got an idea!" She puts on her biomancer robes and stows the cucumber God knows where. Then she gets up onstage and starts singing the song. There's that perfect line...let's see, what is it exactly...oh yeah. *I never wanted this one-eyed worm, this penis, or this cock. So now it's time for you and me to have a little talk.* And then she pulls the cucumber out of her robes and starts singing to it! The first time I saw that bit, I laughed so hard I nearly pissed myself.

TB: *It was certainly some...colorful prop use. Especially when she began to caress the...eh, member that she had just supposedly torn from her own body.*

TGTMB: But that's just it, Thoriston, my wag. Give 'em something to think about, then give 'em something to ogle over. It's what you call dialectical theater.

TB: One thing that really struck me about the show is just how true to life it feels. You know, I actually met the real Grandteacher Hope and Lord Chamberlain Pastinas myself once.

TGTMB: You may have mentioned that fact on a few occasions.

TB: Yes, well, I bring it up now to emphasize just how struck I was by the masterfully authentic performances that were given. In particular, Miss Lymestria's rendition of Grandteacher Hope struck me as astonishingly accurate. That lush sensuality combined with an almost feline ferocity is exactly how I remember the grandteacher when I met her.

TGTMB: Is that so? Well, I'm glad to hear it, old pot. Your son wasn't bad as Red either.

TB: He worked very hard on the part, insisting on actually frequenting the infamous Drowned Rat tavern for several weeks!

TGTMB: I daresay he also learned quite a bit from Lymestria, keen? She's always wanted a little lacy pet of her own, and now she's got one. Seemed to work out for everyone. I just hope you've got a big kitchen up there in Hollow Falls. That molly can pack it away!

TB: What? I hadn't heard—

TGTMB: Never mind, old pot. Anyway, yeah, I tried as best I could to honor the truth of what those brave toms and mollies have done for us all.

TB: And of course you couldn't resist recounting your own role in shaping events with that most moving duet, "The Wisdom of the Theater." I'm fond of your line

just before the song begins. **What are we fighting for,
if not the right to make our art? What are we making
art for, if not to help us fight?** *Truly, my mind reels at
the thought that this man sitting humbly before me had
such an impact on history.*

TGTMB: [*chuckles*] You know I practically raised
the *Lord Chamberlain* for a period when he was
just a young and foolish tom more interested
in chasing mollies than chasing justice. I didn't
spend a great deal of time with Hope, or Dire
Bane, as she was calling herself then. But she
showed up on my doorstep at what I reckon was
a real turning point in her life. I gave her the best
advice I could, and it seemed to work out for her.

*TB: Quite so! Sometimes even the greatest of women
need the firm hand of a man to guide them!*
TGTMB: I would not recommend saying that, or
anything like it, in her presence.

TB: No?
TGTMB: Trust me.

Acknowledgments

I finished the first draft of this book in the aftermath of the 2016 presidential election. It was a shocking and tumultuous moment in history, and I'm not sure what the world will look like by the time this book sees print. So I am writing to you from the past, and like Hope, who is (nearly) always true to her namesake, I want to believe, despite the harsh reminder that hate and small-mindedness are still very much present, that as you read these words, the world is an even more beautiful and wondrous place than the one in which I'm currently living. A place full of possibility. Not because it must be, but because we make it so. This story of Hope and Red has been my humble contribution toward that end.

First and foremost, I want to thank my publisher at Orbit, Tim Holman, who has been tremendously supportive, especially during the stressful transition period between editors. Thanks also to Anne Clarke, deputy publisher, for pinch-hitting as editor during that transition. And of course, a huge thank-you to Brit Hvide, my awesome new editor who jumped right into the Empire of Storms with both feet like she'd always been there. Thanks also to my mapmaker, Tim Paul; my cover illustrator, Bastien Lecouffe Deharme; and my book designer, Lauren Panepinto, who have been responsible for making this entire trilogy look supercool. I also want to thank my agent, Jill Grinberg, and the incredible staff at JGLM for all of their support and encouragement. Lastly, and most importantly, I want to thank my sons, Logan and Zane, who continue to keep me sane and whole. More or less.

extras

orbit

meet the author

J<small>ON</small> S<small>KOVRON</small> is the author of several young adult novels, and his short stories have appeared in publications such as *ChiZine* and *Baen's Universe*. He lives just outside Washington, D.C., with his two sons and two cats. The Empire of Storms is his first adult fantasy series.

if you enjoyed

BLOOD AND TEMPEST

look out for

THE TETHERED MAGE
Swords and Fire: Book 1

by

Melissa Caruso

CONTROL THE MAGIC, CONTROL THE WORLD.

In the Raverran Empire, magic is scarce and those born with power are strictly controlled—taken as children and conscripted into the Falcon Army.

Zaira has lived her life on the streets to avoid this fate, hiding her mage mark and thieving to survive. But hers is a rare and dangerous magic, one that threatens the entire empire.

Lady Amalia Cornaro was never meant to be a Falconer. Heiress and scholar, she was born into a treacherous world of political machinations.

But fate has bound the heir and the mage. And as war looms on the horizon, a single spark could turn their city into a pyre.

Chapter 1

Here, my lady? Are you sure?"

As the narrow prow of my boat nudged the stone steps at the canal's edge, I wished I'd walked, or at least hired a craft rather than using my own. The oarsman was bound to report to La Contessa that her daughter had disembarked at a grimy little quay in a dubious corner of the Tallows, the poorest district of the city of Raverra.

By the time my mother heard anything, however, I'd already have the book.

"Yes, thank you. Right here."

The oarsman made no comment as he steadied his craft, but his eyebrows conveyed deep skepticism.

I'd worn a country gentleman's coat and breeches, to avoid standing out from my seedy surroundings. I was glad not to risk skirts trailing in the murky water as I clambered out of the boat. Trash bobbed in the canal, and the tang in the air was not exclusively salt.

"Shall I wait for you here, my lady?"

"No, that's all right." The less my mother knew of my errand, the better.

She had not precisely forbidden me to visit the pawnbroker who claimed to have a copy of Muscati's *Principles of Artifice*, but she'd made her opinion of such excursions clear. And no one casually disobeyed La Contessa Lissandra Cornaro. Her word resonated with power in every walled garden and forgotten plaza in Raverra.

Still, there was nothing casual about a Muscati. Only twelve known copies of his books existed. If this was real, it would be the thirteenth.

As I strolled alongside the canal, my mother's warnings seemed ridiculous. Sun-warmed facades flanked the green water, and workers unloaded produce from the mainland off boats moored at the canal's edge. A bright, peaceful afternoon like this surely could hold no dangers.

But when my route veered away from the canal, plunging into a shadowy tunnel that burrowed straight through a building, I hesitated. It was far easier to imagine assassins or kidnappers lurking beyond that dim archway. It wouldn't be the first time I'd faced either in my eighteen years as my mother's heir.

The book, I reminded myself. Think of the book.

I passed through the throat of the tunnel, emerging into a street too narrow to ever see direct sunlight. Broken shutters and scarred brickwork closed around me. The few people I passed gave me startled, assessing glances.

I found the pawnbroker's shop with relief, and hurried into a dim wilderness of dusty treasures. Jewelry and blown glass glittered on the shelves; furniture cluttered the floor, and paintings leaned against the walls. The proprietor bent over a conch shell wrapped with copper wire, a frown further creasing his already lined face. A few wisps of white over his ears were the last legacy of his hair.

I approached, glancing at the shell. "It's broken."

He scowled. "Is it? I should have known. He asked too little for a working one."

"Half the beads are missing." I pointed to a few orbs of colored glass still threaded on the wire. "You'd need an artificer to fix it if you wanted it to play music again."

The pawnbroker looked up at me, and his eyes widened. "Lady Amalia Cornaro." He bowed as best he could in the cramped shop.

I glanced around, but we were alone. "Please, no need for formality."

"Forgive me. I didn't recognize you in, ah, such attire." He peered dubiously at my breeches. "Though I suppose that's the fashion for young ladies these days."

Breeches weren't remotely in fashion for young ladies, but I didn't bother correcting him. I was just grateful they were acceptable enough in my generation that I didn't have to worry about causing a scandal or being mistaken for a courtesan.

"Do you have the book?" I reminded him. "Muscati's *Principles of Artifice*, your note said."

"Of course. I'd heard you were looking for it." A certain gleam entered his eye with which I was all too familiar: Cornaro gold reflected back at me. "Wait a moment, and I'll get it."

He shuffled through a doorway to the rear of the shop.

I examined the shell. I knew enough from my studies of artifice to trace the patterns of wire and understand the spell that had captured the sound of a musical performance inside the shell's rune-carved whorls. I could have fixed a broken wire, perhaps, but without the inborn talent of an artificer to infuse new beads with magical energy, the shell would stay silent.

The pawnbroker returned with a large leather-bound book. He laid it on the table beside the conch shell. "There you are, my lady."

I flipped through the pages until I came to a diagram. Muscati's combination of finicky precision in the wire-work schematics and thick, blunt strokes for the runes was unmistakable. I let out a trembling breath. This was the real thing.

The pawnbroker's long, delicate fingers covered the page. "Is all in order, then?"

"Yes, quite. Thank you." I laid a gold ducat on the table. It vanished so quickly I almost doubted I'd put it there.

"Always a pleasure," he murmured.

I tucked the book into my satchel and hurried out of the musty shop, almost skipping with excitement. I couldn't wait to get home, retreat to my bedroom with a glass of wine, and dive into Muscati's timeworn pages. My friend Domenic from the University of Ardence said that to read Muscati was to open a window on a new view of the universe as a mathematical equation to be solved.

Of course, he'd only read excerpts. The university library didn't have an actual Muscati. I'd have to get Domenic here to visit so I could show him. Maybe I'd give the book to the university when I was done with it.

It was hard to make myself focus on picking turns in the mazelike streets rather than dreaming about runic alphabets, geometric diagrams, and coiling wirework. At least I was headed in the right general direction. One more bridge to cross, and then I'd be in polite, patrician territory, safe and sound; and no lecture of my mother's could change the fact that I'd completed my errand without incident.

But a tense group of figures stood in the tiny plaza before the bridge, frozen in a standoff, every line of their bodies promising each other violence.

Like so many things in Raverra, this had become complicated.

Three broad-shouldered men formed a menacing arc around a scrawny young woman with sprawling dark curls. The girl stood rigidly defiant, like a stick thrust in the mud. I slowed to a halt, clutching my satchel tight against my side, Muscati's edge digging into my ribs.

"One last chance." A burly man in shirtsleeves advanced on the girl, fists like cannonballs ready at his sides. "Come nice and quiet to your master, or we'll break your legs and drag you to him in a sack."

"I'm my own master," the girl retorted, her voice blunt as a boat hook. "And you can tell Orthys to take his indenture contract and stuff it up his bunghole."

They hadn't noticed me yet. I could work my way

around to the next bridge, and get my book safely home. I took a step back, glancing around for someone to put a stop to this: an officer of the watch, a soldier, anyone but me.

There was no one. The street lay deserted. Everyone else in the Tallows knew enough to make themselves scarce.

"Have it your way," the man growled. The ruffians closed in on their prey.

This was exactly the sort of situation in which a young lady of the august and noble house of Cornaro should not involve herself, and in which a person of any moral fortitude must.

Maybe I could startle them, like stray dogs. "You there! Stop!"

They turned to face me, their stares cold and flat. The air went dry in my throat.

"This is none of your business," one in a scuffed leather doublet warned. A scar pulled at the corner of his mouth. I doubted it came from a cooking accident.

I had no protection besides the dagger in my belt. The name Cornaro might hold weight with these scoundrels, but they'd never believe I bore it. Not dressed like this.

My name meant nothing. The idea sent a wild thrill into my lungs, as if the air were alive.

The girl didn't wait to see what I would do. She tried to bolt between two of the men. A tree branch of an arm caught her at the waist, scooping her up as if she were a child. Her feet swung in the air.

My satchel pulled at my shoulder, but I couldn't run off and leave her now, Muscati or no Muscati. Drawing my dagger seemed a poor idea. The men were all armed, one with a flintlock pistol.

"Help!" I called.

The brutes seemed unimpressed. They kept their attention on the struggling girl as they wrenched her arms behind her.

"That's it!" Rage swelled her voice. "This is your last warning!"

Last warning? What an odd thing to say. Unless...

Ice slid into my bone marrow.

The men laughed, but she glowered furiously at them. She wasn't afraid. I could think of only one reason she wouldn't be.

I flattened myself against a wall just before everything caught fire.

Her eyes kindled first, a hungry blue spark flaring in her pupils. Then flames ran down her arms in delicate lines, leaping into the pale, lovely petals of a deadly flower.

The men lurched back from her, swearing, but it was too late. Smoke already rose from their clothing. Before they finished sucking in their first terrified breaths, blue flames sprang up in sudden, bold glory over every inch of them, burying every scar and blemish in light. For one moment, they were beautiful.

Then they let out the screams they had gathered. I cringed, covering my own mouth. The pain in them was inhuman. The terrible, oily reek of burning human meat hit me, and I gagged.

The men staggered for the canal, writhing in the embrace of the flames. I threw up my arm to ward my face from the heat, blocking the sight. Heavy splashes swallowed their screams.

In the sudden silence, I lowered my arm.

Fire leaped up past the girl's shoulders now. A pure, cold anger graced her features. It wasn't the look of a woman who was done.

Oh, Hells.

She raised her arms exultantly, and flames sprang up from the canal itself, bitter and wicked. They spread across the water as if on a layer of oil, licking at the belly of the bridge. On the far side of the canal, bystanders drawn by the commotion cried out in alarm.

"Enough!" My voice tore out of my throat higher than usual. "You've won! For mercy's sake, put it out!"

But the girl's eyes were fire, and flames ran down her hair. If she understood me, she made no sign of it. The blue fire gnawed at the stones around her feet. Hunger unsatisfied, it expanded as if the flagstones were grass.

I recognized it at last: balefire. I'd read of it in Orsenne's *Fall of Celantis*.

Grace of Mercy preserve us all. That stuff would burn anything—water, metal, stone. It could light up the city like a dry corncrib. I hugged my book to my chest.

"You have to stop this!" I pleaded.

"She can't," a strained voice said. "She's lost control."

I turned to find a tall, lean young man at my shoulder, staring at the burning girl with understandable apprehension. His wavy black hair brushed the collar of the uniform I wanted to see most in the world at the moment: the scarlet-and-gold doublet of the Falconers. The very company that existed to control magic so things like this wouldn't happen.

"Thank the Graces you're here! Can you stop her?"

"No." He drew in a deep, unsteady breath. "But you can, if you have the courage."

"What?" It was more madness, piled on top of the horror of the balefire. "But I'm not a Falconer!"

"That's why you can do it." Something delicate gleamed in his offering hand. "Do you think you can slip this onto her wrist?"

It was a complex weave of gold wire and scarlet beads, designed to tighten with a tug. I recognized the pattern from a woodcut in one of my books: a Falconer's jess. Named after the tethers used in falconry, it could place a seal on magic.

"She's *on fire*," I objected.

"I know. I won't deny it's dangerous." His intent green eyes clouded. "I can't do it myself; I'm already linked to another. I wouldn't ask if it weren't an emergency. The more lives the balefire consumes, the more it spreads. It could swallow all of Raverra."

I hesitated. The jess sagged in his hand. "Never mind. I shouldn't have—"

"I'll do it." I snatched the bracelet from him before I could think twice.

"Thank you." He flashed me an oddly wistful smile. "I'll distract her while you get close. Wits and courage. You can do it."

The Falconer sprinted toward the spreading flames, leaving the jess dangling from my hand like an unanswered question.

He circled to the canal's edge, calling to get the girl's attention. "You! Warlock!"

She turned toward him. Flame trailed behind her like a queen's mantua. The spreading edges crawled up the brick walls of the nearest house in blazing tendrils.

The Falconer's voice rang out above the clamor of the growing crowd across the canal. "In the name of His Serenity the Doge, I claim you for the Falcons of Raverra!"

That certainly got her attention. The flames bent in his direction as if in a strong wind.

"I don't belong to *you*, either!" Her voice was wild as a hissing bonfire. "You can't claim me. I'll see you burn first!"

Now she was going to kill him, too. Unless I stopped her.

My heart fluttering like an anxious dowager's handkerchief, I struggled to calm down and think. Maybe she wouldn't attack if I didn't rush at her. I tucked my precious satchel under my coat and hustled toward the bridge as if I hoped to scurry past her and escape. It wasn't hard to pretend. Some in the crowd on the far side beckoned me to safety.

My legs trembled with the urge to heed them and dash across. I couldn't bear the thought of Muscati's pages withering to ashes.

I tightened my grip on the jess.

The Falconer extended his hand toward the girl to keep her attention. "By law, you belonged to Raverra the moment you were born with the mage mark. I don't know how you managed to hide for so long, but it's over now. Come with me."

The balefire roared at him in a blue-white wave.

"Plague take you!" The girl raised her fist in defiance. "If Raverra wants my fire, she can have it. Let the city burn!"

I lunged across the remaining distance between us, leaping over snaking lines of flame. Eyes squeezed half shut against the heat, I flung out an arm and looped the jess over her upraised fist.

The effect was immediate. The flames flickered out as if a cold blast of wind had snuffed them. The Falconer still recoiled, his arms upraised to protect his face, his fine uniform doublet smoking.

The girl swayed, the fire flickering out in her eyes. The golden jess settled around her bone-thin wrist.

She collapsed to the flagstones.

Pain seared my hand. I hissed through my teeth as I snatched it to my chest. That brief moment of contact had burned my skin and scorched my boots and coat. My satchel, thank the Graces, seemed fine.

Across the bridge, the gathering of onlookers cheered, then began to break up. The show was over, and nobody wanted to go near a fire warlock, even an unconscious one.

I couldn't blame them. No sign remained of ruffians in the canal, though the burned smell lingered horribly in the air. Charred black scars streaked the sides of the buildings flanking me.

The Falconer approached, grinning with relief. "Well done! I'm impressed. Are you all right?"

It hit me in a giddy rush that it was over. I had saved—if not all of Raverra, at least a block or two of it—by myself, with my own hands. Not with my mother's name, or with my mother's wealth, but on my own.

Too dangerous to go to a pawnbroker's shop? Ha! I'd taken out a fire warlock. I smiled at him, tucking my burned hand into my sleeve. "I'm fine. I'm glad I could help."

"Lieutenant Marcello Verdi, at your service." He bowed. "What is your name, brave young lady?"

"Amalia Cornaro."

"Well, welcome to the doge's Falconers, Miss..." He stopped. The smile fell off his face, and the color drained from his bronze skin. "Cornaro." He swallowed. "Not...you aren't related to La Contessa Lissandra Cornaro, surely?"

My elation curdled in my stomach. "She's my mother."

"Hells," the lieutenant whispered. "What have I done?"

if you enjoyed

BLOOD AND TEMPEST

look out for

AGE OF ASSASSINS
The Wounded Kingdom: Book 1

by

RJ Barker

To catch an assassin, use an assassin…

Girton Club-Foot, apprentice to the land's best assassin, still has much to learn about the art of taking lives. But his latest mission tasks him and his master with a far more difficult challenge: to save a life. Someone, or many someones, is trying to kill the heir to the throne, and it is up to Girton and his master to uncover the traitor and prevent the prince's murder.

In a kingdom on the brink of civil war and a castle thick with lies, Girton finds friends he never expected, responsibilities he never wanted, and a conspiracy that could destroy an entire kingdom.

Chapter 1

We were attempting to enter Castle Maniyadoc through the night soil gate and my master was in the sort of foul mood only an assassin forced to wade through a week's worth of shit can be. I was far more sanguine about our situation. As an assassin's apprentice you become inured to foulness. It is your lot.

"Girton," said Merela Karn. That is my master's true name, though if I were to refer to her as anything other than "Master" I would be swiftly and painfully reprimanded. "Girton," she said, "if one more king, queen or any other member of the blessed classes thinks a night soil gate is the best way to make an unseen entrance to their castle, you are to run them through."

"Really, Master?"

"No, not really," she whispered into the night, her breath a cloud in the cold air. "Of course not really. You are to politely suggest that walking in the main gate dressed as masked priests of the dead gods is less conspicuous. Show me a blessed who doesn't know that the night soil gate is an easy way in for an enemy and I will show you a corpse."

"You have shown me many corpses, Master."

"Be quiet, Girton."

My master is not a lover of humour. Not many assassins are; it is a profession that attracts the miserable and the melancholic. I would never put myself into either of those categories, but I was bought into the profession and did not join by choice.

"Dead gods in their watery graves!" hissed my master into the night. "They have not even opened the grate for us." She swung herself aside whispering, "Move, Girton!" I slipped and slid crabwise on the filthy grass of the slope running from the river below us up to the base of the towering castle walls. Foulness farted out of the grating to join the oozing stream that ran down the motte and joined the river.

A silvery smudge marred the riverbank in the distance; it looked like a giant paint-covered thumb had been placed over it. In the moonlight it was quite beautiful, but we had passed near as we sneaked in, and I knew it was the same livid yellow as the other sourings which scarred the Tired Lands. There was no telling how old this souring was, and I wondered how big it had been originally and how much blood had been spilled to shrink it to its present size. I glanced up at the keep. This side had few windows and I thought the small souring could be new, but that was a silly, childish thought. The blades of the Landsmen kept us safe from sorcerers and the magic which sucked the life from the land. There had been no significant magic used in the Tired Lands since the Black Sorcerer had risen, and he had died before I had been born. No, what I saw was simply one of many sores on the land—a place as dead as the ancient sorcerer who made it. I turned from the souring and did my best to imagine it wasn't there, though I was sure I could smell it, even over the high stink of the night soil drain.

"Someone will pay for arranging this, Girton, I swear," said my master. Her head vanished into the darkness as she bobbed down to examine the grate once more. "This is sealed with a simple five-lever lock." She did not even breathe heavily despite holding her entire weight on one arm and one leg jammed into stonework the black of old wounds. "You can open this, Girton. You need as much practice with locks as you can get."

"Thank you, Master," I said. I did not mean it. It was cold, and a lock is far harder to manipulate when it is cold.

And when it is covered in shit.

Unlike my master, I am no great acrobat. I am hampered by a clubbed foot, so I used my weight to hold me tight against the grating even though it meant getting covered in filth. On the stone columns either side of the grate the forlorn remains of minor gods had been almost chipped away. On my right only a pair of intricately carved antlers remained, and on my left a pair of horns and one solemn eye stared out at me. I turned from the eye and brought out my picks, sliding them into the lock with shaking fingers and feeling within using the slim metal rods.

"What if there are dogs, Master?"

"We kill them, Girton."

There is something rewarding in picking a lock. Something very satisfying about the click of the barrels and the pressure vanishing as the lock gives way to skill. It is not quite as rewarding done while a castle's toilets empty themselves over your body, but a happy life is one where you take your pleasures where you can.

"It is open, Master."

"Good. You took too long."

"Thank you, Master." It was difficult to tell in the darkness, but I was sure she smiled before she nodded me forward. I hesitated at the edge of the pitch-dark drain. "It looks like the sort of place you'd find Dark Ungar, Master."

"The hedgings are just like the gods, Girton—stories to scare the weak-minded. There's nothing in there but stink and filth. You've been through worse. Go." I slithered through the gate, managing to make sure no part of my skin or clothing remained clean, and into the tunnel that led through the keep's curtain wall. Somewhere beyond I could hear the lumpy splashes of night soil being shovelled into the stream that ran over my feet. The living classes in the villages keep their piss and night soil and sell it to the tanneries and dye makers, but the blessed classes are far too grand for that, and their castles shovel their filth out into the rivers—as if to gift it to the populace. I have crawled through plenty of filth in my fifteen years, from the thankful, the living and the blessed; it all smells equally bad.

Once we had squeezed through the opening we were able to stand, and my master lit a glow-worm lamp, a small wick that burns with a dim light that can be amplified or shut off by a cleverly interlocking set of mirrors. Then she lifted a gloved hand and pointed at her ear.

I listened.

Above the happy gurgle of the stream running down the channel—water cares nothing for the medium it travels through—I heard the voices of men as they worked. We would have to wait for them to move before we could proceed into the castle proper, and whenever we have to wait I count out the seconds the way my master taught me—one, my master. Two, my master. Three, my master—ticking away in my mind like the balls of a water clock as I stand idle, filth swirling round my ankles and my heart beating out a nervous tattoo.

You get used to the smell. That is what people say.

It is not true.

Eight minutes and nineteen seconds passed before we finally heard the men laugh and move on. Another signal from my master and I started to count again. Five minutes this time. Human nature being the way it is you cannot guarantee someone will not leave something and come back for it. When the five minutes had passed we made our way up the night soil passage until we could see dim light dancing on walls caked with centuries of

filth. My own height plus a half above us was the shov-
elling room. Above us the door creaked and then we
heard footsteps, followed by voices.

"...so now we're done and Alsa's in the heir's guard.
Fancy armour and more pay."

"It's a hedging's deal. I'd sooner poke out my own
eyes and find magic in my hand than serve the fat bear,
he's a right yellower."

"Service is mother though, aye?"

Laughter followed. My master glanced up through
the hole, chewing on her lip. She held up two fingers
before speaking in the Whisper-That-Flies-to-the-Ear so
only I could hear her.

"Guards. You will have to take care of them," she
said. I nodded and started to move. "Don't kill them
unless you absolutely have to."

"It will be harder."

"I know," she said and leaned over, putting her hands
together to make a stirrup. "But I will be here."

I breathe out.

I breathe in.

I placed my foot on her hands and, with a heave,
she propelled me up and into the room. I came out of
the hole landing with my back to the two men. *Seven-
teenth iteration: the Drunk's Reversal.* Rolling forward,
twisting and coming up facing guards dressed in kilted
skirts, leather helms and poorly kept-up boiled-leather
chest pieces splashed with red paint. They stared at me
dumbly, as if I were the hedging lord Blue Watta appearing from the deeps. Both of them held clubs, though
they had stabswords at their sides. I wondered if they
were here to guard against rats rather than people.

"Assassin?" said the guard on the left. He was smaller
than his friend, though both were bigger than me.

"Aye," said the other, a huge man. "Assassin." His grip
shifted on his club.

They should have gone for the door and reinforcements. My hand was hovering over the throwing knives at my belt in case they did. Instead the smaller man grinned, showing missing teeth and black stumps.

"I imagine there's a good price on the head of an assassin, Joam, even if it's a crippled child." He started forward. The bigger man grinned and followed his friend's lead. They split up to avoid the hole in the centre of the room and I made my move. *Second iteration: the Quicksteps.* Darting forward, I chose the smaller of the two as my first target—the other had not drawn his blade. He swung at me with his club and I stepped backwards, feeling the draught of the hard wood through the air. He thrust with his dagger but was too far away to reach my flesh. When his swipe missed he jumped back, expecting me to counter-attack, but I remained unmoving. All I had wanted was to get an idea of his skill before I closed with him. He did not impress me, his friend impressed me even less; rather than joining the attack he was watching, slack-jawed, as if we put on a show for him.

"Joam," shouted my opponent, "don't be just standing there!" The bigger man trundled forward, though he was in no hurry. I didn't want to be fighting two at the same time if I could help it so decided to finish the smaller man quickly. *First iteration: the Precise Steps.* Forward into the range of his weapons. He thrust with his stabsword. *Ninth iteration: the Bow.* Middle of my body bowing backwards to avoid the blade. With his other hand he swung his club at my head. I ducked. As his arm came over my head I grabbed his elbow and pushed, making him lose his balance, and as he struggled to right himself I found purchase on the rim of his chest piece. *Tenth iteration: the Broom.* Sweeping my leg round I knocked his feet from under him. With a push I sent him flailing into the hole so he cracked his head on the edge of it on his way down.

I turned to his friend, Joam.

Had the dead gods given Joam any sense he would have seen his friend easily beaten and made for the door. Instead, Joam's face had the same look on it I had seen on a bull as it smashed its head against a wall in a useless attempt to get at a heifer beyond—the look of something too stupid and angry to know it was in a fight it couldn't win.

"I'm a kill you, assassin," he said and lumbered slowly forward, smacking his club against his hand. I had no time to wait for him; the longer we fought the more likely it was that someone would hear us and bring more guards. I jumped over the hole and landed behind Joam. He turned, swinging his club. *Fifteenth iteration: the Oar*. Bending at the hip and bringing my body down and round so it went under his swing. At the lowest point I punched forward, landing a solid blow between Joam's legs. He screeched, dropping his weapon and doubling over. With a jerk I brought my body up so the back of my skull smashed into his face, sending the big man staggering back, blood streaming from a broken nose. It was a blow that would have felled most, but Joam was a strong man. Though his eyes were bleary and unfocused he still stood. *Eighteenth iteration: the Water Clock*. I ran at him, grabbing his thick belt and using it as a fulcrum to swing myself round and up so I could lock my legs around his throat. Joam's hand grasped blindly for the blade at his hip. I drew it and tossed it away before he reached it. His hands spidered down my body searching for and locking around my throat, but Joam's strength, though great, was fleeing as he choked. I wormed my thumb underneath his fingers and grabbed his little finger and third finger, breaking them. I expected a grunt of pain as he let go of me, but the man was already unconscious and fell back, sliding down the wall to the floor. I squirmed free of his weight and checked he was still breathing. Once I was sure he was alive I rolled his body over to the hole.

"Look out, Master," I whispered. Then pushed the limp body into the hole. I took a moment, a second only, to check and see if I had been heard, then I knelt to pull up my master.

She was not heavy.

For the first time I had a moment to look around, and the room we stood in was a strange one. Small in length and breadth but far higher than it needed to be. I barely had time for that thought to form on the surface of my mind before my master shouted,

"This is wrong, Girton! Back!"

I jumped for the grate, as did she, but before either of us fell back into the midden a hidden gate clanked into place across the hole. Four pikers squeezed into the room, dressed in boiled-leather armour, wide-brimmed helms and skirts sewn with chunks of metal. Below the knee they wore leather greaves with strips of metal cut into the material to protect their shins, and as they brandished their weapons they assaulted us with the smell of unwashed bodies and the rancid fat they used to oil their armour. In such a small room their stink was a more effective weapon than the pikes; they would have been far better bringing long shields and short swords. They would realise quickly enough.

"Hostages," said my master as I reached for the blade on my back.

I let go of the hilt.

And was among the guards. Bare-handed and violent. The unmistakable fleshy crack of a nose being broken followed by a man squealing like a gelded mount came from behind me as my master engaged the pikers. I shoved one pike aside to get in close and drove my elbow into the throat of the man in front of me—not a killing blow but enough to put the man out of action. The second piker, a woman, was off balance, and it was easy enough for me to twist her so she was held in front of me like a shield with my razor-tipped thumbnail at her throat. My master had her piker in a similar embrace. Blood ran down his face and another guard lay unconscious on the floor next to the man I had elbowed in the throat.

"Open the grating," she shouted to the walls. "Let us go or we will kill these guards."

The sound of a man laughing came from above, and the reason for the room's height became clear as murder holes opened in the walls. Each was big enough for a crossbow to be pointed down at the room and eight weapons threatened us with taut bows and stubby little bolts which would pass straight through armour.

"Open the grate. We will leave and your troops will live," shouted my master.

More laughter.

"I think not," came a voice. Male, sure of himself, amused.

One, my master. Two, my master . . .

The twang of crossbows, echoing through the silence like the sound of rocks falling down a cliff face will echo through a quiet wood. Bolts buried themselves in the unconscious guards on the floor in front of us. Laughter from above.

"Together," hissed my master, and I pulled my guard round so that we hid behind the bodies of our prisoners.

"Let me go, please," said my guard, her voice shivering like her body. "Aydor doesn't care about us guards. He's worse than Dark Ungar and he'll kill us all if he wants yer."

"Quiet!" I said and pushed my razor-edged thumb harder against her neck, making the blood flow. I felt warmth on my thigh as her bladder let go in fear.

"Look at them," came from above. "Cowardly little assassins hiding behind troops brave enough to face death head-on like real warriors."

"Coil's piss, no," murmured the guard in my arms.

"Your loyalty will be remembered," came the voice again.

"No!"

Crossbows spat out bolts and the woman in my arms stiffened and arched in my embrace. One moment she was alive and then, almost magically, a bolt was vibrating in front of my nose like a conduit for life to flee her body.

"Master?" I said. Her guard was spasming as he died, a bolt sticking out of his neck and blood spattering onto the floor. "They are playing with us, Master."

Laughter from above and the crossbows fired again, thudding bolts into the body in my arms and making me cringe down farther behind the corpse. The laughter stopped and a second voice, female, commanding, said something, though I could not make out what it was. Then the woman shouted down to us.

"We only want you, Merela Karn. Lay on the floor and make no move to harm those who come for you or I will have your fellow shot."

Did something cross my master's face at hearing her name spoken by a stranger? Was she surprised? Did her dark skin grey slightly in shock? I had never, in all our years together, seen my master shocked. Though I was sure she was known throughout the Tired Lands— Merela Karn, the best of the assassins—few would know her face or that she was a woman.

"Drop the body, Girton," she said, letting hers fall facedown on the tiled and bloody floor. "This is not what it seems."

As always I did as I was told, though I braced every muscle, waiting for the bite of a bolt which never came.

"Lie on the floor, both of you," said the male voice from above.

We did as instructed and the room was suddenly buzzing with guards. I took a few kicks to the ribs, and luckily for the owners of those feet I could not see their faces to mark them for my attention later. We were quickly bound—well enough for amateurs—and hauled to our feet in front of a man as big as any I have seen, though he was as much fat as muscle.

"Shall I take their masks off?" asked a guard to my left.

"No. Take any weapons from them and put them in the cells. Then you can all go and wash their shit off yourselves and forget this ever happened."

"I think it's your shit, actually," I said. My master stared at the floor, shaking her head, and the man backhanded me across the face. It was a poor blow. Children have hurt me more with harsh words.

"You should remember," he said, "we don't need you; we only need her."

Before I could reply bags were put over our heads for a swift, dark and rough trip to the cells. *Five hundred paces against the clock walking across stone. Turn left and twenty paces across thick carpet. Down two sets of spiral stairs into a place that stinks of human misery.*

Dungeons are usually full of the flotsam of humanity, but this one sounded empty of prisoners apart from my master and I. We were placed in filthy cells, still tied though the bonds did not hold me long. Once free I removed the sack from my head and coughed out a wire I had half swallowed and had been holding in my gullet. It was a simple job to get my arm through the barred window of my door and pick the lock. Outside was a surprisingly wide area with a table, chairs and braziers, cold now. I tiptoed to my master's cell door.

"Master, I am out."

"Well done, Girton, but go back to your cell," she said softly. "Be calm. Wait."

I stood before the door of her cell for a moment. An assassin cannot expect much mercy once captured. A blood gibbet or maybe a public dissection. Something drawn out and painful always awaited us if we were caught, unless another assassin got to us first—my master says the loose association that makes up the Open Circle guards its secrets jealously. It would have been easy enough for me to slip into the castle proper and find some servant. I could take his clothes and become anonymous and from there I could escape out into the country. I knew the assassins' scratch language and could find the drop boxes to pick up work. Many would have done that in my situation.

But my master had told me to go back to my cell and wait, so I did. I locked the door behind me and slipped my sack and bonds back on. I imagined a circle filled with air, then let the top quarter of the circle open and breathed the air out. I let go of fear and became nothing but an instrument, a weapon.

I waited.

"One, my master. Two, my master. Three, my master . . ."

DEC 1 2 2017,